Date Due

AUG.28.1984			
FEB 0 9 1988		OCT 1 3 2007	
SEP 2 4 1993			
FEB 2 2 2005			

BRODART, INC. Cat. No. 23 233 Printed in U.S.A.

CHAIN REACTION

Also By Nicholas Guild

The Lost and Found Man
The Summer Soldier
Old Acquaintance
The Favor
The President's Man

CHAIN REACTION

Nicholas Guild

St. Martin's Press New York

 For information, address St. Martin's Press, 175 Fifth Avenue, New York, N.Y. 10010.

Design by Laura Hammond

Library of Congress Cataloging in Publication Data
Guild, Nicholas.
Chain Reaction.
I. Title.
PS3557.U357S48 1983 813'.54 82-17000
ISBN 0-312-72780-1

First Edition
10 9 8 7 6 5 4 3 2 1

This one is for Nettie.

. . . namque tu solebas
meas esse aliquid putare nugas . . .
(Catullus, 1, 3–4)

CHAIN REACTION

I

It was after ten o'clock when the submarine finally broke through to the surface. The gray water washed back and forth across its deck, hissing down the conning tower as the massive shape rocked from side to side and then was still. The darkness closed around it, as if it had been there forever. A light snow was drifting down. There was no sound.

Meyersdorff had ordered the running lamps extinguished, so nothing was visible from the coastline when the hatch opened. First one man and then another came out, looked around for the landfall he had expected to see but which gave the impression of having been swallowed up into a seamless, distanceless void, and shoved his hands further down into the pockets of his greatcoat, as if he couldn't imagine what he should do next. The cold was appalling, and not even the stars were out.

"Kapitän," one of them said in a low voice, turning back to address the blank space occupied by a third man who had only just joined them on deck, "do we risk a searchlight? How will we even know in which direction to paddle?"

Meyersdorff shook his head, perfectly aware that that too would be lost in the darkness. "You are a sailor, are you not? Use a compass, and you will find the shore quickly enough. It is no more than a hundred meters."

"Yes, Kapitän."

And then, quite suddenly, like the next sentence in their conversation, the cloud cover parted, allowing the moon to flood them with a pale, silvery light. Meyersdorff grinned.

"Is that better, Hopf? Now you will have no difficulty seeing the shore, and if there is anyone on the shore he will have no difficulty seeing you."

"Yes, Kapitän."

Another two men climbed out through the hatch, and then two more, making the narrow wooden deck almost crowded. The last man reached back inside and pulled up an awkward bundle that someone must have been pushing from the other end.

"Be quick, Sauter," Meyersdorff whispered hoarsely. "There is no need to be all night about this business—the Americans doubtless patrol these waters."

Sauter dragged his bundle to the prow of the ship, opened a valve, and stood back as the raft unfolded like some obscene, flabby jungle flower. Somehow, in the dim moonlight, it was a profoundly disgusting thing to witness.

Two of the men standing on the deck were not dressed in naval uniforms. They wore topcoats and civilian hats, and they carried suitcases. One of them was making his way through the little crowd that had assembled in front of the conning tower, shaking hands with each in turn and murmuring "Auf Wiedersehen" with almost machinelike efficiency. He was in his early twenties—about the same age as most of the crew—and a shock of dishwater-blond hair stuck out from beneath the brim of his hat. He had large hands, with thick, short fingers, and nothing about his figure suggested much agility.

The other man stood a little apart, as if waiting for these ceremonies to be finished. He was perhaps as much as ten years older, slender and dark. His face, under the shadow of his hat brim, was rendered somehow even more handsome by the thin, careworn lines that looked as if they had been scratched in around his eyes and mouth with an awl. Except for the eyes, which moved restlessly from one object to another, he stood so still that he hardly even seemed to be breathing.

Meyersdorff came up to him and touched him on the elbow.

"Well, Niehauser," he said gently, the way one might have spoken to someone recovering from a long illness, "we are here, my friend. Seven weeks across from Kiel, and there it is. You have everything you need?"

It was one of those questions one asked simply to be asking something, because a certain kind of relationship demanded it, because, aside from Wentzel, who was still only a boy, they were the only two officers aboard. Because of the kind of intimacy that grows up at sea between two men who know they will probably never meet again, and who for that reason alone find it possible to speak frankly. It was, on the face of it, a stupid question—they both knew that in an undertaking of this sort there were no charms against the unforeseen—but von Niehauser nevertheless understood, and smiled and nodded his head.

"Yes—well. . . . At least you will have enough money."

"Did he show it to you?" The smile on von Niehauser's lips had died, and he seemed almost angry. "But he would, of course. Fifteen thousand American dollars—he managed to convince the SS we would need as much as that for living expenses if we were kept longer than six months. He is not without guile."

Meyersdorff found it possible to laugh.

"Perhaps he feels it might be too much trouble to conquer America. Perhaps he plans simply to buy it."

"I think there is little enough chance of our managing either."

It was a long moment before either of them spoke again—it was as if they both were trying to ignore the fact that anything of the kind had been said.

"You should learn to be more discreet, Niehauser."

"You forget my privileged position," he answered, smiling again, a smile that had taken on the character of a disguise. "If I fail, the Gestapo will be saved the trouble of hanging me. And if I succeed . . ." His right shoulder moved in an almost imperceptible shrug, indicating how little he would have to fear from the Gestapo then.

"Do they put such importance on it, then?"

"It would seem so."

Meyersdorff asked no more questions. He was very far from being a fool—he understood as well as anyone how the fuel shortages had curtailed operations, especially in the Navy. And von Niehauser had had a submarine placed at his disposal. Such an extravagance would have had to be cleared through Dönitz himself. Yes, it would seem they put a very great importance on it.

As if the same idea had occurred to both of them, they watched the blond young man's back as he stood in conversation with a couple of the crew—it couldn't have been much of a conversation, since Stafford understood hardly any German.

"You had better take care with him," Meyersdorff said, turning aside slightly so that he was speaking almost directly into von Niehauser's shoulder. "That one will get you killed if you aren't careful."

Von Niehauser nodded slowly, as if he had pondered the matter for hours and come to a similar conclusion.

"The SS is quite satisfied that he is genuine, but what does that mean? Those idiots seem able to convince themselves of anything. For myself, I can't decide which would constitute more of a threat—if he turned out to be an American agent or if he didn't."

Meyersdorff looked at him questioningly, but for several seconds von Niehauser hardly seemed to notice.

"Patriotism is a matter of instinct," he went on finally. "A man who will turn his back on his own country like that is not to be trusted in anything. You may be sure I will be careful."

He smiled again, and then happened to glance down and saw that Meyersdorff was holding a small automatic pistol in his hand. It simply rested there on the flat of his palm.

"Take it," Meyersdorff said. "I have been carrying it around with me ever since the start of the war, and I have never had a reason to fire it. Perhaps you can put it to better use."

Von Niehauser shook his head. "Thank you, my friend, but I will be better off without it. It isn't the sort of thing I should care to have found on me, and there are plenty of other ways of gaining the same end. Thank you just the same."

"You're quite sure?" Meyersdorff, who was the best soul in the world, actually seemed disappointed.

"Quite sure. Good hunting on your way home."

A quarter of an hour later the raft scraped ashore, and von Niehauser and Stafford jumped out onto the beach, their shoes making a harsh crunch on the gravel. And then the sailors who had done the rowing jumped out, and one of them made a joke about how now they would be able to tell people that they had invaded America. Everyone laughed except Stafford, and then von Niehauser translated the joke for him and he laughed too.

"Good luck, Herr Baron."

Both the sailors were standing at salute, and von Niehauser couldn't be sure which of them had addressed him, so he put out his hand to the one who looked like he might have been a year or two the elder, who took it rather hesitantly, and then shook hands with the other man. No one spoke again.

And then the two sailors turned their raft around and started back toward the ship, which was only a dull gleam in the shining blackness of the water. In a few minutes they were almost invisible, and the sound of their oars was dying away. Von Niehauser and Stafford picked up their suitcases and disappeared into the woods.

It wasn't a very pleasant walk. The snow was probably five or six inches deep, and neither of them was wearing anything except ordinary street shoes. And it was cold, probably ten or fifteen degrees below zero. The slightest breath of wind seemed to go straight through their overcoats.

But von Niehauser felt very little inclination to complain—at least they were off that damned submarine. Seven weeks. Seven weeks, with never more than an hour or two each day in the fresh air, and all the rest of their time lived within the narrow iron walls of the ship. There had hardly been room to stand up, and von Niehauser, who was a tall man, had noticed that he was continually scraping himself on bulkheads and the edges of tables.

It had been torture—the constant smell of ozone and other men's bodies, the eerie yellow light that made everyone look like a corpse—it had been like being shut up in a mass grave. He had found that he slept hardly at all and was subject to disturbing dreams when he did sleep. That had been the worst part of it—there had been too much time with nothing to do except to brood.

It had almost been enough to make him miss the Russian front.

But still, these woods weren't comfortable either. It was difficult to see precisely where you were going—the moonlight threw peculiar shadows across the ground, making it almost impossible to keep from stumbling and running into things. At one point von Niehauser was startled by a loud crash and turned around to find his partner lying on the ground, cursing in a manner frightful to hear in such solitude. It seemed that he had tripped over a fallen log. It would have been funny except for the saving thought that one's life might be put at hazard by this clumsy American. He waited impassively for Stafford to regain his feet.

"God—couldn't they have landed us somewhere a little closer to civilization? We'll probably freeze to death before we get out of here."

Von Niehauser couldn't summon up much compassion. The mortar fragments in his left arm and along that side of his rib cage were giving him trouble, as they always did when he was outside in cold weather. "*They are very small,*" the surgeon at the field hospital had told him, "*and extracting them all would have taken several hours of operating time we need for men whose wounds are critical. Yours is the sort of case that can safely be left until after the war.*" It was the great lesson of the Eastern conflict, that one must learn to bear with one's infirmities. Von Niehauser had learned.

"You would prefer to hang?" His voice was calm, almost scholarly, as if he were offering instructions in tolerance. "In 1942 the Abwehr landed eight men along the south shore of Long Island—they were supposed to act as saboteurs, to dynamite power stations and disrupt communications in the New York area. It was considered a good plan. None of them lasted a week before they were arrested, and none of them managed to blow up so much as a balloon. Be patient, and you may yet live to serve the Reich."

It seemed to work. Stafford nodded glumly and followed along.

"What are we going to do?" he asked.

"You mean, immediately? We are going to push ahead until we find a road. Things will be easier after that, and there are a lot of little towns around here. A hot meal, and a few hours of sleep, and we can catch a bus south. You mustn't worry."

"I'm not worried—I'm just cold."

Von Niehauser smiled to himself, wondering how Stafford would have managed in Russia.

"Quite right. There isn't anything to worry about."

Would that it were so.

"He can help you find your way about," Schellenberg had said. *"It isn't every day we get a native American volunteering for espionage work, and too much significance is attached to this mission to entrust it to a single, unaided man. You have your orders, Major."*

It was only in the SS that a hoodlum like Schellenberg would have been able to climb his way up to brigadier and Head of Foreign Intelligence, and all by the advanced age of thirty-three. Schellenberg had never seen a shot fired in anger in his life; everyone knew he was nothing but a desk soldier, a protégé of Reinhard Heydrich, for whose memory no one in Europe had a decent word. One found only two sorts of men in the SS, the buccaneers and the madmen. One hardly knew which was worse.

And now, on what seemed little more than a whim, they had encumbered him with this American turncoat who had visions of himself as the stuff of the Wehrmacht officer corps. A mere boy, clearly unsettled in his mind, who steps off a merchant ship in Lisbon and turns himself over to the German consulate with some story about wanting to serve the Fatherland. What could they have been thinking of?

Von Niehauser had been keeping watch for any signs of another human presence, but found nothing. Except for their own, there were no tracks in the snow, which unfortunately was hard and crusted and would probably show a footprint for days. There were no fences or NO TRESPASSING signs, no beer bottles or crumpled, half-burned newspapers, nothing to suggest that they ran any risk of being seen. And yet, so one was told, this part of the Maine coast did a modest tourist business in the summer months. Schellenberg had been reasonably clever on that point—no place on earth is more deserted than a summer resort in January.

He shifted his suitcase over to his left hand and instantly felt a stab of pain along the inside of his arm. For a few seconds, until he had made the adjustment, it was difficult even to breathe. It had been necessary, however; his right arm was getting tired, and he didn't want to stop and rest—one had to think of young Stafford's flagging morale.

The boy was an inconvenience—perhaps he was something worse, for all that the SS so trusted him—but perhaps there, too, Schellenberg had been right, up to a point. Since 1933, the Americans had probably gotten used to the odd accents of European refugees—in the big cities, he imagined, he would hardly be the object of much attention—but perhaps just at the beginning it would be better to let Stafford speak for him.

"Where did you learn English?"

The question was so unexpected, and so perfectly in accord

with his own train of thought, that it was difficult for von Niehauser to fight down the disagreeable suspicion that Stafford must somehow have been able to read his mind.

"In England," he answered, with tolerable calmness. "I went to school there. My father was attached to the embassy for five years."

"I just wondered—you sound like a duke or something."

Was Stafford trying to flatter him? Could he be so obvious as all that? It was a disturbing enough thought about one's partner in espionage.

Or perhaps there was a touch of hero worship mixed into it —he was rather fixated on martial glory, was this young American, and there had been other evidence that he had not failed to be impressed with the fact that von Niehauser was a decorated veteran of the Russian campaign. Apparently someone had shown him a dossier, because for the week they had trained together back in Holland, until von Niehauser had gotten so sick of it that he had been forced to say something, Stafford had pestered him with personal questions, had even asked to see his medals. On top of everything else, it had been an intolerable liberty.

At any rate, it was one of the reasons von Niehauser found it impossible to like him. To be chums with a person like Stafford was simply more than he could manage. Still, one was obliged to try.

"I was introduced to the Duke of York once," he said, forcing himself to smile. "That was in 1925, and today he's the King. I remember that he stuttered."

"Well, I didn't mean anything like that."

"I know you didn't. Have you ever been to England?"

"Four months ago. My ship stopped off for forty-eight hours on the way to Portugal, but I figured to hell with the damn English. They're the enemy, aren't they?" The question carried all the sullen vehemence with which Stafford usually freighted his political remarks and must have been so endlessly reassuring to the SS. He had a knack for making it seem that, really, it was your own patriotism which was open to doubt. "By then all I wanted was to get to Germany and join up. Anyway, I never got out of Southampton."

"Ah, then. . . ."

But by that time they had come to a road. It wasn't much of a road, just a couple of lanes of asphalt, but it was a road.

"God, my feet are freezing."

Von Niehauser hardly even looked at him.

"In Russia," he said finally, as if speaking to himself, "sometimes when it was really bad the leather of our boots would freeze. Solid, as if they had been cobbled out of brass. You couldn't even unlace them—you would have had to cut them off with a saw, if you could have found a saw, and you didn't dare because you would never have seen another pair. Half the Army marched on blood-soaked rags. When we could finally find somewhere warm, and put our feet up against a fire to melt the ice, we would find men who were grayish-black from the ankle down. You could smell the rot as soon as they had thawed out. At the merest touch the flesh would slough off in a single piece, just fall away, all the way down to the bone."

Stafford grunted derisively. To him, it was just a story. "Yeah, well, this isn't Russia."

"Then we mustn't complain."

They walked on in silence after that. The road seemed to be deserted, and the only sound was the grinding of their shoes on the snow. There was nothing near them, just endless distances of empty road, leading nowhere. It was like the landscape of a dream. Finally, Stafford began to mutter—very quietly at first, as if ashamed he might be overheard, but loud enough in time.

"How far is it to the next town? God, don't you *ever* get tired? We must have come five miles."

"We have come perhaps two," von Niehauser stated quietly, simply as a neutral fact. "And there should be a place called Sullivan no more than three or four miles along this road. We will be there in another hour, no longer."

"An *hour?* Jesus, we'll freeze to death by then."

"We will not freeze; we will merely be uncomfortable. If we sat down and fell asleep, with our backs resting against a tree, then we might freeze. But we will not do that."

No, they would not freeze. But, still, it was cold enough to make you forget the possible existence in the world of anything except misery. Von Niehauser wondered what sort of life Harry Stafford must have been leading all these years to make him look with such offended surprise on a little common inconvenience. In Russia, boys of sixteen and seventeen, fresh from home, had slept in shell holes on nights that froze the very hair in your nostrils —boys who by then had forgotten all about serving the Fatherland and the Führer, or turning aside the wrath of the godless Bolsheviks; who had forgotten everything except that they were expected to be men. Some of them had died, with their heads down as if they were praying and their hands clasped around their rifles, but they hadn't complained.

It was close to eleven before they saw the headlights in the distance. At first it was merely an uncertain glimmer through the trees, and then there was the low, sullen groaning of an engine. Before they knew it, it was almost upon them.

But they still had time. Von Niehauser took Stafford by the arm and started back toward the cover of the trees. Two yards off the road and no one would see them. Why should they? Who would be looking for anyone out on foot on such a night?

But Stafford had other plans. He pulled himself free from von Niehauser's grip with a jerk and turned around, glaring at him.

"Are you kidding?" he asked, his voice unnaturally shrill as he stepped back a pace. "We can catch a ride."

And by then, of course, it was too late. Even as Stafford spoke he had come into the field of moving light. The driver of the car must have seen him by then: a man standing directly in your path isn't the sort of thing anyone would miss.

There was nothing else he could do. Von Niehauser stepped

out from the edge of the road, where the lower part of his body was immediately washed in the hard glare of the headlamps. He took off his hat and held it in his left hand, feeling the sort of embarrassment one might experience at being forced to witness some pointless cruelty one was helpless to prevent.

"Leave it to me," he murmured, turning his head a little toward Stafford but keeping his eyes on the approaching car. "Just stay where you are and let me deal with it."

It was obvious that Stafford didn't have any inkling of what he meant.

Von Niehauser raised his arm, holding the hat over his head and waving it back and forth. He tried to smile, to look the part of the stranded traveler grateful for this chance of being rescued, but he found the effort was beyond him.

For an instant he thought whoever was driving might not stop, might do the sensible thing and keep right on going, just as if he, too, might not relish an encounter with strangers on a lonely road. Von Niehauser almost hoped that he would.

But it wasn't to happen that way. The car slowed gradually, trying not to fishtail on the patches of ice that dotted the road here and there, and stopped almost directly in front of the spot where von Niehauser was standing. He could almost have reached out his hand and set it on the brow of the right headlamp.

It wasn't a new car. Except for the staff limousines of the SS, you didn't see new cars, not since before the start of the war; it was probably the same in America—but someone had obviously gone to a great deal of trouble to maintain that particular survivor in pristine condition. Even in the dark the paintwork seemed to glow under uncountable coats of wax, and, if the sound of the engine slowing to an idle meant anything, the same kind of care had been lavished there too.

Von Niehauser could see the driver now, peering out through the windscreen at him. It was an unpleasant surprise to realize he was hardly more than a boy, just a fresh-faced farmer's son with a shock of reddish-brown hair hanging heavily down over his forehead. He couldn't have been more than about seventeen, and he was watching him with the unsuspecting alertness of someone who had not yet learned to mistrust the adult world.

"Problem, mister?" he asked, rolling down his window and thrusting his head and left shoulder out through the opening.

A glance back at Stafford insured there would be no trouble from that quarter. He merely stood where he was, his hands thrust deep into his overcoat pockets as he stamped his feet against the edge of the pavement in a profitless effort to strike up a little warmth in them. He was too absorbed in his own misery and too happy at the prospect of getting in out of the cold to interfere. He would let his partner deal with the specifics.

Von Niehauser walked around the front of the car, forcing himself to appear relaxed.

"Our car has broken down," he said as he approached the door on the driver's side. He moved slowly, with a deliberate weariness, all the time appalled at the transparency of the deception—couldn't the boy hear his accent? Couldn't he see the danger? What sort of fool stops in the darkness, in the middle of nowhere, for men who could be anything? "I wonder if you could perhaps just take us to a phone? I could call a mechanic, and . . ."

He had his hand on the doorlatch now, just resting it there casually, as if it were something he did unconsciously, merely to support his weight as he leaned down to have a word with this healthy, accommodating, apparently rather stupid youth.

If the boy suspected anything, he gave no sign. His arm still rested along the top of the door and he was still smiling, the way anyone might smile at a poor stranger in distress.

"Sure, mister. If you — "

But he never had a chance to finish. He had been leaning against the door and suddenly it was gone, just as if it had disappeared. The sound of its opening was like a pistol shot.

Von Niehauser took him by the back of his collar, jerking him the rest of the way out onto the road. He was a big lad, tall and solid, but surprise and balance were all against him; he simply fell, like so much dead weight. He struck the pavement with his shoulder and chest, without even the time to cry out.

After that it was simple. Von Niehauser brought the heel of his shoe down just a little to one side of the boy's spine. There was a hoarse little bark, something between a cry and a gasp, as his ribs pulled loose and the air shot out of his lungs. He was alive and conscious, but that kind of pain would render anyone as helpless as a sucking babe. There would be no resistance now.

Von Niehauser turned him over onto his back, almost gently. Already it was like handling a dead body; the eyes were large and frightened but seemed to be looking out at nothing. Already the boy and his murderer seemed to inhabit different worlds.

"My God! You . . ."

It was Stafford, of course. He had been attracted by the sound of a struggle—or perhaps just by the sound. Perhaps he had been half afraid of being left behind. In any case, he was there now, looking down at them, apparently too astonished to speak.

Von Niehauser glanced up at him, the expression on his face conveying nothing. It was only an instant. And then, with a sharp, delicate movement that was almost too quick to be seen, he broke the farmboy's larynx with the back of his fist—it made a noise like the crushing of a walnut.

It was impossible to know whether the boy felt anything. After a few seconds he tried to roll over on his side, and a heavy trickle of blood ran out of the corner of his mouth. He seemed to struggle for a moment, like a man drowning, and then he was still. His eyes were still wide open, but no one had ever looked like that while he was alive.

Stafford retreated a few paces, his movements rusty like those of an old man, as if he were afraid of falling. He looked at the dead body on the road, and then at von Niehauser. He seemed to be trying vainly to swallow. Von Niehauser rose to his feet.

"Yes." He stood with his arms dangling at his sides; he gave the impression he couldn't have raised them if he had wanted to. "Yes—as you see, I've killed him. What did you expect? He saw our faces. He could have placed us, here, tonight. How should we have explained ourselves? Did you imagine no one would think to ask us?"

He turned away, as if in disgust, and stared down at the dead farmboy, whose limbs were twisted around at odd angles.

"You did a stupid thing, my friend," he went on, his face, which was still illuminated by the harsh yellow light from the car's headlamps, was as rigid as a mask. "And because of that, I have found it necessary to do this."

II

Ever since Pearl Harbor day, George Havens' desk had been the dumping ground for every screwball report on German espionage activity, anywhere in the Eastern United States. Havens was the man who had to follow through on all the anonymous tips about mysterious radio transmissions that turned out to be "Yiddish Theater of the Air" and all the rumors of massed, brown-shirted stormtroopers every time there was a Boy Scout rally in New Jersey. If the Bureau got it, Havens got it.

"Sometimes I think it's just Mr. Hoover's way of getting even with me," he said, leaning back in his chair, his shoulders barely touching the wall behind him as he thrust his hands morosely into his trouser pockets. "I don't think he's ever forgiven me for trying to enlist, so I'm benched for the season."

Sam Fraser passed a hand over his perfectly bald head as he calculated the chances of the chair collapsing under his subordinate—it had happened once, and these days office furniture was difficult to replace. His eyes narrowed, giving him, for the moment, an uncanny resemblance to Vladimir Lenin.

"Your timing could have been better. Tuesday, December the ninth, 1941." He shook his head ruefully. "You're lucky you're not in Kansas City right now, polishing filing cabinets. You should have known."

"Yeah, well . . ."

Fraser, the careerist, who hadn't spent a working day away from his desk in twelve years and had no discernible ambitions except to live to collect his pension, could still feel sorry for him in an abstract sort of way. After all, it was different for George —George was a field man. It had been an act of cruelty to promote him out of the New York office, where he had been having the time of his life as head boy for counterintelligence, but the war had changed all that. There wasn't much work for spy hunters these days.

And George was right about the Director—he *had* hit the ceiling. God forbid that anyone anywhere should ever get the idea that he could serve the war effort better than in the FBI. Apparently it was a matter of bureaucratic prestige. So that was that; there would be no resignations. Anyone who tried would find out that the Army and the baseball teams weren't the only ones with authority to draft.

"I have this vision of myself," Havens went on. "It comes to me now and then: I'm on the bridge of an aircraft carrier, looking out to the edge of the horizon. The water is an unbroken, soundless surface in every direction, and everyone else on board is asleep. It's the morning of the Battle of the Coral Sea."

"That's very poetic." Sam Fraser's mouth compressed in a thin, bloodless line.

"Good God, Sam, this is one of the turning points in the whole history of the world." The front legs of Havens' chair came back down to the floor with a snap and he leaned forward, resting his elbows on his knees so that his slender body seemed lost in a tangle of limbs. He was no longer quite a young man, but he seemed young as his pale blue eyes lit up his face, making you think for a moment you were witnessing a religious conversion. "Everybody knows the Allies are launching an invasion into Northern Europe this spring. What happens over the next six or seven months might just settle things for the next hundred years, and here we are sitting in Washington, reading reports."

"What happened to your aircraft carrier in the Coral Sea?"

Havens only glared at him.

"Look, George, it isn't that I don't sympathize." Sam Fraser smiled, tilting his head to one side like a pantomime clown. "But it can't all be cowboys and Indians; the Germans won't land a boatload of saboteurs every week just for your personal amusement. There are probably some pretty slack times out on the Pacific too."

"Yes. That was lovely, wasn't it."

"What was lovely?"

Havens laced his fingers together and dropped them over the top of his head, as if he wanted to keep it from floating away. His face took on a dreamy look; he might have been recalling the beauty of some long-lost passion.

"June, 1942. Wasn't that what you were talking about? All those wicked Nazi spies paddling around by East Hampton in their rubber boat. They didn't amount to much as villains—remember the one who phoned us up to tell us how he really didn't like Hitler and would we please let him surrender? But we had *such* a marvelous time running the rest of them to earth. It was just like before the war."

"Yes, well . . ." Fraser sniffed impatiently, frowning at the tip of the pencil he held in his left hand. "You weren't the one who had to do all the paperwork on that."

"God knows, though, I've done enough of that in the meantime."

They regarded each other accusingly for a moment, and then Sam Fraser made a gesture with his hand as if sweeping away a cobweb.

"All right, but be reasonable," he said, the least little edge of annoyance in his voice. "All I want to know is if it would be too much to expect to have my desk cleared by tomorrow night. You know how Ida's likely to take it if I tell her we have to put off visiting her mother in Myrtle Beach."

"Myrtle Beach?" Havens wrinkled his nose. "I thought you didn't like Ida's mother."

"I don't, but I like staying in Myrtle Beach—it's warm there, donkey. You can go swimming and sleep with the windows open. Now, am I going to get to go or not?"

Havens lifted himself slowly out of his chair. His every movement conveyed the impression of weariness and boredom.

"I haven't checked the morning's cables yet," he said, stopping for a moment by the door and speaking over his shoulder. "But I can't remember the last time we had a good cable, so Ida can probably start packing her beach towels. Hell, what are you going to do, take the train? That must be an eight- or ten-hour trip."

"Twelve, not counting delays. Then another five hours from Columbia in my mother-in-law's 1932 Chrysler station wagon, the one with no shocks."

"Christ, Sam, I envy you the high drama of your life." Havens raised his hand in what looked like a casual caricature of a salute and started back toward his own office, where he could spend the rest of the morning locked up with the crank mail.

The hallways in that part of the Bureau headquarters were painted a cream yellow that reminded you quite forcefully of Mom's hominy grits. A spidery network of cracks was visible in the ceiling, and all around the door frames and light switches there were hundreds of overlapping handprints. In places the linoleum floor had been worn away almost down to the glue.

A year ago, he probably wouldn't have noticed, but the intervening time had brought George Havens to one of those astonishing revelations by means of which we discover ourselves surrendering our youth—he had found that he was getting bored with his job.

He had been with the Bureau ever since his graduation from law school in 1934. It had never occurred to him to go into anything else—he loved the Bureau. But for about a year now, ever since it had finally gotten through to him that he was going to have to sit out the war, he had felt increasingly restive. He wanted to do something, and they weren't going to let him. He was going to stay in Washington, writing polite letters to the little old ladies in White Plains, right up until the last day of the war. It was like being dead.

After the war, he had decided, he would quit. They couldn't very well stop him then; he would draft Mr. Hoover a well-behaved little letter of resignation and call it a day. He would go back to New York, enter private practice, and grow old watching the World Series. He didn't see how he could stay with the Bureau after this—it was like the failure of a marriage. He felt betrayed.

But until then he would school himself to be like Sam Fraser. He would go through the motions while he waited to be set free.

Having collected a cup of coffee from the urn in the secretarial pool, he picked up a manila folder from his mail slot and went to the little partitioned-off space on the third floor where he had a desk, a filing cabinet, and two chairs. He sat down, opened the envelope, took a sip of coffee, and started going through that morning's collection of hot tips from the local constabularies.

He was a little less than halfway through the pile, and about ready to knock off for lunch, when he found the telegram from the Hancock County Sheriff's office.

Probably with so much of the country's violence having been exported to Europe and the atolls of the Pacific, the police were having a pretty dull time of it; that and the fact that so many cops had gone into the Army and been replaced by middle-aged amateurs was the only way Havens could account for the quantities of hysterical nonsense that came in for him over the Teletype. Sometimes it seemed that half the little towns on the Eastern Seaboard were populated almost exclusively with suspected Axis spies.

Most of it was just junk and could be dismissed out of hand —some loony's neighbor was named "Schmidt" or listened to Wagner or owned a dachshund, and the Bureau was supposed to run a background check to verify it wasn't really Hermann Göring out there in East Stroudsburg. He wondered if the Gestapo had these problems.

But Sheriff Ernest A. Bilson of Ellsworth, Maine, didn't sound like a nut.

"We have an unexplained homicide," the cable read. "The victim, Randall S. Tucker, aged 18, was killed sometime after 10:30 P.M., Saturday, January 22. No leads on perpetrators, but tracks were found leading from probable scene of crime to shore of Frenchman's Bay. Circumstances suspicious. Additional information on request."

It seemed to strike a chord for some reason. George Havens searched through his memory and then through a folder he kept on embassy reports and military news, until he came up with the item he was looking for.

It had arrived yesterday, a couple of lines about a Canadian freighter out of Halifax that had been attacked and sunk almost at dock's edge a few minutes after sunset on the twenty-fourth. The freighter, poor old thing, had been taken completely by surprise—she hadn't even made the rendezvous with her escort yet—and sank in about thirty minutes. The report assumed a submarine; maybe somebody had seen the wash from the torpedoes. They had sent out a couple of planes, which had dropped some depth charges, but they hadn't scored. Probably the submarine had gone straight to the bottom to wait them out, and they never would have been able to find her in the darkness.

There hadn't been a German submarine sighted in North American waters since August, so this was an unusual enough occurrence to make itself noticed. The wolfpacks were staying out in mid-Atlantic to avoid the shore patrols. The war had been going so badly for them that they couldn't even expect to be refueled at sea—so what was a Jerry U-boat doing that far outside its normal patrol area?

It was the conjunction of the two events that intrigued him. A couple of unknowns turn up in Maine—the sheriff had written "perpetrators," hadn't he? yes—and some kid ends up the evening dead. Then, a little less than forty-eight hours later, an enemy submarine, way off its beat, kills a freighter just outside Halifax harbor. That was . . . how far?

He took the road atlas from the bottom drawer of his desk and tried measuring it off with his thumb. Maybe three to three hundred and fifty miles, as the fish swims. The average German submarine probably did seven or eight knots submerged—and that close to an enemy landfall, it would want to run submerged—so in two days it could probably make such a distance with no trouble at all. As a matter of fact, the time and distance were just about right.

It was still a few minutes before noon, so probably Sam Fraser wouldn't have left for lunch yet. Havens picked up his telephone—these days you had to have a travel voucher for a trip to the men's room.

"Sam, I don't know how to break this to you, but maybe you'd better not count on Myrtle Beach. . . ."

"This is where we found the Tucker boy's body."

Sheriff Bilson turned out to be a man in his late fifties with heavy black hair and a comfortable expanse of belly under his plaid hunting jacket. He had a habit of smiling absentmindedly as he thought his way through something, and his eyes would almost disappear into the deep creases in his face. He pushed back a clump of bushes with his arm and pointed down at a patch of bare earth. There was nothing to suggest that anything extraordinary had happened there.

"The kid was frozen solid—they had to wait until he'd thawed out before they could do the autopsy, but anybody could see what'd happened. Somebody'd busted his windpipe, crushed it just as neat as you please."

He straightened up, allowing the bushes to close.

"I'll tell you somethin', Mr. Havens," he said, the edges of his mouth pulling back in a mirthless, unconscious smile. "I was a cop in Chicago for nine years before the wife talked me into movin' back here, and I've seen a lot o' dead guys. But I never seen a one of 'em that got it this way." He touched his larynx with the tip of his little finger. "This was a real elegant number—he knew what he was doin'. Somebody who kills a kid to steal his car and four or five bucks out of his wallet ain't gonna do such a lovely job."

"You found the car?"

"Oh, yeah." Sheriff Bilson nodded impassively, as if assenting to something perfectly obvious. "The next afternoon, in a parkin' lot in Ellsworth. Not five blocks from my office. We got the crime lab people from Bangor goin' over it for prints an' stuff, but they won't find nothin'."

Havens grinned at him, as much in admiration as anything else, and dug his hands into the pockets of his overcoat. He couldn't understand how people kept from expiring from the cold up here—and the sheriff wasn't even wearing a hat.

"You sound pretty hopeless."

"Maybe—but, like I said, I been around. We had some pretty hard boys back in Chicago, and I know a pro when I see one. This guy was a pro."

"Show me the tracks."

"Sure."

The woods were even colder than the road, if that was possible. And snow-laden tree limbs kept taking swipes at you, trying to drop their loads down the back of your neck. But Sheriff Bilson just went swinging right along in his heavy boots, not seeming to realize that he ought by rights to have been chilled to the bone.

"This is where they must've come onto the road," he said, pointing to a small clearing through which it was just possible to see the wet gleam of asphalt. Sure enough, looking down you could still see where the snow had been disturbed by several sets of footprints. The snow had thawed and refrozen once or twice, probably, but the weather had been clear that week and the characteristic marks of human passage had not yet been filled in.

Two men—the sheriff had been right about that. And then, about five feet off to the side, running parallel to the others, a fresher set of tracks that were probably Bilson's own.

"Are you making inquiries?" Havens asked. "Has anyone reported seeing any strangers?"

The sheriff nodded, not seeming to resent the question at all. "I got my two deputies on it. We don't get a lot o' pilgrims through here in the winter. If they stayed long enough to buy a meal or even just to light a cigarette, somebody'll remember. Look—I figure one of 'em must'a tripped over the log there."

They stopped in front of a patch of ground that looked as if the snow had been gone over with a roller. Several twigs had been broken off a nearby bush, and you could see where a thin strip of snow had been scuffed away from the top of the log.

Glancing around him, Havens reflected that even this brief little leg through the woods probably wouldn't have been much of a treat in the middle of the night. It was brushy country and the ground was broken up with rocks and narrow fissures and was half buried under the snow. If the gentlemen in question had only taken one spill they had gotten off lucky. God knows, they must have had a hell of a good reason for being out here.

The wind started to rise and all at once he could smell the ocean, a faint gritty dampness that inevitably suggested gray sand and tangled, rotting masses of seaweed and, somehow, a certain hopelessness. He couldn't see anything through the trees, but the sense of being at the land's edge was very strong.

Havens turned up the collar of his overcoat and wished he were back in Washington. He was cold and he hated being cold, and the hissing of the wind through the treetops made him uneasy. He was a city boy. As a kid, growing up on the edge of Brooklyn, his idea of the wilderness had been Central Park, and he felt himself at a disadvantage so far from the nearest telephone.

"What do you do up here to keep from going crazy?" he heard himself asking as he stamped his feet to shake off the snow. He looked around at Sheriff Bilson and found that apparently he had said something funny.

"Wait for spring." The creases in the sheriff's face widened as he smiled. "But it ain't as cold as Chicago. You ever been to Chicago?"

"Once. But that was in summer, and I was only there long enough to make a collar."

"Well—Chicago, now that's cold. Sometimes I miss it, though."

He seemed on the verge of confiding something, some personal anecdote perhaps, implying some personal weakness, however slight. Havens merely waited, trying to keep his face as unreadable as he could.

"You know, my missus was born up here," the sheriff began, hooking one gloved thumb over his belt and gazing down at the crusted, black-edged snow. "She talked me into movin' back because she said Chicago wasn't no fit place to raise kids—well, hell, I'd seen enough walkin' a beat on North Clark Street to think maybe she was right. And now this happens."

In the almost perfect silence around them, Havens at last was able to make out behind him the muffled sound of waves dying against a shingle beach. The sheriff, when at last he raised his eyes, seemed to be searching between the trees for some glimpse of water.

"I sure hope you catch these guys. I got a son of my own just Randy Tucker's age—they played on the high school baseball team together. This whole business hits a little too close to home."

It was possible to feel sorry for him. The big-city cop had lived in this peaceful backwater long enough to have lost a policeman's natural cynicism, and now the casual murder of a teenager on a lonely road had stripped him of his last illusion.

"Your boy plays baseball?" Havens asked, smiling, he imagined, somewhat fatuously—he was only trying to be kind. "What position?"

"Third base. This'll be his last season, though—I expect he'll enlist as soon as he gets out of school."

The idea didn't have a very cheering effect. After a moment the two men started walking again, following what was left of the tracks.

They stopped just at the snowline, where high tide would have washed the stones clean. You walked down the narrow pebbled beach, and you found yourself at the water's edge. Whoever had killed young Tucker that night obviously hadn't come by cab.

"How deep is the water out there?" Havens asked, looking around to where his guide was standing on a fallen log just at the top of the landfall. He found the sight of the slate-gray waves strangely exciting, as if he had discovered something unexpected. In his mind's eye, he could see the submarine, a black shape against the horizon as it nosed in toward the land.

Sheriff Bilson merely shrugged. "How deep do you want it? Eighty, a hundred feet—deeper in places."

There wasn't a doubt in George Havens' mind. After the disastrous failure of the '42 mission, the Germans had licked their wounds for eighteen months and now they were landing another team of agents. All that way, just to put two men up on a beach in Maine—only the second attempted penetration of the whole war.

"It makes you wonder," he murmured to himself. "What they could be looking for that would make it worth their while."

III

It took only forty minutes and two long-distance calls between Maine and Washington, D.C., before George Havens had the permission he needed to go ahead. He wouldn't have been at all surprised if that was a new Bureau record.

"We could track them right down to the water's edge, Sam," he said, sitting at one of the desks in Sheriff Bilson's office and staring out through the window at Ellsworth's main street. A storm had blown up while they were driving back from Frenchman's Bay, and by late afternoon the passing cars were churning up great plumes of dirty snow. It was nice to be inside. "Somebody went to a lot of trouble about those two. I can't imagine they're just here as tourists."

He waited through the long silence at the other end of the line, wondering if the whole business wasn't nonsense after all, wondering if this wouldn't turn out to be another black mark against him in Mr. Hoover's little book, another step toward that assignment polishing filing cabinets in Kansas City.

"Have I got your number there?" Sam Fraser asked, and Havens repeated it for him. "Then sit tight and I'll call you back in half an hour. I'll have to check on this with the Director."

"I'm sorry about the vacation, Sam."

"Fine—then you can explain it to Ida."

Just as Havens hung up the phone, the door opened and Bilson came in, brushing the snow from the shoulders of his jacket. Apparently he had been home in the meanwhile, because he was wearing a red knitted ski cap that hadn't been in evidence before. He whisked it off almost immediately and stuffed it into his pocket, as if he were ashamed of it.

"We got somethin' that might interest you," he said, in the tone of a man catering to the whims of his guest. "A witness—waitress over at Cowper's diner says she served dinner to a pair o' strangers late Saturday night, says they asked about the bus to Portland. You want to talk to her?"

"What do you think?" Havens was halfway into his coat before he remembered the telephone. Sam had said half an hour, but Sam might not be the one who called back. What if it were Mr. Hoover himself? That was possible, and he didn't want Mr. Hoover getting angry and pulling him off just because he wasn't there to pick up the phone—he did things like that.

So he sat down again. The sheriff's witness would have to wait. It was exactly twenty-eight minutes before the phone rang again, and it wasn't Mr. Hoover after all—only Sam.

"Follow it up, George. The Director says you can borrow whatever you need in the way of manpower from the local offices along the trail, but that he won't be too surprised if your spies, when you find them, turn out to be a couple of weekend fishermen."

"I don't think so, not these jokers. Don't you worry, Sam. When we pull in this catch we won't have any trouble squaring things with Mr. Hoover."

"It's not Hoover I'm worried about. It's Ida."

Havens grinned as he sat there listening to the buzz from the broken connection. He felt like a man reprieved from death.

"Let's go visit your waitress," he said to Bilson, who was leaning against the door frame, studiously investigating his fingernails. "I'll even buy you dinner, courtesy of the FBI."

At five-fifteen in the afternoon Cowper's diner was already about half full, which meant that either Friday nights started early in Ellsworth or the food was good. There was a counter, where most of the stools were occupied by solitary men in overalls hunched over their coffee cups like misers, and there were booths around three walls. Havens opted for a booth.

The two policemen sat down on opposite sides of the dark wooden table that carried the scars from generations of water glasses and hot plates and little boys who wanted to purchase immortality at the price of a few scratches with a dinner fork. Bilson sighed heavily and took a cigarette from his shirt pocket; it was the first time Havens had seen him smoke, so maybe it was a little ritual associated with being off duty. From here on, this was to be Havens' caper. The sheriff crooked his finger to summon the waitress—presumably *the* waitress—but after that, he seemed to imply, his part was over.

"Sure—two guys, right?" She handed them a couple of menu cards, written out in a peculiar greenish ink, and while she waited for Havens to respond, or maybe just to make up his mind about the meatloaf and mashed potatoes that were the special of the day, she used the eraser end of her order pencil to scratch just behind her right ear, all the time staring vacantly out through the big plate-glass window at the street, where it was only a few degrees above zero and nothing moved. "They closed the place up last Saturday—asked about the bus to Portland. We don't get that many strangers this time of year."

She favored him with a tentative smile that suggested that under the right circumstances she might look with kindness on a stranger. She was probably about twenty-three and not bad at all if you liked them with straw-colored hair that came straight out of a bottle, but Havens much preferred her as an eyewitness. He took out his badge and showed it to her, and the smile just withered away.

"Sit down, miss, and tell me all about them. Did they say specifically that they were going to Portland?"

"No, but that's where it goes." The sheriff made room for her and she slithered onto the bench and leaned forward on her elbows. "Hey, what is this anyway? Who were they—crooks or somethin'?"

"We just want to ask them a couple of questions. Could you describe them for me?"

Oh, yes, she could describe them. Especially the older one, who seemed to have made something of an impression.

"Like a movie star—you know what I mean? The whole number—tall, dark, and handsome. He reminded me a little of Tyrone Power—have you seen *The Black Swan* yet? Dreamy. A nice smile when he took the trouble, but most of the time you could have thought he was alone in the place. Never said a word, not one—at least not to me. Like ice. Still, I wouldn't have minded . . ."

"And the other one? What was he like?"

"Oh, *him.*" The waitress raised her upper lip in distaste. She didn't care for younger men, apparently. "All *he* wanted to do was get a peek down the front of my blouse—fat chance of *that.*"

"What did he *look* like?"

Havens smiled tolerantly, thinking he wouldn't have minded a peek in that direction himself, and the waitress raised her frizzy brown eyebrows and sniffed. She seemed rather to resent the suggestion that she might have noticed.

"Blond hair, kind of thick through the face. . . . He had little tiny eyes, and he blinked a lot—what can I tell you?"

"Who paid the tab?"

"The older one."

"Dreamboat?"

"That's right, smart guy—the good-looking one."

"And you never heard his voice?"

The waitress shook her head. "No, never."

Well, that was interesting—a suggestion, just a suggestion, that the older one was running the show. You would expect that, of course. And, for whatever reason, he preferred not to speak.

"Blondie—you heard him, though. What did he sound like?"

"*Sound* like?" She shrugged her shoulders, and the eyebrows once more crept up her forehead. "*I* don't know—what does *any* body sound like?"

"So he didn't have an accent?"

Obviously, she didn't even know what he was talking about.

So—maybe they weren't German agents after all. Maybe he had gone and made a big deal out of nothing, and they *were* just a couple of fishermen. Score a point for Mr. Hoover.

And maybe not. After all, the older one hadn't spoken. Maybe he had his reasons. And you didn't necessarily have to be a German, or sound like Erich von Stroheim, to be a German agent.

"What do you want to eat?" Havens asked, turning to Bilson.

"I don't know," he said as he studied the menu card meditatively. "But I'd stay away from the meatloaf if I was you."

"Is that *all?*" The waitress seemed scandalized, but Havens only nodded.

"For now—I'll have the corned beef—but don't worry, honey; this is only the first inning. I'd pack a bag when I got home tonight if I were you. I think you're probably going to be spending a couple of days away from home—a little vacation, a treat from your Uncle Sam."

"Gee."

Three-quarters of an hour later, Havens and Sheriff Bilson trudged back through the four-inch-deep snow to Bilson's office. There was no wind, and the cold wasn't as bad as Havens had expected. Perhaps he was just growing hardened.

"You gonna wait for the bus driver?" Bilson asked.

"You think he would be the same one?"

"Hell, I don't know." Bilson shook his head. For some reason the action reminded you of a buffalo. "Could be, but I don't know."

"Could you do me a favor and find out? And if it is the same one, see if you can't get word to him that he should call the Bureau office in Portland—right away."

"Is that where you'll be?"

"I suppose so." Havens looked around him at the storefronts along both sides of the narrow street. They gave the impression of having been deserted for good and all, as if the events of the preceding week were as inaccessibly past as the age of dinosaurs. "We've got a trail that's nearly six days cold. Catching these guys is going to be a close thing."

Havens requisitioned one of the two county cars assigned to the sheriff's office and drove down to Portland. It was a trip of only about a hundred and fifty miles, but he didn't get in until close to midnight because large stretches of the road were still unplowed. Almost as soon as he was inside the door, they handed him a transcript of their telephone conversation with the bus driver.

The driver remembered picking up two men in Ellsworth, neither of them his regulars, not half a block from Cowper's diner. That was about three-forty in the morning—he had been running late on account of the weather—and what they had done with themselves in the hours since the waitress had closed up after them at midnight was anybody's guess. They must have found somewhere in out of the cold, because obviously they hadn't frozen to death.

They sat by themselves, he remembered, all the way in the rear of the bus. The younger one was asleep most of the time.

By ten that morning they were on their way south again, with tickets for Boston. Havens himself talked with the woman from the ticket window in Portland, getting her name and address from the bus company and driving over to her rooming house to wake her out of a sound sleep. She, too, like the waitress, remembered the tall, handsome—and silent—man who had sat on one of the station benches for over an hour and a half, moodily staring at his hands. She had thought it strange that the two men, who were obviously traveling together, should hardly have spoken in all that time.

"He was a looker, the dark one," she said, blinking owlishly as she huddled at one end of the sofa in her two-room flat, her bathrobe wrapped around her like a shroud. At about sixty, she was as desiccated as a mummy, but apparently she still took an interest.

"That seems to be the general opinion."

Havens gave her his card and told her to phone him if she remembered anything more, and she was resolute that he should stay for a cup of coffee and a small square of fudge brownie. It was well after three in the morning, but she kept him there for a good twenty minutes, telling him what a shocking thing it was to work for the bus company and how he ought to investigate them. It was pathetic in a way—she seemed to welcome the disturbance.

He didn't reach Boston until the next afternoon—you had to get some sleep sometime—but the local office had their instructions and had already confirmed that two men answering the general description of Havens' suspects had indeed arrived in town on the afternoon of January 23. It looked like they were getting cagey, because they had checked into a hotel five blocks from the bus station, vanished almost immediately, and were finally traced to a room all the way over in Cambridge, where they stayed for two nights before taking a bus down to Providence, Rhode Island, where they caught the train.

The train went to New York, but they got off at New Haven. Dreamboat—you had to call him something—bought a newspaper at the stand right there in the station and engaged the vendor, who was a Basque refugee, in a long conversation in French. It was as if he wanted to be remembered as having disembarked at that stop, should anyone be interested enough to inquire.

"Did he speak good French?"

"Oh, yes, *très bien.* Very good French." The paper vendor's eyes widened in his leathery old face. His mustache was thick enough to cover his whole mouth, but you had the impression he was smiling underneath it. "He was a gentleman, was that one."

"Where would you say he came from?" The old man looked puzzled—did he imagine he was being quizzed about train schedules?—so Havens decided to rephrase the question. "What nationality?"

The paper vendor shrugged. "Oh, well . . . as to that, with a gentleman it is always difficult to say."

Where they went next was an open question, but Havens believed they must have gotten back on the train and gone to New York.

After all, it made sense. Certainly they hadn't stayed in New Haven. Bureau people had been all over town and hadn't turned up a trace of either of them. Nobody at the ticket windows remembered them, but quite possibly they could have purchased their tickets on board from the conductor. They would need to stop somewhere long enough to buy new clothes and get their bearings, and New York would be the point of departure for almost anywhere they would want to go next. Besides, they would want to be a little careful before they indicated too clearly where they were bound. They would want to see if they were being followed. New York would be a good place for that.

So Havens went on to New York, where there wasn't very much to do except wait. He had both the newspaper vendor and the waitress from Ellsworth run into the Boston office, where they helped a Bureau artist put together a composite sketch of each of the two subjects. They had a lot of trouble agreeing, and neither of them retained any very vivid impression of the younger one—and now guys with badges were all over Manhattan showing copies of the sketches to ticket sellers and rooming house landladies. There weren't any guarantees that they hadn't already left the city, provided they had stopped there at all, but that was the best bet going at the moment. If they weren't there, they weren't anywhere.

Havens requisitioned a force of ten men, figuring he could probably hang onto them for no longer than a week before Mr. Hoover would want either the spies or his hide, and there were limits to what you could do with ten men in a week. They were making the rounds, and the train and bus stations were being watched; it was as far as you could go without throwing out a regular dragnet—running the sketches in the newspapers, alerting the taxi drivers, that sort of thing—and it just hadn't developed into that big a deal yet. Mr. Hoover would never have stood for it.

So all Havens could do—all anyone could do—was to keep his fingers crossed and wait. It was the sort of thing that drove you buggy by slow degrees.

He rented a room up on Eighth Avenue, but it was small and dark and silent, and by the second day he couldn't stand it anymore. It was even worse at the Bureau office; he could sit by the telephones and listen to them not ringing. By the middle of the afternoon he found he just had to get away for a while.

He took a walk, but a cold wind had blown up since yesterday—it really wasn't very nice out. So he bought a cup of coffee and a copy of the *Times* at a lunch stand on East Thirty-seventh Street and sat down at the booth nearest the window and read about what was happening in the world.

As always, the headlines only depressed him. The Pacific Fleet had begun its invasion of the Marshalls, and the British had evidently gotten within sixteen miles of Rome. All of this while George Havens was sitting around in New York, waiting for a couple of jokers who might or might not be spies, and might or might not be in town, to stick their heads up out of a hole. It wasn't fair.

Outside, people on the sidewalk were pulling their hats down over their ears as they bent into the wind, their coattails swirling behind them. Havens took a sip of his coffee, which looked and tasted like motor oil, and turned to the sports pages.

Like the fulfillment of prophecy, there was an article headlined "BRADLEY IS SKEPTICAL ABOUT 1944 BASEBALL." Well, what else was new?

"Alva Bradley, one of organized baseball's frankest magnates, advised major league owners today to suspend operation for the duration rather than present 'a low form of comedy' during the 1944 season."

Oh God, that was all the country needed was for some purist to shut down the World Series. Then there really wouldn't be anything left to live for.

Leo Durocher was going overseas to entertain the troops, the paper said, and Joe Tinker was in a hospital down in Florida, dying of influenza. It was enough to make you take a vow against reading anything except *True Detective Stories*.

He refolded the pages with almost fussy deliberation and laid the newspaper down on the seat next to him. The virtue had gone out of everything.

The girl at the cash register smiled and took his receipt and a dollar bill and gave him a Mounds bar and ninety cents in change. A Mounds bar, for Christ's sake—maybe it was his lucky day after all. He couldn't even remember the last time he had tasted a Mounds bar.

As he walked along the pavement, in the general direction of the Forty-second Street Library, it occurred to him that this was almost the first time he had been in New York since his divorce. No wonder he wasn't enjoying himself very much.

Poor Karen. What she had wanted more than anything was a nice, steady sort of husband who steps off the commuter train at 6:05 every evening and doesn't stir from the front parlor until it's time to go to bed, and what she got was the Lone Ranger.

"I'm in the spy-catching business, sweetheart—just like 'Terry and the Pirates.' The Nazis don't keep bankers' hours, so I can't very well either."

"But you could be home for dinner *once* in a while. I roasted this lovely saddle-of-lamb, and the Gormers were coming over in the evening to play Parcheesi, and you never even *phoned.*"

"Yeah, well . . . things got a little rushed."

So, after two years, four months, and twenty-two days, Karen decided she had had enough and moved back in with her widowed mother. Havens hadn't even gotten a card from her in over a year —probably by now she was married to a bus conductor, if she could find one who was 4-F.

And her ex-husband had applied for a leave of absence to go fight in the big war across the water, and Mr. Hoover—damn his eyes—had issued his pointed refusal, and now the George Havens who had been the terror of the Abwehr spent most of his time behind a desk in Washington answering nut phone calls about whether the Japanese had invaded New Rochelle. It was by no means certain that Karen would have appreciated the irony.

God, how he wished these Nazi sons of bitches, if that was what in fact they were, would do the decent, sporting thing and give him a peek—just a peek, so he would know the game hadn't been called on account of rain. It was the waiting around that made an old man out of you.

The cement lions at the Fifth Avenue entrance to the library looked patient and faintly sleepy, as if content to wait for the snow to melt. Each of them seemed to be ignoring the other's existence, and the thin stream of harassed-looking and, at that hour, mostly female pedestrians passed back and forth beneath them with almost insulting indifference. Havens trudged up the steps, feeling like a petitioner on his way to court.

Actually, all he wanted to do was to use the men's room.

When he was finished, he found he was no longer able to withstand the temptation and hunted up a telephone. Probably there was nothing stirring. There never was. It was like waiting for prices to go down.

"Mr. Havens?—no, sir, no sightings yet." The voice belonged to a kid named Irving who was fresh out of Quantico and keen as mustard. "But we got a kind of screwy call about forty minutes ago; some guy said he wanted to talk to Mr. Hoover about spies. We gave him the standard pitch about Mr. Hoover being out of the office just then and would he like to talk to one of his assistants, and finally he decided to settle for that. But not today, thank you—he said he'd call you back."

Havens studied the initials carved all over the inside of the phone booth—"N.H." "J.G." "L.D. + R.W." "P.D.Q."—and wondered whether espionage hadn't become the exclusive property of the demented. There weren't any real spies anymore, only a bunch of crazies who thought they were in on Final Secret. Why did they always think they could insist on talking directly with Mr. Hoover?

"Do you think he was just a nut?" he asked wearily.

"No, sir. He was scared, but he wasn't crazy—at least, I don't think so. He said something about a submarine."

"What time did he say he'd phone back?"

"Nine o'clock in the morning, sir."

Havens hung up, feeling better than he had in days.

But nine o'clock was a long way off, and sitting on one of the wide benches in the main corridor, right next to the entrance to the Oriental Room, was what was generally referred to as the Genuine Article. She had blond hair that swept back behind her ears and fell down between her shoulder blades in a roll, and she was perched there with her legs crossed, reading a magazine. She didn't look all that busy.

Mr. Hoover had rules about this sort of thing. You were supposed to be as pure as Shirley Temple, married or not. And if you were married, it was supposed to be to the right kind of girl, the kind who was a good trooper, loyal to Mr. Hoover, the flag, country, and your own sweet self in just about that order. Well, it hadn't worked out that way. Mr. Hoover hadn't been pleased —divorces weren't exactly rejoiced over, even divorces that resulted from spending too much time on the Bureau's business and not enough on your own—and Mr. Hoover wouldn't have been pleased now, since girls who let themselves get picked up outside the Oriental Room probably wouldn't have qualified in his mind as good troopers. But what Mr. Hoover didn't know wouldn't hurt him, and Havens was in the mood for an easy steal.

The doorway from the telephones and the elevators was about fifteen feet high; he stood next to it, waiting for her to notice him. Finally she looked up—she had blue eyes and a red, full mouth, which was very nice. And she smiled.

Havens sat down beside her and fished around for a moment through the pockets of his overcoat. He was smiling too. He wondered whether she would feel like splitting a Mounds bar.

IV

It had been snowing at intervals ever since lunch. Von Niehauser stood behind the rear window of his apartment, looking down at the corner of Eighty-first Street and Lexington Avenue, hardly able to see a thing for the smears left behind by thousands of half-melted snowflakes that had traced their way across the dusty glass.

He was in his shirt sleeves and a pair of light gray flannel trousers that looked a size too large for him, and his hands were locked together behind his back. He hadn't stirred in perhaps as long as twenty minutes. He was quite alone, staring through the clouded windowpane with almost painful concentration.

All day long he had been prey to a kind of anxious melancholy that was quite new to him. It was like a warning, but against what he couldn't have said. Stafford was gone—off amusing himself with the money he had swindled from the SS. Perhaps, von Niehauser found himself thinking, perhaps, after all the weeks of enforced intimacy aboard Meyersdorff's submarine, he had lost the knack of being alone. Perhaps he was no longer used to the solitude. Yes, perhaps it was something as simple as boredom.

His father had used to do the same thing sometimes—stare out through one of the sitting room windows at home, sometimes for hours. Especially after the death of von Niehauser's mother. Had that been boredom, too? Was it simply that without the baroness the world had become empty? Or had his father been visited by some harsher ghost?

But, no. The late Rolf, Baron von Niehauser, had died a lieutenant general in the first heady days after the invasion of France, so he had been spared everything that was to follow. He had never had to face the world Hitler had made of Europe since 1940. For him it had been simple, nothing more than a second chance to fight yet once again the Great War of 1914–18—and his sons, all of whom had seen service in Poland, had kept the truth of that conflict from him. He had thus never known about the wholesale executions behind the lines, about the work of the *Einsatzgruppen,* about the whole sickening spectacle. And when a land mine had blown up under his staff car, he had been able to die in innocence.

So he would never have understood.

His father, had he lived and been compelled to witness what the last of his line had come to, would probably have turned away from him in disgust. What, after all, should a von Niehauser have to do with espionage and murder? When you were the head of one of the oldest families of the Prussian nobility, members of which had worn the red trousers of the General Staff in unbroken succession ever since the time of Frederick the Great, your traditions were those of honorable combat and blameless service to the state. What had any of that to do with stolen cars and the police and the butchery of farmboys? What indeed?

But the son was not the father. The son had known the contagion of sin this war had brought to the world, and had lived to see himself that strange thing, the hunted fugitive.

"I can't stand this," Stafford had said, whispering between his teeth as they sat in the almost deserted railroad car while it pulled slowly away from the station at a place called Milford. It had been a long day, and Stafford's apparently infinite capacity for panic was beginning to take its toll. "They could be on to us already, you know. They could be following us right now, just waiting to see where we lead them."

Von Niehauser had looked up over the edge of the newspaper he had purchased in New Haven. Finally he shrugged his shoulders.

"Then we will shake them off. We will step up over their heads."

Stafford hadn't understood. But then, fortunately, very little depended on what Stafford might or might not understand. And, in any case, how could something like that be explained? It was one of the advantages of breeding.

The last of the von Niehausers, who had followed his parents to London and Copenhagen, to Paris and Madrid, to all the places where his father had been posted as a military attaché, had been allowed to come to manhood without seeing life from the narrowing perspective of someone born to a uniform. He was the third son—it had hardly mattered, since the tradition was safe, so the baron had raised no very serious objection when little Joachim's interests had drawn him in other directions. But perhaps, unprotected as he was by the gold braid of an officer's epaulets, he had grown up more alert, more apt to notice things.

And one of the things he had noticed was that the police were great believers in the virtuousness of the upper classes. Out of habit and self-interest, they sought their criminals among the socially defenseless. They looked up to the rich and the powerful or, rather, they hardly looked at them at all. At a certain economic level, you became invisible.

And it was just as true in the other direction. Von Niehauser doubted very much if his father had ever noticed a policeman in his life. Why should a baron and a member of the German General Staff notice the police?

But, then, his father had never been a spy.

Notwithstanding, one of the first things von Niehauser did after he and Stafford arrived in New York was to rent a large furnished apartment in a respectable neighborhood. He had sent

Stafford around to the closest branch office of the National City Bank and had him establish a checking account. They had paid out the first six months' rental in advance—after all, the SS could afford it.

Then, the next morning, he had set out for a men's clothing store on Madison Avenue, one he had passed while walking up from Grand Central Station and which gave the impression that it didn't cater to the working classes, to buy himself a suit. Both of the ones he had brought with him from Germany were copied out of American magazines, and he felt some misgivings about their perfect accuracy. It took only a trivial mistake, something as insignificant as the width of one's lapels, for someone to notice and remember, and von Niehauser didn't want to be noticed. So he would buy a new suit—and a new overcoat and shoes and shirts and underwear—and set his mind at ease.

The precaution was unnecessary with Stafford, since all of his clothes dated from before his defection. Stafford presented other difficulties.

It had been a pleasure picking out the suit. The store carried only a limited selection, but he found a gray pin stripe that would require very little tailoring and could be ready the next afternoon.

"Wartime scarcities," the tailor assured him, folding his hands together apologetically. "We can't get the cloth."

He was an elderly Jew who spoke heavily accented English with a kind of wheezing murmur, his shoulders assuming a gentlemanly stoop as he adjusted von Niehauser's lapels, making him feel at once homesick and ashamed. From the shape of his vowels anyone could have guessed that he was from Breslau. One wondered what his history could have been.

"Yes, tomorrow, around four." He helped von Niehauser out of the jacket. "It just needs a little taking in."

And it really was a good suit. Von Niehauser had only worn it once, but he liked to leave it hanging from the hook on the outside of his closet door, simply because it gave him so much satisfaction to look at it. It was the first purely personal item of clothing he had bought since before the beginning of the Polish campaign, and its purchase had been like the rediscovery of some forgotten emotion.

Finally, that was the most vivid impression of this country, something that came to one gradually, like an object recognized as one's eyes adjusted to the dark—the war seemed so distant. It was almost possible to imagine that the world had returned to normal.

"I read in the paper that they'll probably lift meat rationing by May," he had overheard a woman saying to the man, possibly her husband, who sat next to her on the subway. "*Then* you'll see the butchers change their tune!" The newspapers even talked about what would happen in what they referred to as the "postwar period," as if they had already won. As if it were over.

And why not? Except, perhaps, for the dying, perhaps it was.

New York was a long way from Berlin, where all you had to do was to walk to the next block to see the evidence of the previous night's bombing raid: the broken buildings, the stunned, sleepless families setting up their furniture on the sidewalk because there was nowhere else. All over Germany, people would start at the slightest sound. The whole country was under siege.

People there wondered when it would end. They all knew how it would end, and they couldn't imagine any kind of life for themselves beyond that. Hitler was right—everyone in Germany was a soldier now. They all knew that the final defeat would be theirs too.

But Stafford was an American. He had been shielded by thousands of miles of ocean from the consequences of war; he understood nothing of defeat. It was merely a word to him.

"Do you think we'll get a medal for this?" he had asked once. "You probably don't care—you've probably got a chestful of medals. They told me at the training school that you had the *Ritterkreuz.*"

The submarine had been nearly four hundred miles beyond the Irish coast, far enough away from enemy territory to risk surfacing for a few hours in daylight, and von Niehauser had been taking what advantage he could of the cold winter sun. He had been alone on the conning tower for about twenty minutes, just watching the way the prow split through the slate-gray water, when Stafford joined him. He turned around and smiled thinly.

"Hitler has given the *Ritterkreuz* to his physician, who, they say, injects him with amphetamines and bull semen. Be content to do the thing we are being sent to do, and to come away alive. There will be glory enough in that."

"What *are* we being sent to do?"

If you looked at Stafford for longer than a few seconds, he would always grin at you. Probably it was nothing more than embarrassment—he had an almost pathetic need for approval—but von Niehauser took it simply as a sign of weakness. Stafford couldn't keep his countenance; he was constantly the victim of self-betrayal. Whatever his loyalties might be, whatever he might imagine them to be, he was not a man to be trusted.

This time, von Niehauser did not smile.

"Be thankful you have been spared that knowledge. What you need to know, you know—be content with that."

No second warning had proved necessary.

Or perhaps it had. He didn't know—he couldn't read a man like Stafford. The motives of such a person were a mystery to him.

He rested the palm of his hand against the windowpane, surprised somehow to find it so cold. He could feel the little drops of condensation trickling down between his fingers. It was too hot in the apartment. One would have thought that in time of war . . .

But here it seemed to be no one's war but his own. He wondered where Stafford could be, what he was doing. He didn't trust the man unless he was right there before his eyes. Perhaps, now that he was home, Stafford had forgotten all about the fact that they were here as agents of the Reich.

"What *are* we being sent to do?" he had asked, actually expecting to be told. It had been a wise precaution to exclude him from that particular secret.

But perhaps Schellenberg hadn't trusted Stafford quite so far as he had pretended—perhaps Stafford had grinned at him too. Or perhaps it had been the simple prudence of his trade. After all, vulgar little climber that he was, Schellenberg had never shown any signs of being a fool, and this particular assignment required the kind of specialized technical training one normally didn't pick up in the hold of a merchant ship. Stafford was there merely as decoration.

"We need a man who knows what he's doing," Schellenberg had said, "someone with the proper background. You studied under Schleiermacher at the Kaiser Wilhelm Institute, didn't you?"

As they walked along together, he peered around at von Niehauser, cocking his head to one side just as if it had been a real question. But, of course, he already knew the answer. There seemed to be precious little about von Niehauser that he didn't know.

"Yes, right up until 1938, when he lost his professorship."

"Ah, well. . . ." Schellenberg smiled to himself. He had a handsome, rather infantile face, and the soft boyishness of his smile was supposed to be one of the reasons he had been able to climb so high so fast. "That, as it turns out, was something of a mistake."

They continued on in silence for a while, walking across the hospital grass in perfect step, their hands clasped behind their backs. Despite the difference in their uniforms, anyone would have thought they had been comrades in arms for years.

"I wouldn't wish to be in your place," Schellenberg said finally, as if the idea had just occurred to him. "Of course, it would have been impossible for you to refuse—a man like you couldn't, could he? —but, still, I shouldn't like to be the one to go. Aside from the danger, there's the responsibility. There's every chance you might end up settling the fate of Europe for the next thousand years."

"I thought the Führer had already done that."

"Well, yes. . . ." And he had smiled again, seeing the joke. Precisely because he was such an opportunist, it was possible to talk to Schellenberg—a real Nazi would never have seen the joke. "But you might actually make it happen. We could still win the war—or, at least, keep from losing it, which comes to the same thing. We could keep Britain and the United States at bay, and that would mean we could hold on to what we have in the East. And that was always the plan anyway. *Lebensraum,* remember? We could still have it all."

"And you think I might be able to give it to you?"

"Well . . . you might be lucky enough to be the instrument of your country's salvation—yes. I needn't tell you what will happen if you fail."

And Schellenberg, who had never seen combat, visibly squared his shoulders, as if in preparation for that end which, doubtless, he could hardly imagine.

But von Niehauser had no trouble imagining it. What had Russia been but a massive preview? Starvation, misery, death in the full range of its horror. The land a vast waste, populated only with corpses and broken, burning machines. No men left, only instances of wretchedness.

And the Russians would extend that all the way across the face of Germany. Germany would be like a second Carthage. The Russians would lead the people away as slaves and sow the ground with salt. There would be no mercy—why should the Russians show them any mercy?

That was what his father would never have understood: war as the totality of existence, the absolute condition of life. It wasn't just an affair between armies anymore. For Hitler, everyone was the enemy, and the fate of an enemy was extinction. And he had taught that lesson to the Russians.

No, there would be no mercy. The Germans would not be forgiven so soon again.

Once, just a few months before a random mortar round put an end to his military career, von Niehauser had been extended the rare privilege of two weeks' leave. Except to attend his father's funeral, he had hardly been home since the beginning of the war, and he had just been decorated a second time, so perhaps they decided he had earned it. At any rate, he was given two weeks—just enough time to get home for a day or two to refresh the spirit. That was the idea.

By then, of course, he thought he had seen it all. He had been spared nothing, it seemed. Conquest had been bad enough, but defeat . . .

He had always imagined that losing must be so simple. It had never occurred to him that it would take so long and turn out to be so astonishingly intricate. But it left you no time for anything else—everything was going wrong and there were no replacements and your men were dying around you like rats from exhaustion and the cold and the sudden early-morning attacks of the partisans. There wasn't even time to think.

That was all he wanted, really—just a little time to think. After all, there was nothing at home. Since the deaths of his two older brothers, he was the last of the von Niehausers. There would be no one to whom he needed to explain anything, no one to offer the distraction of a friendly word. He would be quite at liberty. Perhaps the nightmare would come clear to him if he could just give it a little time.

He was lucky enough to have a cousin attached to Governor-General Frank's staff, who arranged his passage for him through the conquered territories; he traveled with a couple of colonels in the *Sturmbanne* who were returning from a tour of inspection. During the journey they had all stopped off at a place called Treblinka. The colonels had insisted. They seemed to be under the impression they were offering him some sort of treat.

"This will give you a story or two to tell your grandchildren," one of them said, and they both laughed.

That was the day von Niehauser had learned that this time not even God would pity them if they lost.

He had hardly spent an hour at his family estate before he

realized that he no longer belonged there.

Görlitz was too insignificant a place to have suffered much from the Allied bombing raids—of course, Dresden, which was only about a hundred kilometers away, was another matter—and his home was to the northeast, almost half an hour by car. He could stand in the middle of his mother's drawing room, the room where she had died of a heart attack the last year he was a student at the Institute, and imagine, for a moment, that the war was simply something he had dreamed. It couldn't possibly have really happened. Presently Egon and Kurt would come striding in, tanned and arrogant from a day of grouse shooting, and everyone would laugh and drink sherry while they waited for dinner to be announced. During the meal, his father would sit at the head of the table, listening silently—only nodding now and then—while Kurt talked about Army politics.

Except that Kurt had burned to death under his half-track during the second Battle of El Alamein, and Egon, poor Egon, who had never had very much to say if there was anyone else to do the talking and who would, on the whole, have preferred breeding horses to a career in the military, poor Egon had been blown to atoms six months later when the officers' mess at Gukovo found itself under point-blank Russian artillery bombardment.

An hour—the familiar feeling of safety lasted an hour, no more—and then von Niehauser felt as if he had somehow blundered into a museum after closing hours. Nothing here had anything to do with him any longer. He slept that night in his old bedroom, where his school diplomas still hung on the walls and against one corner of his closet leaned the cricket bat he had used during his four terms as a student at Winchester. The next morning he packed up his kit and caught a troop train back to Russia—running away as if to a place of refuge.

And then, six weeks later, the mortar round that had almost killed him. And then all those months in the hospital at Bitterfeld, where there had been nothing to do but to turn over his memories, one at a time, like old photographs with torn corners and the indelible smudges of unnumbered fingers. Memories oddly impersonal, as if they belonged to someone else's life.

And then, as the brown leaves began to curl and the weather turned cold again, and he found he was once more able to raise his left hand above his shoulder, along had come Schellenberg, smiling and boyish in his carefully tailored Brigadier-SS uniform, offering a path back from the tyranny of foreboding.

"Yes. I'll do it. You knew that before you asked. But I have a condition."

Schellenberg's eyebrows shot up—doubtless he was thinking of the price, whether in money or promotions or immunity for friends; that was simply the way his mind worked.

"I wish to resign my commission first. This is not the sort of business with which to sully a uniform my family has worn with honor for two hundred years. I should prefer to go as a civilian."

"Yes, well, I imagine something of the kind can be arranged."

It had rained all the night before, and the hospital grounds were covered with shallow pools of water in which the grass seemed to be lost in shadow. As they walked along, Schellenberg was taking great care to keep his boots dry.

"I suppose they are ready to let you leave this place," he said, glancing around with very evident distaste at the row of chair-bound patients that lined the front porch.

"Oh, yes." Von Niehauser smiled mirthlessly. "I haven't any idea why I've stayed so long already. Except—one feels rather at loose ends. . . . I had hoped for another posting to Russia, but they tell me that a return to active service is out of the question."

The brigadier looked surprised, as if he suspected he was being lied to. The impression passed away quickly enough.

"Well—I imagine you'll see enough active service in America. And at least the winters there aren't as bad."

Of course, at that time he had said nothing about Stafford. There had been a good deal that had been left unsaid.

It was hard to believe, with the whole world at war, that there could still be anyone left who would be so affected by the shedding of a little blood. Schellenberg might have warned him.

What an exhibition Stafford had made of himself, as if the hazard should have been in any way changed by the murder of a farmboy.

To be fair, though, it was no more than the natural reaction. One had to remember—Stafford was really still nothing but a civilian.

"What are we going to do?" he had gasped, leaning with both hands against the roof of the car, his head dropping down between his arms—anyone would have supposed he was exhausted. "What the hell are we going to do?"

It wasn't a practical question, since they had already done almost everything that the situation demanded. Von Niehauser had driven the car far enough off the road so that it wouldn't be noticed by any passing motorists, and then the two of them had carried its late driver's corpse about thirty yards back into the woods and set it face down behind some bushes. There wasn't even much blood, only a single dark patch on the asphalt that von Niehauser had been able to clean away nearly completely with a little snow and a tree branch.

"He won't stay hidden very long," he had said as they walked back to where the car was hidden. "A day or two, no more than that, and someone will find him. They'll probably start looking as soon as they miss him."

But his partner hardly seemed to hear. Stafford merely stumbled along beside him, breathing noisily, almost as if he were running. For him, apparently, the problem was not one of dealing with immediate contingencies. But von Niehauser had tried to be consoling.

"His name was Randall Tucker," he went on, holding up a small, rectangular object. It was the boy's wallet. "There are four dollars in here, enough to provide the police with a motive. We'll drive the car a few miles and then abandon it, with the empty wallet on the front seat. That will seem to suggest a simple robbery; perhaps no one will think to look beyond that."

Stafford hadn't appeared very consoled. He glanced up, turning his head to the side so he could gaze blindly over his shoulder, and even in the dark it was impossible to overlook the terrible slack weariness in his face. It took some people like that—fear assuming the aspect of an almost physical prostration.

Von Niehauser had seen easily enough that now was not the time for explanations or bracing encouragements. For the moment at least, Stafford was beyond the reach of words.

"Get in," he said, in a voice loud enough to break through this coma of dread. "Get in the car, Harry, it's time to go."

They had driven back the way they had been going, in the direction which, presumably, would take them to the nearest town.

"See if there is a map in the dash. No, leave your gloves on. Nothing is to be gained by providing the police with a set of fingerprints."

Because by then, of course, Stafford had come a little way out of his trance. No one had need of any maps. Those had been furnished by the SS, to be memorized and left behind with the charts aboard the submarine, but it was just as well if he were provided with something to occupy his mind. He groped around, found a flashlight, turned it on, and reported that there were no maps.

"Why? Are we lost?"

Von Niehauser pointed to a road sign that was coming up on their right side: SULLIVAN—5, HANCOCK—9, ELLSWORTH—18.

"No. Since we have the car, I think we might as well drive straight on through to Ellsworth and leave it there. Bangor would have been even better, but I doubt if we have enough petrol—excuse me, *gasoline*—for that. The SS, in their wisdom, neglected to provide us with any ration coupons. At any rate, Ellsworth will do."

The suggestion didn't seem to excite much enthusiasm. Stafford's eyes were glassy with fright. He had forgotten to turn off the flashlight.

"But, the police! This car . . ." He was panting so hard he couldn't seem to finish a sentence. "What if they . . ."

"Calm yourself, Harry. The police will not be looking for anything for several more hours. No one but you and I have any idea that young Mr. Tucker isn't safely home in bed, and Ellsworth is no more than thirty or forty minutes away. We will attract less attention in a larger town, and we can abandon the car where no one will notice it for some time. We should be on the bus and very probably out of the state before morning."

"But if they catch us, they . . ."

"It will make remarkably little difference, my friend." Von Niehauser turned to him, his lips parted in rather a cruel smile. "If they catch us at all, what difference do you imagine Mr. Tucker will make? We are spies, remember? And you are a traitor. In time of war, either of those is quite sufficient to put us in the condemned cells."

They had already been together for weeks, through the journey and the training before that, but in an odd way that evening on a snow-covered road in Maine they seemed finally to have discovered one another. It hadn't been a very encouraging experience.

Von Niehauser decided to open the window. It had stopped snowing, and their living room was like an oven. He gulped down the cold air, leaning out over the roof of the next building, across which unused clotheslines were swaying heavily in a fitful, half-hearted wind. It was a few minutes after three, the slack middle of the afternoon when the sidewalks below were almost deserted and even the intersection, a piece of which was visible around the side of the next apartment house, seemed for the moment to be empty of traffic.

They had been in New York for nearly five days. That had

been the plan from the beginning, to go to ground for a while somewhere, catch their breath, and make sure they hadn't attracted any attention. It would have been pleasant enough, except for the feeling of nakedness that probably afflicted every agent in a hostile country. It was impossible to be comfortable when you wondered every moment who might be watching you and, as a result, von Niehauser tended to spend most of his time in their rooms. This narrow little view of Lexington Avenue had become one of the important pleasures of his life.

Of course, Stafford was not so handicapped. He was home, so there was no reason for him to be troubled by von Niehauser's sense of strangeness. In fact, the apartment seemed to make him nervous.

This, however, was the longest he had yet stayed out of contact. There hadn't been a word since yesterday morning.

Was that the problem—that Stafford was home? Perhaps it had been a mistake to stop in New York. Perhaps it would have been better to have kept him on a tighter rein.

Von Niehauser went into the kitchen and took a bottle of ginger ale out of the refrigerator. In England, during his youth, they had had something similar; he had been quite fond of it. But the American version turned out to be pale and rather insipid. He opened the bottle and, without tasting it, set it down on the kitchen table. He appeared to have forgotten its existence.

"Where the devil is he?" he whispered to himself, staring angrily at the half-open cupboard that contained their meager supply of dishes. "What in God's name can he be doing?"

V

He awoke with a start. Had he made a noise? Screamed? No. Well, thank God for that. And now he couldn't even remember what he had been dreaming, except that it had scared the hell out of him. Maybe it had only been the sunshine, streaming in through the hotel window.

Stafford sat up in bed, sweating, waiting for his heart to quiet down. He was wide awake now—or would be, as soon as he could convince himself that the dream, whatever it had been, was gone. He was glad he hadn't screamed.

His watch was lying on the night table. It was still a few minutes shy of seven, and the girl he must have picked up last night was lying with her face to the wall, quietly snoring. God, he couldn't even remember her name. He couldn't even remember where he had found her. Was she going to expect to be paid, or what? God, he was going to have to stop drinking so much. All he could remember of last night were little snatches.

He needed a drink of water. There was a thick film all over the inside of his mouth, and the taste was like something had crawled in there to die. As quietly as possible—he didn't want to wake her, whoever she was; he didn't want to have to talk to her, not yet—he put his legs over the side of the bed and padded into the bathroom. The floor was strewn with underwear, and there was a brassiere draped over the arm of a chair. They must have had themselves quite a time at least.

He turned on the cold water and dabbed a little on his face.

It made his eyes sting. In the mirror he looked terrible. His skin was as yellow as wax, and the flesh under his jaw seemed all bloated. He was going downhill almost from morning to morning.

And then he remembered Joachim von Niehauser, and the unfocused terror of his dream came back to him with sickening immediacy. The nightmare had been real.

That kid back in Maine, with the blood leaking out of the corner of his mouth—he had been real. How was it possible to kill someone like that, so that he hardly even made a sound?

In Europe, millions are dying. Whole nations. Don't speak to me of your squeamishness over a little blood. Soon enough, and we will all be up to our necks in it.

Whatever Stafford had expected when he stepped off that merchant ship in Lisbon, it hadn't been Niehauser. All he had wanted was a little German glory—to be a soldier, and wear a uniform, and fight—and, instead of that, here he was back in the States, not twenty miles from the place where he had been born, taking orders from this crazy man who didn't even like Hitler and went around murdering people as calmly as anyone else would put out a cigarette.

We are spies, remember? And you are a traitor. In time of war, either of those is quite sufficient to put us in the condemned cells.

Ever since they had gotten to New York, and it had become possible to get away from Niehauser once in a while, Stafford had been living it up. Clothes, the best restaurants, the best liquor—whatever women he could get his hands on. If you work at it hard enough, he figured, it might be possible to forget for a while that you've been an accomplice to murder, and that Niehauser has as much as told you that you were next on the list. For a while.

He had to do something—that was all. He had to do something before he ended up in jail, or at the bottom of an air shaft somewhere with his neck broken. Niehauser scared the hell out of him.

He went back into the bedroom and sat down on the edge

of the bed, wishing he had a cup of coffee. The girl was still sleeping with her face to the wall; her back, where it was uncovered by the sheet, was pitted with acne scars. He was developing a headache. He wondered if it wouldn't be possible to dress quickly and be gone before she woke up.

No, it wouldn't. She rolled over toward him and smiled. It was a lazy, deliberately provocative smile, and she made not the slightest attempt to cover her breasts. Yes, she was going to expect to be paid.

"Morning, Harry," she said. She had a wide, shiny face, and her black eyebrows grew together over the bridge of her nose. He must have been pretty drunk.

Good God, had he been drunk enough to tell her his real name?

He didn't answer. Somehow he doubted that she'd take it very much amiss; she didn't seem the type to view these matters personally. He started gathering up his clothes, keeping his back to her as much as he could. At the moment it seemed that the only worthwhile thing was to get out of there.

"What's your hurry? Why don't you come back to bed?" He turned around to look at her and found that she had drawn back the sheet for him, exposing herself all the way down to her knees. For the first time he noticed how old she was—she could have been in her middle thirties. There were stretch marks on her belly. "You want somethin'? Best way in the world to start the day. You're a nice boy—an extra ten bucks and you can do anything you want with me."

The subway out to Queens was crowded; there almost wasn't room to raise your arm and grab hold of one of the straps. At that hour everyone was going home.

Stafford hung on to one of the polished steel poles next to the doorway, feeling curiously grateful for the anonymous crush. For a while, at least, he was just one more in a congregation of strangers, an object of interest to no one, unnoticed except as another body. He had returned to the confused boredom of everyday life. He was like everybody else.

Of course, it was going to end with the train ride. After the Jamaica station he would once more be the traitor and fugitive that Niehauser said he was. That was real—safety was the illusion. Still, he couldn't quite see himself as a German spy. He had gotten into a hell of a fix, but all this business was just more than he could quite make himself believe.

"It would be better if you put all that out of your mind," Niehauser had said. "Avoid places where you might be known, but, for the rest, try to imagine that you have just taken up your old life again. There is nothing which attracts notice so quickly as fear."

Yes, well, maybe it was different with Niehauser. What on God's earth should someone like Niehauser be afraid of?

Stafford waited for a moment at the mouth of the subway entrance, blinking stupidly. Jamaica's main street was lined with buildings of only two or three stories, and they let in the cold, white winter sunshine that somehow, in Manhattan, never seemed quite to reach down to the sidewalk. Suddenly everything seemed to have gained a strange and painful reality, as if until that moment he had been feeling his way in the dark.

He had been given explicit instructions: two blocks east of Mayhew Drive, west on Eightieth Street, number 4257, the second store from the corner and right next to Floria's dry cleaning, but it was only through an exercise of the will that he was able to convince himself to take the first few steps. It was like striding out into a wilderness.

It occurred to him that his presence here was as clear a demonstration as he could wish that he hadn't exactly made much of a success of his life. After two years of college, a six-month tour with the Navy—his enlistment terminated "for the good of the service," as they put it—and close to fourteen months in the Merchant Marine, Harry Stafford's adult friendships had dwindled down to this one. There was literally no one else. His mother was probably hoping he had drowned or something, so curiosity about his movements was now largely restricted to the German Foreign Office, the police, and his draft board. And now, maybe, Pete Kirchhof.

For a brief space they had been roommates at Rochester Tech, until Stafford had pledged a fraternity and then, almost immediately, dropped out of school. It had been Kirchhof who had gotten him started on the glories of the German Wehrmacht. Kirchhof's father had been in the first war, fighting for the Kaiser and the Fatherland, and the son seemed to think that cast a glow over the whole family. All that had been in 1941, when an admiration for the Nazis hadn't yet taken on the scent of treason, but it hadn't made Kirchhof any more popular. Like Stafford, he hadn't graduated, and he had returned to Queens to work in an uncle's appliance store. Apparently the armed forces hadn't wanted him either.

"Come after five," he had said. "The old fart always leaves me to close up."

It didn't look like a very prosperous business—there was dust inside the display window, and the store itself seemed gloomily vacant, as if no one had bought so much as a vacuum cleaner bag in months. Stafford peered in through the weather-streaked pane of glass that occupied the upper third of the front door and saw a dim little figure in an apron and a white shirt, waving a bony arm at him like someone trying to frighten away a mosquito.

Three hours later, after dinner and a fruitless search for a brothel that was reputed to be just off Kissena Boulevard, they were in a very noisy bar in Flushing, and Stafford was trying to explain, yet once more, about von Niehauser. It wasn't easy because Pete Kirchhof kept breaking into a drunken giggle and laying his head down on the table in a puddle of beer.

"I don' believe the part about him bein' a *baron*—hee hee hee! Jesus, I don' believe a fuckin' *word.* You made it up, di'nt you. Di'nt you, Harry? You made up the whole fuckin' thing—hee hee hee!"

They were at a table in the back, conveniently close to the men's room. There seemed to be about five parties going on simultaneously, and just half an hour earlier there had been a short but furious fistfight; so the place offered plenty of distraction. You could have plotted the bombing of the Manhattan sewer system in there, with the diagrams spread out all over your table, and no one would have noticed. It was that kind of establishment.

Which was just as well, because anywhere else Pete Kirchhof would have been the center of interest. He was a skinny little creature who gave the impression he was merely inhabiting his clothes—the dark gray suit he wore didn't seem to be in contact with his body anywhere. His face was as narrow as an ax head, which somehow had the effect of making him appear slightly cross-eyed. It was only when he was drunk that he attracted much in the way of attention to himself—he wasn't a decorous boozer.

Mercifully, so far this evening he had refrained from throwing up, but such luck couldn't hold forever; in college it had been a fairly regular event. About four hours into the party he would start staggering toward the bathroom, green and bewildered. It was perfectly possible that in college that had been held against him even more than his sympathy with Hitler.

Stafford watched him with growing uneasiness. Lately, for some reason, drunkenness only made him warier. It was doubtful he would have told Kirchhof anything about his association with German intelligence if he hadn't been cold sober at the time, and now, as he could feel his head beginning to buzz, he had almost come to the conclusion that he had committed a terrible mistake. Kirchhof, he had decided, was not someone he felt comfortable trusting with his life.

"Come on, Harry, you c'n tell me. He can't really be no fuckin' *baron*, can he? Hee hee hee!"

"Oh yes he is, pal," Stafford said quietly, almost to himself. In fact, he was reasonably sure that nothing that wasn't actually shouted could be heard anywhere in that room, even across the length of a table. And, besides, Pete Kirchhof didn't give the impression he was listening very closely. "He is, every bit of it. And I think he's probably going to kill me."

"Fuck'm." Kirchhof leaned forward on the table, supporting himself with his hands. He looked half blind, and his speech was badly slurred. "Fuck'm, the son of a bitch. If he gets frisky, sell'm to the cops."

And then, with a kind of clumsy dignity, he got to his feet. His hands still rested on the table, and he stared out at nothing.

"I gotta puke," he said, growing visibly paler. Tiny beads of sweat were breaking out all over his gray face.

Stafford never moved. He was transfixed, like a man who has been within sight of the divine. Kirchhof might have been the Messiah.

"What did you say?" His voice, as he looked up at the slightly swaying figure above him, was hardly more than a strained whisper.

"I said, I gotta puke."

Kirchhof lurched away, tangling a foot in the legs of his chair and nearly knocking it over as he tried to disengage himself. It was an open question whether he would make it as far as the Gentlemen's before he reached his crisis. His jacket hung loosely on his thin back, as if it had been cut for a much larger man.

I'm safe enough, Stafford thought to himself, watching the dismal figure of his friend as it stumbled out of the light. Tomorrow he won't remember anything—or he'll think it was all bullshit. What, after all, would have prepared Pete Kirchhof to believe there were people in the world like Joachim, Baron von Niehauser?

"Fuck'm." That was what he had said. "If he gets frisky, sell'm to the cops." And for the first time in days, it occurred to Harry Stafford that there might, after all, be a way to safety.

It was four o'clock the next afternoon before he made the call. It was something he had to nerve himself up for.

He had gone back to the apartment that night, getting in around three in the morning, and Niehauser had been sitting in a chair in the front room, waiting for him. As he watched the slow, tolerant smile forming on Niehauser's lips, Stafford was glad not to have sobered up much on the taxi ride home. Niehauser seemed almost relieved, as if he found it easier to trust him when he was drunk. God, what a mistake it would have been to have spent another night out on the tiles!

"I'm sorry," Stafford murmured, trying to grin sheepishly. "Maybe I should have called. You weren't worried, were you?"

He sat down, sagging slightly at one end of the divan that their landlord had had brought up the day after they moved in —it was meant as a sort of housewarming present, apparently. Niehauser hardly moved. You could tell he was struggling not to betray anything like anger.

"Perhaps you should have called." He made a slight, dismissing gesture with his left hand. "I want you to relax and enjoy yourself—the journey here has been very long, but . . . well, one is subject to special anxieties on a mission like this. I like to know where you are."

He lapsed back into a granite calm, a stillness that would have been hard to manage with conscious effort. Perhaps he hadn't been angry after all. Perhaps that, more than anything else, was what made Stafford so afraid of him. He could never guess what Niehauser was thinking.

"You must be tired," he said finally. "Go to bed, Harry. In any case, we will be leaving here in a few days."

Stafford undressed and went to bed and just lay there, conscious every minute that Niehauser was right across the hall. The sun was up before he could bring himself even to close his eyes.

Was Niehauser asleep? Did that man ever really sleep? It was an open question. It was hard to imagine him the prey of such an ordinary human weakness.

In any case, we will be leaving here in a few days. What the hell did that mean? It didn't take much of a leap to imagine that, if they did leave, it might be in very different directions—Joachim von Niehauser out of town, and Harry Stafford out of this life.

That Niehauser was planning to kill him had gradually hardened into something very like a working assumption. He was excess baggage—Niehauser didn't really need any help. The baron spoke better English than most Americans; if anyone noticed his accent, they would probably just assume that he was English. He sounded English, and God knows the country was full enough of Englishmen just then. And he knew it, too. Niehauser wasn't the least little bit shy anymore about talking to people. And what else could he need poor Harry Stafford for?

At just a few minutes after noon, when for the fourth time Stafford had been awakened by the sound of the truck horns blaring down on Eighty-first Street, he gave up the fiction that he was resting and went into the bathroom to take a shower. When he was dressed and had decided that he needed some coffee and something to eat to steady his nerves, he found Niehauser waiting for him in the kitchen. It was rather like being startled by a spider.

"I have some work to do at the library," Niehauser said, smiling kindly. "Perhaps we could meet somewhere for dinner and then go to the cinema—it would be amusing to watch the newsreels."

He was dressed in his new suit—apparently dinner was to be something of a celebration—and he stood resting his back against the door frame, his arms crossed over his chest, looking for all the world like one of the clothing ads in the magazines. He reflected so completely the unconscious authority of the aristocrat by birth that it was impossible even to envy him. One could only admire. When it came to that, would even the police have the temerity to arrest him?

Stafford swallowed hard and tried to keep from flushing. It was at moments like this that he realized just how completely he was in Niehauser's hands. "Sure—why not?" He even managed a single noiseless syllable of laughter. "Where should we go?"

"Anywhere—a bistro perhaps. Somewhere we can have onion soup and fish and a little white wine. Somewhere with music—real music. A violin perhaps. Are there such places in this country?"

"I don't know. There must be."

"Then we can find one."

All the rest of the afternoon, Stafford kept restlessly to the sidewalks. It was a cold, windy day, but he could no more have stayed in one place than he could have stopped breathing. He had never been so scared in his life. Niehauser had tried so hard to put him at his ease.

He'll kill me, he thought, staring at his own reflection in a plate-glass shop window. There were pouches under his eyes and his skin looked gray, but that could have been nothing more than the cold. Niehauser is going to kill me. I could be dead by this time tomorrow.

If he went back that evening, there was no way he would be able to get loose before the next morning. And there was no way he wasn't going back—he wouldn't have had the nerve to do anything else.

We can meet somewhere. . . . God, the man was letting him go, giving him five whole hours to taste the illusion of freedom, knowing perfectly well he would come back.

Because it was one of the axioms of Harry Stafford's new existence that he was Niehauser's creature. If he strayed too far, Niehauser would find him. There was no safety until Niehauser was either dead or behind bars—until then, if he suspected that his poor puppet was getting ready to betray him, Stafford wouldn't give a nickel for his life. It amounted to a superstition.

So he would wait, and make his deal with the cops, and when Niehauser was theirs . . .

Dinner was a nightmare. Von Niehauser took him to a restaurant down on Second Avenue that had a strolling gypsy violinist, complete with a gold ring in his ear, and then spent half the evening buying the guy drinks and trading jokes with him—

Stafford couldn't even tell what language they were speaking. He bought wine and talked about his school days in England and how wonderful life had been before the war. He was terrifyingly human. As they were leaving, he took Stafford by the elbow and told him in a low, confiding voice that he was sure he was a good fellow and everything would go very easily from that point on. Who wouldn't be scared?

Afterward, they went to a movie house on Fifty-second Street and saw *I Married a Witch.* Von Niehauser seemed to enjoy everything, even the news films of the American landings in Italy.

"Wouldn't you agree that Veronica Lake is a beautiful woman?" he asked as they walked back to their apartment; it was freezing, but von Niehauser didn't seem to notice. "Not a very intelligent face perhaps, but striking."

Stafford didn't know what to answer, so he merely shrugged his shoulders, digging his hands further down into his overcoat pockets. Von Niehauser didn't seem to be paying attention anyway.

"*I* think she is beautiful," he went on, his tone slightly offended. "She reminds me of a girl I knew when I was at the Kaiser Wilhelm Institute. She was studying the cello, and we met at a concert—Furtwängler was conducting the Brahms *Double Concerto,* and she told me during the intermission that she thought the soloists had played like pigs. 'Like pigs'—that was just the way she phrased it. She was Norwegian, I think. God knows what must have become of her by now."

That night, von Niehauser stayed up until nearly three o'clock in the morning, just sitting in the front room listening to classical music on the radio. After a while Stafford couldn't stand it anymore and went to bed. Not so much to sleep as merely to get away.

The next morning, grateful simply to be waking up alive, he looked at his watch and discovered that it was a quarter after eight.

"I think I'll have breakfast out. I feel like French toast," he said, smiling and trying not to sweat. Von Niehauser, who—thank God—had already eaten, merely stared at him for a moment.

"As you wish. Don't be gone too long; we'll be leaving this evening."

He stumbled along Lexington Avenue, almost blind to the other people on the sidewalk, looking for a telephone booth. Then he discovered that he couldn't remember the number and turned into a drugstore.

"Have you got a phone book?"

The man behind the counter, who was at least two hundred years old, scratched his Adam's apple as, apparently, he considered the matter and then pointed toward a small wooden table in one corner, on which rested an ancient telephone and, underneath that, the Manhattan directory.

"You want to use the phone? It'll cost you a nickel if you want to use the phone—this is a business we're runnin' here."

Stafford only smiled and shook his head. The old man scowled at him, as if the matter constituted a personal and longstanding grievance.

The number was located under *F* in the United States Government listings, and this time, just to be on the safe side, Stafford hunted through his pockets until he found a piece of paper on which to copy it out. Then he would find himself somewhere a little more private to see what kind of a deal he could expect.

Somewhere more private turned out to be one of the vast, crowded corridors of Rockefeller Center. He climbed into a booth, dialed, and waited.

"I'd like to speak to Inspector Havens, please. . . ."

When he hung up, not more than five or six minutes later, he felt as if the weight of the world had been lifted from his shoulders. In just a few hours he would be safe. He balled up his slip of paper, dropped it into a cigarette canister—it wasn't the sort of thing he would feel right about carrying around with him

—and headed back outside to get a cab. Niehauser would be out on business most of the day, so the apartment would be the safest place to wait. He would go there.

God, he felt like a new man. Maybe the Feds would even offer him a reward. As he walked along through the lobby the heels of his shoes clicked against the stone floor; it was a sound repeated over and over in that sea of movement. The offices and shops were just beginning to open up, and the tempo of a thousand footsteps echoed faintly from the walls.

Von Niehauser waited, shielded behind the rushing, purposeful crowd. It was easy to lose oneself in New York, easy to keep from being seen. But an idiot painted yellow could have followed Stafford—the poor booby had never even turned around.

In a moment, when he was sure Stafford was safely outside, he walked over to the cigarette canister and, feeling around for a moment in the sand, produced the small, tightly wadded piece of paper that Stafford had been at such pains to be rid of. It was a telephone number, naturally enough. It was all so obvious that von Niehauser actually felt a twinge of disappointment.

He would call, and see who answered. But life really held very few surprises, and who would Harry Stafford have to call in such secrecy except the police? It was all so pathetically like him. He would have been safe enough if he had simply managed to keep a grip on his fear. He had given himself away with every gesture, with every word that he spoke. The poor fool.

Everything now would take on its own logic. It was useless to wish that their journey could have ended some other way, because events had resolved themselves down to the workings of personality and, whether they liked it or not, each of them had chosen his own fate. Von Niehauser could only feel his powerlessness, and his shame.

VI

An oily film had formed over the surface of his coffee, which by then was stone cold, and the guy behind the counter was beginning to treat him to funny looks. It was difficult to figure why, since there wasn't another patron in the place and you would have thought he'd be glad of the company. It was a quarter after two on the big wall clock over the door, and this guy Stafford hadn't shown up yet. That wasn't a terribly promising sign.

Havens had a seat near the window, where he could be seen and where he could keep a casual watch on both sides of the street for anybody who could possibly be his man. Sometimes they were like that; they would hang around in the neighborhood, pacing off the sidewalks for a couple of blocks in every direction, waiting to see if maybe there were more cops around and they were walking into a trap, or maybe just screwing up their courage to risk everything and come inside.

But why did they always have to pick a lunchroom? Why couldn't it ever be the bar at the St. Regis or a nice table for two at Delmonico's? Why did it always have to be coffee and a fucking sweet roll?

"I'll meet you at Charlie's," he had said. "I have breakfast there a lot, so I know the layout—it's on Lex and Seventy-seventh. One-fifteen. You know I'm the genuine article, but I don't sell you Niehauser over the phone. He's a big-ticket item."

Well—at least now they had names. That was something.

There hadn't been time for a background check, not that it

mattered. Maybe Stafford had planned it that way, but Havens didn't think so; the guy hadn't impressed him as clever enough for that. He was strictly minor league. Havens had seen a million just like him. He had something to trade and he wanted to trade it for his life.

You had the distinct feeling he was more afraid of his partner than he was of the law, that he would cut the best deal he could and be grateful just to keep breathing. Joachim von Niehauser must be quite a customer.

"You've gotta grab him first. There's a lot I can tell you, but I don't want him walking around loose. And I don't want to have anything to do with it. I'm not gonna be bait in anybody's trap. You get the baron on your own."

The *baron?* Good God, the joker seemed to think he had a bit part in a Flash Gordon serial. Havens had to force himself to keep from laughing over the phone.

"Okay, but we'd better talk first."

"Then we'll talk—I told you where."

And then the line had gone dead and Havens had been left to consider the frailty of all human endeavor. Here the Germans had gone to all that trouble—submarines, secret landings, so much razzle-dazzle to cover their tracks—and now it was all going to go pop because somebody in Berlin had made a mistake and picked a gutless wonder to act as tour guide. It made you feel almost sorry for them.

Havens took another sip of his coffee, which was terrible, and glanced up at the wall clock again, which said it was twenty after. He wondered what had gone wrong, or if Stafford was just trying to be cagey. Maybe it wasn't all going to be as easy as he had thought.

"You want some more coffee?"

The counterman was frowning at him, holding the pot in his hand as if he were trying to decide how much it weighed. He was bald and didn't seem to have any eyebrows and looked as if his last job had been on the mat at Madison Square Garden.

"What would I want with more coffee?" Havens grinned rattily, folding his hands over his left knee as he turned from the window.

"I wouldn't know, since you haven't drunk the cup you've got. What should I do, start chargin' you rent?"

"You could try, but I wouldn't fancy your chances."

Havens turned back to his survey of the traffic—he had lost interest in the conversation. He preferred to worry. The wall clock said twenty-five minutes after two, and still he was sitting alone at his table at Charlie's.

Stafford wasn't going to show up. He couldn't have said how he knew, but nevertheless he knew. He could wait there until Labor Day, but Stafford wasn't going to show up.

"Have you got a pay phone?"

"A *pay* phone?" The counterman's nonexistent eyebrows shot up, wrinkling his forehead—that was absolutely the only way you would have known—and he wiped his hands with a dishtowel in a manner suggestive of the most extreme astonishment. "You sure you want a *pay* phone?" Everybody, it seemed, was an ironist.

Yes, it was finally established, there was a pay phone back by the toilet, and Havens called his office on the off-chance that Stafford might have tried to get a message to him. There was nothing, of course. He had half the New York Bureau waiting around on stand-by, and Stafford hadn't shown himself. It was the bottom of the ninth, and the home team was two down. Mr. Hoover wasn't going to be at all pleased.

Walking back toward Eighty-fourth Street, where he had left his car parked—one didn't like to be obvious about these things—Havens did the best he could to talk himself out of the notion that Stafford's calls might have been nothing more than an attempt to draw official attention away while he and von Niehauser made good their escape. Had Stafford played him for a sucker? It was the sort of question that made him profoundly uncomfortable.

It didn't seem likely, however. For one thing, Stafford had

no real reason to suppose that he was blown, let alone that he had been traced to New York. Indeed, the main effect of Stafford's making contact had been to confirm his presence in the city. The Bureau had made arrangements to have the call traced, and he had stayed on the line long enough for them to establish that he had been phoning from somewhere in the midtown exchange.

It just didn't make any sense to assume anything except that he had been more or less on the level. Probably at the last minute he just lost his nerve.

Except that he had called *twice*—once in the afternoon and then again this morning. He had had plenty of time to suffer through the terrors of indecision, and then he had picked up the phone and set up a meeting. There wasn't any rule that said he couldn't subsequently chicken out—it wouldn't exactly have been a unique instance—but somehow Havens had trouble getting himself to believe it. Stafford had sounded so eager, as if the really scary thing was to stay out on the loose with von Niehauser.

That was what Havens was really looking forward to—meeting Joachim von Niehauser. Guys like Stafford were ten to the penny, but von Niehauser sounded like rather an exotic specimen. After all, how often in this business did you get to collar a baron?

It was a fine, brisk weekday afternoon. The lunch hour was over, and in this largely residential neighborhood everyone was either back at work or home taking care of the laundry. The sidewalks weren't particularly crowded; you didn't have to dodge around people's shoulders as you strolled along, wondering what to do next about a couple of Nazi spies that were loose in the country. It was almost relaxing.

As he crossed the intersection at Seventy-seventh Street, a man came around the corner from the Park Avenue side, brushed past him, and took the stairs down the entrance to the subway. For a moment their eyes met, as sometimes happens with people you pass on the street, and then he was gone. He was a handsome man in a dark, otherworldly sort of way, but probably, Havens thought to himself, the only reason he had noticed him was that he happened not to be wearing a hat. Perhaps he didn't mind the cold—somehow he rather looked the type who wouldn't. And, of course, he had the sort of face that made you ask yourself where you had seen him before.

Havens had almost forgotten him, and was nearly halfway up the block, before he remembered. And then it struck him with such force that for those brief few seconds the breath seemed to have gone out from beneath his ribs.

"Like a movie star," the waitress had said. "The whole number—tall, dark, and handsome. He reminded me a little of Tyrone Power. . . ."

He spun around so fast that he almost tripped and fell over his own feet, and an elderly woman with a shopping basket full of oranges—probably he would carry the memory of the expression on her face with him to the Last Judgment—had to dodge out of the way as he ran to the subway entrance, jumping down the stairs four at a time.

"My God, my God, my God," he kept repeating, whether out loud or simply in his mind he had no idea, "let him still be there. Let the bastard still be there."

He thought he could hear the roar of a train—was it on this side, or the other? or maybe it was the express on the lower level—and he hit the platform at a dead run. People were pushing past him, turning back to stare.

Maybe the roar was merely the sound of the blood pumping in his ears. Maybe there was still time.

But there was no time. From the barricade he could see the back of the last car pulling away. He was too late.

He clambered over the turnstile, hoping against hope that maybe, for some reason, von Niehauser might have missed this one, might have gone to the men's room, might still be out there, waiting for the next train. Panting for breath, Havens glanced around him, but the crowd was all moving toward the exits. There was no one waiting—no one who mattered. Strike three.

"Hey, buddy, you can't *do* that." He felt a hand on his

shoulder, and turned around to find himself in the custody of one of the station guards.

What was the half-wit talking about?

"You wanna ride, you gotta pay a nickel just like everybody else. Come on."

The guard started to lead him back to the barricade, but Havens wasn't going anywhere.

"Can you stop that train?"

The guard, who had reddish hair and huge freckles but otherwise seemed to be all arms and shoulders, peered at him out of tiny, pale blue eyes that registered nothing except bewilderment.

"*Stop* it—man, why should you want me to *stop* it? Keep your shirt on. There'll be another one along in a couple o' minutes."

Havens hardly knew what to do, until he remembered that he was a cop. He was a federal agent in pursuit of a criminal. He fished around in his pocket until he found his badge case, flipped it open, and held it up in front of him like a priest with a cross.

The guard stared at it and then, as if as an afterthought, lifted his hand away from Havens' arm.

"One more time—can you stop that train?"

"*Stop* it," the guard repeated, this time with a kind of unfocused anguish, as if he personally might be held responsible. "Man, by now they're already most of the way down to Fifty-ninth Street. How the hell am I supposed to stop it?"

"Have you got a phone?"

"Sure I got a phone. In the booth."

It was useless. What was he supposed to say, that Joachim von Niehauser, wanted for espionage and murder, had been last seen in the vicinity of the Lexington Avenue subway line? But he had to try. There wasn't anything left to do except to try.

"Cover the railway and bus stations—I don't care how many men it takes. And I think we'd better bring New York's Finest in on this. If he gets out of Manhattan, then we might as well forget it because we'll never get near him again."

As he hung up the phone, he wondered if the subway platform at Seventy-seventh Street wasn't as close as anyone was ever going to get to von Niehauser, ever again. Had the man realized he was being hunted? Was that what that split-second of recognition had meant?

Havens took the composite sketch out of his inside coat pocket and spread it out on the table inside the token booth to look at it. The expression on von Niehauser's face seemed by its very blandness to mock him.

But the artist had done a good job—the baron might have sat to have his portrait painted.

I'll meet you at Charlie's. I have breakfast there a lot, so I know the layout.

Von Niehauser comes down Seventy-seventh Street from Park to catch the subway, and Stafford is a regular at a greasy spoon nearby. This had to be their home turf—not very many other conclusions were possible.

So everything might not be lost after all. Havens smiled at the printed sketch that had grown creased and grubby with constant handling; it was as if the issue between himself and the calm, refined face had become somehow intensely personal.

At the corner of Seventy-seventh and Park he took the green light as an omen and started uptown. He would do five blocks up Park and then cross over and do ten down the other side of the avenue. Then he would double back and, if he came up dry, start in on the side streets. It was bound to take hours, but it was better than sitting around on his hands back at the office and—who could tell?—his two spies might not have fled their nest for good and all. If he found the place, it would certainly be worth putting under guard. Besides, he might even stumble on a few clues—the odd, scribbled-over piece of notepaper perhaps, or the ever popular coded set of instructions hidden in a tube of toothpaste. After all, he didn't know the man; von Niehauser might be that melodramatic, or that careless.

But it didn't take hours—only about twenty-five minutes. The custodian at 947 Park Avenue recognized "Mr. Wemberley" as soon as he saw the sketch.

"Sure. He and the other gentleman share number seven, quiet as mice. They rob a bank or somethin'?"

Havens had had to track him down to his little utility room in the basement, where he was sitting in his undershirt, hunched over a plate of brown lumpy paste that could have been absolutely anything. He blinked inquisitively, shrugging his hairy shoulders as if to testify to his harmlessness. Havens shook his head.

"I just want to talk to him—him or his friend. Why don't you just loan me your key."

The badge once again worked its magic, and Havens got the key. The custodian wanted to come along, "just to make sure that everything's all right"—was he just curious, or did he think there was a chance Havens might walk off with the spoons?—but Havens told him in his best and most official-sounding policeman's voice to stay down in the basement and keep out of trouble.

He took the stairs up, on the theory that elevators were noisier, and inserted the key in the front door lock as silently as he could. The door swung open, and Havens rolled into the living room in the manner he had learned at Quantico and came to rest behind one end of a rather large sofa, his revolver pointing menacingly at the fireplace. No one shot at him.

Nothing moved. There was no sign that anyone was even living there. The furniture had that slightly worn look that one associates with hired rooms, and the air was stale. The place was like a burial vault. Finally, feeling a little foolish, Havens got up and ventured into the next room.

It was a kitchen, and nobody was hiding in the refrigerator. If anybody was home, he was awfully good at holding his breath. Still, something wasn't quite right. You could almost smell it.

At the end of the short corridor there were three doors. Havens tried the one on the right-hand side and discovered it was a bedroom—probably that was the arrangement, two bedrooms with a bathroom in between.

He would have bet any money that von Niehauser slept in here. Somehow he had never been able to think of von Niehauser as anything except a soldier and this was a soldier's room, for all that there wasn't anywhere in sight an item as personal as an open magazine. The bed was covered with a single blanket, and the sheets had been drawn as tight as drumskin. There was one chair, made of wood, without so much as a cushion, as though the man had lost the habit of personal comfort. Havens closed the door respectfully.

He found Stafford in the bathroom, hanging by his necktie from the showerhead. His eyes had almost started out of their sockets and his hands looked swollen. He seemed so surprised.

There was a reddish bruise on his throat, just half an inch below where the necktie was digging into the flesh. Havens took him lightly by the wrist and found that rigor mortis had already begun to set in. At the merest touch the corpse began turning slowly in an arc from right to left, his shoes tapping against the sides of the bathtub.

"Well, Harry," he murmured to his unhearing companion, who seemed to be surveying the room as slowly he twisted at the end of his necktie, "it looks like the baron won't be coming back after all."

VII

For the rest of the afternoon and evening von Niehauser's apartment was full of New York City homicide detectives, so Havens retired to the kitchen where, for some reason, nobody bothered to come looking for evidence. There was a telephone in the kitchen and, given that, he could keep track of his people just as well there as he could have downtown at Bureau headquarters and, in any case, the city police carried the major responsibility for the dragnet—they had the manpower and it was their sandlot. Besides, Havens wanted to stick around for a word with the coroner.

"No, you idiot, don't *cut* him down. Get up there and untie the fucking thing. And get him out of these clothes first—we'll want to do a fiber screening. *Gently,* you moron."

Watching Harry Stafford make his slow way down from the showerhead wasn't a terribly appetizing business. When they got him out of his trousers you could see that his legs were all covered with postmortem bruises, and when they had finally lowered him into the bathtub, and loosened the necktie by which he'd been hanging, he started to belch. It was just trapped gas escaping from his stomach, but he sounded like he was snoring. One of the detectives found it so unnerving that he had to step out of the room.

The coroner was a small, precise man with a pencil-line mustache, thin brown hair plastered carefully across his skull, and the eyes of a bird of prey. The cuffs of his white shirt were carefully turned back as he examined the corpse, which by then was as rigid as a brick.

"I'd say he's been dead about three hours," he said, handing a thermometer back to his harassed assistant. "When did you say you found him?" He turned around to look at Havens, who was crouched just behind his right shoulder.

"About ten minutes after three."

"Then you must have arrived not more than forty minutes to an hour after the murder." The coroner smiled faintly, as if the fact represented some sort of personal triumph. "That wasn't rigor mortis you noted; that was cadaveric spasm. The stiffening comes at the moment of death, usually because the victim is badly frightened. He must have been petrified of whoever killed him."

"Then you're ruling out a suicide?"

"Oh yes—look at that." He pointed to the bruise directly over Stafford's windpipe. It looked like someone had painted it on. "That was what did the damage. See the difference in color from the marks left by the necktie? He didn't hang himself. He was already dead."

"That checks." The voice came from the bathroom doorway, which was entirely filled with a detective lieutenant named Phelan whom Havens remembered from before the war. "We found a patch of blood about the size of your hand in one of the bedrooms. The killer must have dragged him in here afterward—what did you say his name was, Havens?"

"Von Niehauser. Joachim von Niehauser. He killed a kid up in Maine ten days ago."

"The same way?" Phelan's heavy black eyebrows raised slightly, but otherwise the expression on his meaty face remained unchanged. He was interested, but only professionally. Havens nodded.

"Broke his larynx. Apparently Herr von Niehauser knows what he's doing."

"So it would seem."

A few minutes later Harry Stafford was inside a canvas bag

and on his way to the icebox at the city morgue. With its guest of honor gone, the party began to lose some of its sparkle. Except for the few technicians, who were dusting everything in sight for fingerprints and worked as silently as moles, there was almost no one left in the apartment except Havens and Lieutenant Phelan.

"You know, I hate them when they're like this," Phelan said, sitting down rather heavily on one of the kitchen chairs. "We've got our one and only suspect, and if he's really a spy like you say the city won't even have the expense of trying him. There's nothing left to do except to catch the son of a bitch. It's too easy —it's like something you get out of a can."

He scowled, and his forehead crinkled into heavy folds. He was leaning against the kitchen table and the fingers of one huge hand were curled over the edge. The simplicity of the case seemed to depress him horribly.

"What I can't understand is why he even bothered to try making it look like a suicide. What did the stupid bastard think it was going to buy him?"

"A little time, maybe. Most likely it would have if I hadn't happened to spot him ducking into that subway entrance." Havens smiled, trying hard to sound like the detached observer—it was odd, however, how he felt a proprietary interest in von Niehauser's good name.

"And I think you'll find that he turns out to be anything but stupid. He may be a bastard, but he's a clever one. It made good sense to string Stafford up like that. If the body had been discovered in the normal course of things, you might have missed the broken larynx until autopsy and been stuck with the presumption of suicide for another couple of days. And how much more of a head start do you think he would have needed?"

"Well, he didn't get much, did he. Don't worry your head about it; we'll have him down in the Tombs before the weekend."

"I admire your confidence."

"We'll catch him." Phelan looked up, his eyes reflecting the unblemished certainty of a man stating the unassailably true.

"Why shouldn't we catch him? He's a man on his own, without a soul who would lift a finger for him, and we've got men turning this town on its ear. The bus and train stations are being watched, even the subways out to Long Island and up to the Bronx. The tollbooths on the bridges and tunnels have been reinforced. Manhattan is an island—where can he go?"

Underground—underground. Von Niehauser rode the subways, more or less at random, trying never to stay too long in one station, until he was sure it would be dark outside. When he ventured back to the surface he found himself in Greenwich Village. It was a clear, cold night, and music seemed to be coming from every doorway. For some reason it reminded him of his student days in Göttingen.

There were crowds on the sidewalks; their presence was oddly and unreasonably consoling, as if no force on earth would think to take him from the midst of these sympathetically indifferent people. He walked along the southern edge of Washington Square, a stranger among strangers.

He stopped for a moment a few blocks away, at the entrance to what seemed to be a public recreation area of some kind, although it was surrounded by a high chain-link fence and the surface was covered with asphalt, making it look more like the yard of a concentration camp. Several boys were playing a game which involved throwing a large ball through a hoop suspended three or four feet over their heads from a pole. Whoever had the ball kept bouncing it against the ground as he ran around, trying to approach the hoop for a throw, and the others all seemed bent on taking it away from him, although none of them ever touched him. It was a curious game—he had seen it only once before, at the Olympics in Berlin. He couldn't remember the name; he could only assume it was something indigenous to the country.

Two old men were seated on a wooden bench just outside the fence. They appeared to be arguing, although they were speaking in a language von Niehauser couldn't remember ever having heard before so it was impossible to be sure. One of them was gesturing with a heavy cane he held very near the crook in his clenched left hand—there was nothing threatening in it; the cane was merely for emphasis. Von Niehauser decided that he was hungry.

There was an Italian restaurant located in a cellar on West Twelfth Street. The Italians had recently defected from the Axis, but it had been the sensible thing to do and von Niehauser saw no reason to hold a grudge. He descended the staircase and was met by the heavy smells of tomato sauce and garlic.

A waiter wearing a white jacket and an apron that reached within a few inches of the floor showed him to a table, and he ordered veal and pasta and a small green salad and a bottle of Asti. Against the back wall was a framed print of Garibaldi.

He was halfway through the meal before it occurred to him to reflect on his own callousness. By now he was probably being actively hunted by the police—how long, really, could he expect them to remain fooled?—and less than five hours before he had killed a man, and neither, apparently, had had any effect on his appetite. The condition, of course, was not new. In Russia death and danger had been around him constantly and, like everyone else, he had felt little enough inclination to starve himself. It is only the novelty of these things which makes them upsetting; after a while, one begins hardly to notice.

About Stafford he cared nothing at all. Stafford had invited his own death. It had been a matter of simple self-protection.

"I was scared—I was just gonna turn myself in. I wouldn't've told 'em anything about you, honest."

Von Niehauser hadn't had to say a word. All that was necessary was to walk in the door and look at him, and Stafford had begun confessing his sins, pleading for forgiveness as if it were some minor matter of personal trust between them. He had made a disgusting sight. Von Niehauser had killed him, as much as anything, simply to make him hold his tongue.

Hitler was right about that—they were all soldiers now. A

soldier breaks faith and must pay for it with his life, and that ends the matter. In a conflict such as this, no one had a right to consider his own survival. That had been Stafford's offense, to imagine that he could possibly matter.

There was a cat which apparently belonged to the restaurant, since it worked its way from table to table with perfect impunity. Von Niehauser never even noticed the creature until he felt it rubbing its back along the bottom of his right trouser leg. He took a few strands of spaghetti that carried a taste of the Bolognese sauce and held them low underneath the tablecloth, as if it were the most guilty action of his life. In a few seconds he could feel the cat's rough tongue licking his fingers. The experiment was such a success that he cut off a tiny piece of his veal cutlet and offered that as well.

For dessert he ordered *zabaione* and a cup of the thick, sweet coffee favored by the Italians. The taste of the Marsala was almost like the ache of longing.

In 1933, the summer before his mother died, he had taken the train down to Viareggio, where she could have the warmth and the sea air that his father believed might save her life. He had been twenty-four and almost at the end of his training at the Kaiser Wilhelm Institute. They had already offered him a *Privat-dozentur,* to be taken up as soon as he had finished his dissertation. He was to be a theoretical physicist and could afford to ignore the sordid concerns of politics. Hitler seemed to matter very little.

But that had been all his father had wanted to talk about—what was happening in Berlin, what it all might mean for the Army. He remembered thinking how boring it all was, wondering how his father could possibly concern himself with this new government which was so obviously bound to collapse within the next half-year.

And his mother would sit on the veranda of the house they were renting and look out over the beach and the sea beyond. She was forbidden coffee, but a little wine was supposed to be good for her and there was a place in the next street that served a particularly delicious *zabaione* of which she was very fond.

"Enjoy yourself, my dear," his father would murmur to her across the table. "It will give you strength—put the roses back in your cheeks." And his eyes would have an anxious, haunted look that von Niehauser had never seen there before. She was wasting away right in front of them.

And in the late afternoon, he and his father would put on white trousers and stroll along the breakwater. Somehow his father always looked uncomfortable in mufti, as if he were conscious of having assumed a disguise.

"I don't know," he would say, his hands clasped behind his back in a way that would have revealed to anyone that he was a member of the Prussian officer caste. "I received a letter from Blomberg a few weeks ago, and Blomberg thinks very highly of him. He says the new regime will be good for the Army."

"And, after all, there is still President Hindenburg."

"Hindenburg is a senile husk who is completely under the spell of his son Oskar. You mustn't look in that direction." And the general smiled and put a hand on his youngest boy's shoulder. "You should spend less time with your precious particles, Joachim, and live more in the world. Hindenburg—what an idea!"

All of that seemed so very long ago, more than a single lifetime. His mother had never wanted him to be a soldier. "You are too sensitive," she would say. "Leave it to Kurt and Egon; they haven't your eye for things. The Army would be the death of you." And now his mother and father and Kurt and Egon were all dead, and he was a soldier after all. Ten short years and a whole world had been swept away. It had been longer than a single lifetime.

Von Niehauser sat lingering over his coffee, in no hurry to be finished. What did he have to hurry him along except a renewal of his difficulties with the police? Earlier in the week he had studied a map of Manhattan, considering all possible avenues of escape should his presence be discovered, and he could only assume that by this time they had all been effectively sealed. The SS had not done well in settling on New York as his first place of refuge. It would seem that he was trapped.

However, there were always limits to the power and imagination of the police. Even in Hitler's Germany, where they enjoyed unlimited opportunities for the perfection of their art, they had proved unable to arrest everyone who was found obnoxious to the regime. It was well known that political dissidents for whom the Gestapo had fingerprints and photographs on file had still, in some cases, managed to evade capture for months at a time. Why should the Federal Bureau of Investigation fare any better than the Gestapo? In a democracy, one supposed, they had less practice.

It had been a pretty, feminine voice that had answered him when he called the number Stafford had written out on that slip of paper. "Federal Bureau of Investigation," she had said. Von Niehauser had never heard of such an organization, but at least now his pursuers had a name.

Perhaps he could simply wait them out, go into hiding for a few weeks until they lost interest or assumed he had slipped past them. It was perhaps even the safest course.

But the war would not wait. In the spring the Allies would most certainly invade France, and then the Reich's life would be counted out in months. "There's every chance you might end up settling the fate of Europe for the next thousand years," Schellenberg had said; and von Niehauser would not do that hiding in a coal cellar. No—if he waited much longer it would matter very little whether the Americans caught him or not.

He had called ahead—there was a train leaving Pennsylvania Station for Washington, D.C., at a few minutes after midnight. The destination hardly mattered; all that was important was to get out of Manhattan and somewhere he couldn't be bottled up quite so completely. He would board at the last possible moment and would buy his ticket from the conductor. People did that all the time.

There were certain obvious precautions to be taken. On leaving the restaurant he had looked around in the cloakroom for a hat of approximately the right size and walked away with it; running from the apartment, he must have been more shaken than he was aware because there was no other reason why he should have left his own behind. He was a tall man, so it couldn't be counted on to do much toward hiding his face, but in winter people expected to see a man wearing a hat.

Also, he went to a chemist's—a *drug* store, rather—and purchased a bottle of hair dye. If they had his description, as he must assume they did, they would be looking for a man with black hair. After forty minutes in the lavatory of a sleazy hotel room on West Twenty-third Street which he rented for no other purpose, he was able to bring his hair to a reddish blond. He nearly blinded himself trying to do the eyebrows, but the results were passable. In the station he would be sure to walk with his hat off.

The one point on which he found it difficult to make a decision was luggage. It seemed reasonable that anyone taking a late train to a city over two hundred miles distant would wish to take at least a suitcase, if only to be provided with a clean shirt and a few toilet articles. But a new suitcase might be as conspicuous as none—the police would be looking for something of the kind.

The problem was solved when he happened to pass a pawnshop. He bought what in England they called a Gladstone, worn threadbare by decades of service. A couple of tablecloths—stained but serviceable, and selling for fifty cents apiece—padded it out quite well.

For the rest, he would simply have to take his chance.

The next few hours were passed in a kind of frantic aimlessness. Von Niehauser was tortured by the unfocused suspicion of every hunted man, the feeling that every eye was upon him, that everyone he passed on the sidewalks or stood beside as he waited for the traffic lights to change must know everything about him, that he had become somehow preternaturally conspicuous. He found himself looking for mirrors and studying himself in shop windows to check the color of his hair; he half expected to see a halo of black coming through every time he took off his hat. The image that stared back at him seemed so strange—could anyone actually look like that?

He tried to stay off the streets as much as possible—one never knew how large a force this Federal Bureau of Investigation might have at its disposal, or where they might be patrolling—but at the same time he felt the danger of lingering in any one spot too long. He would take a chair in a restaurant, making sure his back was to the door, order a cup of coffee, stay as long as it took to drink half of it, and then leave. Always he kept moving closer and closer to Pennsylvania Station.

At five minutes to twelve, he crossed Seventh Avenue and started toward the main entrance. He knew it was too soon, that he should have waited another two or three minutes, but somehow it was impossible—he had to begin to make his escape.

The huge foyer was as large as the central square in von Niehauser's native village, and walking down the stairway from the street he felt hideously exposed. There must have been three or four hundred people down there, and any one of them had merely to turn his head—he felt like an actor on a stage. His eyes scanned the crowd, trying to spot the policemen he felt certain would be there.

No one stepped forward to arrest him as he crossed the floor. Perhaps they hadn't seen him yet. Perhaps they were only waiting to corner him. At any rate, no one came near him.

The great board listing arrivals and departures directed him to track five. He bought a newspaper along the way, tucked it under his arm, and set out for his train.

Even at that time of night, the train was crowded. Almost every seat was taken, and von Niehauser found he had to sit with his bag across his knees because there was no room left in the overhead racks. The man next to him seemed to be asleep, with the side of his head resting against the window.

The carriage was uncomfortably warm. Below the main foyer had been the waiting areas and the entrances to the tracks, and below them the trains themselves; like Dante's Inferno, each level, as you descended from one to the next, was progressively hotter. And in the train, with so many people packed so tightly together, it was like the furnace room of a ship; von Niehauser could feel the sweat trickling down his back under the heavy overcoat. It was like the submarine all over again. It was difficult to catch one's breath.

And the train hadn't begun to move. He looked at his watch—it was six minutes after midnight, and the doors were still open. They should have been underway four minutes ago.

The temperature seemed to rise. There was no sound except the droning of the ceiling fans. Von Niehauser checked the time again—it was ten minutes after twelve. He could feel his heart pounding.

The man sitting next to him had begun to wake up, gradually pulling himself into an upright position and twitching through the shoulders and arms, as if he were being jolted awake by degrees. Finally he opened his eyes and began looking around with hostile boredom. Von Niehauser took the opportunity to attract his attention.

"We appear to be delayed," he said quietly, trying not to seem intrusive. "I wonder if there could be some difficulty."

"It's the war—where've you been, buddy?" The man shrugged sleepily. His voice was nothing but a husky murmur, but he seemed to be addressing himself to the coach at large. He might have been summarizing the grievances of the whole of the traveling public. "I don't know," he went on. "They schedule trains at these crazy hours, and then you get on board and wait. I think they do it on purpose."

He didn't seem to expect a reply—he looked rather as if he

might actually resent one—so von Niehauser remained silent, thinking that probably the fellow was right. After all, it was wartime, even in America, and war was the mother of inefficiency. In Berlin . . .

But there was that something else which wouldn't allow him to relax. In Russia, during the successive withdrawals that had constituted the whole recent history of German arms, he had learned to trust his instincts. It was the logic of defeat that you should have been killed a dozen times over, and if you lived it was because you could separate out from the fear that never left you that inner voice that whispered that somewhere, somehow, you had been given a warning. Von Niehauser was hearing that voice now, just loud enough to keep him prickly with apprehension.

The other passengers were becoming restless. You could see it in the faces of women as they held their sleeping children and stared out the windows at nothing. For all that the ceiling fans could do, the air was growing grayish-blue with cigarette smoke.

It was twenty minutes past the hour. Von Niehauser hadn't seen a conductor since he had come on board.

Presently the door that led to the car in front slid open, and a young man in a hat and an open tan topcoat came in. He wasn't in a hurry; he glanced around for a moment and then began making his way toward the rear of the coach. He kept his hands in his coat pockets. His face was set, as if the muscles had hardened with disuse. Only his eyes were alive.

They always gave themselves away, von Niehauser thought to himself, suddenly quite calm. In that there seemed to be no difference between this Federal Bureau and the Gestapo—even when they were trying to disguise themselves they always carried with them the same arrogance, as if they had been set apart from the rest of the breed. And perhaps they had.

It was the hands that betrayed this one. Anyone else walking through a train, even while it rested in the station, would have guided himself down the aisle by holding on to the outside corners of the seats; it would have been a reflex, something done without thinking. But this one never took his hands out of his pockets. Why did police everywhere have this obsession about their hands, as if to show them openly might be a damaging admission of their all-too-common humanity? Perhaps they wanted to be like primitive idols, simply an outline.

They were searching the train.

VIII

It was all over in a moment. The policeman—and there could be no question of his being anything else—passed down the aisle and into the next coach. Von Niehauser heard him closing the door behind himself.

There had been no arrest, of course, nor even the hint of recognition. But that, of course, meant nothing. He would have to posit that von Niehauser was armed—he would be mistaken, but he would have to be a fool to suppose anything else—and he would hardly care to risk armed resistance aboard a crowded passenger train. He would want reinforcements.

The alternatives, therefore, were perfectly straightforward. There was no point in running because if he were observed he would never make it out of the station. So it came down to this: he could simply wait where he was and hope that he had gone undetected, or he could assume the worst and attempt to deal with this one man before he had a chance to call in any others. Either way, the risks were appalling.

The gentleman next to him had apparently gone back to sleep, so von Niehauser rose quietly, leaving his bag and his newspaper on the seat behind him. After the fashion of travelers, everyone else was either too tired or too excited or too preoccupied with their own problems and discomforts to notice his departure. After all, he would be right back; hadn't he left his things?

The policeman was still in the next car behind. Von

Niehauser could see him through the open door as he walked past.

It was odd how one never seemed to think of them as ever having had a youth. In one's imagination the law was always middle-aged, heavy and humorless. But this specimen couldn't have been more than twenty, for all that he had already mastered the policeman's masklike blankness. His hat was pushed back on his curly, light brown hair, and there was still a childlike agility in his movements.

And it seemed that he had yet completely to comprehend the craft of his profession.

Because why, after all, would anyone walk *through* a train that still hadn't left its station? The side doors to all the coaches had been left open, and the platform outside was wider and far less cluttered—anyone going from one coach to the next, even to the one immediately behind, would step out onto the platform. No one would walk *through* except if he wished the opportunity to study each face at his absolute leisure. In short, no one but a policeman.

And it wasn't as if the windows were caked with dirt, or the size of portholes. An experienced man would have seen everything he needed to see from outside—but this one, it would appear, wasn't sure enough of himself for that. In his policeman's arrogance he simply walked through the aisles, assuming, one gathered, that no one would notice. Or perhaps not caring whether they did or not.

In a way, it was almost insulting. Did they suppose they were dealing with a child? Or one of their native cutpurses, perhaps, who could be expected to stay within the rules?

But perhaps it didn't matter. Perhaps this one was young enough to have been fooled by a bottle of hair dye and hadn't noticed him. It would seem so, since he was still looking. Perhaps it would be just as well for von Niehauser to return to his seat and leave things as they were.

The platform was a gloomy, faintly infernal place, illuminated on the one side through the windows of the train and overhead by lamps that threw down narrow yellowish pools of light. The air was warm and stale and smelled of tar and chewing gum and wet winter clothing, and the only sound to be heard above the confused buzzing of people and machines was the occasional sharp gust of steam from the train's braking system. It was a strangely sinister atmosphere, a passage from light into darkness.

It was a cruel perversity of timing that made the conductor choose that moment to come outside. Von Niehauser had more than half decided that enough was enough, that there was no necessity for him to take any drastic action, that he was safe. He had paused for just a moment and was watching the policeman's back and thinking that there was no reason why he couldn't return to his seat and make a start on his crossword puzzle when the conductor leaned out from the walkway between coaches and raised a hand to attract his attention.

"You wanna board, sir? We're about set to go."

He was a Negro, with a broad face and very spruce in his dark blue uniform, and in the garish overhead lighting the inside of his hand looked as pink as coral.

The policeman, who was still inside the coach, must have heard him because he turned around to look. There was nothing but a window between him and von Niehauser—they couldn't have been more than twenty feet apart—and this time a flicker of recognition did appear in his face, a kind of half-formed consciousness that here was someone of interest, a tightening of the eyes that a few years' more experience might have taught him to suppress. For that instant he and von Niehauser stood studying each other, just as if they were about to be formally introduced.

So—there was not to be any easy way out after all. And there was precious little point in trying to get away either, so once more it came back down to finding a way to silence this one policeman, this boy who carried a pistol and imagined himself the embodiment of the state.

Von Niehauser smiled at him, almost tauntingly, and turned

back in the direction from which he had come.

He was astonished and even a little amused at his own calm, as if he were someone else admiring the progress of a protégé. The worst thing that can happen is he will kill me, he thought. The idea was somehow strangely comforting.

The whole secret was to treat each new situation as if it were a training exercise, to judge oneself on performance and concentrate on the form of the thing. Nothing was real; there was no danger. There was nothing at risk beyond one's self-conceit.

Because, of course, he had formulated a plan. It had come into his mind unbidden, and he was rather pleased with it. Its hazards—its very incompleteness—made him like it all the more.

It all hinged on two facts or, rather, a fact and an assumption. Or perhaps, more accurately, a hopeful guess. The fact was that he could hardly afford to take any sort of action in full view of a trainload of people. Except if he was to be dragged away in chains, any resolution would require privacy.

The guess was that his young friend would have the full confidence of youth.

And would it be fair to add as well that possibly this paladin of the law wasn't overly bright? It seemed likely—it was a good fifteen or twenty seconds before von Niehauser heard the faint noises of a commotion behind him and he knew that the policeman had at last made the connection. He turned around to look. He wasn't being coy about it; he wanted the other man to see.

They were both out on the platform now, separated by a little less than the length of two cars. It was a calculated distance, far enough to put von Niehauser out of effective pistol range—his adversary would have to be more than just a simpleton to try a shot under these circumstances—but close enough to constitute a provocation. Because this was the moment of decision. The policeman could either go for help, risking the possibility that von Niehauser might escape him, or he could have faith in his own powers and attempt to make the arrest on his own. It was a choice upon which more depended than he realized.

"Hey, YOU!"

Apparently he hadn't made up his mind. His arm shot up, as if that would be enough by itself, and he put one foot out in front of the other in what seemed like a threat of pursuit. He was just on the edge. All he needed was a little encouragement.

Von Niehauser took a step backward, and then another. Yes, it was working. He turned around and continued toward the head of the train, listening for the footsteps behind him.

As he walked he counted. There were four more passenger coaches, and then what looked like a freight car—at any rate, the windows were dark—and then the engine. The thing was to reach at least the middle of the freight car. They would be out of sight there; the light was poor, and with the train almost underway that end of the platform was deserted. They would be quite alone.

In the confusion of sound it was difficult to sort out the footsteps of one man—and, of course, there was no question of looking back—but he had the impression that he wasn't as yet being chased. A running man makes a good deal of noise on a concrete surface, and there was none of that yet.

And there wouldn't be. There would be no wild pursuit—not just at first—and there would be no shooting. Because this policeman couldn't be sure; it might be anyone, this figure with the wrong color hair, who might or might not resemble a drawing on a handbill. And he would have no more than that, merely a description. Germany would have been another matter, but in the West they wouldn't begin to shoot on so little as that.

There were two short blasts from the train whistle—von Niehauser was close enough to the front now that he experienced the sound as an almost physical pressure—and a kind of shudder passed along the line of carriages. Very slowly, the thing had begun to move.

Von Niehauser risked a glance over his shoulder. He was very near the freight car, and as if on signal the policeman broke into a loping run. His hand was thrust into the pocket of his tan overcoat, which flapped around his body like a pair of clumsy, strengthless wings. Von Niehauser quickened his pace.

He stopped just a few steps ahead of the engine and turned. They were facing each other again, and the other man began to slow. The train was crawling forward, seemingly by inches, and von Niehauser allowed himself a pace backward, and then another and another. There was so little time now.

"You—I want to talk to you." The policeman was coming closer, drawn along the darkened platform by von Niehauser's receding figure. His hand was still in his pocket, the elbow slightly bent, as if he couldn't quite make up his mind to show the pistol. Only a few feet separated them now. "I want to . . ."

It was over in an instant. Von Niehauser stopped—for a minute particle of a second the other man stopped too; he seemed paralyzed, as if suddenly everything had changed. And then, as von Niehauser took a step forward, he regained possession of himself and his hand began to slide out of his pocket. They were so close to the edge of the platform that the train, as it slowly drew forward, seemed ready to brush against them.

But it was too late. He knew he was too late; you could read it in his eyes as he realized the dimensions of his error. Von Niehauser's left hand darted out, catching him by the wrist, and then, taking full advantage of the surprise, the fingers of his right closed into a hard mass and snapped forward into the policeman's throat.

A man can hang between life and death, powerless as he watches the world darken and fade before him. He stands straight, struggling to remain alive, but the force has gone out of him.

In this man's face there was only the one, inevitable, incredulous question. How could this have happened to me? How?

In what amounted to a spasm of revulsion, von Niehauser grabbed him by the shoulder, throwing his weight against him so that the policeman toppled backward. Von Niehauser released his grip and, like a dead tree in the wind, the man began to fall. His foot slipped on the edge of the platform and he seemed to turn, as if he were trying to see into the gulf opening beneath him—but perhaps he was already beyond that, already dead. He just sank through the air, down onto the tracks below, and the train, still dragging itself forward, covered him with its weight.

From the threadbare luxury of the lounge car it was possible at certain moments to make out the lights of Harrisburg, Pennsylvania, glittering softly in the distance. The train would sway gently around a curve and there they would be, a vague smear of white in the early morning darkness, far, far ahead, something to disappear again when the tracks began to straighten out. At least, the porter had said it was Harrisburg. It might have been anywhere—anything. It might have been a military installation, or a tourist camp, or the Second Coming of the Redeemer for all von Niehauser would have been able to recognize the difference.

He could not adjust himself to this spectacle of brightly lit cities. It seemed unnatural. After sunset the whole landscape of Europe was plunged into blackness—it had been that way now for years, and bombing raids had come to seem as essential a hazard as the winter frost. Except that, finally, the winter went away, and the Allied planes never did. In the East it was the Russians, in the West the Americans and the British. But they never went away, and to show a light after dark was to invite annihilation.

But here he was, safe and sound in the bosom of America. And whom should Harrisburg, Pennsylvania, fear after dark?

In the end, his escape had been so easy. He had merely to walk away, to wait with the milling crowds for the departure of the next train—to anywhere, since destination didn't really matter—and to step aboard as it pulled out, exactly according to plan. If there had been any more police, this time they had missed him. This time.

Pallida Mors aequo pulsat pede pauperum tabernas regumque turris. It was one of the fugitive lines that had stuck in his head from schoolboy Latin: Pale Death strikes with an impartial foot the hovels of the poor and the palaces of kings. Pale Death.

He had seen enough of that—the gray, frozen corpses of his soldiers lying in the snow around Morozovsk. It had been the beginning of the great Russian counteroffensive, and they had received one of those mad orders to hold at all costs. It went on for eleven days, eleven days during which he and his men never even closed their eyes, but they held. Seventy percent of the battalion had been killed or wounded—and on that front the one usually amounted to the other—but they held. And when the order finally came to evacuate, General Manstein had been reduced to tears of impotent rage when he saw the condition of his army as they marched back behind the lines. He had stood there and wept.

But von Niehauser had not wept. His mind had been too stunned for that, and when the Führer had hung the *Ritterkreuz* around his neck all he had been able to feel was contempt for this flabby little Austrian corporal who really seemed to believe that there was something glorious and ennobling about men blowing each other to pieces.

And for himself as well, because after all it was a base thing to survive where so many others had died.

But he had kept the medal. And even now, in the midst of the enemy, he held it in the palm of his hand, its black ribbon wound through his fingers, and he turned it this way and that so the shiny enameled surfaces could catch the light. It was madness to carry it with him like this, but some things were impossible to surrender. He was a soldier after all, even now. His father and brothers had been soldiers, and they, like him, had been members of the Order of the Iron Cross. No one could abandon everything.

Pallida Mors.

So, when the policeman had gone under the train's wheels and been ground to bloody atoms, von Niehauser had merely looked away for an instant and then walked off. He had refused to hurry, and the blood hadn't drummed in his ears. He had merely left the platform, as calmly as if nothing had happened, and no one had thought to interfere with him. Nothing *had* happened. He had killed men before—as a soldier it was his profession to kill men—and he was haunted by enough terrible memories that one more couldn't matter.

IX

Sam Fraser ran a hand across the top of his bare skull, wishing the heat in his office weren't turned so high. The whole floor was regulated by some guy down in the basement who seemed to have his own ideas about comfort, and he wasn't very amenable to reason.

It was hot for everybody, apparently. Across the desk from him, leaning his chair back against the wall, George Havens sat with his fists lying in his lap like hunks of mangled iron, his face a tragic mask as he stared down at the floor. He hadn't moved or said a word in ten minutes.

"It wasn't your fault, George."

"The hell it wasn't." Havens continued his gloomy inspection of the linoleum as the furrows in his brow deepened. "There's a German spy running around somewhere because I didn't catch him when I had the chance. I blew it."

"You didn't blow it. The NYPD blew it—it was their show."

"But he was my spy!" He jerked forward in his chair, excited and flushed, as if he were about to get it all off his chest. But then words seemed to fail him and he lapsed back into silence.

"He was my spy," he continued finally, his voice little more than a whisper. "I should have declared von Niehauser a federal fugitive and run the dragnet myself. I fucked it, and that's why Mr. Hoover's going to ship me off to Kansas City to polish the filing cabinets. And damn right too."

Fraser wiped his skull again, all the time watching the radiator with distaste and wishing to God he could just get through life without the enthusiasts. People like George Havens, with their ups and their downs, with their goddamned earnestness, were the ruination of police work. It was a nice job as long as you didn't let it get to you, but some people . . .

"Mr. Hoover's not going to do that," he said soothingly. "He's just glad it wasn't one of our people your boy pushed under that train—it would have looked so bad."

"It didn't look very good anyway. I watched them hosing down the tracks after the Fire Department finally got the poor sucker out of there—Jesus. He must have been ground to jelly."

"Don't tell me about it." Fraser winced suddenly, almost as if someone had struck him. "Just be glad it wasn't you."

Fraser's office door was closed, but outside you could hear the secretaries returning from their three o'clock coffee break. The two men sat quietly, as if listening to the clicking of the high-heel shoes and the sounds of voices and, occasionally, laughter. Havens, slouching forward in his chair, seemed to regard the unseen parade with fierce, sullen resentment, but in fact he was merely tired.

He had stayed in New York until eight-thirty in the morning, long enough for the coroner to confirm from as much of him as was left that Detective Abner Gorley had probably had his larynx broken *before* the 12:05 to Washington finished him off —what more did anyone need to confirm that von Niehauser had made good his escape?—and then he had phoned in his preliminary report and been ordered back to Seat of Government for a 4:00 P.M. appointment with Mr. Hoover himself. It had been a long drive. There had been time upon arrival for a shave and a shower and a change of clothes, but no sleep.

"You really look beat, George. You better watch yourself in there—don't get careless. You don't want to throw your career away, not for a few ill-chosen words, and if there's anything Mr. Hoover can't stand it's a bad mouth."

Havens only smiled. A few minutes later he lifted himself

slowly out of his chair and brushed off his trousers.

"He doesn't like to be kept waiting either," he said calmly, as if he were stating some law of nature. "And neither do I. But don't despair, Sam. Maybe if I play my cards right I can goad him into firing me. I don't suppose the Army would much mind my leaving here under a cloud."

"Are we back to that again?" Sam Fraser shook his head. "Is that what you're after, the chance to get killed in this precious war of yours? You really are deranged."

"Maybe so, Sam. My love to Ida."

The waiting room to Mr. Hoover's office had obviously been designed with certain specific psychological effects in mind. It was a large, square space, lined on three walls with leather sofas. The walls were a blank yellow and covered with framed photographs: Mr. Hoover with President Roosevelt, Mr. Hoover testifying before a Senate subcommittee, Mr. Hoover receiving various unidentified foreign military dignitaries. There was nowhere the eye could turn without encountering massive evidence of the importance, the power, the virtually inhuman rectitude of J. Edgar Hoover—even Shirley Temple was up there, shaking Mr. Hoover's hand and gazing up into his amused, benevolent smile.

The point of the huge room, of course, was to emphasize for you your own insignificance; and just as obviously the point of everything else was to impress upon you that in ten or fifteen or thirty minutes—or after whatever interval of time happened to strike his fancy—you were going to be ushered into the presence of the Living God. Presidents and all the rest of us might come and go, but the Director of the Federal Bureau of Investigation was there eternally.

And most of the time it worked, especially with Bureau personnel. Agents summoned in from the provinces had been known to faint dead away in this room—one poor sucker even had a coronary. Almost no one was immune.

George Havens had been twenty-six the first time he was

summoned to an audience with the Great Man. Only the week before he had arrested the man who had stolen the Cantanflas bomb sight; it had been his first big pinch and was all over the papers, and he was being called in to receive the Director's personal congratulations. He remembered that he had bought a new suit for the occasion and gotten his hair cut twice in four days. That was just the way it affected people.

But since December 9, 1941, the Director had become nothing more than the bastard who was powerful enough to yoke him to a desk in Washington. Their conversation on that day had reduced Hoover for all time to the merely mortal. His capacity to reward or punish had been exhausted by the simple act of refusing to accept a letter of resignation, and George Havens had learned to hate him in much the same way he would have hated anyone else.

So Havens didn't pay much attention to the photographs. Instead, he sat down on the sofa directly across from the door that led through the secretarial offices into Mr. Hoover's own, closed his eyes, and promptly fell asleep.

"Mr. Havens."

It was beautiful. He was alone, shipwrecked on this island in the South Pacific—well, almost alone. There was this big, luscious blonde with a bunch of green grapes in her hand—did they have blondes in the South Pacific?—and she kept nudging his shoulder with her jugs while he lay under a palm tree, watching the surf come in. Did she want him to finish the grapes, or was she just being chummy?

"Mr. Havens."

An eyelid fluttered open, and he saw that it wasn't a blonde at all. It was Miss Crisp, who hardly had any jugs at all to speak of and was one of Mr. Hoover's dogbodies. Her smiling, faded, fiftyish face was only a few inches from his own and she was speaking in what almost amounted to a whisper, out of kindness no doubt. God, what would happen if J. Edgar found out that a member of *his* Bureau had been caught asleep in the waiting room! The waiting room was for waiting.

"Yes, Miss Crisp—just coming." He sat up and ran his fingers through his hair as a kind of gesture in the direction of tidiness, and then he checked his watch. It was 4:25, so Hoover had kept him dangling for nearly half an hour. Havens grinned, thinking with some pleasure how angry the Great Man would be if he knew that his poor, quaking subordinate had been snoozing the whole time. The wise man took his revenge where he could.

The Director looked much as he always did—as if about to explode in the next few seconds. His wavy, dark brown hair was carefully slicked back, which somehow only succeeded in emphasizing the heaviness of his petulant, babyish face. His lower lip was protruding slightly and his thick hands were placed palms down on his desk. That was not a good sign.

There was another gentleman in the room, a heavyset soldier in his late forties, with the stars of a major general on his shoulders. He wore a mustache and sat on a small, uncomfortable-looking chair against the far wall. Hoover seemed to ignore his presence—perhaps he was offended by the mustache—and the general was making no claims on anyone's attention as he leaned slightly forward, his left hand resting on his knee.

"I haven't yet received your report," Hoover snapped, making it sound like a court-martial sentence. Havens only smiled at him, in a way calculated to make him furious.

"No, sir, that's because I haven't written it yet."

The Director remained unfazed at this impertinence, as if he had expected it, even counted on it, but the general seemed embarrassed. His face assumed that expression of tense, deliberate vagueness that you see in people who are unwilling to intrude on someone else's domestic squabble, and out of respect for his feelings Havens allowed the smile to die away.

"No, sir."

"I take it this von Niehauser individual is now definitely out of bounds?" Mr. Hoover's eyes widened slightly—it wasn't really a question. "One could have hoped the local police would do a little more professional job, but we've never had good cooperation from those people."

Those people—probably Mrs. Vanderbilt used the same emphasis when mentioning the IWW.

"It was my case, sir, and my dropped ball. I was the one who called in the NYPD."

"It was *their* case, Mr. Havens. Officially, we don't have enough to support a charge of espionage, and murder is not a federal offense."

"Yes, sir."

Havens stood staring at the wall behind Mr. Hoover's desk, his face as blank as he could make it. If the Director didn't want to admit in front of a third party that anyone working in his Bureau could be anything less than infallible, that was his business. For the record, Special Agent Havens was the victim of other people's incompetence. Still, Special Agent Havens noticed that he hadn't been invited to sit down.

Anyway, it could have been worse. You weren't allowed to argue with the umpire, even if the only side he favored was his own, and at least he wasn't sending anybody back to the dugouts. If it wasn't going to be the Coral Sea, at least it wasn't going to be Kansas City either.

There was a manila folder directly under Mr. Hoover's right hand. He opened the cover delicately, the way anyone else would have removed the housing from a land mine, and frowned at the first page.

"We have here the available information on your spy," he said, glancing up at the blameless Special Agent Havens with an expression that might have been mistaken for hatred. "The name seems to have rung a bell in certain circles of Military Intelligence —everything after 1939 is a blank, but there are one or two points that might interest you. . . ."

The Director ran his finger down the first page, just as if he had never happened to glance at this particular dossier before. It was a little routine of his, intended no doubt to suggest that he was merely seeking confirmation of something he had known already from ages past.

"Yes, well—born, March 12, 1909, in Görlitz, Prussia, third son of a military family. The mother was the granddaughter of Helmuth von Moltka, the head of the Prussian General Staff during the Franco-Prussian War. The father was decorated in the last war and served abroad as a military attaché.

"Education: Le Rosey, 1919–23; Winchester, 1923–26; Göttingen, 1926–28; the Kaiser Wilhelm Institute, 1928–33, taking a doctor of philosophy degree in physics. He stayed on the faculty there until the beginning of the war, when apparently he entered the Army. Does any of this suggest anything to you, Mr. Havens?"

The Director's eyebrows crept up about half an inch, implying that any sharp young man—any young man with the stuff of a Bureau agent in him—should have been able to deduce the rest.

"No, sir." Special Agent Havens shifted his weight from one foot to the other. He disliked guessing games.

"Nothing, Mr. Havens?" The son of a bitch was genuinely pleased.

"Nothing, sir. Except that he sounds like kind of a big fish to be wasted as a spy. Could be he got in wrong with the regime, though."

" 'He got in wrong with the regime. . . .' " There was that in Mr. Hoover's inflection to suggest that maybe von Niehauser wasn't the only one. "You can't do any better than that, Mr. Havens?"

"No, sir."

"Well, be that as it may, Mr. Havens, Herr von Niehauser has managed to do for you what you never succeeded in doing for yourself. He's managed to get you transferred to the Army."

The Director was looking at Havens, who was perhaps lucky that looks couldn't kill, but Havens was looking at the overweight major general who all this time had been sitting against the wall, who hadn't said a word or moved a muscle, who didn't officially seem to be there at all. Havens was grinning at him.

"This is General Leslie R. Groves," Mr. Hoover announced, rising from his chair—it was only when he was standing that you remembered how short he was. "General Groves, you'll be interested to know, was the one who brought von Niehauser's background to our attention. You belong to him now, Mr. Havens, and I wish you joy of each other."

Havens waited, wondering what was going to happen next, but what did happen was the last thing he would have expected.

Because Mr. Hoover walked out of the room. He actually left, surrendering his office, the *sanctum sanctorum,* closing the door behind him with angry violence. It didn't seem to make any difference for the first few seconds—his presence was like an image that doesn't just suddenly disappear but fades slowly away.

Nevertheless, he was gone. It was like finding oneself in the presence of a miracle.

For a moment after they had the office to themselves, both Havens and General Leslie R. Groves—ask for it by name—seemed to be trying to pretend that each was alone in the room. Or perhaps they were just waiting for the vibrations to subside. Anyway, it was Groves' show now, and he wasn't inviting anybody to sit down either. Havens caught himself wondering what the "R" stood for.

Finally the general ventured so far as to look in his direction; he might have been examining a piece of furniture.

But two could look as cheaply as one. The insignia on General Leslie R. Groves' jacket lapels indicated that he was with the Corps of Engineers. Havens sighed as his last best hope deflated in front of his eyes. So much for combat.

"What is it you want with me, General?" he asked at last, more out of irritation than from any feeling of curiosity. "What does the Army care about von Niehauser, and what's it got to do with me?"

The general smiled.

"Son, I don't suppose you've ever heard of the Manhattan Project?"

X

The general turned out to be actually rather a decent sort, something the hierarchy of the FBI didn't prepare you to expect from a boss.

The two men had dinner together that night, around a conference table in an office on the fifth floor of the War Department. A secretary brought in a couple of paper bags full of little cartons of Chinese food and then left, ostentatiously closing the door behind herself. Havens was really too tired to be hungry, but Groves made up for him.

"Naturally we don't get much intelligence on it," he was saying as he felt around in one of the cartons for another fried shrimp, "but there's reason to believe that the Germans are every bit as interested as we are in building such a bomb—and they've got a head start. They're beaten in the field and they know it, but you can imagine the consequences if Hitler manages to get his hands on a weapon like this."

Yes, he could. The general had been quite eloquent on that score: a device maybe not much bigger than a steamer trunk that would be capable of destroying most of downtown Washington, that might poison the earth for a generation and go right on killing. A fireball that might even be able to ignite the atmosphere and burn up the whole planet.

Or maybe he couldn't. Maybe nobody could. Maybe that was what made the thing so horrible—a weapon that couldn't be controlled or even imagined. Just endless devastation.

"We really don't have much of an idea what it might be able to do—it's all theory at this point. But I don't think the Nazis would hesitate to use such a device against, say, London, if the alternative were losing the war. If they can't have the world, they might be willing to watch it go up in flames."

Havens leaned against the table, propping his head up between his hands. It was a novel sensation to be half asleep and scared to death, both at the same time. The two together created a strange feeling of panicky helplessness—this was probably what it felt like to be drowning.

"That still doesn't tell me what makes von Niehauser such a big threat. How do you know that he's even interested in your device or would know where to look?"

"Figure it out for yourself. Last November we bombed the heavy water installation at Vemork, Norway. The place had been under tight Wehrmacht security ever since '42, with production increased a couple of hundredfold, and it's all been going to about four research facilities, all of them associated in the past with atomic physics. Do you follow me so far?"

"No. Sorry, but I was an English major."

General Groves smiled suddenly. It was the smile of someone who understood the limits of the humanly possible. "You want to go to sleep for a few hours? We can continue this in the morning."

"No. Just tell me—do you use this 'heavy water' to make bombs?"

"Sort of." Groves leaned back in his chair, and the smile faded away of its own accord. He picked up a pencil which had rolled against his hand, holding it delicately between thick first finger and thumb. "All of that is complicated and classified. The point is that Vemork was their only source, so let's just say that they need it and all at once they haven't got it anymore."

"Okay. Let's say that."

Suddenly Havens felt like apologizing. He hadn't meant to sound like a smart ass; he must be getting punchy. But Groves didn't appear to have noticed.

"Then two months later we get a visit from Herr von Niehauser." He looked at the younger man as if he expected that everything had been made clear, but Havens merely stared at him.

"*Post hoc, ergo propter hoc,* General. 'After this, therefore because of this'—it's a classical error in logic. Von Niehauser's appearance may have nothing to do with your bomb. There must be all kinds of other things the Jerries would like to know about over here. And the fact that he used to be a physics teacher doesn't mean very much either; he can't know anything significant about their project or they'd have to be out of their minds to have sent him. Would you risk dropping one of your bright boys into the Third Reich?"

"I might not have any choice—and neither might they." Groves smiled again, his blue eyes almost disappearing in the folds of his heavy, tanned face. He had been over all this terrain before, apparently, so he knew where he was. "You can't just smash open a safe somewhere and then grab the papers and run. We guard our secrets better than that, and so do the Germans. It's not what's written down that matters but what's in people's heads—there are hundreds of men involved in this project, and we can't keep them all under lock and key. And to get anything from any of them, von Niehauser is going to have to know what they're talking about."

He sighed heavily and shifted his weight in the chair. The subject seemed to make him uncomfortable.

"The atomic physicists," he went on, "used to be like a private club before the war. There weren't very many of them and they all knew each other. They'd meet for conferences and write each other letters about their work, right up to the invasion of Poland. They've got their own language and their own values, and they trust each other a lot more than they trust any government. They don't know the meaning of the word 'security'—if I told you the trouble I've had with some of them . . . Anyway, the point is that von Niehauser is a member in good standing. He wasn't *just* a physics teacher."

Havens glanced sleepily around the office, thinking that it was a drab little place to be discussing the survival of the world. There was a green carpet on the floor, and the walls were painted the usual institutional buff. Through the Venetian blinds were visible a road and, beyond that, the Arlington cemetery. *Memento mori.*

"Well, then, I hope you catch him, General." He reached out a tentative finger and tipped one of the cardboard cartons far enough toward him that he could see inside. It was about half full of fried rice. He let it go with a shudder of disgust, and it rocked back on its heels like a first-day recruit snapping to attention.

"I'm not going to catch him—you're going to catch him."

There was a moment of almost tangible silence, and then Havens' face split into a grin.

"Don't make me laugh, General. You know what happened in New York. Von Niehauser could be anywhere right now, and recent experience would suggest that right now I probably couldn't catch a cold."

But nobody was laughing. General Groves just sat there in a kind of frigid immobility, as if nothing had been said that called for any response whatsoever. To this man, it seemed, there were no arguable points.

And then, finally, he shook his head.

"I talked to a Lieutenant Phelan in New York this morning," he said, as if he were deliberately changing the subject. "He seems to think von Niehauser got out of the city by some act of levitation. He was very embarrassed; he nearly burned up the phone wires. Anyway, he says you're the best bird dog in the business. Hoover says the same thing. He's not very fond of you otherwise, but he tells me you're good at hunting down spies."

"Hoover's just covering his ass."

"Maybe so." Groves frowned slightly, as if he found the

expression distasteful. "But you were the one who figured out that the Germans had landed an agent, and you tracked him all the way down to New York. And everything we've been able to find out about von Niehauser suggests that he's a clever man—not just book clever, but smart and resourceful. So far, I'd call it a draw."

It was an obvious enough ploy—first the appeal to vanity and the competitive instinct. It was the Military Intelligence version of the pregame peptalk. And it was working.

Havens wasn't kidding anybody. What he wanted more than anything in the world was another crack at von Niehauser. He would never be able to live quietly with himself if somehow he didn't manage to turn the key on this guy. This was his Battle of the Coral Sea, his invasion of Europe. His war had come down to him and Joachim von Niehauser, physicist and spy. And he wouldn't have been surprised if General Leslie R. Groves knew that every bit as well as he did, the bastard.

"This bomb of mine is a priority one item," Groves went on. "I get anything I need—money, men, anything. I got you away from Hoover, so you understand what I'm talking about. And it's priority one with me that you catch this German agent. You can have anything or anybody you want, and no one is going to question you about your methods. Just get him, and there won't be any complaints. But get him."

"And when I get him?" Havens ran a hand through his hair, which he found, much to his surprise, was damp with sweat, and tried to smile again. "It doesn't sound like what we have here is the sort of deal where anyone would much care for having von Niehauser put on trial for espionage. What are you planning to do with him once I've caught the poor son of a bitch?"

Groves raised his eyebrows, as if the question surprised him.

"Does he strike you as the type who would allow himself to be taken alive?"

"Frankly, no."

"Then I don't expect the problem will ever come up." The eyebrows sank back down again, and the general moved the point of his thumb absentmindedly back and forth across the surface of the table, as if he were rubbing out a mark. "I expect you'll run him to ground and that'll be the end of it."

"That's clear enough, General."

"I hope so."

There was an uncomfortable silence that went on for several seconds, as if neither of them cared to be the first to speak again.

"You know, you're going to have to tell me a little more about this project of yours," Havens said finally, glad to have found a means of getting to something else. "I can't go running blind. If I'm to catch him, I've got to know what he's looking for."

"I thought you took your degree in English." The general smiled, just a little condescendingly, but if he expected Havens to be put off he was mistaken.

"But that doesn't make me an idiot—just spell it out for me in layman's terms, how in outline the thing's supposed to work, what sorts of materials it needs, what the problems are, and where your people have got their laboratories. I think I'd like to know that first."

"Do you have any idea what you're asking?"

"In broad terms—yes. But don't worry, General. I don't talk in my sleep."

Groves stared out through the Venetian blinds for a moment and sighed. And then, from one instant to the next, he seemed to grasp the force of Havens' argument.

"All right," he said suddenly, his head snapping around on his thick neck. "I suppose that security clearance was inevitable. After you've heard some of it, you won't thank me."

"We'll see—start with the locations. I want to know where he's likely to turn up."

The general actually laughed—it wasn't a very cheerful sound.

"You name it. You try coming at it from that end, son, and you'll end up in a strait jacket. We've got big installations in Washington State and Tennessee and New Mexico; Berkeley is doing work for us, and the University of Chicago, and NYU, and the Ford Motor Company. And there are small contracts out to dozens of companies, and every one of them has got a security force of its own to make sure people lock the doors."

"Okay, which ones are you the most worried about? You seem to think all this has something to do with their not having any more heavy water. Where would von Niehauser go for that?"

"Nowhere. We aren't using heavy water."

Havens watched him for a moment through narrowed eyes, but there wasn't anything in Groves' face to suggest that he was trying to sandbag anyone. Havens nodded—okay, so heavy water was out.

"All right. Next question—if the Germans have the head start you seem to think they do, they must already have done their own spadework. Where do you feel the most naked? Suppose our boy wants to know about how you plan to put the goddamned thing together, where would he go?"

"New Mexico."

"What's in New Mexico?"

"A converted boys' school with a bunch of certifiable lunatics running around loose." It sounded like a joke, but apparently it wasn't—the general wasn't laughing. "The actual bomb development laboratory is on a mesa just north of Santa Fe. The place is called Los Alamos."

XI

For what felt like the hundredth time that week, Jenny Springer swept the snow from the two concrete steps that led up to the front door of the three-room bungalow she shared with her husband. There was no garden, since there was almost no water. In the spring, when the ground thawed, it simply turned to mud and then, finally, the summer sun baked it hard as concrete. There were no flowers, so one lavished one's attentions on the front steps.

The house was a prefabricated structure, put up with twenty other houses in part of an afternoon, with almost no heat and only the most rudimentary plumbing. Still, to have it at all had to be considered an enormous privilege—more than half of the other enlisted personnel had had to leave their families behind or, what was perhaps worse, to huddle them together in one of the squalid little apartments which had originally been intended as bachelor quarters. But Hal was a sergeant in the Security Section and thus enjoyed more perquisites than some of the officers. The Security Section really ran the installation. And Hal was the sort of person who took advantage of every break that came his way.

It was too cold to linger outside for more than a few minutes, so Jenny retreated back through the door and went into the bedroom to change her dress. It was Saturday, and on Saturday she and some friends pooled their gasoline coupons and drove into Santa Fe for the afternoon. In theory, it was supposed to be a shopping expedition, a safari in pursuit of make-up cases and lingerie and pretty little tile plaques to hang up in the kitchen, but the prices were really better at the Army commissary and the stores in town were nearly empty of such peacetime luxuries and, besides, nobody had the money to waste. Really, what everybody wanted was just a chance to get away for a few hours from the smothering atmosphere of the base.

She opened her closet door, looked inside, and sank down on the corner of the bed, stifled with melancholy. Nobody had told her that it snowed in the desert and all of her warm clothes were in mothballs back home in New Jersey. Nothing had prepared her for this. Suddenly, all she wanted to do was to cry.

But she wouldn't cry. After all, she wasn't a child. It was always the same—every time she had one of these days she ended up feeling horribly guilty. Somehow it didn't seem very patriotic to hate military life quite so much, but she did. Even in the middle of a war, even when she knew everyone else was having to make sacrifices too, she couldn't help herself. She just hated Los Alamos.

And it wasn't even that, really. Everybody hated Los Alamos. She didn't know a single woman there who didn't loathe every square inch of it, who didn't live for the day the war would be over and she could go home. There was a solidarity of misery here, but she doubted if many of her friends collapsed in a panic of depression every time they looked inside their closets. It was the solitude that she felt was crushing her, the necessity of facing every second of it with no resource but herself.

She hated her husband. At least, sometimes she hated him. And it was worse when she didn't.

She couldn't really judge. Even in her own family, she really didn't have any clear idea how her mother felt about her father—her mother wasn't the sort of woman who could have brought herself to talk about something like that. And her friends, well . . .

But at least, from the way they sounded, from what they seemed to assume about their marriages, at least, if they didn't think that the man who came home at night and sat down to dinner in his underwear was precisely a hero of romance, they didn't feel that nothing was possible except silence.

I told Frank that he should have talked to his brother before he bought that car. I told *him. Even his mother told him and, you know, she believes the sun rises and sets on Frank. Frank imagines he knows everything there is to know about cars, but he's* such *a fool. That salesman wrapped him around his little finger, and now he's . . .*

If that wasn't love, at least it was something. It wasn't just an emptiness that was like death.

And with Hal it had been no other way, a desolation, from the first moment. And she had known that it would be. Oh God, why had she married him?

He had been hanging around her parents' house for close to a year without managing to generate much interest. He was a nice enough sort of fellow, but with a kind of cold tenacity that wouldn't listen when she said no. He seemed to think he was irresistible just because he happened to be wearing a policeman's uniform. And then, about six months after Pearl Harbor, one day he showed up in his fatigues and announced that he was through with basic training and had just a week's leave before he was expected to join his unit.

He begged her, almost with tears in his eyes, saying that he had done it for her, that he would face any kind of death for her. It would be Europe, he said, and he wanted to carry her with him in his heart, to give him something to stay alive for. There didn't seem to be anything else to do except to marry him.

It was her own fault, her own stupid mistake. She had let her enthusiasm run away with her, and who wouldn't tell her that she was a fool to marry a man because she thought that afterward she wasn't going to have to live with him?

Except that Hal had known he would never get out of the country—he already had his orders that morning when he showed up with his uniform and his aching eyes and made his last appeal. It had all been a lie, from beginning to end.

Two weeks after they came back from their three-day honeymoon in Connecticut, when she had heard the truth and was busy telling herself that she had no right to resent Hal because he had been assigned to the MPs, when they had moved to Fort Monmouth and she was busy trying to get everything put away in the two-room apartment they had rented in town, she found the letter from the commandant's office, saying that his application had been approved and giving his posting. The date on the letter was a month back. There wasn't anything she could say to him—what could she have said?—so she put the letter back into its envelope and tried to forget she had ever seen it.

But how could she do that? How could she ever do that?

So they had spent that first year of the war at Fort Monmouth, not fifty miles from the place where both of them had lived their whole lives. Hal grew a mustache, but otherwise he might just as well never have left the Newark Police.

Hal. He was a good-looking man, with a dark complexion and black hair and eyes. He was tall and well-built and had been lifting weights ever since his early teens to make the most of it—he could spend half the morning standing in front of a mirror feeling his biceps. When he put on his uniform, he really looked like a soldier.

And during the entire eighteen months of their marriage, every night his uniform had been carefully hung up in their closet and he had never even missed dinner. Sometimes, while she lay in bed next to him, listening to his slow, even breathing, she thought it just possible she might actually suffocate out of sheer desperation.

There was a crack in the bedroom ceiling, just over the closet door—the house hadn't been up longer than five months and already there was a crack in the ceiling. She sat there now, watching it, expecting it to widen in front of her eyes. Half hoping that it would. The house might split open, like the skin on an apple, and then she could get out. And then she . . .

But she was only being stupid again. She was always being

stupid—it was a trait that seemed destined to decide the whole pattern of her life.

Marrying Hal was supposed to have been a gesture, you see. It hadn't been something she had thought through very carefully—that was obvious enough by now, even to her—but she had seen it as in some sense a contribution to the war effort. The idea, on some level or other, had been that she would sacrifice herself, her private reluctance—after all, Hal might have been sacrificing his life. But it hadn't turned out that way. This wasn't the war she had signed on for.

Nobody even seemed to know what they were doing here. Not even Hal. One gathered there was some sort of top-secret research program up on the mesa, but they could be up there making mud pies for all anybody really knew for sure. And a military detachment of some two or three hundred men had been assigned as baby sitters. There was almost no contact between the military base and the others, the ones who were involved in what was called simply "the Project," but it must have been the same for them too. All those hundreds and hundreds of people, sitting out here in the middle of the New Mexico desert—the battles in Italy and the Pacific were just things you read about in the newspapers.

Hal would be endlessly mysterious on the subject of the Project. He didn't have any idea what it was either, but its importance—and therefore, indirectly, his own—was something he accepted as an article of faith.

"It," he had on the highest authority (probably no higher than the scuttlebutt in the sergeants' mess), was going to win the war all by itself. "It" was just something he needed to believe in, so that no one could criticize him for being here rather than at Anzio.

It was impossible to believe that anything that happened here was going to make any difference in the history of the world. They were both of them just wearing away their lives. Los Alamos was just a pointless suspension, something they had to get through and then try to forget about as quickly as they could. It was just a place they happened to be, where they could allow themselves the luxury of not thinking about what would come next.

Jenny Springer pressed her hands down against the mattress, forcing herself to remember that her friends would be by to pick her up in less than half an hour, that she was driving into Santa Fe for the afternoon, that she had better step on it or she would hold everybody up and ruin the one day a week that held the promise of escape.

She got up and took the brush and comb from the top of the dresser and began working on her hair, which fortunately never took very much work. She brushed it straight back over her ears, and it was a color somewhere between brown and blond that didn't need to be washed every day. Water was scarce at Los Alamos, and even shampoo was something of a luxury item, unavailable at the PX, sometimes for weeks at a time, and not easy to find even in Santa Fe.

And she had to wear her hair short to make her face seem fuller. All her life she had envied girls with long hair—she had even tried it once, but it only made her look like Wanda the Witch. Even now, as she combed out the ends and studied herself in the mirror, she was conscious that she had started losing weight again. Her brown eyes were getting so large that she looked like a startled child. It happened every time she had something to worry her; she began forgetting about food and thinning away to nothing. You didn't get to be a beauty queen that way.

And that was just one more thing to worry about. It was like a merry-go-round you couldn't get off.

She would wear her brown wool suit and the tan coat. She always wore her brown wool suit and the tan coat on her Saturdays in Santa Fe, simply because there wasn't anything else. In another three or four months, when Hal got his furlough and they could get home to New Jersey for a week or two, she would gather up the rest of her winter clothes. But by then, of course, the cold weather would be over, and by April she would be back to fighting the snakes and the Gila monsters for the little patch of shade provided by the canvas awning over her back door. Probably by then it wouldn't seem worth the effort anymore.

It was just ten minutes before eleven when she heard the car horn sounding—one short little squeal so as not to wake the neighbors' children. It was time to go.

The ride down into town was pleasant enough—five women in a car with the windows rolled up could at least keep themselves warm—and, before they split up and went their separate directions, they all had lunch together at a tiny Mexican restaurant about three blocks from Palace Street. The tablecloths were like horse blankets and the single ceiling fan creaked like a rusted hinge, but it was cheap and the food wasn't bad. Mindy Applewhite spent the whole meal talking about her husband's probable promotion to T-5.

Outside, where the sidewalks had been scraped clean of ice, the sunshine was bright enough to make your eyes tear. Wilma Bragg, who was thirty-seven and the wife of a second lieutenant who had been promoted up through the ranks too slowly ever to have made the social transition from enlisted to commissioned, took Jenny by the elbow and began guiding her toward the center of town. As if by prearrangement, the others had all scattered up and down the various side streets, but Wilma, it seemed, wasn't averse to a little company.

"I don't know why we come down here," she said brightly, smiling like a milkmaid. "You can see everything there is in Santa Fe inside of forty-five minutes. I've been looking for a pair of size nine elastic-sided rain shoes for Pauley ever since we got here and I'm not even getting warm. You have anything special on today, dearie?"

Jenny laughed, perhaps a trifle nervously, and shook her head. She liked Wilma Bragg.

"No, I'll probably end up going to the movies. I saw in the paper that they're playing *Springtime in the Rockies,* and at least the theater will be warm."

"Betty Grable in the middle of the afternoon—oh God, no, not for me! Are you sure you wouldn't rather come and help me inspect the rubber dish drainers?"

"I'm sure," she answered, still smiling. "What time do we meet to drive back?"

"I should think four would be soon enough. Why? Impatient to get back to the nest?"

It was only a joke—after all, what did Wilma Bragg know about her domestic troubles? But Jenny thought of the sullen, silent dinner she and Hal would eat at their general-issue composition-board kitchen table, and her heart seemed to go cold within her.

"No. Nothing like that."

"Well, then, figure on four. That is, if Mindy doesn't take all night at the hairdresser's again—imagine such a silly waste of time and money, and in the middle of a war. . . ."

It was after one-thirty before Jenny finally got away by herself, which was all she had wanted from the beginning. And she had never intended to go anywhere near *Springtime in the Rockies,* but one had to tell Wilma Bragg something. *Springtime in the Rockies* would keep—movies were the principal staple of entertainment at the base, with screenings two or three times a week, and Hal was a fan. So it was a pretty safe bet that Betty Grable would have her chance.

From the look of the sky, they would have snow for their return trip. If you could get an unobstructed enough view north, you could see the clouds gathering behind the Jemez Mountains. But it was still clear and windless in Santa Fe. The sidewalks were crowded, and people seemed to be taking advantage of the nice weather. Jenny browsed in front of the shop windows until she was absolutely sure that no one who knew her was anywhere within sight, and then she cut across the street, went down two more blocks, and stepped into the lobby of the La Ventana Hotel.

There wasn't much there to tempt you to linger—just a

couple of tired-looking blue-gray sofas resting on a tan carpet, a few low tables covered over with that morning's newspaper, and the front desk. It wasn't even the sort of place where you could buy a pack of cigarettes.

Jenny couldn't have said whether the clerk noticed her or not, so resolutely were her eyes fixed on the staircase. If he had he wouldn't have bothered to make any inquiries of her—it wasn't that sort of a place either.

The door to Room 227 was painted over with so many coats of white that the moldings around the edges were almost completely filled in. Jenny noticed every detail—the dirty smudges above the knob, even the brush marks—as she stood there, trembling with dread. Finally she summoned up the courage to knock, twice, hardly loud enough to hear herself. She waited, wondering whether to knock again, wondering whether to leave, hoping and fearing that no one would answer.

But someone did answer. After what felt like an eternity, and was probably no more than eight or ten seconds, the door swung open and revealed a man standing in his shirt sleeves, one hand thrust into the pocket of a pair of baggy brown trousers. He was only a little over average height, but, poised there in the doorway, he seemed to fill the room behind him. The door seemed to open onto him and nothing else.

His face was wide and strong and very tanned, but it was possible to see already a certain slight puffiness around the angles of his jaw, presaging that he would run more and more to fat as he approached middle age. But that was still all in the future—he was young yet. He couldn't have been more than twenty-nine or thirty and was handsome in an obvious way. And whenever he smiled, and his brown eyes crinkled a little around the corners, he revealed that he knew it. He was smiling now.

"I was beginning to think you wouldn't come," he said, in an accent that turned his "w"s into soft, liquid "v"s. But it wasn't the accent that kept you from entirely believing him. "I'm glad to see you."

He stepped aside, and Jenny Springer walked across the threshold into the room, and the door closed.

The room's only window faced west and threw a thin bar of hard yellow light across the carpet, which was tan, just like the one down on the lobby floor, and dotted here and there with cigarette burns. The light cut the bed in half lengthwise, as if to divide one side from the other, but no such precaution was necessary now. Jenny Springer was in the bed alone. The sheet was pulled up to cover her breasts, but no one was looking at her—the man who had spent the afternoon lying beside her was up now, standing in front of the bureau with his back to her, tying his necktie in the mirror.

She reached over to the night table and picked up the wristwatch her parents had given her as a high school graduation present. It was twenty-five minutes after three.

"Erich—Erich, I have to leave pretty soon."

He turned around to look at her, and smiled. He was only reacting to the fact that she had spoken; probably he hadn't even been listening. Probably he didn't give a damn whether she stayed or went.

"What will you tell your husband?" he asked, his voice smooth and musical—almost feminine—and his accent correct but obviously European. He smiled again, as if the question were part of a little joke he was having on Hal Springer, whom, as far as Jenny knew, he had never met.

When she didn't answer, Erich Lautner turned back to his mirror. She watched him for a long time, as he finished with his tie and began the careful business of combing his hair. He was like an artist, putting the finishing touches on a masterpiece, she thought, and then flushed with shame the next instant. What an idea to have! Was that what it was like to be an adulteress, not to think well of anyone? Apparently.

She had been to bed with Erich twice before, often enough for him to feel he had established a kind of claim on her. So now she was trapped, both by her marriage and by this affair with Erich. God, how could she have been so stupidly blind? Now all she wanted was to be left in peace, and even that was no longer possible. Stupid, stupid, stupid!

She slipped her feet over the edge of the bed and began feeling for her shoes. If she hurried, there would be just time enough for a shower. Oh the blessed luxury of it, with plenty of hot water and soap—she knew she would feel better after a shower. Erich never even glanced at her as she made her way into the bathroom.

Five minutes later, when she came back out, she found him fully dressed and sitting on one of the room's two chairs, waiting for her.

"When will I see you again?"

It wasn't the question she wanted to hear. She thought of what it would be like that night when she got home, she thought of Hal, grunting under a barbell in his khaki underwear. He would probably want to make love to her, which he did as if according to a recipe, as if she were simply something to be handled, to be turned this way and that, which would give her no pleasure at all—she might as well be a block of wood.

And Erich, who thought he was so much the technician of lovemaking, wasn't much better. What he forgot was that it was hard to feel pleasure—to feel anything—where there was no love. She despised herself all the more because she couldn't manage even a little spark of guilty sensuality. She wasn't meant for adventures in motel rooms.

When she was seventeen there had been a boy. . . . She had never told anyone; it was her secret. He had been a cousin of a friend, someone there for a month one summer. He had been her only other experience—they had done it twice, on the back seat of a car he had borrowed from his uncle, and each time she had been overwhelmed with shame. She had been glad when he went home again. She had promised herself she would never do anything like that again, and she never had. Not until Erich.

But there had been pleasure on that back seat, an aching, desperate kind of pleasure. Everything after had been a crushing disappointment, but at least she knew that it was in her to feel passion.

"I don't know," she said quietly, turning her eyes a little away from the full force of Erich's smile. Why did he always have to smile like that, as if he thought he could read her mind? "It's so hard to get away. I don't know how you do it—I thought everyone was supposed to work on Saturday."

And it was true. Hal was working today. All the men at Los Alamos worked six days a week. Sometimes right through Sunday. But Erich always seemed to be able to get away.

"I can come and go as I please. I am a theorist—they pay me to think, and I can do that anywhere. Besides, a bachelor . . . I have a right to come into town once in a while to get my shoes resoled. When will I see you again?"

"Look, Erich, this is no good. This is . . ."

"Is it your husband that worries you?" He closed his eyes, and an expression of weary boredom came over him—even his shoulders seemed to sag imperceptibly. "I think we have little enough to fear from him. Or perhaps you have decided that you love him. Is that it, Jenny? Have his embraces suddenly become so very dear to you?"

She hated him when he was like this. Erich was good-looking and clever—he was the most intelligent man she had ever known—but he could be so arrogant, so sure he could have his own way in everything.

That was part of the charm for him. She suddenly saw it. If she hadn't happened to be married to one of the base security officers, he probably wouldn't have enjoyed his little affair with her half so much. Stolen meetings in sleazy little rented bedrooms were all very well in their way, but what really made it for him was the fact that he was putting one over on a man who walked around the grounds at Los Alamos with a .45 automatic hanging from his belt. She wished sometimes that Hal would find out, just to see how Erich Lautner, doctor of philosophy, would handle that.

Her clothes were draped over the back of the other chair. She turned her back a little to him, trying not to be too obvious about it because she didn't care to be teased about her few remaining scruples of modesty, and took off her towel. She didn't speak as she stepped into her panties—she really didn't know what to say.

When she was dressed, and was zipping up the suit skirt, she could face him calmly enough again.

"It doesn't have anything to do with Hal," she said. "But we can't go on like this."

"Are you suggesting I should marry you?"

She shook her head. No, she wasn't suggesting that—and neither was he. It was just more of his sly mockery.

"No—I don't want you to marry me. When the war is over, I don't know what I'll do about Hal, but I don't imagine that will last. No, you don't have to marry me, Erich."

It did begin to snow on the way home. As the car wound its way up the mountain road, and the flatland fell away to leave them naked and exposed against the rising ground, the wind stiffened toward them and hard flakes struck against the glass with a sound that was audible even over the growl of the engine. They were all glad to get back inside the confines of the base housing complex, and when they dropped Jenny off in front of her bungalow she ran for the front door as if for dear life. The snow pelted the backs of her bare legs like sharp little stones.

Even after she was inside, after she had hung up her coat and turned on the electric heater in the bedroom, she still stood with her arms clasped around her shoulders, she was still quaking—it was as if an icy hand had reached up inside her to lay its fingers against her heart.

She wasn't cold—she was afraid.

It would have been different if she had had the courage

simply to throw the whole thing away—the marriage, Hal, Erich, everything—and go back to her parents' house in New Jersey. But she didn't. She knew she didn't, and there was nothing she could do about it. It was a weakness, a species of cowardice, but she didn't want to be the little tramp of a soldier's wife who had made a fool of herself with some smoothie of a European scientist and got dragged through the divorce courts. Hal wouldn't be nice about a thing like that—it wasn't his fault, but he just wouldn't have it in him—and she was afraid of what her parents would think. She was afraid of admitting to anyone that kind of a failure.

And Erich was the type who would probably like to brag about his conquests, who certainly would brag if she ever wounded his masculine vanity by somehow slipping away from him. As long as she was his mistress, and he had the secret satisfaction of having a military policeman's wife at his beck and call, he would be silent, but if he lost that . . .

"Why shouldn't we go on as before?" he had asked, smiling his crafty, contemptuous smile. "You don't love your husband—why should you deny a little measure of affection to a poor fugitive from the Nazis?"

XII

On the second story of the base security office, where the floors were unfinished plywood and the walls had been painted a mustard yellow, Hal Springer sat with his feet up on his desk, staring resentfully at a letter one of the project scientists had written to his wife back in Massachusetts. The goddamned thing was in cipher.

They did stuff like that all the time, just to be annoying. It was sort of a game with them—make the work just as difficult as you can for the snoops, let the snoops know every day of their lives just how pointless it is trying to keep a leash on such a bunch of bright boys. Springer knew perfectly well that if he went over to this one's office and demanded an explanation the little snot-nose would probably just sigh dramatically, reach inside his desk, and pull out a code key, and that would be that. He was a mathematician named Stanley and his wife was an assistant professor of statistics at Radcliffe—it said so right on the envelope—so presumably she would have been able to figure out the letter without a key. But Springer wasn't going to play their little game. He wasn't going to give anybody a chance to make a fool out of him. He just wasn't going to forward the letter.

He balled the thing up and threw it in his wastepaper basket, wondering why the whole world seemed to conspire against him. In the five months since he had come out from the East, he had learned to hate the project scientists worse than he ever could have hated the enemy. He couldn't understand why they all wore civilian clothes, why they hadn't all just been drafted and put under direct military authority so they wouldn't be able to fuck around like that without landing in the brig where they belonged.

And he couldn't understand what they were all supposed to be doing up here in the first place. Everybody just called it the Project and tiptoed around like guests at a funeral, but nobody—at least nobody he had talked to—had the faintest idea what it was about. Nobody. He was a security officer, so they told him, but what was he supposed to be protecting? What was the big deal?

God, he should never have joined the Army. They might have let him off if he'd told them about his old hernia operation. He should have stayed with the cops in Newark, busting drunks and whores and handing out parking tickets along Wilson Avenue. Nobody needed him to be a night watchman out in the sticks.

And he would have stayed back in Newark if it hadn't been for Jenny: it was all because of her; she just had to be so gung ho about the stupid war. All she could ever seem to talk about was how she had joined the Red Cross and who had enlisted and what was happening in the Pacific. What should she care? Jenny had never even seen the Pacific.

But he had gone and joined up, just because he knew she wouldn't even look at a man she thought wasn't serving his country—and hadn't he been serving his country by running in the cruds who pissed on the bus station walls?—and now everything had gone wrong. He was a good soldier and a good husband, but the people he was assigned to guard did everything they could to make him look stupid and his wife didn't seem to care about him.

The night before he had made love to her. He was a proper man; he had waited until she had come to bed and turned out the light on her night table, and then, while she lay there in the darkness with her back turned to him, he had reached out and put his hand on her arm, just below the shoulder. He hadn't forced her, and she had come to him willingly enough, but she did nothing. She was just there, lying beneath him; he couldn't even hear her breathing.

It was always like that. It seemed to be something that she simply accepted, like meat rationing. She wouldn't even allow him the consolation of being resented.

The Army had been unaccountably lavish in its use of windows for the security office, and from where he was sitting Springer had an almost panoramic view of the entire mesa. He knew that if he got up and walked the fifteen or so feet to the front of the building he would be able to see part of the roof of his bungalow, hiding behind a three-story bachelor apartment building in the next block. When they first came to Los Alamos, he used to do that a couple of times every day. It had given him a special kind of feeling to look down there and know that Jenny was at home, doing whatever it was that women did in their husbands' houses. It had been love and the pride of ownership and a certain feeling of triumph, that he had won out at last. Now he could barely stand to go near that side of the room.

It wasn't supposed to come out this way; marriage was supposed to settle everything. He had always believed that if he could just get Jenny to marry him—it didn't matter how—that everything else would work out. She would love him then. She would have to love him.

Marriage, he had always believed, was the happy ending, not the start of some new contest. Life was supposed to return to normal, but Jenny just seemed to refuse to understand that. It was like there was something wrong with her.

And now some smart-ass little cocksucker of a college boy wanted to send his wife love letters in cipher. Jesus.

"Doesn't it make you feel like a peeping Tom?" she had asked him once, a couple of weeks after they first arrived, when he had started to work in Mail Screening. She had been standing in front of the sink in the kitchen, her back turned to him, scrubbing potatoes for dinner.

"What kind of a question is that?"

"I don't know," she had answered, her voice perfectly conversational and easy—they had gotten along better in those days. "I just wondered how you felt about it."

"I don't *feel* any way about it at all. What've feelings got to do with it? It's just the job I was assigned—somebody's got to keep the eggs from telling everybody on earth what they're up to over there."

But Jenny hadn't understood. She was as smart as anybody he had ever known, man or woman; she probably would have gone on to college and become a teacher if her old man had had the money—it was what she said she had wanted. But she hadn't figured out that the eggs were just a bunch of rotten, spoiled little brats who had to be watched every second or they would commit treason and call it "kidding around."

For Jenny it was very simple: it just wasn't nice to open other people's mail. She didn't seem to understand that they weren't back in New Jersey anymore, that there was a war going on. He had pointed that out to her once.

"Are we at war with the eggs?" she had asked. "I thought it was the Japanese and the Germans."

You couldn't explain anything to a woman.

There was still a stack of manila envelopes on his "in" tray—the work came like that, bundles of letters tied up in manila envelopes; you had to watch what they received as well as what they sent out. Springer took the top one, unfastened the clasp, and let the contents spill out over the surface of the desk. The sight of it all made him feel faintly sick. God, life in the Army.

"I feel funny in this uniform," he had told her, only half joking. "It's the wrong color."

He had known her then for about a year. He used to come and visit her a couple of times a week, taking her out to a movie sometimes but mostly just sitting there with her on her parents' big porch swing. Sometimes she'd tell him that he shouldn't come around so often, that he ought to give the other girls a chance, but she didn't seem to mind so much—at least, not enough to warn him off for good and all. Not that he would have listened to that. He wouldn't always stay very long, usually just an hour or half an hour, just long enough to establish a kind of claim without seeming to force himself in.

He had thought it all out, and what he wanted to do was to become a fixture, somebody that everyone was used to. If that happened people would get the idea that he and Jenny were a settled issue, and then the other guys would stay away. It had worked up to a point—one or two he had had to warn off by shaking a night stick in their faces, and some just wouldn't take a hint. But she was his girl, whether she knew it or not and whether she liked it or not. Nobody was going to beat his time.

But he had to be careful, because Jenny just didn't seem to warm up the way he had expected. She seemed to think he was okay—he was tolerated, but she wasn't exactly falling into his arms.

So they had sat there on the porch swing that morning. He remembered that she had worn a filmy green summer dress and held her arms crossed over her chest while he tried to talk her into marrying him. May was always pretty in that part of New Jersey. She had liked the uniform.

"Do you know yet where you'll be going?" she had asked, looking up at him with interest—more interest than he had ever seen in her face, in all those months of trying. Jenny was very big on the war.

"No—Europe, I suppose." He had smiled, wondering whether she could tell that he was lying. "You hear rumors all the time, but . . ."

Probably he would wonder until the day he died what she would have said if he had told her the truth. But he hadn't wanted to take the chance, and he had pressed his advantage. He already had his posting, and the military police insignia were in his suitcase, just waiting to be stitched on. It had been the luckiest break in the world—the idea of combat turned his guts into ice water—but Jenny wouldn't have seen it that way. So he had smiled and lied.

And now Jenny was his wife and sat alone in his house in New Mexico, feeling cheated because her husband hadn't gotten his head blown off in Sicily. And nothing made any sense anymore.

That morning, when the alarm went off, he had put an arm out in the bed to find her, but she was already up. He lay quiet for a moment, and finally he could hear her; she was in the kitchen making breakfast. She always beat the alarm. He wondered sometimes whether she didn't go back to bed for an hour in the middle of the day, just so she wouldn't have to be there with him when he woke up.

"Good morning," she said when he came in. She was just putting the eggs on his plate, and she hardly looked at him. There was only one place setting; Jenny never ate breakfast, just drank a cup of coffee while she was standing by the stove.

He wondered what it was like with other couples the morning after making love, if it was the same with them, as if it had never happened. Didn't any private smiles pass between them, any unspoken recognition of a more cheerful world? Or was it like yesterday's crossword puzzle in the newspaper, something that passed out of memory because it was too insignificant to remember?

So he ate in silence and left, letting the screen door slam shut behind him as he set out on his walk to work. They hardly ever spoke at all anymore.

And what plagued him the most was that he knew that Jenny was doing the best she knew how by him. She attended to his needs—kept his clothes and his house clean, made the best use of his money, never let him sit down to a cold meal, let him have his way with her in bed. She was trying, almost painfully hard, so he could accuse her of nothing except that she didn't love him. It was like there was something wrong with her.

"I suppose you've got a boyfriend or something, somebody you like better than me."

That had been back at Fort Monmouth. His voice had been angry, but that had been a lie too. He hadn't even believed it himself.

But perhaps she had. She had been sitting on the edge of the bed, in nothing but her slip, combing her hair, and her arms had stopped moving and her back had assumed a kind of rigid stillness. And then she had begun combing her hair again. What had passed through her in that moment was as closed to him as everything else she felt or thought. As far as he could know, she might be dead inside.

"You haven't got anything to complain about," she had said, without turning around. He hadn't chosen to pursue the subject.

The jumble of mail on his desk—envelopes of various shapes and colors, postcards, even a few advertising circulars—seemed to mean nothing. He swept his hand carelessly over the pile, spreading them out, and picked a couple up to look at. A letter with the address written out in a sprawling, feminine hand, an overdue notice from a library in New York City—the usual unintelligible garbage.

The war seemed a long way distant.

XIII

The morning wind was just beginning to pick up as Erich Lautner started out on the eleven-minute walk from his room on the second floor of Bachelor Quarters J-6 to the desk he occupied in the cavernous building that housed the Bomb Physics Division. Like everyone else at Los Alamos that winter, he complained about the ghastly weather and the lack of heat, but largely out of nothing more than an instinct to conform. Until he was eighteen and had gone to Berlin to pursue his studies, he had lived with his mother and father in an apartment over a paint store in Hamburg, so he was used to cold rooms and damp, windy streets. Besides, he had a heavy tweed coat that he had bought in England in 1939 and a pair of fur-lined gloves. Nothing bothered him.

The roads were only thinly covered with asphalt, and along the edges they were already crumbling like pie crust. Wisps of snow, as dry as sand, snaked their way across the black surface, driven along by the harsh, fitful wind that blew over the mesa all day long, only changing direction in the early afternoon.

Lautner was almost alone as he walked by the side of the main artery that led to the lab compounds—he had slept late and everyone else was already at work. Nobody would mind; there weren't any time clocks at Los Alamos. They put in fourteen- and sixteen-hour days, six or seven days a week, but the scientific staff still adhered to the customs of the various European and American universities from which they had been gathered—people set their own schedules. They were like the Hitler Youth in their wretched enthusiasm, but at least there was a certain measure of disorganized freedom.

"It's the desert," Oppenheimer had said, glancing around in that preoccupied way of his, as if with half his mind he were casting about for some avenue of escape. And then he would glance at you with his strange, startled eyes and smile. "Beautiful country, but a wilderness. And we'll be working for the Army. Would you like to come?"

That had been at Princeton, where Oppenheimer had come recruiting. No one had needed to be asked twice. It was going to be a run for the grand prize—there would never be another chance like it in the history of the world. And if they failed . . .

All the brightest stars would be there: Fermi, Teller, Bethe, von Neumann, finally even Niels Bohr. So Lautner had signed on. He had applied to his department for a leave of absence, had bought his railway ticket for Lamy, where a corporal in sport clothes had picked him up for the drive into Santa Fe, and he had turned himself over to Oppie's brilliant dream.

And in the evenings they could try to get drunk, or listen to Teller play Beethoven on the hopeless little upright piano in the common room and describe in excruciating detail his idea for a super "fusion" bomb, or return to the endless task of trying to get the sand out of their bedclothes, but Lautner did not complain. After all, wasn't he supposed to be an anti-Fascist refugee in good standing? Wasn't he expected to do his part toward seeing that Hitler didn't develop the bomb first? One fulfilled the role assigned.

He stepped out of the road for a moment as a couple of MPs in a jeep drove past, heading for the perimeter wire. They were always doing that, checking the fences as if there were the most imminent danger that the Wehrmacht might mount an assault right there in New Mexico. One wondered what particular variety of fool these Americans must be.

"You will find you have little or no difficulty making yourself believed," Heydrich had said. "The Yanks are the most trusting people on earth."

And then he had smiled, showing his teeth, and his blue eyes had glittered like pieces of broken glass. Everyone in Germany had heard the stories about him and, standing on the other side of his desk at the Berkärstrasse, watching him smile, one was tempted to believe that they all had to be true.

"Your story will be that you are following your teacher into exile—now that Schleiermacher has lost his professorship, he will certainly follow the others. First to Bohr in Copenhagen, then to England, then to the United States. It will be the same with you—this business with Schleiermacher has simply been the last straw; you want to wash your hands of the New Germany. It is precisely the sort of sentimental claptrap that will appeal to the Jews, and once they have accepted you the Americans will welcome you like a hero."

And, again, it had been a question of fulfilling one's role in life. The SS controlled everything, didn't they? You couldn't expect a decent career in the universities if you didn't go along with them—they owned you. So when Heydrich had summoned him on that February afternoon in 1939, there hadn't been any question of refusing.

"They say that this new discovery of Hahn's—what are they calling it?" He raised his eyebrows in a gesture of contemptuous inquiry. The light from the window behind him formed a kind of demonic halo around his head, and the expression on his face became strangely blurred.

"Uranium fission, Herr Obergruppenführer."

"Fission? Yes, exactly. They say there is considerable potential for weapons development to come out of this, and now so many of the best brains have gone over to the enemy. War is inevitable now; you know that, don't you?"

"Yes, Herr Obergruppenführer."

"Inevitable. And I shouldn't imagine the Americans, when

they come in, will be at all backward about working up one of these fission bombs. They will come in, you know—this idea that they'll simply stand aside and let England go down the drain is just a lot of whistling in the dark. What does that suggest to you, Lautner?"

"Herr Obergruppenführer?"

"We will need to know what they are up to," he answered, showing his teeth again. Suddenly Lautner realized what made the man's smile so oddly sinister—the lower lids of his eyes were unnaturally thick, giving him an almost Oriental appearance. "We will need to place a spy in their midst. Someone who will be trusted, someone with the requisite technical background. Someone like you."

He could hear the dull hum of an automobile engine and the sound of tires on the loose gravel, and he turned around to see a tan prewar Dodge swerving over toward his side of the road. The side window rolled down, and Louis Slotin stuck his head and thin shoulder out through the opening and grinned.

"You want a lift?" he asked, his glasses flashing like railway signals as he shook his head. "When are you Europeans ever going to get used to taking cars to work?"

It was a joke. Lautner laughed politely and walked around the front of the Dodge to get in the other side. It was nice to come in out of the cold. Slotin, who was a Canadian and therefore put a premium on his physical comfort, had the heater turned up almost to the last notch.

"We're supposed to be saving gasoline, to aid the war effort."

"That's terrific. If we build the gizmo, they won't have to worry about gasoline."

"That's very true." Lautner closed the door, and the car jerked forward and back onto the road. Within a few seconds, it seemed, they were out of sight of the residential compound.

By the middle of the morning, which came early at this altitude, the sky over the mesa was always luminous. It didn't seem to matter what the weather was. Already the clouds were gathering around the Jemez Mountains, and they glowed with a dark, pearly luster. They would have snow by evening. Lautner closed his eyes and sighed; tonight, by the time he was finally able to get away from his desk, the roads would be a sodden horror.

"We have been impressed with your agility," Heydrich had said. "I don't believe you have ever actually joined the Party, have you, Lautner?"

"No, Herr Obergruppenführer—my position . . ."

"I quite understand." The Obergruppenführer had smiled his peculiar, sinister smile and shrugged. "You have not wished to offend Schleiermacher. As things have turned out, it is just as well. And yet I have read reports to the effect that you attend meetings of the Student Organization—I assume, then, that your allegiance is clear?"

"Yes, Herr Obergruppenführer."

In the moment of silence that followed, Heydrich had regarded him with what was probably meant to be understood as tolerant contempt. The man was very far from being stupid, and he doubtless knew an opportunist when he saw one. But, in this instance, who but an opportunist would serve?

"Good, then." He picked up a pen that was lying in front of him on the desk, looked at it for a moment, and set it down again. "Then we understand one another. The Party, of course, will see to your career when you come back. I suppose we can guarantee you a professorship—you won't have to wait until you're sixty. And there will be plenty of money; we know how to take care of our friends. As a protégé of the SS, you will lead a very comfortable life. All you have to do is to go to America and learn all you can. When the time comes, we will make arrangements to get you out."

He had made it sound so seductively easy, sitting there in his office in Berlin, smiling his lazy, contemptuous smile. And now he was dead, shot down by Czech partisans the summer before last—there had even been a movie made about it; Lautner had seen the thing in Chicago just before coming to Los Alamos. He might have hoped, under the circumstances, that the SS had forgotten all about him, but it would seem not.

When the time comes, we'll make arrangements to get you out.

The Obergruppenführer had made it sound as simple as jumping aboard a tramcar out to the suburbs.

"Do you think we will ever actually build the gizmo?" Lautner heard himself asking. He was a little surprised at the sound of his own voice.

"Oh yeah." Crouched over the steering wheel, Slotin was nodding vigorously. One almost had the impression that he was addressing someone on the other side of the windshield. "Why not? By the time Fermi can make us enough plutonium we'll have the triggering mechanism worked out. What's left but a few technical problems? I figure it should be ready by the end of the year. Make a nice Christmas present for Hitler, don't you think?"

He turned to Lautner and grinned. It was a joke—everybody at Los Alamos talked about the bomb like that. It was the gizmo and would end the war, but nobody thought about it, really thought about it, as anything except an interesting theoretical exercise and a great laugh on the Germans. When it finally went off—*if* it finally went off—and some city somewhere simply vanished from the face of the earth, the bright young men of the Project were going to have a frightful surprise. But in the meantime they slept well enough.

They drove on in silence, and a few minutes later the car slowed down in front of Bomb Physics. Slotin worked in Ordnance, which was several blocks farther along.

"You going to the party on Saturday?" he asked. It was the sort of question that could only be answered in the affirmative, so Lautner nodded and smiled.

And it was true that the parties at Los Alamos were among the saving graces of life there. Saturday night on the Hill tended to be a weird hybrid between an orgy and a seminar. Strange concoctions out of the available liquor supply would be mixed together in wastepaper baskets and drunk down by the beakerful. Where else in the wide world could you see so many Nobel laureates, so sodden, in a single room? There would be singing that drowned out the record player, and wild, manic dancing. And around one-thirty in the morning, Enrico Fermi, grinning and rolling up his shirt sleeve to show off his muscles, would probably issue a general challenge to arm-wrestle. And all the time, in little groups of five or six, people would stand around in corners and whisper about the endlessly fascinating theoretical problems of achieving nuclear rupture.

And everywhere there was Oppenheimer, looking like a cross between a film star and an Indian holy man. Everyone was as fascinated with Oppenheimer as they were with the Project—he had the magnetism of royalty.

Lautner waved as the car drew away. He stood there for a long moment, and when his hand came down it settled over his heart where, even through the heavy fabric of his overcoat, as if it were of steel and heated to the burning point, he could feel the outline of the postcard he had received in the mail that morning. On the back was the printed form, filled in to indicate that he owed the New York Public Library seventy-two cents in accumulated fines for a book titled *The History of Florence* by Francesco Guicciardini. He hadn't been anywhere near New York in more than eighteen months.

When the time comes, we'll make arrangements to get you out.

It appeared that the time had come.

XIV

It was an obvious enough piece of deception, but Schellenberg had described it in a manner that suggested he thought perhaps you might want to break out into spontaneous applause. The SS were always very easily impressed with themselves.

It was a book code. The details had been agreed upon in Berlin in 1939. When Lautner knew where he was going he was to transcribe the location into Guicciardini's *History,* underlining a single letter on every seventh page. And then his "travel agent," as Schellenberg called him, would send an overdue notice to his academic address, on the perfectly reasonable assumption that it would be forwarded by whatever circuitous route the American military authorities might think best, and he would know to make himself available. Everything had been settled.

So all von Niehauser had to do was to wait until the girl at the circulation desk was called away for a moment, reach over the counter, and take a couple of the cards. They were in plain view —why should anyone wish to steal them?

All of this had been done the day before his escape from Manhattan, so presumably Lautner would be ready for him by the time he reached Santa Fe, New Mexico. It would be a strange corner of the earth for two alumni of the Kaiser Wilhelm Institute to hold a reunion in the middle of a world war. Von Niehauser had to admit that until that moment in the Fifth Avenue Library he had never heard of Santa Fe, New Mexico. He couldn't imagine what it would be like. It seemed to be located in the middle of a vast desert, but all he had to guide him were the carefully edited newsreels of the war in Libya he had seen between a couple of mindless comedies during a slack few weeks in Russia. It had been a propaganda blunder to show them, even to that audience of hardened professional soldiers; everyone had been consumed with envy at the marvelous time Rommel and his men seemed to be having out there in the sunshine and the hot sand.

Would Santa Fe be like that, or would it be winter there too? Von Niehauser looked out through the window of the dining car as his train pulled away from the suburbs of Chicago, where the ground was blinding white with snow. God, how Russia had taught him to hate and fear snow.

He had hated Chicago too. Even in America the war was having some slight impact on freedom of movement—there was a two-day wait for the next train to Santa Fe, and he had had to bribe the ticket seller to get on that. The delay wasn't completely unwelcome, however. It would hurt nothing if he spent a few days making absolutely certain that he really had gotten away from the trap set for him in New York, that his movements were of interest to no one. So he checked into the Palmer House, which had the largest advertisement in the telephone directory, and tried—tried—going out for a walk.

Perhaps the blood had thinned since Briansk. Perhaps the wounding had taken more out of him than he had realized. In any case, the cold wind of that Chicago street was almost more than he could bear. It made him ache, particularly through his rib cage and left arm, where the tiny slivers of Russian shrapnel he still carried felt like razor blades—he had the impression they were twisting frantically, to cut their way in deeper to the warm core of his body. It made him feel positively ill, and he had pushed his way through the revolving door of a department store and stood leaning against the wall for several seconds until he was sure the sensation had passed off. He was surprised to discover, when he brought his hand up to his forehead, that he was sweating heavily.

So Chicago had been the confines of the Palmer House, where he spent the greater part of one afternoon in his bathroom, dying his hair back to black. His experiment in disguise had not been a great success; it hadn't kept the policeman in New York from recognizing him, and the color looked so artificial that he felt ridiculously conspicuous. For the rest, he would sit in the lobby and read newspapers. If he felt like eating outside the hotel, he would make a hurried visit across the avenue, down which the wind poured like ice water through a sluice. He had always heard Chicago described as a large city, but how could people live in such a place?

And on the third morning he had arrived at the train station with his ticket carefully folded away inside his wallet. He was so glad to be on his travels again that he would happily have journeyed the whole distance to Santa Fe, via Kansas City, Topeka, Hutchinson, La Junta, Trinidad and, finally, Lamy—they were only names on a schedule—in a day coach, sleeping in his seat. He would have done it sitting on mail sacks if that had been necessary, but he found himself the beneficiary of that chaos engendered by war. Trains were few and irregular, but there was nothing to be had on that particular one except Pullman berths. He would have a whole compartment, to be shared with only one other traveler. In such times it was so luxurious as to be almost embarrassing.

There was already a suitcase in the narrow little closet next to the bathroom; it was very old, and kept closed with two leather straps, but the owner was nowhere in evidence. Von Niehauser slipped his own bag under the seat and went to look for something to eat. He was cold and hungry and hadn't slept at all well the night before. He would meet the companion of his journey soon enough—introductions could wait.

As he sat over his scrambled eggs and toast—who but the Americans had eggs anymore?—he wondered if Lautner would know him, or if both of them had been so changed out of all recognition by nearly five years of war that they would meet as total strangers.

Of course, Lautner had spent his five years in this land of milk and honey, where the trains still had dining cars with white tablecloths, so probably he was just the same. Von Niehauser had never liked Lautner.

"You mistrust him because he is a guttersnipe from Hamburg, Joachim," Professor Schleiermacher had said, smiling behind his rimless glasses, his hands thrust down into the pockets of his threadbare sweater as he sat in his study. There was a cup of tea on the desk in front of him, but it was coated with dust and as cold as tap water; he had forgotten about it hours ago. "Erich suffers from the disability of not being a Prussian aristocrat. Is it any wonder you suspect the quality of his intelligence?"

"I wasn't aware that his intelligence was at issue."

"Well . . ." The Professor had shrugged, as if the distinction was not important enough to bother drawing, and finally one small, chubby hand came up and smoothed back the few strands of gray hair that still grew across the top of his skull. "Then let us say the perfect disinterestedness of his motives. His father sells cans of paint over a wooden counter, and the son is ambitious for academic distinction and the upper-middle-class security of a university career. He cannot affect your detachment."

That had been in February of 1936, when Schleiermacher's Austrian citizenship still protected him from the consequences of having had a Jewish mother, when it was still possible to believe that the Nazi regime was something that would disappear as suddenly as it had come.

In the strictest confidence, von Niehauser's father had informed him of the Führer's plan to occupy the Rhineland, expressing his own belief that it would lead to disaster.

"The French will resist," he had said, standing uncomfortably in the exact center of his son's apartment sitting room. He kept glancing down at the Persian carpet, as if afraid that the pattern might come off on his uniform. "Why shouldn't they? Our Army is no match for theirs. It will be a rout, a humiliation."

"Good. Then perhaps the General Staff will come to their senses and remove the lunatic."

The baron had looked grave, almost disapproving. He was perhaps not accustomed to hearing the head of state spoken of in such terms.

"Yes, perhaps you are right."

But, of course, he had not been right. Hitler would simply take a little longer to achieve the final ruin of Germany.

And Schleiermacher had not been right either. No one could have been more astonished than he when, two years later, after the *Anschluss,* he lost his professorship and, finally, when the months after *Kristallnacht* brought his danger home to him, he found himself packing his suitcases for the journey into exile. For the learned scientist and Nobel laureate, politics had always been as unreal as witchcraft.

"I have been offered a post at Princeton University, in America," he announced, slouched over a wooden crate full of books —von Niehauser had come over to help him prepare for the loading van.

"You will like it there. Einstein is there—it should be like old times for you."

Schleiermacher had smiled wanly, as if at a rather tasteless joke.

"It will never be like old times."

And then, in the kitchen, over a couple of glasses of cognac —the last in the bottle—the surprise.

"They tell me I am invited to bring a research staff, that everyone will be offered 'assistant professorships'—isn't the American terminology interesting? Erich Lautner has already agreed. I don't suppose I could tempt you as well, Joachim? Theoretical science is not going to fare very well under this regime."

"Lautner?" Von Niehauser set his glass down on the rough

wooden table that the Professor had once told him had been the first purchase he and Frau Schleiermacher had made after their marriage—the *liebe Gattin* had been dead since 1925. "I should hardly have thought that Lautner . . ."

"Would have a political conscience? You always underestimated him, you know."

"Perhaps." The sun was setting, and it cast a patch of pinkish light on the kitchen's back wall. Von Niehauser watched it for a long moment, wondering why he felt as if he were about to commit a breach of decency. "But we cannot all leave. You have no choice, and Lautner has nothing to lose, but some of us have nothing else we can do. I am a Prussian *Junker,* Herr Professor—my responsibility is here."

"I understand. I knew you wouldn't be able to come."

And he had understood. "I shouldn't like to think that the Nazis are being left quite at liberty," he had said, smiling and shaking von Niehauser's hand as he boarded the train for Denmark. To stay had not meant to side with the barbarians.

And there had been a steady stream of correspondence, almost up to the moment when the Polish crisis had forced the young *Privatdozent* to revert to type and put on the uniform of an Army officer. After September, 1939, von Niehauser no longer had a regular mailing address, and master and student lost track of each other. Perhaps it was just as well.

But, in any case, Schleiermacher had been wrong about Erich Lautner too.

Von Niehauser had read the transcripts in Berlin. Heydrich, who seemed not to have been a fool, had recorded all of his conversations with Lautner on wire. There couldn't be any doubt about it; the Herr Professor Doktor's loyal pupil, who had so willingly followed him to the wilderness of Princeton, New Jersey, had all the time been a creature of the SS. "The Party will see to your career when you come back," Heydrich had said. Two such perfectly unscrupulous villains; they must have understood each other to a nicety.

The dining car was oppressively hot. Von Niehauser found it impossible to eat anything and pushed his plate away from him. "Was everything all right, sir?" the waiter asked, his black face puckered with concern as he cleared the table. His voice was deep and rich and touchingly human. Von Niehauser almost started, the man had been so silent. He managed to smile.

"Everything was fine. It seems I've lost my appetite."

"You might be coming down with something—it's the flu season, you know, sir. You want me to bring you some aspirin?"

The door to his compartment was slightly ajar when he returned, and he could see a pair of long thin legs in khaki trousers stretched from the wider of the two seats to almost the precise center of the floor. It gave von Niehauser a decided thrill of anxiety to realize that his traveling companion was apparently a British Army major.

For an instant, he thought he might be walking into a trap —the British were the enemy too, after all—but then he saw that the man was asleep, his shoulder jammed into the corner of the seat and his head resting peacefully against the wall. His hands were folded in his lap.

Well, the Army had to travel too, and not even the British were so relaxed that they took naps while waiting to arrest people. Von Niehauser found his seat, allowing the air trapped in his lungs to escape into a faint sigh. This one was no immediate danger.

He was career officer from the look of him. It was the sort of thing you could always detect if you took the trouble. The hair was sandy, with white at the bottoms of the closely shaved side-burns, and the mustache was florid. The complexion was brick red, even to the eyelids—he had that indefinable look of a man who has spent a fair part of his life in a tropical climate. From the condition of the hands, and particularly the fingernails, it was clear that this was not someone born a gentleman.

Also, he was, from all appearances, about fifty—too old to have been drafted. And even asleep he carried himself with that slight rigidity that becomes second nature to the professional soldier and that civilians, even after years of war, never seem to acquire.

It was a conclusion in which von Niehauser found a certain degree of comfort. He was a member of the caste himself—at least by birth—and he supposed he understood that species of man as well as any. And the British were, after all, the British.

In the end, culture was everything. A German officer might have been a formidable adversary; in Germany it was the best minds that went into the Army. But the British were a nation of civilians. Soldiers were, as a whole, distrusted, and the career military—with the possible exception of the Navy; in his years in the country, von Niehauser had met relatively few sailors, so he didn't feel himself in a position to judge—didn't attract the best and the brightest.

This one, snoring slightly through his pursed lips, didn't look as if he had been the type to take a First at school. So perhaps it would be possible to relax a little. Perhaps they could simply ride along together to Kansas City, or wherever it was that the major was going, and pass the time playing two-handed bridge.

The man's jacket was hanging up in the narrow little closet next to the lavatory—that much von Niehauser had seen simply upon entering the compartment—and his suitcase was in the rack overhead. An officer carries a pistol when he goes armed, but this one certainly didn't have one on his person. When the opportunity presented itself, von Niehauser would have to check the luggage and the closet. It was the sort of thing one felt better for knowing.

The train began going around a wide curve, and apparently that slight shift in the center of balance was enough to jar the major awake because suddenly he jerked into an upright position and opened his eyes. He didn't seem particularly happy to see von Niehauser, who smiled.

"Did I wake you?"

"Damned trains—never could sleep on 'em." The accent was Edwardian country squire, just a little too thick to be quite real. He scowled, as if the reflection had left a bad taste in his mouth, and then he did what no genuine English gentleman would have done and stretched out his hand across the width of the compartment. After a split second of astonished hesitation, von Niehauser took it.

"Major Archie Dowland."

Major Archie Dowland grinned, revealing a pronounced space between his two front teeth and a good deal of gold bridgework. His palm was hard with calluses, and it seemed that no one had ever taught him that a crushing grip wasn't always taken as certain evidence of manhood and veracity. Still, von Niehauser wasn't such a snob that he couldn't appreciate the obvious friendly intention.

"Paul Bayle," he answered, smiling gamely as his arm was jerked up and down like a pump handle, wondering if that particular forged passport—one of four he had been issued in Berlin—happened to be the one he was presently carrying in his wallet.

Archie turned out to be a pleasant enough sort. They went to the lounge car together, and the waiter, after explaining the eccentricities of the Illinois liquor laws and accepting a two-dollar bribe, kept them supplied with Scotches and water, and by the time they made it to the dining car for a late lunch von Niehauser had heard practically the whole story of the major's life and career. He was unusually confiding for an Englishman: before they were halfway through their meatloaf and mashed potatoes, Archie had retailed the history of his three collapsed marriages, complete with a word-for-word account of the judge's summary in the last case, and had described the fiasco that had gotten him shipped off to the States to work in "supply liaison." Of course, that might only have been the liquor.

"Stupid business," he announced thickly, wiping the fringes of his mustache with the side of his index finger. "The bloody

Johnnie had no business going over my head like that. Still, could have been worse I suppose—'cept that I can't see how. Can't stand the bloody Yanks."

Having accepted von Niehauser's story about being an exiled Dutch journalist, Dowland seemed to feel perfectly at liberty to express his distaste for all things American—the solidarity of Allied Europe was something he seemed willing to take on faith. One had the impression that this was probably someone who really didn't much like anyone who wasn't British, middle class, career military, and somewhat less than middling successful. Von Niehauser was careful not to antagonize him.

"I'm not very fond of them myself," he said, raising an eyebrow and pantomiming a stealthy look over his shoulder. "But one can't always choose one's friends."

"I'm surprised you're not with the Free Dutch, a young man like you." Dowland's face was a mask of friendly contempt until von Niehauser laid a hand across his left shoulder and arm.

"They wouldn't have me anymore. I was shot up pretty badly when the Germans came, so I was mustered out. Fortunes of war."

XV

Von Niehauser wondered if it might possibly rank as one of the central misfortunes of his life that in all likelihood he would never know what Missouri looked like. The winter sky was already as impenetrable as a wall by the time they crossed over the state line from Illinois and, as far as he could make out in the odd moments when some glimmer from an unseen farmhouse thinned the darkness, the horizon was nothing but a flat black line.

But he was happy enough simply to stare out into the night and feel the train rocking beneath him. Dowland was asleep again, snoring heavily. There was no need to pretend to anyone that he was a Dutch resistance hero, and he could lie quietly on the upper bunk and allow his mind to empty.

Von Niehauser was not such a fool as to fail to appreciate the advantages of traveling with someone—a man alone somehow seemed to attract more attention—but he found the major tiresome. He was glad the poor clown had drunk so much and was sleeping so soundly; it meant that he would be undisturbed until late in the morning, probably.

It would be late the following evening before the train arrived in Lamy, where von Niehauser would change for the short run to Santa Fe. Dowland was going on all the way to Los Angeles. His war, thank God, seemed to be in the Pacific. Because, of course, it would be impossible to stay in anyone's company for very many days without arousing their suspicion. There were simply too many things about which it was necessary to remain vague.

So it would be just as well if the major slept late tomorrow morning. With any luck at all, given the headache with which he was likely to wake up, he might even decide he could live without breakfast.

Would he remember very much of what he had said the night before? It was difficult to imagine he would—he had to have been fairly far gone in drink to have given so much of himself away. Perhaps the whole evening would be nothing more to him than a clouded impression, a buzz of words that meant nothing. That would, on the whole, be better.

Because no man entirely trusts the receptor of his confessions; he begins looking for some secret stain in you, something to redress the balance. And von Niehauser had no wish to stand that kind of close examination.

Besides, he didn't have any illusions about how far he could rely on the good will of Archie Dowland—this was no sterling character.

The major said—he *said*—that what had gotten him into trouble with the Indian command in Kanpur had been certain irregularities in his dealings as a supply officer with some of the native merchants. *It's the old kickback system, you see. The little yellow bandits expect a chap to grease their palms.* Yes, von Niehauser had seen. He simply wondered whose palm it was that had expected to be greased.

So Dowland had escaped court-martial and had been shipped over to the States where, presumably, he would be out of harm's way. *I have a cousin in the War Office, you see—well, one hand washes the other. A chap's family ought to be good for something.*

It had been a tissue of lies, of course; but it wasn't the sort of story anyone would have told about himself cold sober. So one could only hope he would have forgotten telling it by the morning.

But the morning was a distant consideration, an unreal event that could, for the moment, be viewed in perfect seriousness as something which might never take place at all. In a darkened sleeping compartment, looking out into the blackness of an empty landscape, it was possible to dismiss the future. There was only now.

In the morning, Archie Dowland was sitting disconsolately on the edge of his bunk, his head held between his hands. He did not seem pleased with life.

"My God, what a thumper."

"I have some aspirin in my kit," von Niehauser said quietly. "Would you like a few?" He smiled, trying to appear sympathetic.

"Can't take the stuff. Upsets the tum." Dowland looked up at where von Niehauser was standing in the doorway to the tiny lavatory, and there were large purplish bags under his eyes. He really looked bad. "What'd set me up'd be a spot of coffee. Only thing is, I'd never make it to the dining car—all those damned bumping pneumatic doors. It'd kill me."

"I'd be happy to go fetch some for you."

"Oh, that's a chap." For the first time, the major was able to manage a pained smile. "But no hurry—when you've finished your breakfast. I don't think I'd be able to keep it down just yet anyway."

It was five cars up to the diner. Von Niehauser ordered a bowl of Cream of Wheat, and the waiter brought him a pot of strong tea.

"Is that still Missouri?" he asked. The ground outside the dining car window was a checkered pattern of snow on plowed fields. There was hardly even a road to be seen.

"No, suh, that's Kansas," the waiter replied. He seemed to find nothing astonishing in the question.

"And then we're in New Mexico?"

"No, suh, not yet. First we go through Oklahoma, then Texas, and *then* New Mexico."

"And was Missouri anything like this?"

"Jes' the same."

Perhaps people breakfasted later when they traveled by train, because the diner was only about half full. There were mainly couples, mainly middle-aged, and they sat and ate with intense concentration.

In Europe, when people traveled by train, they kept an anxious watch out the window, searching the sky for bombing planes—the Allies seemed to love attacking trains; nowhere were you in perhaps as much danger as aboard a train. But these people seemed to be nothing more than hungry and bored—they hardly glanced outside. It was as if something were missing from them, some basic thread of their humanity.

For some reason, the corridors were much colder on the way back. Von Niehauser clutched the little paper cup of scalding coffee the waiter had made up for him, trying to keep from squeezing the sides in as he swayed from side to side in an effort to keep his balance. His feet were freezing.

It was nine in the morning. In fourteen hours he would be in Lamy, and he would get off the train. For fourteen hours he would remain reasonably safe, and then everything would once more be at hazard.

He opened his compartment door and stepped inside. The first thing he noticed was that the bunks had already been closed back up; the second was that Archie Dowland was sitting next to the window, in the seat facing the engine, and was pointing a revolver at him.

"I bet you thought you were wonderfully clever," he said, through his teeth, almost whispering. "You Jerries always think you're such a brainy bunch of chaps."

For a second or two, von Niehauser stood perfectly still, and then he sat down. He was directly opposite from Dowland—their knees were almost touching.

"You've been going through my suitcase," he said casually, simply as a statement of fact. It wasn't the sort of thing that could be denied, because the suitcase was still lying on its side on the floor, and the lid was popped open about three inches.

"Of course—what did you think, that you had me fooled? I had you spotted for a ringer the second you stepped on the train."

Archie Dowland's eyes were very wide and moist, and even after he had stopped speaking his lips continued to move slightly. He was holding his service revolver as if he wasn't quite sure how it worked. Suddenly von Niehauser understood everything.

"You're lying. You simply went through my things looking for something to steal."

"That's a bloody lie, you bastard." But there was no conviction in the words, and hardly any anger. Dowland was past being mortified that that particular truth should be known about him. The slight flickering away of his gaze was the real truth.

What had happened? Dowland had searched the bag, looking for anything—money, jewelry, letters of credit, anything. And what he had found was von Niehauser's collection of forged passports; there hadn't been anything else that could have given the game away.

And it had rocked him back on his heels. You could see that in his face, even now; he hadn't known what to do. So he had gotten out his gun and had sat down to wait, his mind too filled with his discovery to understand what he should be about. He was in a kind of limbo, paralyzed by the suddenness of it all.

And when that moment had passed off, von Niehauser would be as good as dead.

So he smiled. He had to keep Archie Dowland amused while he had a chance to think.

"You were looking for something to steal," he repeated. "That's what happened to you in India, isn't it? Somebody caught you with your hand in the petty cash box."

Archie Dowland seemed to have led a troubled life, because this time his reaction wasn't anger, either real or assumed, but a general slackening depression. The creases around his mouth deepened; his shoulders sagged—he took on the appearance of a man accepting the return of a familiar burden. One could almost pity him.

And then von Niehauser remembered that he was holding a cup of still very hot coffee. There was a little cardboard lid over the top, but what did that matter? He gave the side of the cup a faint squeeze with his thumb and, sure enough, the lid came loose. And Major Dowland, supply officer, wasn't holding his service revolver like someone prepared from one second to the next to pull the trigger; it was perfectly possible he had never fired the thing in his life. It was worth a try.

"It's all right, Archie. I understand."

Dowland looked up at him in blank amazement—he had forgotten all about forged passports and German spies. Von Niehauser smiled at him, waited about half a heartbeat, and threw the coffee straight into his face.

It worked like a charm. Dowland didn't fire—he could have, but he didn't—and before he even had a chance to do more than open his mouth to cry out, von Niehauser had reached out with his left hand and grasped the revolver, holding the cylinder tightly enough that it couldn't turn.

It wasn't until Dowland could open his eyes again that he worried about the revolver. And then, when he tried to pull the trigger and nothing happened, he really looked astonished. Von Niehauser twisted it out of his hand, and Dowland gave a little scream when his finger broke with a snap in the trigger guard, but by then he wasn't thinking about fighting back anymore. He was just a victim. He couldn't seem to get over what was happening to him.

Von Niehauser rose slightly out of his seat and drove his fist into the man's throat. Dowland jerked backward, and his head hit the seat cushion behind him with enough force to make a quite audible thud. For a few seconds he slumped back against his seat as if he were trying to catch his breath. By the time the blood began to trickle down from the corners of his mouth he had lost the look of someone living in this world; he was just staring out in front of him, his eyes glazing over as you watched. And then he tried to cough—you could hear the blood gurgling in his windpipe—and then, very slowly, he began to slide over sideways as he died. After that he never even twitched.

Von Niehauser got up and closed the compartment door, which had been standing open the whole time. Apparently no one had been in the corridor, since no one was screaming for the porter and the police. There wasn't a sound anywhere. And he was alone, on a crowded train, in the middle of an enemy country, with a man he had just murdered.

"You want me to come in and tidy up, suh?" The porter peered inside through the two or three inches von Niehauser had been willing to open the door. His eyes rolled up toward the figure on the upper bunk, covered to the shoulders with blankets, its face turned toward the wall.

"I don't think so, thank you," von Niehauser answered, smiling and pressing a twenty-five-cent piece into the palm of the man's hand. "My friend isn't feeling terribly well—I'd rather just let him sleep."

The porter gulped, staring down at the coin—was it too large a tip or too small? Had it made him suspicious?

"Yes, suh. I c'n come back later."

"Oh, you needn't trouble yourself. I expect we'll be able to manage." Von Niehauser smiled again—the muscles in his face felt as if they were stretched to the breaking point—and closed the door. He waited for several seconds, hardly able to breathe, until he heard the tap, tap, tap of the porter's knuckles on the door of the next compartment down.

It had been a bad moment. A dead body in the upper bunk, the bathroom sink filled with blood-soaked towels: the porter would have been in for a delightful surprise. But perhaps now, von Niehauser could hope, he had purchased himself a few more hours of safety.

Fortunately, these Pullman cars were uncarpeted, because Archie Dowland had spilled a considerable quantity of blood on the floor when von Niehauser tried to move him over to the bed. It had simply poured out of his mouth and nose, and the linoleum floor had been covered with it. Right at that moment, the major was resting comfortably with a washcloth stuffed down his throat, just to make sure there would be no more little accidents. God, what a mess!

But the porter had seen nothing. At that precise instant he was busy making up the beds next door; von Niehauser could hear him through the wall, humming to himself like a man without a trouble in this life.

Von Niehauser sat down on the narrow seat on which Archie Dowland had died; he held his hands knitted tightly together to keep them from shaking, and he forced himself to breathe with a long, regular rhythm. It had been half an hour, and his reaction had been postponed as he had tried to prepare things for the porter's inevitable visit, but now it was on him with accumulated force. It was cold in the compartment, but he could feel the sweat popping out on his brow and under his armpits. Was the strain of these last few weeks beginning to tell? Was he losing his nerve? It wouldn't do. It wouldn't do at all.

No—he was going to be perfectly fine. Anyone was entitled to a moment or two in which to allow the tension to pass off. Even the officers of the German Wehrmacht were only made of flesh and blood.

Simply to give himself something with which to occupy his mind, von Niehauser took out Archie Dowland's little leather valise, undid the straps that held the lid in place, and began going through it.

There wasn't a great deal, and what there was wasn't of the highest quality. Like their owner, Major Dowland's possessions had that slightly down-at-heel look of things retained beyond their useful life span. Underwear, a couple of tan shirts, a khaki tie, a small box containing an assortment of inexpensive men's jewelry, a shaving kit. At the bottom, carefully folded, a spare uniform. A five-year-old copy of a magazine called *La Vie Parisienne,* the pages containing illustrations of naked women. All the sorts of things one would expect.

In one of the side pockets, along with half a dozen handkerchiefs, was a small bound parcel of letters.

A few of them were from a woman whom one could only assume had to be Archie Dowland's latest ex-wife, nagging, nasty propositions concerned exclusively with threatening demands for money and allusions to the major's failures as a husband. One was bound to wonder what had possessed him to keep them—a few were as old as a year—but perhaps they had represented for him some last lingering personal attachment. No one was ever going to know now. The rest were from a solicitor in London.

"I haven't yet convinced the Appeal Board to schedule a second hearing, but I have every confidence that our petition will be attended to as soon as the court-martial calendar has cleared. It might even be to our advantage to seek a delay, since in the present atmosphere . . ." The date was December 16, 1942.

So it would seem that the incident in India had been a little more serious than Major Dowland had led him to believe. The uniform, the mess talk, the expressions of concern for "the rough time my old mates are having over there" were all a pretense. Archie had gotten himself cashiered.

Von Niehauser rose out of his seat and took Dowland's military jacket from where it hung in the narrow closet next to the lavatory. There was a thin billfold in the inside pocket; it contained twenty-three pounds and about fifty dollars in notes and a set of heavily creased identity papers dating from before the war. As expected, the papers did not include a photograph—that particular security refinement was of a later vintage.

On a sudden impulse, von Niehauser tried on the jacket. It was a trifle roomy, but the arms were of approximately the right length. And most of the world's soldiers went around in ill-fitting uniforms; that sort of thing was almost one of the defining characteristics of war. It was possible that half the British officer corps had lost significant amounts of weight since 1939.

The germ of an idea began to stir in his mind.

Under the best of circumstances, it was a difficult proposition to dispose of a dead body, and the sleeping compartment of a moving train wasn't the best of circumstances. Obviously there were only two choices, either to get off at the next stop and leave Archie Dowland where he was or to throw him out the window and hope no one noticed.

The first option would have been the simpler, but ultimately the risks were greater. How long after he disembarked, von Niehauser wondered, would the porter find the body? He would probably be in here within half an hour to make up the bed for the night; he would have witnessed von Niehauser's departure, perhaps wondering why the party with a ticket for Lamy, New Mexico, was getting off somewhere in Oklahoma. Within two hours at the latest, von Niehauser could expect himself to be the object of a police dragnet—and he had been through that particular experience once already, thank you very much.

So Archie was going to have to make an unscheduled disembarkation through the compartment window.

It was simply a question of whether to do it now, in broad daylight, or to wait for the covering darkness. Which was greater, the danger of being seen at ten-forty in the morning or of being discovered before, say, eight in the evening? Von Niehauser decided he would wait.

It was a long day. He missed lunch; he missed dinner—he simply didn't dare risk leaving the compartment. Around two in the afternoon the porter made another try at getting in to clean up.

"Really—I have the impression it's the flu or something. It might be best if as few people were exposed to him as possible. No—no, I don't think it's serious enough to warrant a doctor. Thank you."

And he smiled and pressed another quarter into the man's hand.

By seven he judged it was dark enough. He opened the window—in an instant the whole compartment was freezing cold—and stuck his head out to look back and check if the windows behind were lit up. Fortunately, all the rest of that side of the car seemed to have their shades drawn; probably, since there was nothing to see except a vague horizon line, they had all decided to try keeping the heat in.

He began pulling the late Major Dowland off the upper bunk and discovered that his eyes were still open, which was disconcerting enough, and that he was as stiff as an iron rod. The washcloth was still stuffed into his mouth; von Niehauser took it out and threw it through the window, along with the blood-soaked towels—there wasn't going to be any more bleeding at this late hour.

It was like pushing a plank of wood through the window. When Archie was about halfway through, the wind caught him, twisting him out of von Niehauser's grasp. His foot caught for an instant on the window frame, and then he was gone. Von Niehauser looked back after him, but he was lost in the darkness.

Three and a half hours later, the train pulled into the station at Lamy, New Mexico. There was only a tiny station house there, and only half a dozen or so people got off. Among them was a thin, handsome man in the uniform of a British major. He carried a battered leather valise held together with two straps. There was no one there to meet him, and he stepped off the platform almost immediately and started in the direction of town, out of the pools of pale light that illuminated the railway yard. No one noticed him.

XVI

"I don't think we're going to get anywhere if all we do is try to track him down. He's already got the jump on us there, and he isn't the stupidest man I've ever had the pleasure of hounding to his doom. What we've got to do is to start at the end and work our way backward."

That was how he had explained his plans to General Groves, but as George Havens sat in the dark Park Avenue apartment, which he had entered illegally and where he was waiting for the second secretary to the Mexican Legation to return from a visit to his mistress, he found himself entertaining certain doubts.

After all, von Niehauser might be planning to make it out of the country entirely on his own. Or he might have devised some other method of getting his information back to Germany, such as short wave or even the mails. Perhaps it had been a mistake to concede the first innings to him so completely.

But really there wasn't any choice. No one had ever disappeared from Pennsylvania Station so completely without a trace as Joachim von Niehauser. At that moment he could be anywhere.

"I've informed the security offices at all the more important installations that we've got a German agent on the loose," General Groves said as they drove together to the Washington railway terminal—the general had to be in Chicago the next afternoon and he didn't like to waste time in transit, so they held the last part of Havens' briefing in the car. "They don't have to be told to keep on the alert."

"And I'll try to have my own teams in place by this evening. Then all we can do is wait."

Well—not quite all. After seeing the general off, Havens hitched a ride back to Seat of Government. He had a friend in Records.

"Smitty, who's the number-one Axis sympathizer in the Latin American diplomatic community right now? I want somebody who really knows what's going on with that crowd."

Smitty, whose thin hair was so pale that his head looked positively naked, who was probably more overweight than anyone else in Mr. Hoover's employ, folded his hands across his belly as he leaned back in his oversized swivel chair, blinked a few times, and ended up blowing a gust of air out through his puckered lips.

"José Ernesto de Rivera del Suñer," he said finally, as if the name had been on the tip of his tongue all along. "A couple of times there's been talk about asking the Mexicans to have him recalled, but it seems he's got a lot of drag with *el Presidente.* We know he went to Germany a couple of times in the last two years before the war, and he's never made any particular secret of his ties with the Abwehr. He's your man."

"Can I see his file?"

"Sure."

There was a lot there—transcripts of telephone calls, photographs, lists of contact points and times. Several of the names were familiar; Suñer was posted to New York, and that had been Havens' bailiwick before Hoover had moored him to a desk in Washington. Suñer had been a very bad boy.

"Come on, Smitty—where's the rest of it?"

"What *rest?*" Smitty's voice, which was hardly more than a high-pitched squeak to begin with, went up another fourth as he wriggled uncomfortably in his chair. "There is no *rest.* That's the file, George."

It was almost pathetic. Nobody likes to lie to his friends, and it was worse somehow when there was no real intention to deceive. Smitty didn't even expect to be believed.

"You wouldn't kid a kidder, would you, pal?" Havens grinned his best ratlike grin. "You know as well as I do that with this much on him Suñer would have been on his way back over the border a long time ago if J. Edgar didn't have him in his pocket. *El Presidente* be damned. Come on—I want to know what The Boss has got on him. I want to see the special file, Smitty."

"I can't give you *that.* It's my ass if I give you *that.*" Smitty pressed his hands into his lap, as if it were really another part of his anatomy that he was worried about, and his eyes glittered with apprehension. But Havens remained unmoved.

"Ask him."

"*Ask* him! Are you out of your *mind?*"

But if he was, he was persistently so. Finally Smitty gave in and made a call to the dreaded office on the fifth floor.

"Yes, sir . . . That's what I told him, sir . . . No, sir, I mean, yes, sir, I know that . . . That's what he said, sir . . . Yes, sir . . . Yes, sir. . . ."

By the time he had hung up, the assistant chief clerk of Records was as pale as water and his breath was coming in little gulps, as if he had just had his foot cut off. As soon as there was room in his face for anything except fear, he looked up at Havens with genuine reproach.

"I think you've just cost me my pension, George. But you can see the goddam file."

Havens took it with him. It made very interesting reading while he was being driven back to his apartment.

He had already made up his mind about what he needed to do, and after that the choice of personnel more or less made itself; the list of specialists for operations of this kind was reasonably short. Half a dozen phone calls to old friends from the race-and-chase days before the war and he had things lined up, both in New

York and Washington. It was wonderful to be back in the game, but the best part was not having to work everything around the Director. A couple of the people he talked to, guys who had finally had it up to the eyebrows and gone into business for themselves, agreed to help only after they had been assured that it wasn't going to be Hoover's show.

"I'm not lifting a finger to polish his halo," one of them said. "Not so that he can grab all the glory and keep the world conned into thinking he's the world's greatest G-man. I mean it, George. You tell the old fart to go out and catch his own crooks."

"J. Edgar's not in on it, and there won't be any glory for anybody. I seem to be working for the Army right now."

"Okay, then—count me in."

The Washington end was easier. That was simply a matter of monitoring police reports, and there were plenty of people inside Seat of Government who could do that. By about three in the afternoon everything was ready.

He had to be back in New York by the next morning, and that meant another long drive at night. But he just wasn't up to it yet—he had to have a couple of hours in the sack first. As he lay on top of his bed, fully clothed, waiting for sleep to come, he kept thinking about that cop they had scraped off the rails in Pennsylvania Station. How many would that final darkness cover before this crazy business was finished? How many . . .

"He left the señora and their kids back in Mexico City—maybe he thought they'd just get in the way, and from what I've been hearing they probably would have. He seems to fancy himself as the Latin Lover."

Dick Stevenson was a private detective these days, with an office down in Greenwich Village and a long list of fashionable clients. Since leaving the Bureau he had made kind of a specialty of divorce work, but time was when he had been the number one man in Bunco. He'd probably put more con men in the slammer than anybody else in the Western Hemisphere, and nobody could touch him when it came to laying a sucker trap.

They sat together on the front seat of Stevenson's 1938 DeSoto, on Sixty-eighth Street just around the corner from Park Avenue, where they had a perfect view of the awning over the door of Suñer's apartment building—you could almost make out the design on the brass buttons of the doorman's overcoat—and Stevenson was calmly chewing on a wad of antacid gum. He always claimed that it was Hoover who had given him his ulcers.

George Havens kept checking his watch. Five minutes to eight. Now three and a half. Now two.

"Relax." Stevenson turned a little to the right and his face came partly out from underneath the shadow of his gray felt hat; it was the face of a ribbon clerk at Woolworth's—soft, slightly pockmarked, forgettable. His face was one of his great professional advantages. "He'll be along. He's a very punctual man, even in his lechery."

"You ought to know."

Stevenson laughed, and the dull brown eyes suddenly flickered into life. "That's right, pal. I ought to know."

And, sure enough, at about thirty seconds after eight the man himself strode out from under the awning, accepting the doorman's salute like a grandee. He turned left and an instant later was out of their line of sight.

"He was the same way the whole time I tailed him on account of that upholstery tycoon's wife. They had a suite they were keeping for just that purpose up at the Waldorf Astoria—there's nothing cheap about this hombre—and you could set your watch by his walks there and back."

"Did the tycoon get his divorce?"

"No." Stevenson shook his head, showing his teeth in a pitiless smile. "As it turned out, the wife had just as much on him and, besides, there was the little matter of diplomatic immunity. He couldn't haul the señor into the dock, so the wife got a big allowance and a boat ticket to the Virgin Islands, which struck me as just a trifle snide. I don't think Suñer ever even found out that the jig was up, not that he would have much cared."

"Well, I suppose I'd better get going—you're sure that back door is taped open?"

"Would I lie to you?"

The rear of the building faced onto an alley not much wider than your shoulders, the walls of which were coated with soot, and at the far end it opened up into a tiny courtyard, about the size of first base, which was stacked with empty wooden crates that looked like they must have been left there by the original settlers. The door, which was covered with about eighty coats of green paint, yielded with a push.

"The service elevator is on the other side from the laundry room," Stevenson had said. "The custodian's room faces that way, and he usually leaves his door open a few inches, but he plays the radio so fucking loud that you could march a battalion through there without him ever suspecting. I used to take that way so often you would have thought I was one of the tenants, and he never even stuck his head out."

Havens hadn't taken a step inside before he heard an audience laughing at a joke about Fibber McGee's closet—Stevenson had been right. All the way up to the seventh floor, he never saw a soul.

There were little skills that weren't part of the curriculum at Quantico but that you were supposed to pick up along the way, and one of them was knowing how to do without keys. Techniques differed, but Havens had learned to carry the needle probe from the dissection kit he had bought for college biology. It did the job; Suñer's kitchen door had a lock that would have opened with a sharp look.

You'll have two hours—tons of time. As soon as I spot him coming back, I'll call you from that telephone booth across the street. Two rings.

Two minutes would have done it. Havens was only interested

in making sure Suñer didn't have any revolvers stuck away in a desk drawer—in such circumstances people had been known to panic.

The living room had to be seen to be believed. The walls were covered with fuzzy red paper, and all the furniture was upholstered in black leather; right in front of the fireplace was—you guessed it—a white bearskin rug. There were liquor stains here and there on the carpet, but otherwise the place was impressively clean and tidy. The total effect was one of vulgarity raised to the level of high art.

There wasn't so much as a knitting needle anywhere, so nobody had anything to worry about. Havens collapsed into a huge, thronelike chair that creaked under him like a saddle. There wasn't anything more to do but wait.

He whiled away the time trying to estimate how much an apartment like this one would cost every month in rent—probably more than Havens brought home in half a year. And Suñer didn't have to break into people's kitchens in the middle of the goddam night. Maybe Karen had done a smart thing when she had pushed off in search of her bus conductor from Queens.

And maybe divorced Special Agents should stay the hell out of New York. God, that woman—what a laugh it would probably hand her that her ex- was still up to his old tricks, and still hadn't gotten over being sent to the outfield. He wondered if the war made any difference, or if women all over the country were shucking their husbands as they went off to fight the enemy. It didn't seem very likely. Maybe Karen had been an exception to the rule and the world was really full of the self-sacrificing ladies that Mr. Hoover had always recommended so highly. Of course, there was always the draft to consider. Maybe not having any choice was viewed as an extenuating circumstance.

It was two minutes after ten when the telephone rang. Once, twice, and then silence. Suñer was probably already walking across the lobby.

Havens got out his .38 police special and rested it on his

knee. He had no idea how he was going to explain himself to anyone if for some reason he should have to burn down the second secretary, but there was nothing like pointing a revolver at a man for commanding his undivided attention. With any luck at all he wouldn't have to wait very long before Suñer realized that the possibility of catching just one bullet in his New York apartment was going to be the least of his problems.

He tiptoed over to the front door, pressing his ear against it, and listened for the whisper of the elevator. He could hear the cable rattling in the shaft and then the grinding sound of the doors opening. Suñer's apartment took up the entire floor, so the second secretary only had to walk a few paces to be on his own threshold.

Even before he heard the sound of the key being inserted into the lock, Havens had stepped back so he would be behind the door when it opened. He was holding his revolver like a club, but then he thought better of the idea; the time for guns might come later, but right at the moment he didn't want to take a chance on killing the poor guy.

Suñer came inside and closed the door. His back was to Havens and he was taking off his overcoat—all that was visible was a thick head of black hair, threaded here and there with silver. Perhaps he heard something as Havens stepped forward, because he began to turn slightly. Havens chopped him on the back of the neck and he pitched over, just exactly as if his feet had been kicked out from underneath him. His face seemed to be the first thing to hit the floor; the impact sounded like someone clapping his hands. After that he didn't move.

Havens rolled him over, thinking how proud his instructor in hand-to-hand combat would have been.

"Wake up, señor. Rise and shine." The one hall light that Suñer had turned on when he first entered bathed the carpet and walls in a soft pinkish glow. Probably that was the first thing the second secretary saw when finally he opened his eyes. When he saw Havens grinning at him, his face contracted in pain and he brought his hand up slowly to cover his cheek. "Come on, señor, it can't be that bad."

He was an elegant little man, with lightly tanned skin and a pencil-line mustache. His nails were cut short and seemed to have some sort of clear polish on them—it was the first time Havens had ever seen a man wearing nail polish—and his hands were small, sensitive, and faintly pudgy. In all, he looked a man very much devoted to the care and comfort of José Ernesto de Rivera del Suñer.

Fine—it just made life easier. This wasn't anybody who was going to sacrifice himself to anybody's sacred cause.

"*Dios,*" he said quietly, apparently to no one in particular. And then his eyes focused on the revolver in George Havens' right hand; it was lined up on a spot just a little to one side of his nose. "This is going to bring you a great deal of trouble, my friend."

"We can discuss my problems some other time—I'm not the one staring down the muzzle of a .38."

Havens made an impatient gesture, and Suñer took the hint. Turning it into a great production, he picked himself from the floor and threw himself down on one corner of the black leather sofa that seemed to be about fifteen feet long. He groaned quietly, just in case you should forget how much he was suffering, and leaned forward to support his forehead against the palm of his hand. He was almost good enough to make you believe him.

"If you're thinking about trying to jump me, forget it." Havens sat down on the chair opposite, crossed his legs casually, and smiled. The .38 was resting on his knee, not pointed at anything in particular. "The distance is lousy; besides, if you're not a good boy it'll be *el Presidente* who shoots you, not me. We know all about your involvement in that bungled coup d'état back in '41—don't you think he'd love hearing about that?"

Perhaps it was just some trick of the artificial light, but Suñer's eyes seemed to turn yellow with fear. Suddenly he was sitting up very straight. It was as if he could already feel the bullets from the firing squad tearing through his body.

"Are you from Mr. Hoover?" he asked finally. He appeared to be having a certain amount of trouble getting his tongue to work.

Havens shook his head, not really sure whether he was lying or not.

"No. But I have Mr. Hoover's file on you—I've even got wire recordings of some of your telephone conversations back and forth to the military reservation at Tocula. For a man who planned to have himself made foreign minister, you weren't very cagey."

"And what do you plan to do with all this—this innuendo?"

" '*Innuendo*'? Is that what you call it?" Havens allowed himself a short, ugly laugh. "I'll tell you what, pal. Unless I get what I came for, all that 'innuendo' will end up on *el Presidente*'s desk and you'll find yourself on a plane to Mexico City—I'm sure there won't be any trouble about having you deported. I'll leave it to your imagination what's likely to happen when you arrive."

There was one of those unpleasant silences that could go either way. You never really knew how a particular man responded to that kind of a threat until you tried it out on him. Suñer seemed to be considering whether it might still be possible to bluster it out; he was sitting very quietly, and his cheeks puffed out slightly as he breathed through his mouth.

"And what was it that you came for?" he asked finally, his voice hardly more than a murmur—he was even smiling.

No, this was not someone interested in the martyr's crown.

"There's a German agent running around loose in this country." Havens shifted uncomfortably in his chair, wondering why he felt so disappointed. "He's here to gather intelligence on certain classified government projects and then, presumably, to return to the Fatherland. The most reasonable conjecture is that he'll attempt to make his escape through Mexico, and for that he'll need help. You're going to find out where and when he plans to cross the border, and then you're going to sell him out to us."

The smile on the second secretary's face was beginning to

look as if it were being held in place with surgical wire.

"What makes you think I would be able to come by that sort of information, Mr.—?" A pink tongue felt along the edge of Suñer's lower lip—it was the sort of nervous gesture that spoke volumes. Havens decided to wait on the formal introductions.

"Come *on.* Spare me the coy demurs. We have it that you're very thick with the Fascist sympathizers, that they have you marked down for great things in the New Order—you shouldn't have any trouble."

It was odd, but Suñer seemed flattered. It seemed to make him feel better, as if Havens had come to him for a favor. He could resume thinking of himself as a big wheel.

"I might perhaps be able to do something," he said, his face growing serious as he reached up to smooth down his tie—the man's self-conceit was almost awe-inspiring. "Of course, you understand that I can offer no guarantees, but it should be easy enough to make a few inquiries."

Havens laughed all over again, more out of discomfort than anything else.

"Well, it's a good thing then that I'm not asking for any guarantees," he said, putting the revolver back into the waistband of his trousers. He really didn't like Suñer at all. "I don't think we need any guarantees, because if we don't bag this guy—if you fuck up, or get any surges of loyalty to the cause, and he makes it out of the country alive—we're not going to be interested in any guarantees. If you deliver, then that's fine; we'll be very grateful. If you don't, I think you can more or less count on being stood up against a wall."

It was a few minutes after one in the morning by the time Suñer was fully briefed. By then he knew almost as much about Joachim von Niehauser as Havens did himself—he even had copies of the one photograph of von Niehauser known to exist. Suñer promised he would have at least some preliminary information within twenty-four hours.

"Well, don't take any siestas between now and then—time is on his side, not ours."

By a quarter after one, when Havens closed the rear door of the apartment building behind himself, he was almost grateful for the cold, clear winter air. As he walked along the side street up to where he expected to find Stevenson's car parked, he felt more tired than he ever had before in his life.

"I called that number you gave me for your exchange," Stevenson said as he turned the ignition key. The engine coughed into life, and the headlamps, focused on a narrow patch of roadway and sidewalk, seemed to shut out the rest of the world. "They said you should call someone named Pearson—they made it sound pretty urgent. Who's Pearson?"

"A kid I've borrowed from the Bureau to read police reports for me. It can wait until I get back to the hotel."

Havens slouched down in his seat, allowing his hat to cover his eyes.

After Stevenson had dropped him off, and he had climbed the three flights of stairs to his front door, he seriously considered just leaving Pearson until the morning—hell, that wasn't more than four or five hours away in any case—but then he thought better of it and picked up the phone.

"The New Mexico Highway Patrol found a stiff about fifteen feet from the railway tracks just outside of a place called Clayton—that's about eight miles from the Oklahoma border. The guy was in his underwear, and we haven't got a fingerprint make on him yet, but his larynx had been crushed."

Havens put down the telephone as gently as if it had been a Dresden teacup. All ideas of sleep had vanished from his mind—he had forgotten all about being tired.

Von Niehauser was on his way to Los Alamos.

XVII

Santa Fe turned out to be nothing like El Alamein.

For one thing, it was cold. There were flakes of snow drifting through the air as von Niehauser got off the train, and there were bright little halos around the street lights. The air hurt the inside of his throat. He buttoned up the collar of his khaki overcoat and tried to keep within the shelter of the buildings—there was an irregular but persistent wind that cut like broken glass.

The stationmaster had directed him toward the center of town, indicating that he would find plenty of hotels but that, "none of 'em ain't exactly the Ritz." The stationmaster, a heavy-ish, dissatisfied-looking man in his late fifties, apparently didn't think very much of Santa Fe. Von Niehauser followed the direction he had indicated with a peremptory stab of his finger. He shifted the suitcase over to his right hand, putting his left deep into the overcoat pocket in an effort to keep it warm. His arm and shoulder were bothering him again.

"After the war you can have the rest of the shrapnel dug out," the surgeon at Wittenburg had said. "For the time being you'll find that it's only an inconvenience, and right now we have our hands full with the critical cases." Von Niehauser hadn't objected—after all, anyone who had been to the front lines could see the logic of it—but he had been offended by the man's tone, as if he had wished to make him ashamed.

But, after all, he wasn't dead, and New Mexico wasn't the Russian steppes. At that precise moment the men he had left behind there were doubtlessly suffering far more than he, and that did make him feel ashamed.

Here and there were visible the flickerings of neon signs, and once in a while a door would open to cast a distorted rectangle of white light across the sidewalk—the light from the overhead lamps hardly seemed to make it so far down as that. There were a few cars whizzing by on the streets, and for some reason they all seemed to make the same odd insectlike sound as they passed, as if it had something to do with the quality of the roadway. No one else was out-of-doors, however; at such an hour, and in such cold, that was hardly remarkable.

Finally he came to a place called the La Ventana Hotel. The paint on the outside was peeling, but a British major on furlough wouldn't have a fortune to spend on accommodations.

The man behind the desk was a small, square Mediterranean type with the thinnest tracing of a mustache. He might have been powerfully built once, but now his skin merely looked two or three sizes too large for him. He pushed the registration book at von Niehauser, not even interested enough to glance up.

"I'll be staying for about a week," von Niehauser said gently—for some reason the man gave the impression of laboring under some terrible sadness. "Shall I pay in advance?"

"Fine—suit yourself."

Von Niehauser signed the book as "Major Archibald Dowland" and laid a twenty-dollar bill down over the signature. The clerk whisked it into a drawer with a single deft motion.

"That'll last you through Tuesday," he said, looking with watery brown eyes at a spot just above von Niehauser's right shoulder. He slid the key across the desk. "Two-thirteen. Just take the stairs."

It was a dingy little room, but von Niehauser found it strangely comforting. In the context of present history, elegant luxury would have amounted almost to a reproach. He took off his shoes and lowered himself heavily onto the bed, which creaked like a nail being pulled out of a board.

Certainly the federal police would be looking for him, and it was possible that Dowland's body had already been discovered. It would take them a few days before they would be able to identify it—he wondered, in an abstract way, if he shouldn't have taken the opportunity to cut off Dowland's hands; certainly that would have slowed matters for them. One cannot count on one's enemies being fools. He had four or perhaps five days before they tracked him down and arrested him. His disguise might hold that long.

So. By, say, Saturday afternoon he had to have his business finished and be on his way out of the country. After that, he would in all probability be either dead or in prison, and in either case of no further use to the German war effort.

There was a large light brown patch on the ceiling, probably caused at some time in the past by a leaky pipe. It was the approximate shape of the continent of Australia. Germany was at war with Australia too. Germany seemed to be at war with everybody. Von Niehauser closed his eyes and tried not to think about it.

"We got elk, we got bighorns, we even got grizzlies, if you like that sort o' stuff. You name it."

The hardware store, which doubled as a sporting goods store, was run by a pink, well-scrubbed gentleman with thinning brown hair and rimless glasses. High up on the wall behind his counter was a collection of stuffed hunting trophies which suggested that perhaps he wasn't quite as domesticated as he seemed.

"I'll follow your advice," von Niehauser said, smiling as he set his hat down gently on top of the glass case filled with evil-looking knives with wrapped leather handles. "I've never been out in this part of the world before. We used to have elk in Scotland, but I've . . . What's a grizzly?"

The storekeeper laughed shortly, as if he were being questioned by a child. "Well, that's a kind of bear," he answered.

"Mean as cobs—tear you to pieces soon as look at you. Better stick to elk."

"I've hunted bear. In Denmark once, before the war. Let's not rule anything out."

It seemed to work. The storekeeper stopped grinning and stepped back to a rack of impressive-looking rifles, gleaming with gun oil and polished wooden stocks. Several of them were mounted with telescopic sights.

"What you used to?" he asked, putting his hand over the buttplate of the lowest rifle. His eyes narrowed a little behind the rimless glasses.

"A Steyr-Mannlicher 9 millimeter." Instantly von Niehauser saw that he had made a mistake.

"That a German make?"

"Yes." Von Niehauser smiled again. "A wonderful thing—I bought it in 1931. No longer available, as you can imagine."

"Well, we got nothin' like that. Why don't you try a Winchester 30.06? You like bolt action or lever?"

"Bolt action. It's all I've ever used."

And he bought a box of ammunition, hunting clothes, long underwear, a pair of gloves, boots, woolen stockings, a compass, and a map. The total bill came to almost seventy-five dollars. The storekeeper had forgotten all about the Steyr-Mannlicher; Major Dowland was a gentleman, a sportsman, and his friend.

"Is there somewhere I could rent a truck?" von Niehauser asked, proud of himself for not having called it a lorry. He spread out the map on the counter and used his finger to trace a circle around Santa Fe. "I suppose it'll have to be somewhere fairly close, what with gasoline rationing. What would you recommend?"

The storekeeper seemed to consider the problem for a moment, and then he laid the point of his thumb down on a spot about thirty miles north and west.

"The Jemez Range is good this time o' year. I got a cousin

can swing a truck for you—and all the gas you need at the right price. 'Course, you'll have to stay away from the mesa. Used to be good up in those parts, but the Army's got a base there now and it's all restricted."

It was a hard scramble for a man who had spent most of the last six months inside either a submarine or a military convalescent hospital. The ground was covered with loose rock, and you could never be perfectly sure of your footing. Von Niehauser found he had to rest every sixty or seventy yards—in places he was practically having to climb hand over hand.

The owner of the hardware store wasn't the only one who had mentioned the military installation on Los Alamos Mesa; the clerk at the variety store where von Niehauser had inquired about directions and purchased a tube of lip balm thought that was where they were training the troops for the invasion of Japan. Apparently there were lots of theories.

But if the Army had a major facility in this godforsaken place, it wasn't to get ready to fight the Japanese, not if Erich Lautner was here. They had to be building the bomb.

But that wasn't the sort of conclusion one could afford to draw on the strength of a surmise, so von Niehauser had set out to see for himself.

The truck was a dark blue and covered almost to the windows in mud. It and a full tank of gas had cost von Niehauser fifteen dollars, which was little short of robbery.

"Mind you have it back here at the first sign o' weather," the hardware store owner's cousin had said, squinting into the pale winter sunlight. "We're supposed t' have a real good blow comin' up sometime toward the end o' the week, an' you don't wanta get caught out in that."

He put a lean, taloned hand on the fender of the truck, making it fairly obvious what was the real object of his concern. "You got a good three hundred miles in that tank—hell, you could go to Arizona an' back on less 'n that."

His laughter at his own joke had been a kind of dry cackle, almost as if something had gotten caught in his throat. Von Niehauser hadn't liked him very much.

But the desert had been a species of revelation. In fact, you were hardly justified in calling it a desert at all. Here and there, especially as you began to climb into the mountains, you found considerable stands of strangely twisted pine trees, never very large but possessing a certain grotesque grandeur of their own. It was possible to imagine that in the warmer months the ground might yield forth bushes and grass and even perhaps the odd wildflower. It was very far from being a dead place.

But what was startling were the vistas. Everything was swallowed up in vastness, great empty spaces of stone and sky, blue and purple and gray. Nothing in Europe could prepare a man for this.

Von Niehauser's father had been fond of "scenery." He had not been a man of highly developed esthetic sensibilities—painting, for instance, had always struck him as rather effete—but he liked to take the train down into Swabia for a few weeks every year and he and the baroness would walk along the well-worn mountain paths and enjoy the views of little valleys and distant fortresses from the twelfth century. These things had a certain charm for him. God alone knew what he would have made of New Mexico.

Swabia was merely pretty, the stuff of attractive memories, comfortable, almost domestic. But this land cared for no one. It was inhuman in its loneliness.

"You have a pronounced streak of the morbid in your character, Joachim," his father had told him once. "I think it comes from your mother's side of the family—your grandfather was a great reader of Kleist. It isn't something I should cultivate if I were you."

Perhaps. Nevertheless, von Niehauser found the very austerity of the place deeply appealing. At times, as he had driven over the rutted dirt roads and watched the abrupt changes of landscape, he almost forgot why he had come.

But never quite. It was never completely possible while he skirted along the miles and miles of barbed wire fence, hung with signs indicating the terrible revenge the federal government would exact from all trespassers. Finally, when the truck began climbing into the Jemez Mountains and the great desolate flatlands fell away, he was kept occupied with the idea that the Army might have established patrols beyond the perimeters of what seemed to be one of their testing ranges, that as a foreigner he might be subject to interrogation, that it would lead to no end of trouble if he were forced to leave four or five American soldiers dead along the side of a fire road. He kept thinking of time: a few days, that was all he had before the dogs would be barking at his heels. Less time than that if he was unlucky enough to encounter any serious resistance.

Finally, when the road dwindled down almost to nothing, he drove the truck in behind a mass of scrub pine, took out his rifle, and stuffed the pockets of his jacket with the candy bars he had purchased at a drugstore on the outskirts of Santa Fe. It had occurred to him, almost as an afterthought, that he hadn't eaten anything since breakfast the day before, not since he had been forced to kill Archie Dowland, and it would hardly do for him to start turning shaky in the middle of the wilderness. He estimated that he had perhaps as much as another two miles to cover.

Because, of course, it would have been remarkably poor technique to have climbed the rest of the way on the side of the mountain facing Los Alamos. He had driven around behind and would only come straight to the eastern face when he was near the summit; he wanted to be well above the mesa, so he could have as clear a view as possible. Schellenberg might have told him about the inconveniences connected with being a spy, but—no—he had been left to discover all of that for himself.

Had he really been interested in mountain sheep, he would have found himself presented with several opportunities. He had what appeared to be an excellent rifle, with an eight-power telescopic sight, and several times he caught the poor creatures staring stupidly at him from across a few hundred feet of gorge—the mountain, for some reason, was cut in several places along the sides with huge vertical crevasses. They would watch him for a few minutes, then shake their horns as if to register their incomprehension, and wander away. Perhaps by some instinct they knew that he meant them no harm.

It was odd, von Niehauser reflected, but he had never killed a living creature except his fellow men. He had lied to the hardware storekeeper, drawing on what he had heard around the dinner table from his brothers. All the other male members of his family had been wild about hunting, he supposed because the hunt provided the closest peacetime analogue to war. If Kurt had been here he would have spent the whole winter clambering over these rock-strewn mountains; the American mode of hunting, without beaters and guides, simply one man alone with a rifle, would have appealed to him. But Kurt had died in Africa, and there was only his baby brother, the instructor of physics, to see the wonders of the place and watch the mountain sheep watching him.

There were no trails as such, only narrow little animal tracks covered with loose rock. Von Niehauser lost his footing two or three times: once he fell and slid about eight feet down the side of the mountain before he managed to catch hold of an outcropping of bush. His bad shoulder took most of the punishment—he could feel his ribs on that side throbbing as if the nerves had been laid bare. It was after two o'clock in the afternoon before he reached the summit.

He found a ledge that was shaded from above by scrub pine. He would be hidden there, and the ledge itself was as flat as a tabletop. He sat down to rest, too tired even to look around, and took one of the candy bars out of his pocket. The Americans didn't seem to be very good with chocolate, but it was better than nothing.

There was a vast stretch of flatland beneath him, a mottled

tan cut here and there with the dark brown slash of a road, and beyond that the Los Alamos Mesa. He was well above it—even from across that enormous divide he could see the telltale signs of human presence, the vague shapes of buildings and a suggestion of order. He closed his eyes and waited for the weariness to pass off. He didn't want to look just yet.

The telescopic sight on his rifle was as powerful as any of the sets of field glasses that had been available in Santa Fe, and it was perfectly adequate for his uses. The top of the mesa snapped into focus; he could even see individual people, although not distinctly enough to have recognized anyone—it occurred to von Niehauser with a stab of very peculiar emotion that if this really was the American fission bomb laboratory there probably were men down there whom he had known for years, old friends some of them.

But they would not be that anymore. They were the enemy now, scientists and technicians who were preparing the destruction of his country. He remembered what Heisenberg had said in 1939, the first time he had ever heard the possibilities of such a weapon discussed: "It might not be any larger than a pineapple, and could probably destroy a city the size of Stuttgart, simply turn it into a blackened crater. Such a thing must never be allowed to happen."

Such had been the arrogance of the German scientific community that it had of course never dawned on Heisenberg that there was any possibility of the Americans perfecting the device first—his only thought had been to keep such power out of the hands of the Nazis. Germany, of course, would be safe enough.

But it hadn't worked out quite that way.

The people in Santa Fe believed that this was an Army base up on the mesa—at least, some of them did. Perhaps there was a military contingent somewhere, but that was by no means the main purpose of so vast a complex.

The son of a general should certainly be able to tell a military base when he saw one. They were all the same, everywhere in the world. There were barracks and a few administration buildings and vehicle shops and parade grounds. You drilled soldiers; that was what they were for. You marched them up and down and had them fire their rifles and crawl through trenches and under barbed wire. You held tank maneuvers and raised great quantities of dust out on the artillery ranges.

But there was no parade ground on the Los Alamos Mesa.

The place was huge. It was obvious that millions of dollars had been spent here and apparently, if one could believe the locals, all within the last year and a half. Row upon row of new buildings, thrown together in a chaotic patternlessness that suggested a project adjusting itself to unforeseen needs. An Army base reflected the order and discipline of military life; this gigantic complex had as its driving energy some other vision.

He watched a small group of people walking along one of the roads. They wore civilian clothes; one of them was smoking a pipe —even at this distance von Niehauser could make out the clouds of heavy gray smoke. Every once in a while they would all stop and cluster together, their heads and arms moving in excited little jerks as, apparently, they talked. The wind, which swept across the mesa with hideous relentlessness, pulled at the hems of their coats, but they paid no attention. Soldiers didn't behave that way.

How many times in his life had he seen and participated in such discussions? At Göttingen, and the Kaiser Wilhelm Institute. In Rome, when Schleiermacher had taken him on a visit to Fermi.

These were scientists in the grip of an idea, an intellectual abstraction. They were happy because they had fallen in love with death.

XVIII

It was going to be one of those days. Last night they had found the water pipes clogged with ice, and in the morning Hal discovered a badger had crawled in under the bedroom floor and died. And the radio said that there was a storm gathering down in Mexico and that it would bury the whole state sometime within the next three or four days.

For the last week or so, Hal had been just about unbearable. He had thought the dead badger was hilarious and had made some disgusting joke to the effect that that wasn't the only reason their bedroom stank. Jenny wondered if it wasn't somehow possible that he had heard about Erich Lautner.

The main waterline came up out of the ground behind the house, just to the side of the kitchen door, and about two and a half feet of it was exposed to the air. That was why it froze every time the weather turned snappish, but Jenny had heard from a neighbor woman that you could fix that by wrapping the pipe to a couple of inches thick in old blanket. She didn't have a blanket to spare, but Hal's mother had sent him a new bathrobe for Christmas because the old one was ready to be cut up for cleaning rags. A worn-out bathrobe would serve just as well. She would go down to the commissary and see if they didn't have some duct tape, and maybe she could get that particular problem taken care of before Hal came home for lunch. The dead badger was already wrapped up in a burlap sack in the garbage, so that left only their marriage to be attended to.

Because Jenny had come to a few decisions about the direction of her life—she was going to stop allowing things to get to her so much. She was going to learn to deal with the facts as they were. After all, three-quarters of the women she knew claimed not to love their husbands and still managed to muddle through somehow. Illicit sex in hotel rooms didn't seem to be the answer either, so if she couldn't have the grand passion she would settle for a little quiet desperation.

Whatever was wrong, it was almost certainly more her fault than Hal's. There wasn't any point in punishing him. He had a few rights, and if she couldn't work up very much enthusiasm for his weightlifting and his job reading other people's mail that wasn't something he should have to answer for. After all, he was her husband. She had married him.

The truth was, Erich was beginning to scare her. Maybe it came down to the fact that she wasn't quite the hot number she had thought she was, but having a lover was more than she found she could handle. Erich didn't care anything about her, and he wasn't even a particularly nice person. She was just another conquest as far as he was concerned; he wouldn't have any hesitation about wrecking her life if she gave him the chance.

"Would it really annoy you so very much if your husband discovered the truth?" he had asked once, smiling that amused, contemptuous smile of his. "What difference could it make to him—or to you?"

There was always the implied reminder that she had placed herself in his power, that sometime or other, in his urbane disregard for her small-minded American scruples, he might just casually let it be known that Jenny Springer was his mistress.

And there, of course, was the problem. It was all very well to make resolutions about leading a new life, but how did you disentangle yourself from the old one? It wouldn't do any good simply to explain the situation to Erich and appeal to his better nature. Where women were concerned, he didn't seem to have a better nature.

So she had made up her mind that she wouldn't see him anymore. On Saturday, when he would be waiting for her in that horrible little room at the La Ventana, she just wouldn't appear. She didn't have the faintest idea what he would do about it—or if he would do anything at all; it was possible he would just smile, damn him, and dismiss her from his mind—but she had lost control over her life a long time ago. It was possible he might even go to Hal, and that would probably be the end of everything, but at least she would have stopped being somebody's weekend whore.

Really, she couldn't see anything else to do. It frightened her, the way everything had begun frightening her lately, but there just didn't seem to be much else that was possible.

She took Hal's old bathrobe down from its hook in the bedroom closet and, holding it by the hem, tried to start a tear. It didn't work; she wasn't strong enough. She would need a pair of scissors, or a knife. She didn't have a pair of scissors big enough, but there was a knife in the kitchen. If you thought about it for a moment, you could always improvise a solution.

By ten-fifteen she had a very satisfying little pile of six-inch strips of dark blue terrycloth on the kitchen table. The house was clean and there wasn't another thing to think about until twelve-thirty, when Hal would be home wanting his lunch. She would go down to the commissary and buy the tape, then, and possibly she would have that all taken care of by noon. It would please Hal when he saw that she had done something about the water pipe; he only needed a little encouragement to believe that their life was everything it should be.

There hadn't been any snowfall that day, but it was bitterly cold outside and the wind was steady and strong. It was nearly half a mile to the commissary.

Jenny put on her coat and a pair of knitted gloves and tied a scarf over her hair, wishing that Hal hadn't left his car behind in New Jersey. The walk would take about eight minutes, by which time she probably wouldn't be able to feel the surface of her face.

The commissary was just inside the front gate of the base; the Project, whatever it was, was another mile farther up on the mesa, well within the Army compound that was supposed to protect it. On an ordinary day the main road would be busy with soldiers' wives either going to or returning from their grocery shopping—provisions were so haphazard that almost everyone made the trek three or four times a week. The walk back and forth was almost a social occasion. But today, except for the official cars that were almost as regular a feature as the dust they blew up, the road was virtually deserted. Probably there weren't many other women who would be prepared to venture out in such weather just to pick up a role of duct tape so they could fix a pipe to please their husbands. Probably that was part of the definition of being happily married—not feeling the need for that sort of gesture.

It really had been stupid to come out. She was wearing her heaviest shoes and already the soles of her feet were freezing—it was like walking barefoot over ice. The wind was blowing from the south, so you had to face directly into it, walking slightly bent at the waist like an old woman. Jenny never even noticed the car that was pulling up behind.

"MRS. SPRINGER—CAN I OFFER YOU A LIFT?"

She turned to see who was shouting at her, and at first all she saw was the open side window of a blue 1937 Pontiac. And then, in the dark interior, the framed smiling face of her lover.

"Get in, Jenny. I want to talk to you," he murmured. Suddenly she realized that the road wasn't as deserted as she had imagined. "Get in—don't force me to make a scene."

Before she realized what she was doing, she had her fingers inside the door handle. Perhaps a hundred feet in front of them was Mindy Applewhite, pushing along her two-wheeled shopping basket; Mindy was a terrible gossip, and she was beginning to turn around. There was no way out now—it would look even more suspicious if she backed away.

Jenny forced herself to return the smile, the way one might with a casual acquaintance, and opened the door. As she sat down,

Erich Lautner reached across to close it, and she could feel the pressure of his arm against her and smell his body; it was almost a kind of intimidation. The car pulled back out onto the road, and Jenny forced herself to sit with her eyes straight ahead as they passed Mindy Applewhite. She was quite sure she was flushing a brilliant pink, but that could have been the effect of the cold.

Even in the darkened interior of the car, it was possible to detect a certain appearance of strain in Erich's face. The smile on his lips was a little too fixed and the skin stretched a little tightly around the eyes. His jawline was puffy, as if he had been drinking, and around the edge of his brown hair was traced a thin pale line, giving the impression that the healthy tan was some sort of mask. He was gripping the steering wheel and leaning slightly forward.

"I'm going into town," he said, in the tone of someone issuing an order. "Come with me—we could be back by the middle of the afternoon."

"I can't—I . . ."

It seemed to be the last thing he had expected to hear. His head snapped around, the eyes widening with something between incredulity and anger, and his knuckles slipped a little farther forward on the steering wheel, as if he were trying to brace himself.

"What do you mean you can't? Why can't you?"

"Hal will be coming home for lunch. He's . . ."

"What difference can *that* make?"

Somewhere inside of herself Jenny found the resources not to look at him.

"It does make a difference," she said calmly. "He expects me. What am I supposed to tell him when I do get home? That on a whim I went into Santa Fe with Erich Lautner? It's possible he may have his suspicions already; what do you want me to do, give a name to them?"

For several seconds the only sounds came from the engine and the tires on the asphalt roadway. To the south, even at that hour of the morning, the horizon was lost in a dark line.

"I was going to the commissary. You can drop me off there."

For a moment or two it was easy to imagine that he wouldn't, that he was planning simply to keep going, right through the camp gates and on to Santa Fe; but then, at the last moment, he twisted the steering wheel to the right and pulled up with a lurch in the commissary parking lot. He was wearing a heavy tweed overcoat, the collar of which was turned up almost over his ears, but that wouldn't have accounted for the tiny beads of perspiration that were visible on his temple. Even over the sound of the engine dying, you could hear his breath—he actually seemed to be panting.

"It's possible I may be leaving here soon," he said, not looking at her. "In fact, it's almost a certainty."

He smiled again, showing the remarkable evenness of his teeth.

"Another project—far, far away from this place. It seems they can't get along without me."

He seemed to be waiting. For what? For her to burst into tears? Did he expect her to plead with him to take her too? Jenny continued to peer out through the windshield, as if there were some intensely interesting object on the car's hood.

"Do you ever wonder what it is we're all working at up there, Jenny? Would you like me to tell you?"

She looked around at him then, probably because now it was possible to face him without seeming to react to the fact that he was leaving her.

"No." She shook her head, as if the question were utterly without meaning for her. Why did she have the impression that he had meant it as a threat? "It's not something I want to hear about. Why should I?"

"Why should you? Why not?" Yes, it was a threat. "We're making a bomb—did you know that? Probably two thousand of us up on the hill, and we're just the point of the spear. There are other installations, just as big, all over the country. Millions of dollars are being spent, so you can imagine the sort of bomb it must be."

The smile had turned quite ugly, a kind of mocking challenge. Jenny sat staring at him with undisguised wonder. She was a security officer's wife, and she was listening to something very close to treason. Treason, apparently, committed for nothing more than its shock value.

"Don't—don't say anything more," she whispered, shaking her head.

"No? Aren't you curious?" His hands caressed the sides of the steering wheel, the way they had caressed her face a dozen times, but the gesture seemed oddly tense, almost resentful. "A bomb worth all that money? They say it will be the technological achievement of the century if we can pull it off—one little firecracker that can end the war. The catch is, of course, that Hitler is working on the same thing. What do you suppose will happen if he builds his first?"

"You shouldn't be talking about it, Erich." Jenny forced herself to look away. She kept her eyes on her hands, feeling helpless and beaten. Was there nothing it wouldn't occur to him to use like this? "I don't want to listen to another word."

Erich Lautner raised his eyebrows in feigned astonishment—the susceptibilities of these Americans were such a bore!

"Very well."

Outside, women from the base were walking back and forth, carrying bags of groceries to their cars, if they were fortunate enough to have cars, or wheeling their shopping carts across the gravel. Several of them Jennie knew at least by sight, and more than a few screwed up their faces to peer in through the windshield of Erich's car. Tonight, in between the silences, they would have something different to tell their husbands over the pot roast and boiled potatoes. "You'll never guess what I saw today. You know that Mrs. Springer whose husband works in Security . . . ?" And Mrs. Springer's dominant emotion, taking place even over her fear of exposure, was simple jealousy.

Ordinary life—a boring husband, the common vexations of a half-lived domestic existence, the absence of passion and guilt and the drama of suffering. The absence of happiness, of even the appetite for it. That seemed an unreachable happiness in itself. To live in a world that wasn't populated with men like Erich Lautner. To have had the sense never to have entered it.

"It's so cold out, please, you must allow me to help you with those as far as your car," he had said, all those weeks ago, when a gust of November wind had nearly blown her and her packages out into the street. Erich had been passing—he was the faintly familiar face she remembered from here and there up on the mesa, the man who had sat behind them at the Betty Grable movie perhaps—and he had scooped her up just as she was about to fall under the wheels of the Santa Fe traffic. "Well then, if you haven't a car you must allow me to wait with you until your friends come. Here, we can go across the street and have something warming to drink." The play had been so obvious, but she had gone along with it out of embarrassment as much as anything else. And, after all, what had she to be afraid of in a public place?

"This is so pleasant—we ought to do it again. Next week, perhaps. When you come back to town with your friends."

She had said no, more than once, but he had insisted. He would wait for her, right there, in case she changed her mind. They both knew just exactly what he meant, and she had left never intending to see him again. What had prompted her even to let him buy her a drink was something she would wonder about until she died.

All the following week, every day, she had thought that there was no way she would go back. No way. It was a settled thing.

And then, Friday night while they were having dinner in the kitchen, Hal had gone on and on about the war: how it would be over by the end of the year and how afterward everyone would see what suckers they had been to go rushing off to fight. How it would probably end up making no difference to anybody. And she should be glad that he wasn't overseas because this way she didn't have to worry that he'd come home with the clap. It was a big joke.

And in the cold fury of her heart, she thought about Erich Lautner.

"I am a German, you know," he had said. "So I know what Hitler is like. I fight him with science, which is the only weapon I have."

This hadn't been the sort of person she had wanted to become, but still she had gone ahead with it. Erich Lautner and the call of the wild—musty hotel rooms and a feeling of violation—and all with her eyes open. Perhaps she could plead temporary insanity.

"But you will come in tomorrow, won't you?" His voice was insinuating, somewhere between an entreaty and a sneer, and he cocked an eyebrow as if he already knew the answer. "We may never see each other again—I can't let you go that easily."

He reached over toward her. The commissary door opened and three women emerged into the harsh cold, their hands going up automatically to protect their hairdos from the wind. Jenny pulled back from him in a perfectly spontaneous convulsion of dislike.

"Yes," she said quickly, her attention on the door handle behind her. Yes—she was surrounded by familiar faces. Yes, there was no more courage left in her. "Yes, tomorrow. Tomorrow is Saturday, isn't it? Yes—yes, I'll come."

She backed out through the door and closed it with both hands. The click sounded loud enough to command the attention of the whole parking lot. And Erich Lautner's hand slid down to the gear lever, and the car jumped forward with a little start. In a moment she was watching it turn back into the main road. There were tears in her eyes as they followed the little trail of dust disappearing through the perimeter gates.

XIX

It was well after dark before von Niehauser made his way back to his rented truck and, since he had no clear idea of how extensively the area might be patrolled and had even less inclination to attract attention by using his headlamps, he wrapped a blanket around himself and spent the night in the cab. As soon as the sun was up, he shook the stiffness out of his joints and drove back to Santa Fe.

At that hour of the morning New Mexico seemed the most desolate spot on earth. There was no sound except the hum of the truck tires. Nothing was stirring except the wind, and the cold gray sunlight seemed to wash the color out of everything.

He didn't know whether it was the lack of sleep or the excitement at being so near the end of his mission, but von Niehauser felt an uncomfortably pronounced giddiness, the sort of thing one associates with the sensation of falling.

It wasn't a new experience; he had had it before. He had felt much the same dozens of times, two or three weeks into one of those interminable battles on the Russian front, after the boom of their field artillery had penetrated so deep into his nervous system that he simply assumed that he would be blown to atoms sometime within the next several hours and so he stopped thinking about it. The sensation was common enough; a colonel of his, a brave enough soldier who had finally been killed during the retreat from Morozovsk, had called it the last stage of courage, the willingness to lay down one's life on the most trifling pretext. When that was played out there was nothing beyond it—all a man's resources were gone and he had nothing left with which to defend his self-respect.

Having never crossed over that final threshold, von Niehauser could perhaps regard himself as having still a few illusions to treasure.

Still, he was glad this business was nearly finished. In the space of a few days, if he wasn't dead, he would be safely over the border into Mexico. And then the world would have to come to terms with everything that that would bring.

He would be glad to get back to his hotel room to shave and treat himself to the luxury of a hot shower. There would be no time for any sleep—he would be meeting Lautner shortly before noon—and there was no telling if they might not leave immediately. Fortunately, it would not be the first time that he had had to carry on without his beauty rest, and in Mexico he could sleep for a week if he felt like it. In Mexico Lautner would be someone else's problem.

About a mile outside of town he was startled by a jackrabbit that ran across the road, directly under the wheels of his truck. Had the thing come out of it alive? Von Niehauser searched in his rear-view mirror but could see nothing. What could make a creature do something as inexplicably dangerous as that? Was it part of some sort of game? The whole episode struck him as intensely disagreeable—it didn't bear thinking on.

"You took y'r time—get any?"

Von Niehauser smiled and shook his head as, per prior arrangement, he returned the keys to the truck to the man at the hardware store, who didn't seem very glad to see him.

"No. I saw one, but the distance was too great to allow for a shot. Perhaps another day."

There would never be another day.

"It should be a relatively simple matter," Schellenberg had said. "We have many sympathizers in Mexico—the Fascist movement is strong in that part of the world. I'll provide you with a list."

Everything was a relatively simple matter to Schellenberg. Probably, like so many others, he had plans for escaping to South America when Germany lost the war. Just catch a submarine out of Bremerhaven and turn up a few months later in Paraguay. Perhaps he already had money deposited outside the country against precisely that emergency.

"You can contact them and they'll make arrangements for receiving you and Lautner. I should think, with all the practice they must have had over the years, they shouldn't find it too difficult to smuggle the pair of you over the border."

And he smiled his boyish, faintly effeminate smile and used the tip of his riding crop to brush a speck of dirt from his trouser leg. (Why did so many in the SS affect such things? Schellenberg had probably never been on a horse in his life.)

"And of course, Herr Brigadier, it is quite impossible that the Americans might have penetrated the ranks of these 'sympathizers'? I should hate to be arrested because of something so obvious as that."

"My dear Major, you worry too much," Schellenberg answered, clasping his hands behind his back. "American counterintelligence tends to be something of a hole-in-corner affair. They have rather adolescent minds in some respects."

"Yes? I'm delighted to hear it. And just how many agents does the *Sicherheitsdienst* have in that country?"

The head of RSHA VI looked slightly uncomfortable for a moment and then shrugged his shoulders under his heavy black greatcoat, as if the matter were of no importance.

"America is very far away," he answered finally. "And the Führer has never been convinced of its significance for events here in Europe. Believe me, their successes have been no greater than our own."

Nevertheless, von Niehauser decided to be rather cautious in his approaches to the Mexicans.

"There is one man down there in whom we repose perfect confidence—probably you'll want to make your initial contact through him. He seems to be motivated by the purest sentiments: aristocratic prejudice and hatred of the Americans. He's been working for us since 1938 and has never consented to accept a pfennig."

That fact seemed to stand as conclusive with Schellenberg. He gazed about him, surveying the hospital lawns with the air of a proprietor. A man who acts from conviction is always a fool, he seemed to imply, and one can always feel safe trusting a fool.

"Who is this knight of chivalry?"

The Herr Brigadier turned around slightly and looked at von Niehauser as if he were about to say something—to admonish the Herr Major, perhaps, against irony. But then, apparently, he thought better of it.

"We will notify him to expect you," he said, having decided, it would seem, to ignore the question. "He will be told to await a summons from Joachim, Baron von Niehauser, holder of the *Ritterkreuz* and hero of the war in the East. He will be impressed by that—he made his fortune in the leather business, but his wife is from one of the leading families. As you might have gathered, he is something of a snob."

"Really."

That had been one item of business in Chicago, to send the Mexican leather peddler a coded telegram to the effect that he had better make his preparations. By then, of course, von Niehauser had discovered his name.

The late General Rolf, Baron von Niehauser, as was fitting for one whose name had filled a place in German history since the days of Albert of Brandenburg, had had clearly defined ideas about such men.

"Never place your confidence in a parvenu," he used to say. "I make no judgment—were the von Niehausers anything else five hundred years ago?—but those who have come forward only recently are too obsessed with their positions to be reliable. They think too much of the privileges of rank and not enough of its responsibilities; they have no selflessness."

And, one had to admit, there was a certain weight of logic to his point of view. To have been born to a position was like life before Original Sin—there was no fear of falling back into obscurity because obscurity was as unimaginable as death; it was something of which one simply had no experience. But these new men must exist in a constant state of apprehension. They must see the gulf between what they were and what they have become yawning behind them like a chasm.

No, his father had been wise. He would place no confidence in Señor Agustin Gomá.

He had read the dossier in Berlin, and seen the photographs —the best was one taken at the wedding of the leather peddler's eldest daughter to the grandson of the former Minister of the Interior. Gomá was a short, broad man, a tough little peasant in white tie and tails, smiling arrogantly from behind a glass of champagne, his arm linked through the former minister's, who did not look as if he relished the contact.

The rest was rather what one would expect: born January 26, 1890, in a tiny village outside of someplace called Teotihuacan—a note described it as a suburb of Mexico City, but von Niehauser harbored a suspicion that Teotihuacan was probably little comparable to, say, Potsdam. Almost nothing was known about him until he appeared in the capital around 1912 to purchase a shoe factory; no one seemed to have an inkling where he could have gotten the money. By the mid-1920s he was already a millionaire —in pesos, one presumed—and within another decade he was rich enough to begin dabbling in politics. He owned a large ranch near Guadalajara and seemed to fancy himself very much as *el Jefe,* the grand señor. An affinity with Fascist dictatorships was perhaps inevitable.

Beyond the mere mention of their marriage in 1916, there was no information at all concerning the señora. Presumably she was still alive, and presumably she did not figure very prominently in her husband's view of the world, but it was a curious omission for the SS. Generally they were much concerned with things of that sort.

"The new regime, with these jumped-up little men."

Von Niehauser could remember his father on one of their walks through the woods at Görlitz—the old baron liked to sweep the tops of the bushes with his cane in hopes of starting a rabbit. Since he had decided he was too old to continue hunting, it amused him to watch them dart out into his path and then disappear again into the undergrowth.

They had driven home from Berlin together the night before, and the baron took advantage of their weekend alone together to unburden himself. His youngest son, the civilian academic, had become, since the baroness's death, increasingly the one person he felt able to take into his full confidence. During that period they had grown extremely close.

"These capitalists, whose grandfathers made their livings out of pushcarts, they crowd around Hitler like dogs waiting for the table scraps. They smell money to be made in the rearmament—I think they would be prepared to sell the government anything. It appalls me that the destiny of the Reich should be delivered into the hands of such men."

"Yes, but surely the Army remains untouched by all this."

"You think so?" He turned his head slightly, glancing at his youngest child with a curious, pitying expression. "Yes, perhaps, for the moment. But the Party is filled with these jealous nonentities. This fellow Himmler, I shouldn't be surprised if he had ambitions for co-opting us one of these days, turning the Army into merely another subdivision of that hooligan police force of his. Have you ever met Herr Himmler? My God, what a bumpkin!"

No, von Niehauser had never met Himmler. But he had met Schellenberg, the son of a piano manufacturer in Saarbrücken, so we were told, and Schellenberg hadn't struck him as anything like a bumpkin. Von Niehauser found it difficult to share his father's view of the SS as *opéra bouffe.*

And Señor Gomá seemed to be very much the SS's dog.

"I met him briefly in '41," Schellenberg had said. "He came to Spain, and I had him smuggled into France. That sort of personal contact can sometimes make all the difference."

"What was your impression?"

"Do you actually care?"

Schellenberg smiled. The brigadier was two or three years von Niehauser's junior and seemed to have figured out that the major wasn't frightfully impressed by their disparity of rank. Perhaps he too felt the pressure of that aristocratic self-confidence which the late baron had so highly prized as the salvation of the state. Or perhaps that was simply the way the SS fared in its contacts with the regular Army.

After all, in such times, who could feel much deference for a desk soldier?

"Pretend I do—what was your impression?"

"I think he is blinded by his contempt for the democracies," Schellenberg answered quietly, speaking as one might of the moral failings of a friend. His eyes searched the ground in front of him as he walked along, as if worried that it might not bear his weight. "That is a weakness, but from our point of view a useful one. I doubt if he can imagine Germany losing the war, and he seems to think we might make him President of Mexico after the Americans have been humiliated. I didn't like him, but I think he is a man we can trust. One is not required to like one's instruments."

No, that was very true. It was probably better if one did not.

Von Niehauser decided he would go to the post office first, even before returning to his hotel room. Possibly it was bad technique—he was certainly more conspicuous with a day's growth of beard and his face unwashed—but he simply couldn't tolerate the suspense any longer.

The post office was an ugly cinder-block building, painted to look like adobe. An American flag flapped gamely at the end of a short flagpole set in what would have been a flowerbed in a more hospitable climate but here was filled with sharp little mica-flecked stones. The interior was dark and empty. The loudest sound was the clicking of the coil steam heater. Von Niehauser went up to the window marked GENERAL DELIVERY.

"Do you have anything for a Paul Bayle?"

The man inside the cage, who was immensely fat and possessed quantities of kinky salt-and-pepper hair, looked rather stupidly at von Niehauser for a moment, blinked, frowned, blinked again, and stepped wordlessly off his stool to go have a look. A moment later he returned with an envelope, which he slid across the counter as if he were using it to clean off the wood.

"Thank you."

As he walked back toward the La Ventana, von Niehauser hardly did more than glance at the stamp. It was a Mexican stamp. He folded the letter and put it into his jacket pocket; he wouldn't read it yet, not until he was quite alone—not for any practical reason but because he felt the need of the self-imposed discipline. He was just a little ashamed of himself for having yielded to the temptation. His hotel room would be soon enough.

Dear Sir,

The arrangements for your fishing trip are well in hand. If it is convenient, your guests may like to assemble at a lodge we reserve for such purposes. Take Highway 81 twenty-two miles south of Hachita, and you will see a dirt road to your left, marked "private." Five miles on that will bring you to the lodge. We can have everything prepared for your arrival on five hours' notice—simply telegraph our office. We look forward to serving you.

Respectfully,
Raul Cortez

Von Niehauser didn't like it. It was much too explicit. It had all the marks of an amateur production. He was surprised the fools hadn't sent instructions in cipher, so that the Americans—assuming the letter had somehow attracted their attention—could be absolutely sure they were dealing with foreign agents. That was the trouble with dealing with zealots; they always had such a passion for intrigue.

He sat on the edge of his bed, reading the letter through a second time. Then he turned it over and studied the back. Then he took out his pocketknife and scraped the stamp off the envelope to see if there was anything underneath. There wasn't. There was no forwarding address. The whole business was precisely what it seemed. He didn't like it. If he ever got back to Berlin he thought he just might break Schellenberg's neck.

"I don't like him, but I think he is a man we can trust," Schellenberg had said. But Schellenberg had said much the same thing about Harry Stafford.

Von Niehauser decided he would dismiss it from his mind. He would take a shower now, and shave. And then he would take the time to have something to eat. He would be meeting Lautner in a few hours and, the way things seemed to be going, who could tell how that might work out? Perhaps all along the Americans had merely been toying with him. Perhaps they would both be arrested the moment he and Lautner shook hands. He decided he would make a point of enjoying lunch.

He returned the letter to the pocket of his jacket, which was draped over the back of a chair. He carried his medal in that pocket—he could feel the hard edges of the cross against his fingers—so he took it out and looked at it. It was a reminder that honor was a thing which would admit of no degrees.

XX

Within three hours after the end of his conversation with George Havens, José Ernesto de Rivera del Suñer was on a plane headed back to Mexico City. Inspector Havens, if somewhat lacking in polish, had struck him as a serious man, a man to be taken at face value. He said he wanted certain information and if he didn't get it he would go to extremes. It would be a terrible thing for him to do, but the threat had carried conviction. Suñer believed him.

Like everyone of any political prominence in Mexico, Suñer had witnessed executions. He had seen the men being led out behind a priest; he had seen the bullets tearing little pieces out of their chests. The part that had always struck him as the most distasteful was the coup de grâce, the hollow little twang of the pistol shot and the trickling of blood that fell down onto the dust like tears. Suñer had no inclination to end his life in front of a firing squad—his sympathy with the German Fascists did not extend that far. Havens would have his information.

It had been necessary to charter the plane, and inevitably there would be questions about why he had found it necessary to incur such an expense—he was hardly prepared to absorb the cost himself, and that sort of thing went beyond even the rather lavish limits of diplomatic license—but those were all problems he would deal with at the proper time. He would think of some plausible lie.

It was the middle of the afternoon before he could look out through his window and see the outskirts of the capital. Suñer disliked airplanes. He was afraid of crashing and he found it impossible to hold any food in his stomach. But the charter company had provided a stewardess and adequate supplies of liquor, so he had been able to keep himself distracted. The stewardess was blond and cooperative; she sat with him during most of the flight and smiled and didn't object when he slipped his hand up between her thighs. She and the plane would be waiting in Mexico City to take him back, and he had the name of her hotel.

His wife, thank God, was still vacationing with her sister in Veracruz. He hadn't notified her of his intention to return.

It was very cold on the ground. The dry, thin winter air of those altitudes was something of a shock after New York, where you were more sheltered and you were near the sea. There was a film of snow that seemed to have mixed itself in with the dust of the runway, and the few leafless trees that stood by the terminal building seemed to crouch back from the wind like old women shrinking from a blow. Suñer turned up the collar of his cashmere overcoat, squinted at the pale, heatless sun, and wondered if he had any chance at all of discovering the whereabouts of this man von Niehauser, who seemed so very clever and had already killed three men. Havens too struck him as a clever and pitiless man—it seemed a very even contest. Not for the first time it occurred to Suñer that the ground between these two would be dangerous for someone braver and more resourceful than himself, that he had good reason to be afraid.

One of his servants was waiting for him with a car. Suñer gave instructions about his luggage and sat moodily in the back seat while he waited to be driven to his house. He hardly even knew where to begin.

When he got home he ordered dinner to be brought to his room, took a bath, and shaved. He noticed, as he watched himself in the mirror, that he was looking older—in less than twenty-four hours he seemed to have aged ten years. His hair seemed grayer somehow and his skin had taken on a yellowish cast, but it was possible that was merely the artificial light. And he looked as if he had lost weight.

He was being hysterical, that was all. He would have a good dinner and forget all about it.

Apparently the cook had been so taken aback by his sudden return that she had forgotten herself and hadn't left the red peppers out of his chicken. Suñer hated spicy dishes, which he regarded as primitive; he preferred the blandness of food in the United States. In large measure, Mexico had almost ceased to be his home. Perhaps, before he left, he would give directions to fire the cook.

But the dinner was good otherwise, and it was always possible simply not to eat the red peppers. He also had most of a bottle of French white wine, among the last in his cellar—when it was gone, he would have to wait until the end of the war before he could acquire any more. There was almost none left to be had anywhere in Mexico City and, of course, it had been impossible to get in New York for at least a year. Everyone said that the Allies would be invading France sometime during the summer, so perhaps then . . .

When he was finished he made a few phone calls and discovered that there was a reception that evening at the war minister's. The minister was a man of agreeably conservative views, and there were bound to be numbers of people there sympathetic to the German cause. It was as good a start as he was likely to make. He would go there.

His Excellency lived in one of the old palaces in the center of the city. The walls were made of great blocks of rough-hewn stone, and there were no windows on the ground floor; the structure was a survival from the days of the revolutions, when you never knew when the next bandit army would come through, dragging their women and their Gatling guns behind them. There was an iron gate that could be let down over the front entrance —if you looked up, you could see the heavy, pointed tips of the bars—but probably no one had lowered it in twenty years. Probably it didn't even work anymore. Suñer smiled to himself as he stepped across the threshold. In these times, security was an illusion.

"Ernesto, I hadn't expected to see you here tonight. I had thought you were still up north, hobnobing with the gringos."

Ettore Moscardó, whose mother was a cousin of Suñer's and who was believed by many to be the handsomest and most reactionary man in Mexico, showed his beautifully even teeth in a teasing, contemptuous grin. He was almost a foot taller and gave the impression of being all shoulders in his exquisitely tailored dinner jacket. Suñer managed a smile—he and Ettore understood one another, and one's family was, after all, one's family.

"I am only down for a few days," he said evenly. "I wanted to be out of the way for a while. The *norteamericanos* are in a great fright about foreign spies just at the moment, and I thought it would be wiser to be unavailable. How is your mother?"

Moscardó shrugged. It was an elegant, careless gesture he might have spent hours practicing in the mirror. "Much the same. She hardly ever leaves the grounds of her villa anymore."

"Yes—she has taken the death of your father very hard."

The two men's eyes met, and for a few seconds the conversation seemed to falter and die. Leonisa del Rivera had been, as everyone knew, a wild girl before her marriage and, almost as soon as she had been led away from the altar, notoriously unfaithful to her husband, the old General Moscardó. Suñer had himself, in his younger days, been one of her lovers. Her retirement had been occasioned by nothing more serious than a certain petulant vanity —she was merely embarrassed at having grown old and lost her beauty—but family honor required other explanations.

"Are you sure it wasn't some outraged husband?"

Suñer looked at his cousin for a moment, utterly at a loss. What was the boy talking about?

"Is it really the gringo police you wish to avoid, Ernesto, or has your poor wife further cause to complain?"

"Not so much the police as the movement." The second

secretary frowned. He wished Ettore would stop calling them gringos, as if he had just invented the term and expected you to applaud his cleverness. He had no love for the *norteamericanos* himself, but he did not like to hear his relatives calling them vulgar names they might have learned from the kitchen help.

And Ettore should not speak so disrespectfully of other men's wives.

"There seems to be a German spy running loose, and I was being watched more closely than usual. I didn't want anyone coming to me for assistance and ending up under arrest as a return for his confidence."

"I see—yes." Moscardó reached into his jacket pocket and pulled out a gold cigarette case. For an annoyingly long period of time he seemed totally absorbed by the various operations of opening the case, taking out the cigarette, closing the case, tapping the cigarette against the lid, putting it in his mouth, and accepting a light from his mother's cousin. Suñer almost decided to give up on him; the man was so clearly an ass. "There has been much talk of that down here. Just rumors, you understand. But it would seem that something is afoot."

"Talk? Down here? That is bad."

Suñer wished Ettore had thought to offer him a cigarette—he could hardly reach for one of his own without perhaps betraying the enormous excitement that was welling up inside him. He hardly seemed to know what to do with his hands.

"I would advise you to keep free of it," he went on, a little surprised by the pitch of his voice. But fortunately Ettore was too absorbed in his own distinction to notice. "At this stage of the war, I shouldn't imagine the Germans would undertake the risk of inserting an agent into the United States for some trivial purpose. You know the complexion of the present government; they wouldn't hesitate to curry favor with Roosevelt by throwing a few of us in jail. A wise man will stay out of harm's way."

"Oh, I know that, Ernesto." The handsomest man in Mexico smiled again, flourishing his cigarette like a cantina woman.

"I'm content to be an observer in politics—I leave the conspiracies to your side of the family."

I leave the conspiracies to your side of the family. Ettore, the clownish buffoon, what had he meant by that?

All the way home, as he sat in the back of his car and considered how little ground he had gained during the whole long evening, he kept coming back to the same question: What had Leonisa's excessively beautiful man-child intended to suggest by his allusion to "your side of the family"?

If there had been more to learn at the minister's reception, Suñer had failed to learn it—oh, there were rumors enough; there was nothing Mexico City loved as much as a rumor. But no one seemed to know anything of substance.

Or, at least, Suñer hadn't hit upon a means of getting them to tell him. It was like coming up to a blind wall.

Your side of the family.

And then suddenly the solution hit him with all the force of the obvious. He must have grown stupid just talking with Ettore; why hadn't it occurred to him before?

In the morning, as soon as he could be sure she was decently awake, he would go pay his respects to the general's grieving widow.

Leonisa received him in her bedroom, which could hardly have constituted an invitation because the bed was far too crowded with boxes of chocolates, magazines, small dogs and Leonisa to have room for another occupant. She put out her hand to be kissed and waved to him to sit down on a small gilt chair her maid had drawn up so close that it was already touching the backs of his legs while he leaned forward to brush his mustache across madam's fingers. She was wearing a smoky pink peignoir that looked well against her pale, olive skin, and her hair had obviously been brushed and arranged with great care. She was even wearing a suggestion of makeup. Suñer was highly flattered until he remembered that she could not possibly have known he was coming. A life of mourning didn't seem to agree with her; she had grown unattractively heavy.

"My dear," he said, releasing her hand and settling himself in his chair, "you are as breathtaking as ever."

"And you are as much a liar as ever. Come, would you care for a chocolate?" She held out a huge gold-foil box to him, shaking it so that the contents rattled. There seemed to be almost nothing left inside except tissue paper, so Suñer raised his left hand, with the fingers spread wide, and shook his head.

"I saw Ettore last evening at the minister's reception. He does you credit, Leonisa—a young man of great charm. He will go far in the world."

"He is a blockhead, like his father—except that I can't be precisely sure who his father was." Madam Moscardó allowed herself a tight smile, raising an eyebrow as she admitted her old lover to what was a secret from no one. "It might even have been you, Ernesto."

"No, my dear. That was a little before my time."

She looked surprised for a moment, then seemed to reflect, and then nodded. "You are quite right, by a year. But he is still a blockhead—his wife, who is a sensible woman, is presently in love with a taxi driver, and Ettore is too vain and too stupid even to imagine the possibility of such a thing. I really sometimes think he might even be the general's son. . . ."

And she went on and on. Like any woman who has enjoyed the experience of being notorious, Leonisa was a compulsive gossip. Her bedroom, which had once seen traffic of quite another kind, was probably one of the major intelligence centers of the capital. The federal police would have been happy to have discovered half of what was discussed within those four walls. How would Ettore have known anything of German spies unless his mother had told him?

". . . And one understands that your poor wife is still enjoying her extended vacation in Veracruz. Tell me, Ernesto, do you not miss your children?" She smiled again. It was the first time she had paused for breath in at least twenty minutes.

"Yes, I do." Suñer returned her smile. He kept reminding himself that, just at present, he had need of the old harridan, and squirmed slightly in his chair. "I expect to visit them and their mother if my stay is to be longer than a few days. This, however, is not entirely a matter in which I may please myself."

Leonisa was suddenly all attention; one could almost feel the concentration with which she was waiting for the next sentence. And when it did not come, when she was at last convinced by Suñer's placid silence, she leaned toward him, resting on her knuckles like a sprinter. For a moment the only sound in the room was the creaking of her mattress springs.

"What has happened, Ernesto?" she asked breathlessly, almost gleefully. "Are you in disgrace?"

Suñer forced himself to laugh. "No, my pet, I am not in disgrace. The *norteamericanos* are hunting for a German spy, and I have come home to be out of the way."

"Oh—that." The disappointment was obvious in the heavy lines of her once-beautiful face as she allowed herself to fall back against the pillows. "I am so tired of that business—it's a good thing the war in Europe is nearly over. The Germans are such bores; I am sick of hearing about them and their spies."

Nevertheless, by the time Suñer had kissed her hand again and taken his leave he had a pretty good idea of what had been going on and who could lead him to von Niehauser.

"I leave the conspiracies to your side of the family."

Item Number One: On the morning of the previous day, Agustin Gomá, millionaire upstart and political dilettante, had abruptly canceled all his engagements for the following week, including a dinner party which *el Presidente* had been expected to attend.

Item Number Two: Gomá's private secretary, who was an unimpeachable source and also a relative of Leonisa's, had said that the little leather merchant had left for Juarez, supposedly on vacation. Who in his right mind would vacation in Juarez in the middle of the winter?

Item Number Three: Gomá had lately dropped several hints that as soon as Germany won its war against the gringos (Gomá was precisely the sort one would expect to employ such a word), he personally would be in a position to see to it that Mexico's ancient grievances would be answered.

Item Number Four: Gomá's wife was a first cousin of Suñer's own.

Conclusion: By noon, Suñer had sent a telegram to Inspector Havens in Washington and had made arrangements of his own to have the plane he had chartered in New York fly him to Juarez. There was very little time, and Agustin Gomá, to whom under normal circumstances Suñer could hardly bring himself to be civil, suddenly appeared as his last best hope of personal salvation.

Gomá was not difficult to find. He was neither rich enough nor sufficiently well liked to have achieved the sort of political influence that can allow a man simply to disappear. All Suñer had to do was to telephone a friend with business interests in Juarez, and within an hour that friend learned through a local politician in his employ that the gentleman in question was staying at the ranch of an acquaintance about sixty kilometers west of the city. Suñer hired a car and was there by five-thirty in the afternoon. He had the impression that Gomá was not terribly glad to see him.

"*Buenos dias*," he said as he stood with his back to the car, looking up at Gomá, who was standing on the front porch of the house, holding a small glass in his right hand. "I have come a long way for the purpose of saving your life, Agustin. Don't you think it would be polite to ask me inside?"

He smiled, but the upper half of Gomá's body was covered in shadow—it was really impossible to see anything clearly except a pair of dark trouser legs. Finally Gomá moved back perhaps half a step.

"Come in, if that is what you wish."

A servant, dressed entirely in white, opened the door, and a bar of yellow light fell across the porch, revealing the unpleasant, wary scowl that covered Gomá's face.

"You are too kind."

The interior of the house was whitewashed and spartan. There were a few plain wooden chairs, a long sofa that looked as if it had seen much service, and a table covered with magazines, about half of them in English—Suñer noticed that several were three and four years old.

But what he noticed first were the men.

There were three of them, big men in heavy sheepskin coats and thick boots, men with the look of having lived most of their lives out-of-doors. But they were no farmers—they all carried pistols, and one of them had a bandolier draped across his shoulder. He recognized the type. They were mercenaries, ex-soldiers probably, who found work as bodyguards and private thugs and who turned to banditry when times were hard. Clearly, Gomá had not come to this godforsaken place on any vacation.

"Perhaps you would like to send them outside for a breath of air?" Suñer asked, pointing to the one with the bandolier. "They can wait on the porch if that would make you feel safer."

Gomá nodded and, without being told, the three men filed out through the door, filling the space behind them with the sound of their boot heels. The room seemed to expand as they left. Without waiting to be asked, Suñer sat down at the end of the sofa nearest the fireplace.

"What is it that you want, Ernesto? I assume it must have been something truly important to drag you so far away from your comforts."

"Yes, it is."

The second secretary watched the leather merchant with a

certain carefully contained apprehension. Gomá had still not removed the heavy black overcoat that would have been more appropriate to the sidewalks of Mexico City's financial district than to these wind-swept, rock-strewn, pitilessly empty stretches of desert. His wide peasant's face was heavy with weariness, making his eyes little more than slits. He hadn't shaved that morning and his jawline was shiny. It was obvious that for the past few days he had been under enormous strain.

"I know about this fellow von Niehauser," Suñer went on, his voice a marvel of serenity. "Or perhaps you didn't know that that was his name—at any rate, I know that you have been contacted to see to his escape over the border into this country. It will not do, Agustin. You are going to have to turn the matter over to me so that I can allow the *norteamericano* police to catch him."

For several seconds, Gomá seemed unable to move. He simply continued where he was, standing in the exact center of the room, his feet wide apart, as if he had decided to become a permanent fixture. Nothing registered in his expression, not even surprise. It was as if he hadn't heard.

And then, finally, he blinked. It was at least a sign of life. And then he looked down at the floor and frowned—you could have thought that his most cherished illusions had just been swept away for good and all.

"Do you aristocrats believe in nothing?" he asked finally, in little more than a whisper. "I had thought, Ernesto, that you, at least, would have been with us."

"In spirit, yes. But—you must understand, Agustin—I am loyal to nothing more than to my own life. And that is what is at stake here. Not only my life but yours as well."

Suñer did his best to smile, but the effort was simply beyond him. What his face must have looked like, he couldn't have imagined.

"You see, my friend, they have me. The night before last I received a visit in New York from an Inspector Havens of the

FBI, and they have very complete information about my involvement in the Tocula insurrection. They want von Niehauser, and if they don't get him they will turn that information over to *el Presidente* and I will be shot."

"I fail to grasp what that has to do with me." Gomá was still staring at the floor, but it was possible to tell from the tone of his voice that he was frightened, that he grasped perfectly well what it had to do with him.

"Oh, my dear Agustin, you are either very brave or sublimely stupid." The second secretary found himself finally able to relax —for the first time he noticed the heat of the fire on his face, and it occurred to him that he hadn't eaten in several hours. It was like suddenly discovering that you were alive. "You know me," he went on, at last able to manage a convincing smile. "Do you actually imagine that I would go quietly to my death, knowing that you and you alone had it in your power to save me, and that you did not? You had your hand in that sorry business, and I plan to spend my last hours writing out a very complete confession."

And there it was. How many times in a man's life was he presented with a choice of such pristine clarity? It was a moment which, had Agustin been of a more self-conscious disposition, he should have relished.

But Agustin Gomá, it seemed obvious, did not relish this clear choice. Perhaps—and who could blame him?—his experience of them had been rather too limited for him to have developed into a connoisseur. Or perhaps, as Suñer, to his marked discomfort, was coming more and more to suspect, perhaps the two men did not understand the situation in quite identical terms.

"And what would happen if I simply gave orders to have you killed, here and now?" Gomá asked suddenly, his face slowly lighting up with an expression of malignant triumph.

Suñer was disappointed. The man was trying to wriggle out —the esthetic of the thing was ruined. He sighed, and then looked up at the vulgar little leather merchant with as blank an expression as he could manage, bored in advance by the hours of argument and pointless bargaining that must inevitably follow.

"Agustin, my friend, has it not occurred to you that I would not have come here without taking precautions against precisely that contingency? I have left a letter, to be delivered to the minister of police if I do not return to the capital by Monday, and I have already notified the unpleasant Inspector Havens as to where I am, what I am doing here, and with whom. Believe me, if our own government doesn't kill you, Havens will. He is a very uncompromising sort of man. You will not like him. Alas, as you see, there is no third choice."

"Alas, but there is."

There was a silence, during which Gomá appeared to be enjoying himself immensely. And then, all at once, he stamped his foot against the bare wooden floor, and the door opened and the man with the bandolier appeared, holding his sombrero in both hands.

"*Si, patron?*" he asked, although it didn't quite have the inflection of a question. Gomá did not even take the trouble to look at him.

"You have not, I think, considered the possibilities with quite the care you imagine," he went on, quite as if he and Suñer were still alone in the room. "Because, you see, your letter to the minister of police will be too late. Because, you see, when the German gentleman boards the ship that will take him to Lisbon, he will have a companion."

Suñer opened his mouth, as if to say something, but then merely closed it again. There seemed to be some object in his throat; he tried swallowing, twice, and with increasing difficulty, but it was to no avail.

"I have no inclination to stay in my homeland—my wife and children are protected, and the government can do as it wishes toward the confiscation of my property. It will be returned to me when Hitler has won the war and I come back in triumph. I will be a great man then, Ernesto, greater than anything you could possibly imagine. And I have not forgotten your condescension toward me at our last meeting, on the occasion of my daughter's wedding."

His eyes seemed to sparkle, and he stood there, staring at some point beyond Suñer's head, like a man entranced. Then he turned to the armed man at the door.

"You will take the señor out to the barn. You will see to it that the manner of his death is not a pleasant one."

The man with the bandolier nodded, still holding his sombrero and grinning.

"*Si, patron.*"

XXI

Normally the drive from Los Alamos into Santa Fe took better than an hour and a half. The worst part was the road down from the mesa, which was a hair-raising ordeal of switchbacks and blind corners, and always with a sheer drop of several hundred yards not more than six or seven feet from your outside wheel. In some respects it was worse since the Army had brought in their heavy construction crews and paved it over; the slightest whisper of snow would immediately melt and refreeze, making the road like a slalom run with traffic in both directions.

Nevertheless, on that particular Friday morning Erich Lautner clocked himself at fifty-two minutes.

It had been exhilarating. He had listened to the tires squeal as he went around a curve, coasting closer and closer to the edge, not knowing and hardly even caring if another car might be coming right up around into him. He had felt the engine throbbing and fought for control over the vibration that came right up at him through the steering wheel—it had given him an enormous sense of power. When the road flattened out, and there was no longer anything except the long, straight stretch of asphalt into Santa Fe, he had experienced a real twinge of disappointment. It wouldn't be the same going back uphill and, at any rate, by then the mood would have passed off and he probably wouldn't have the nerve to risk all that again.

He would have liked to have had Jenny on the seat beside him. He could almost see the way her face would have looked, white as a sheet of paper. He would have liked to have had someone else be afraid besides just himself.

He was losing Jenny. Even if he weren't going away, he would lose her anyway. It seemed that she too didn't have the nerve for risking it all all over again; she wanted to go back to her husband and forget about her desperate little flirtation with sin. She had begun to look at him as if he were some sort of dangerous criminal.

So it turned out that Jenny was just another conventional little *hausfrau* who didn't care for her husband but hadn't the stomach for the obvious consequences—another Emma Bovary, but without the daring to sustain even that. And it was a great shame because she was a pretty woman.

That was the way he tried to frame it for himself on the drive into Santa Fe, as merely another one of life's unavoidable disappointments, something to be shrugged off and dismissed from one's mind. He tried not to associate it with the temptation toward panic that had been growing in him ever since he had received his summons from the *Sicherheitsdienst.* He wanted to keep the two intellectually separate, to avoid, if he could, the perfectly ridiculous suspicion that Jenny's defection had resulted from her having somehow sensed the truth about him, but it was difficult. It was difficult to be philosophical when so much of one's comfortable world had been torn away so quickly. It was difficult not to imagine that he who had betrayed no one had now been betrayed.

It had been easier when he was coming down from the mesa, when excitement and sheer physical fear had been able to blot out this growing, unfocused apprehension. It had been easier when his heart had been pounding in his throat, when there had been no necessity for being philosophical.

Lautner switched on the car radio and listened first to the weather report—they were predicting a storm, possibly even as early as tomorrow afternoon—and then to some music. They were playing Artie Shaw; Lautner liked Artie Shaw. He liked American music generally; like everything else in this country, it was remarkably comfortable. He wondered what they were playing over the radio in Berlin these days. It didn't seem very likely that it would be Artie Shaw.

He could see Santa Fe up ahead—he had been able to for a couple of miles already; there was little enough out there on the desert to obstruct the view. He would go have lunch as soon as he got into town, one of those huge bland American meals that somehow had the power to dull the senses like an injection of morphine. And then he would go see this messenger from Heydrich—except, of course, that Heydrich was dead—and find out what after all these years the *Sicherheitsdienst* could want of him, damn their eyes.

Would they really want him to come home? There were bombing raids over most of the big German cities these days. You saw them in the newsreels, white puffs of explosions, like smoke rings from a cigarette, over a flat grid of buildings and streets; Lautner found himself trying to recognize places from the aerial photographs—and probably everything was drying up: ammunition, food, pleasure, hope of victory, cigarettes.

"As a protégé of the SS, you will lead a very comfortable life," Heydrich had told him. He supposed he was entitled to wonder just how willing—or, indeed, able—the *Obergruppenführer*'s successors would be to fulfill his promises.

Of course, if he brought them the bomb . . .

From force of habit, he parked his car about half a block from the back of the La Ventana Hotel; it wasn't something he was even aware he had done until he turned a corner and saw the pale neon sign over the front entrance. Of course, Jenny hadn't been the first woman he had taken there, but realizing how automatically he had found his way almost to the threshold was an ugly sensation, like finding himself somehow divided in half, as if he were one self spying on the private life of the other. He had thought he had put all that out of his mind—it was stupid, really—but it would seem not. The little bitch.

The restaurant was one of those small but important discoveries that a man makes if he keeps his eyes open. A tiny place, not more than eight or ten tables, but clean and inexpensive, and the owner had friends in the cattle business and seemed never to have heard of meat rationing. Lautner ate there as often as he could, sometimes after Jenny had gone back up to the mesa with her girlfriends: it would have been instructive to know how many of them were meeting men in out-of-the-way hotel rooms.

On the whole, he preferred to eat alone; he found women under such circumstances an unpleasant distraction, without an idea in their heads that didn't relate back to themselves and their own really rather limited charms. If he wanted to talk he preferred to talk to a man and a scientist, and for the rest he liked to keep to himself.

But the food really was very good. The only disagreeable thing was that they didn't serve wine. He would have liked a bottle of good, heavy-scented red wine. He would have liked leaving for his appointment just pleasantly fuzzy. But it wasn't to be.

When he was finished, he paid and left. As he passed by the window he could see the waiter clearing away his dishes.

The contact codes had been worked out and explained to him almost immediately after he had agreed to defect to the West with Professor Schleiermacher. It wasn't a very complicated business—a bit overingenious, but that was to be expected from the SS. Actually, all Lautner had to do was to appear at a certain place at a certain time, and hope that the plan had not been compromised to the American authorities.

The Santa Fe Public Library was a strange mixture of architectural styles: a cocoa-colored little box with a low, flat roof and brick trim, but with a white, faintly Georgian portico, and a series of balconied windows no more than five feet from the ground and painted turquoise. There was also a bay window and it was painted turquoise as well. All in all, it made a very curious impression. Lautner, whose literary tastes ran mainly to detective stories, had never been inside before, but he discovered he rather liked the place. It was less intimidating than the vast pseudo-Grecian horrors of gray stone to which he was accustomed. One might almost have expected to find a little garden in the back, with a tiny fountain tinkling noisily, except, of course, that gardens weren't usual in New Mexico.

The hallways were of tile and made his footstep sound extraordinarily loud, which, of course, might only have been the work of his imagination. He was thirsty and his hands were sweating; he felt as if he might be coming down with something. He wondered about the man he was supposedly going to meet, whether it could be anyone he knew. But, of course, who would he have known in the SS? It would probably be some thug with a broken nose, the sort who would naturally look with contempt at anyone who was not some version of himself. The whole business was too colossally absurd; they would probably both end up getting killed.

The history section was relatively small, only part of a single room. The books were grouped by country and period. After a little hunting, Lautner found the Italian Renaissance, but he almost turned and fled when he rounded a corner between two rows of shelves and discovered himself staring at the back of a military uniform. The man was leaning against the wall with his shoulder. He seemed to be reading—or perhaps simply waiting. For a second or two Lautner couldn't be sure he hadn't shouted with frightened surprise.

And then the man turned around and smiled at him. The first thing Lautner noticed was that the uniform was British—at least he wasn't about to be arrested. And then his eyes came to rest on the face, and the brief flood of relief seemed to freeze up inside him.

"Hello, Erich," the man said in English, the smile still on his lips. It was odd, but Lautner was sure that this was not someone who had ever called him by his first name before.

Because, of course, he didn't recognize him all at once. This was someone he had known, but not in England, and certainly not in the United States. He searched his memory, and then he realized that it was the uniform itself that had confused him. Yes —he knew him now. Dear God!

"Joachim von Niehauser," he said, under his breath, as much to himself as to anyone. And then, a little louder, "They sent you?"

"Yes, me."

They went to von Niehauser's room, which perversely enough was just a few doors up the hall from the room Lautner regularly took when he was entertaining Jenny Springer. He had been nervous at first and would have preferred conducting their discussion out-of-doors, but von Niehauser hadn't been impressed by his caution.

"You have a great deal to tell me," he had said, "and we could freeze to death. Besides, do you suppose that sitting on a park bench would render you invisible? If they knew enough to be watching us, we would both already be under arrest."

It had its own brutal logic, which von Niehauser articulated with the same dispassionate clarity which had characterized his lectures on particle physics when Lautner was an undergraduate. The voice was the same, but the man had changed. They were in mortal danger with every second, but von Niehauser seemed to have lost the capacity to feel. It was as if the man had died, leaving behind only the intellect.

But, of course, as he himself had explained with such precision when Lautner asked how he of all people had happened to become a spy, Germany was fighting a war.

"I've been in Russia," he said, as if that should have made everything clear.

Still, Lautner, whose blood hadn't, as it happened, been replaced with ice water, felt entitled to worry about the police.

"They have people everywhere," he said, as they walked down the corridor. Von Niehauser hardly seemed to be listening as he took his room key from the pocket of his overcoat. "The FBI . . ."

"The what?" Von Niehauser glanced up, his eyes wrinkled with an instant of perplexity. And then he seemed to understand. "Oh, them—is that what they call themselves? They dress like haberdashers' dummies and lounge around like gypsies. I think I've managed to stay clear of them." Once again a faint, contemptuous smile flickered across his face and then disappeared into his inhuman calm.

But for the most part they talked about the weapon, and there von Niehauser was still the *Privatdozent* from the Kaiser Wilhelm Institute, the man whom everyone had said would be a professor before he was forty, the brightest of the junior men.

Perhaps that was what had undone him. Perhaps a less intelligent, less sensitive soul would have managed to come through the war without losing touch with the desire for life.

"What process have they used to refine the uranium?" he asked, leaning forward slightly as he sat on the edge of the bed. Always the Prussian gentleman, he had given up the room's only chair to Lautner. "Have they found a filtering material?"

"Yes, nickel. But they aren't depending on gaseous diffusion alone; they've built a cyclotron to separate the isotopes."

"It must be huge. Where can they be getting the copper for the electromagnet?"

"They aren't using copper." Lautner allowed himself a short, soundless laugh and shook his head. "They're using silver—six thousand tons of silver, melted down and drawn into wire."

He had expected von Niehauser to be impressed—or surprised, or something—but in that he was disappointed. Von Niehauser merely stared at the floor, as if he were trying to puzzle something out for himself.

"We don't have the copper—or the silver," he said finally, without looking up. "And such an undertaking would require an industrial plant of considerable size." Lautner nodded in agreement, but if von Niehauser noticed he gave no sign. "There is no part of the Reich or the conquered territories free from enemy bombing, and therefore there is no possibility of building such a plant. The Allies would have it flattened before we could even paint the walls."

"Then build a reactor and make the bomb with plutonium."

"What?" Von Niehauser glanced up and his eyes narrowed, as if he imagined Lautner might be having a joke at his expense. "What in God's name is plutonium?"

"Element 94—you bombard uranium with neutrons and some of it will be transformed into a new substance, reasonably stable and extractable by ordinary chemical means." Lautner smiled, and threw his hands out to suggest an explosion. "It will go critical just as well as U-235. You will get just as big a bang."

Von Niehauser shook his head.

"The possibility has been explored; they have been trying to construct a reactor at the Institute for some time, but there is a shortage of heavy water. We must have it to control the reaction, to keep it from going critical all at once, and ten weeks ago the British bombed the heavy water facility in Norway."

The expression on his face was utterly despairing, as if he had seen the end of everything. He stood up from the bed and walked across the room to the door and back, and then remained standing next to Lautner's chair, his arms folded across his chest. He looked like a man awaiting death.

"That was why they sent me," he said, all at once, speaking as if to himself. "We must build a reactor, and we have no heavy water."

"Then use graphite."

"Graphite?"

"Yes—graphite." There was real excitement in Lautner's voice. "Fermi constructed a reactor that went critical in December of '42, using graphite."

"Bothe calculated that graphite would absorb too many neutrons."

"Then Bothe was mistaken."

Von Niehauser sat down again. "Yes," he said. "Then it would be easy, wouldn't it."

"Yes."

After that it became like an interrogation. Von Niehauser was brilliant. He knew exactly which questions to ask, what was important, what lines of research were leading in the right direction. He wanted to know about everything, about theories of critical mass, triggering mechanisms, speculations on the probable qualities of this new element plutonium, everything. It seemed to go on for hours. Finally, Lautner happened to glance toward the window and saw that it was dark outside.

"It's late," he said, like a man offering an apology. "I have to get back, or the security forces . . ."

"Could you leave tonight? We could be in Mexico by tomorrow morning."

But Lautner shook his head. "It would be safer to leave tomorrow. Tomorrow will be Saturday, and Sunday is our day off. I could think of some excuse for coming back into Santa Fe tomorrow, and then no one would notice I was even missing until Monday morning."

"Good." Von Niehauser clapped his hands together. For the first time he seemed genuinely pleased. "Then it shall be tomorrow."

"Do you know what Fermi says about this bomb?" Lautner asked. He hadn't risen from his chair, and his eyes were playing nervously over the carpet. It was as if the question had just occurred to him. "He says that it is theoretically possible that this bomb could ignite the atmosphere—possibly of the whole world—that it could burn away the sky in a few seconds. Can you imagine such a thing, von Niehauser?"

"Yes, perhaps it's nothing more than we deserve."

The light coming in through the room's only window threw sharp, black shadows across von Niehauser's face, giving it a faintly demonic cast. The skin seemed stretched tight over the bone, and the eyes were blind hollows.

"Do you know what they are doing in Europe, Lautner?" he asked, the ghost of a smile on his lips. "Do you know what *we* are doing?"

He didn't seem interested in whether his questions were answered or not. He looked at the other man as if he were an inanimate object, just something occupying space in the room. There was a long silence, during which he remained perfectly still—he might have died, because he didn't even seem to be breathing. And then suddenly he adjusted the set of his shoulders and came back to life.

"I saw something once," he said. "An internment camp in Poland—at least, that was what it seemed at first. Actually it was a kind of antichamber into oblivion, where people's lives were taken away from them a piece at a time so that they hardly seemed to care when they were herded half naked through the snow on their way to extermination chambers where they would be packed together so that they wouldn't even have room to fall down, and then gassed with cyanide. I watched it being done—those chambers were made of heavy iron plate, and you could still hear the people inside screaming. So perhaps the desire for life wasn't quite dead yet—what do you think, Lautner?"

He leaned forward until his face was only a few inches from Lautner's, his cold, mirthless smile still in place, like a mask. He seemed to be studying his former colleague's reaction, waiting to see some sign of comprehension, but Lautner wasn't sure enough of his command of speech to risk opening his mouth. Finally, after what seemed hours but was probably no more than a few seconds, von Niehauser drew back, apparently satisfied, since his tone, when he began speaking again, was calm and friendly, almost confidential.

"I couldn't describe to anyone what that place was like, so I won't try. You wouldn't believe me—why should you? I'd seen enough terrible things in Russia—men with half their heads shot away so that their blood runs out onto the snow in a filthy dark smear, men too shocked and cold and weak to do anything more than sit down somewhere out of the wind and die. I'd seen everything that war could do, but war is madness and you expect nothing better from it. But this—this was orderly and quiet and quite according to plan. The enemy were women and children and old men, and they went to their deaths just the way I've said. Like cattle. And the SS guards stood around and smoked cigarettes.

"I wonder how much those people will care if your bomb sets the sky on fire and turns the whole planet into a cinder. I don't suppose very much. They're mostly Jews—did you know that, Lautner? Or perhaps I hadn't mentioned it. The SS is making good on its word."

"Then why are we going back?"

The words seemed to cling in Lautner's throat like pieces of sticky paper, but he finally managed to ask that one question. Von Niehauser simply stared at him for a moment, as if he wondered whether the poor soul had suddenly gone simple-minded.

"For Germany," he said finally. He was a man stating the obvious. "All of Europe is dying. If the Allies invade, they will be resisted, and everything east of Calais will end as a charred desert, without one brick standing on another and without a single living soul to see. There won't be any fine distinctions left to be drawn in the coming massacre, so don't ask me to pause over the fate of a few million Jews whose deaths are only remarkable for their pointlessness. It has all gone beyond that."

In the clarity of the winter darkness, Lautner could hear music as he walked back toward his car. He didn't have any idea where it came from—it wasn't more than a faint tinkle of sound. But it was Friday night and somebody was having a good time.

Probably, back at Los Alamos, there would be a party going in the bachelor dormitories. There usually was, almost any night during the weekend, even if people had to get up at six-thirty in the morning to go back to work. People would be drinking beer or anything else they could find, and if any women were unwary enough to have come they would probably wake up the next morning with saddle sores. The record players would be turned up as loud as possible, and probably two or three young men would be keeping time to the music by pounding garbage can lids against the plywood walls.

Lautner dreaded going back. He didn't object to those kinds of parties—in fact, he rather enjoyed them—but the thought of having to face another human being on that particular night filled him with dread. He had seen von Niehauser, and that was enough.

Because, of course, von Niehauser was mad.

"How is Professor Schleiermacher?" he had asked. "Is he up there with you working on this device? I can't imagine it would be very much to his taste."

"Schleiermacher died two years ago, at Princeton. It was influenza."

And von Niehauser, who had been to Russia and the extermination camps of the SS, who had seen the future and could describe it all in a calm, steady voice, had looked stricken.

"He was like a father to me," he had said. "He was one of the great men of science."

And then, when their meeting was over, he stood in the doorway of his hotel room and put his hand on Lautner's shoulder and smiled.

"And tomorrow," he had said, "tomorrow we will go. Tomorrow, perhaps, we will settle the war between us."

He was mad. The man was simply mad.

And Lautner knew he had to find some way out. As he walked along the deserted sidewalk, his lips kept forming the words, over and over again. "I have to get out, I have to get out."

But how, when he had shaken hands with the devil?

XXII

George Havens came over the border from El Paso, driving a dark green, unmarked car that belonged to the Army and wondering if he wasn't being suckered. He didn't trust Suñer—he wasn't sure he had thrown enough of a scare into him—and he didn't like staking everything, the whole operation, on this one pitch. If von Niehauser got away from them now, and managed to lose himself in Mexico, where the Bureau had no jurisdiction and people under any circumstances weren't wildly partisan about the gringo war, then they would never catch him.

It had not occurred to him to doubt that von Niehauser would find a way to get whatever information it was that he was seeking—they could build a steel wall around Los Alamos, and it wouldn't be enough to protect their secrets. Von Niehauser would find a way; the concentrated forces of Military Intelligence and the Federal Bureau of Investigation were simply no match for him. He could be betrayed, but he couldn't be outwitted.

And now Havens was on his way to meet the nasty little specimen who was going to do the betraying, conscious that the war, and perhaps even the history of man on this planet, was probably going to turn on this one act of treachery. We wish to lure down the eagle, so we bait the trap with a fragment of rotting meat.

The border policeman on the Mexican side, a huge, swarthy man, almost as black as a Negro, pursed his lips under his Pancho Villa mustache, looked at Havens' vaccination book—probably without seeing it—folded it neatly inside the pages of his passport and thrust them both back through the car window. He grunted and made a sweeping gesture with his arm, as if the idea was to shoo you over the line like a barnyard goose. It was perhaps all the reception to which he felt you were entitled.

"Don't call in the local authorities unless you have to," General Groves had said, "but I don't care who you have to offend, so long as you get our spy. Remember, you're not there to be nice to people."

It was a few minutes after eight in the morning, and the flight from Washington had been just bumpy enough to guarantee that no one on board got any sleep. Havens hadn't been out of his clothes in twenty-four hours. He needed a shave and a hot bath. He needed some rest. He needed a few hours of escape from the idea that the fate of the world had somehow become his personal responsibility. He would settle for a couple of aspirin and maybe a good cup of scalding Indian tea. There wasn't a chance he would get any of them any time soon. He dropped the car into gear and shot across into the crowded, narrow streets of Juarez.

Suñer had said he would meet him in the lobby of the Ritz Hotel—he had said it without a trace of embarrassment, the Ritz. He would wait all day if necessary, he said. He made it sound as if he were doing the biggest favor imaginable.

It was cold outside. The clouds were heavy and the color of pewter; there was the threat of something nasty in the air. No one would be outside on such a morning if he could avoid it, so the only people on the sidewalks—where there were sidewalks; mostly there was only the cobbled street, or the odd strip of crumbling asphalt—were heavy, middle-aged peasant women, wrapped up to their eyelids in Indian blankets. Havens parked his car in a vacant lot beside what purported to be a French restaurant and dropped the keys into his jacket pocket. If the car got stolen, that was the Army's headache. The Ritz Hotel was in the next block.

The lobby was a huge, high-ceilinged room with fake columns running up the sides of the walls and lots of gilt paint. You could hardly move around for the potted palms and the smoking stands and the heavy, voluptuous sofas that looked like they had come out of some Edwardian whore's boudoir. The waiters drifted noiselessly around in morning coats and stand-up collars, but if you looked closely you could see that the carpet hadn't been cleaned in so long that even the coffee stains were faded.

Suñer was nowhere in sight, but it was only half-past eight in the morning, which to that gentleman was probably still the middle of the night. Havens flagged down one of the morning coats and ordered some breakfast—a pot of tea and a couple of croissants and, yes, he would like to be served right there in the lobby, thank you. The waiter sniffed and disappeared, but Havens got his breakfast.

He waited for two hours. He read the newspaper, he ordered another pot of tea, he paced around the edges of the room, he scowled at the day manager who came to inquire if he could be of service. Two hours was a long time.

"He isn't coming," he said finally, apparently out loud because a couple standing nearby turned around to stare. Suñer was either dead or had pulled a fast one on him.

The second possibility was the one that bothered him more. If all this, the summons to Juarez, the appointment in the hotel lobby, the references to an uncovered conspiracy, was just so much camouflage, then von Niehauser was probably already halfway back to the Fatherland.

Because Suñer would have to be buying something with his deception. Even if by then he had put himself out of reach of *el Presidente*'s firing squads, he would still be giving up an enormous amount to keep faith with his Fascist colleagues—how much of your life can you actually carry away with you in a suitcase?

Of course, it was possible that he had simply panicked, that he had discovered nothing and had taken himself off to keep from having to own up, but Havens dismissed that possibility almost immediately. It was too early for that—Suñer simply didn't strike him as the type to skip out on wealth and power and comfort quite that easily.

But if all he wanted was to protect von Niehauser, what was Havens doing in Juarez?

"Meet me at Hotel Ritz, Juarez, tomorrow. Will wait all day. Agustin Gomá is tour guide. Can deal with him." That was what the telegram had said. And Agustin Gomá was a real person—Bureau files had him down as somebody to watch. Why bother with so elaborate a double cross?

And if it wasn't that, then Suñer was probably dead. And if he was dead, then Gomá had probably killed him. It was about as solid a guarantee as you could ask for that Suñer's information had been correct.

All except the part about what a reasonable type Gomá was. Apparently things just hadn't worked out that way.

So—we were in the right part of the world, and we had the right name. So then what?

Havens hunted up a telephone, got hold of the El Paso exchange, and placed a collect call to a special number the Bureau maintained, where the phone was answered by a sweet little old lady in Baltimore—at least, that was the impression. It cut down on the risk that the switchboard girls might get curious and decide to listen in.

"Smitty, have we got any friends in Juarez?"

"Is that you, Havens?" The high-pitched voice at the other end of the line didn't sound very glad to be hearing from him. "What the hell are you doing in Juarez?"

"Looking for friends, pal. Who do we know here?"

"Just a minute."

There was a longish pause, during which Havens could hear the crackle of all those hundreds of miles of phone cable and wondered if he might not be making a mistake. "Don't call in the local authorities unless you have to," the general had said. Well, it might just be that he had to.

"How friendly did you have in mind?" came the voice from

the cellars of Seat of Government. "Will the cops do? I can manage better, but it'll cost—you'll have to get clearance from the Director."

Oh, goody! A chance to annoy Hoover by complying with his mandate from the Army. Life was sweet.

"Tell me about it."

It took some arguing, but within half an hour Havens had his clearance. It was a complicated and nasty business, not at all the sort of thing that polished up the Bureau's image, but times were tough and even Mr. Hoover had to do what he was told once in a while. But he had made it clear that, once the present emergency was over, Havens wasn't likely to be welcomed back into the family with open arms. So what else was new?

The next big question was, how do you go about getting a luncheon appointment with a crime czar?

As it turned out, all you had to do was to ask.

Pepe (the Razor) Romero lived in a house that overlooked the Rio Grande, which geographical and political boundary had always figured very prominently in the histories of the great Mexican crime families. It was said that the Razor was beginning to cast longing glances over at the shores of Texas, where there was money to be made in everything from gambling and women to that exciting new business venture, the importation of heroin. Perhaps that was why he had chosen this particular spot for his house, so he could sit up on the bluff and stare out through the plate-glass window of his living room and dream of the wealth to be garnered on the other side of that muddy little ribbon of water.

Or perhaps he had been moved by strategic considerations—the house was at the center of a compound enclosed by high fences and guarded by men carrying machine guns. The cliffs rising up from the river were so sheer that it would have taken a team of mountain climbers to scale them.

Havens had been delivered by car, straight from the front entrance of the hotel. He had sat in the back seat of a black '38

Lincoln, between a couple of unsmiling gorillas who hadn't even opened their mouths during the whole twenty-seven-minute drive. As he waited in that living room, looking through that plate-glass window at that river, he found himself wondering if FBI agents had quite the same cachet with Mexican hoodlums that they enjoyed in the States. He didn't particularly relish the idea of floating out to sea with the garbage.

"Mr. Havens? Welcome to my house."

He turned around and was pleasantly surprised to find himself facing a small, spare man of about fifty, with a brown face, a neat black mustache, and alert, humorous eyes. The Lucky Luciano of Mexico was wearing a light gray suit that was obviously expensive but managed to keep from shouting the fact at you, and the hand he held out had clean fingernails and wasn't dripping in blood. He looked like any successful businessman—it just so happened that his business was crime.

Havens took the hand and shook it. His business was catching spies, so he had never developed any particular prejudice against gangsters. And, anyway, this wasn't the occasion to be a snob.

"Please—if you will come with me."

Romero took him gently by the elbow, and Havens allowed himself to be led into a small, sunlit dining room, where a table covered with a sparkling white cloth and a silver coffee service had already been set up for them. A servant, an automaton in a black tailcoat and white gloves, stood behind Romero's chair. He leaned forward while Romero whispered something in his ear, and then he disappeared. When he came back he was carrying a couple of covered dishes on a tray. Lunch turned out to be a grilled lamb chop, a little white rice, and a grilled tomato—somehow it was kind of an anticlimax.

"Am I to understand, Mr. Havens, that you are authorized to speak for the American *federales* in this matter?" Romero smiled as he spread a napkin out over his knees—it was just a pro forma question, something to get the negotiations started.

"Your brother-in-law is at this moment being transferred to the prison facilities at Brownsville, Señor Romero. Brownsville, as doubtless I don't have to remind you, is within wading distance of the Mexican frontier. The transfer is entirely under the jurisdiction of the FBI and, while Mr. Hoover cannot of course countenance aiding the escape of a federal prisoner, federal prisoners do escape—it happens all the time."

"And the translation of which is, Mr. Havens?"

"Give me what I want, Señor Romero, and little brother Juan will be escorted to the border and kicked across. Otherwise, he gets five to ten for aggravated assault and interstate flight."

Romero sighed and leaned back in his chair, resting his palms on both sides of his untouched lamb chop. Across the back of each hand, about an inch behind the knuckles, ran a knobby line of scar tissue, as if somebody had once slammed a door on them. That sort of thing probably hurt like the very devil.

"Are you a family man, Mr. Havens?" he asked, his eyes suddenly anything but humorous. Havens decided that there was a good chance he was being threatened, so he grinned.

"Not lately."

"Take my word for it, it is not always a blessing." He spoke as if he really believed it. This wasn't a threat; this was a confession. "He is my wife's youngest brother, the baby of the family. And by the time he was twenty-five, he had already cost me over eight million pesos. I am more than a little tempted simply to let him spend his five to ten—I believe I could use the rest."

They went back to their meal then, and nothing more was said until the servant returned to clear away the dishes and serve the coffee. The silence was almost morose as, presumably, Romero considered which would least ruffle his domestic tranquillity, little Juan lounging around the hacienda or little Juan in the Brownsville jug. Havens couldn't do anything except wait for the issue to be decided.

"It must be an immense favor that Mr. Hoover requires," the crime czar said finally, in a matter-of-fact tone as he filtered a third teaspoon of sugar into his coffee. "He is not famous for his tolerance toward the southern races, and this whole business is really a bit out of character for him."

He raised his eyebrows inquisitively, and Havens breathed a figurative sigh of relief. Little Juan had nothing to worry about.

"It is an important favor, yes, but the risks and inconveniences for you are insignificant. But you're quite right that the Director isn't just thrilled. Even he has to take orders."

"Then why should I believe he can be trusted?"

It was a good question, one Havens would have been just as happy not to have had to answer. But apparently it was time for the guarantees and the threats. Havens forced himself to smile.

"Señor Romero, you'll die a happy man if you never discover what this was all about, but you can take my word for it that if you knew what I know you'd realize that nobody's going to mess up a deal like this just to keep his hooks in a cheap little crook like your brother-in-law. However, if it makes you feel better, as soon as the two of us have struck a deal I'll pick up the phone and you can send one of your goons to the international border to welcome the prodigal home."

Romero seemed genuinely surprised, but probably his world didn't operate very much on trust. Probably he thought that the Federal Bureau of Investigation was staffed entirely by morons.

"Of course, you understand," Havens went on, allowing the smile to die away like a candle flame in an airless room, "that if you in turn decide to double-cross us, you're going to become the private obsession of every Bureau agent in the Southwest. We hear stories that you'd like to expand your operation into the States—you'll be able to forget all about that. Your people won't even be able to come over to watch the dog races without getting collared. Believe me, it won't have been worth it."

The man's self-possession was marvelous. Whatever he felt about what he was hearing, it didn't show—you could have supposed he was listening to a weather report. And then he took a sip of his coffee and set the cup down on its saucer without a sound. And then, with that careless grace unknown among the Anglo-Saxons, he shrugged his shoulders.

"Among gentlemen, Mr. Havens, these things are taken for granted. So tell me, what is this important favor you require. What do you want?"

"I want Agustin Gomá."

XXIII

"Frank got a letter from his brother who works for the OPA in Fort Wayne, and he says they'll probably stop meat rationing by spring. Frank thinks that means the war could be over by the end of the year and then maybe he could get posted back to Springfield, near my mother. I certainly do hope he's right, I *cer*tainly do. I *cer*tainly am getting tired of not having enough water to do the laundry more than twice a month, and you can *keep* the quaint Indian jewelry and the Gila monsters. Just let things get warmed up enough so you can hope to get the chill out of your bones and you have to fight the rattlesnakes for the backyard. Lord! Can you imagine what it'll be like to be able to walk into a grocery store and pick up a pound of butter again? I'm so *damn* sick of this war—you'll pardon my French, girls—but I'm so *damn* sick of this war that I could *scream.* And I think it's all Roosevelt's fault that it's gone on so long; Frank says they could've had the Japs beat last year if they'd . . ."

As was usual during the regular Saturday morning car trip into Santa Fe, Mindy Applewhite was driving everyone into a stunned silence that would last at least until midway through lunch, when patience would wear thin and everybody else would begin talking at once out of sheer desperation. It would be either that or someone would have to tell her to shut up, which had happened once and had lead to an outbreak of tears.

But for once Jenny didn't mind if the back of the car was filled with the clackety-clack of that high, toneless voice. It kept out the sound of other voices and allowed her to let her head rest against the window and feel the cold that came pressing in, almost like the palm of someone's hand, from the pale gray winter that sped past outside. It was all right about Mindy because Mindy provided the perfect excuse to say nothing, to withdraw into herself and try to restore something like a little surface calm. For the last couple of days the complexities of her one little life seemed to be following one of those upward curves that were printed in the newspaper to explain how everything was getting better or more expensive or more dangerous. She kept waiting for the air-raid sirens to go off.

And Mindy went on and on, reciting the gospel according to her husband, just as if he were in on the secrets of the universe, and in the one person who listened the responses had simplified themselves down to simple envy. At least someone in the wide world didn't have any reason to think she had fashioned her own private disaster.

"You must've thought I was really stupid—you must've laughed and laughed. I oughta kill you—I oughta kill the pair of you."

And she had sat on the edge of the bed, not the least afraid, feeling nothing but a dead calm at the center of shame for herself and pity for poor Hal, her husband whom she had wronged with more than her adultery. It struck her, as a species of miracle, that she was probably closer to loving him at that moment than at any time in their married life.

"There isn't anybody else," she had said, lying only a little. "I don't know what's set you off, but if it hasn't worked out for us you don't have to look for anything as melodramatic as that. Don't you think it would be simpler if we just got a divorce?"

He stood there in the bedroom doorway, his khaki undershirt stained with sweat as his chest heaved and the big, raw-looking muscles in his arms looked like they were ready to burst. He had come home early, declined his dinner, and then lay on his back for an hour, straining under a 150-pound barbell before he could bring himself to speak.

"What kind of a woman are you?" he asked, wiping his mustache with the back of his hand. His eyes narrowed. It wasn't a real question—Hal gave the impression of having learned about marriage from the Sunday afternoon matinees, and it was just the sort of thing Melvyn Douglas might have asked Joan Crawford. "Don't you care about anything? Don't you at least care that you're married?"

"What are you getting at, Hal?"

And so he told her. It wasn't something anybody had let him in on—this was an idea he had talked himself into while he sulked and sweated and tried to fix on just where things had come unraveled. And it wasn't even the first time. If he had hit it right, that was just an accident. He had been wrong the time before. It was just the obvious choice, and he was an obvious man.

For a long moment she was silent. She simply sat there on the bed, staring at him, not quite sure what to say. Apparently Hal interpreted that as an angry denial, because he seemed to wilt a little.

"I know there's someone else. I haven't looked at another woman since the night we met, but I guess it hasn't been that way for you." He paused for a moment, seeming to wait for her to answer, and when she didn't he glanced away. "I'm not so dumb I don't know when a woman's making a fool out of me, and when I find the bastard I'm gonna kill him."

And if he wasn't quite as sure as he sounded, that didn't take anything away from his suffering. And if he wasn't going to make good on his threats—and if they both knew it—that didn't speak against him either.

After ten minutes he went slamming out the front door, probably to do the sensible thing and go drinking with his friends. She waited for him until after midnight and then went to bed. He was asleep beside her when she woke up the next morning.

There was no repetition at breakfast, although perhaps that would have been better than the grim silence with which he ate his eggs and hash brown potatoes.

Could he know? Was that possible? She had heard it as the standard warning that was issued to Army brides, over and over, at each of the three bases where they had lived since their marriage—a military post was a small world where it was difficult to keep secrets. So don't have any secrets. Either live as if each day is Mother's Day, or don't care. You would be forgiven anything, it seemed, except trying to have something all to yourself. Life was too short and too dull for that.

Maybe after all someone had seen something and whispered it into Hal's ear—or didn't men gossip like that?

For a moment—just a moment—she wondered if perhaps Erich . . .

But why should he have done that? And how? It seemed unlikely that he would have marched right up to the security office and filled out a form announcing himself as Jenny Springer's lover. Hal would have beaten him to paste, and Hal had spent the evening at home last night, not in the base stockade. His knuckles hadn't even been bruised.

And his accusations had had a vague, made-up quality, as if he hadn't really believed them himself. She "must have a new boyfriend," was the way he had phrased it, which didn't carry a lot of conviction.

Sitting alone in their little prefabricated bungalow, she had been overwhelmed with a sense of what it probably would have been like for Hal if he had believed it. He wasn't a thoughtful man; he would never have been able to explain something like that to himself. It would have become his failure, not hers, and he would have let it twist him around out of all recognition. Nothing, nothing he had ever said or done or failed to do could have entitled her to work that misery on him. If she had to live the rest of her days as his wife, preparing his dinner and listening to the news from his job and sleeping in his bed at night . . . They could never be happy but at least she wouldn't have turned his life into garbage.

So she would have to begin living through Mother's Day.

She took a kind of comfort in the simplicity of it. The terror of having a lover had been its complexity, its endless suspensions of breath while you developed an intimacy with the dread that tainted every moment. Anything was better than that. She wouldn't mind breaking Hal's heart so much, if she could just be sure that that was all she broke.

Lunch, when it finally came to that, was more than she could bring herself to manage, so she begged her way out of it. When they parked the car, and the sound of the engine shutting off snapped her out of her trance, she leaned forward with her left hand resting on the top of the front seat and smiled and said something about breakfast having given her a headache. It wasn't her turn to buy, so no one seemed to mind very much.

The sky that was visible over the tops of the buildings was a sinister, transparent gray, as if it gazed down on the works of men with contemptuous disapproval. Jenny shuffled along, staring down at the sidewalk as it disappeared under her feet, not knowing where to go, feeling as if she should be out of sight somewhere. All the way down, she hadn't really known what she was going to do—Erich would be waiting for her, even now, but she hadn't known if she would have the nerve to go.

And now she did.

Because he too had some claim on her. She had an obligation to tell him, to his face, that it was over between them. It was both the right and the wisest thing to do.

The entrance to the La Ventana Hotel looked just as it had the last time and every other time she had been there. A seedy place, a fitting scene for the sort of affair she had been conducting for . . . how long? With a certain uncomfortable thrill, she realized it had been over two months. The La Ventana hadn't seemed so terrible then.

The man at the desk didn't glance up when she stepped

across the lobby—had she become such a fixture as that? She made her way slowly up the stairwell, forcing herself along, counting the cigarette burns on the carpet to concentrate her mind on each step, as if each few yards contained the end of her journey. She could feel her heart pounding. It was almost painful; she was surprised people didn't come rushing out into the corridor to see what the racket was.

It was the same room. Somehow Erich always contrived to get the same room—perhaps he had come to some sort of understanding with the desk clerk. Perhaps he had brought so many women here that he had developed a certain proprietorship. Their regular patron.

When the door opened, Erich simply stood there. His eyes were wide, and he hardly seemed to know what to do. He seemed surprised to see her.

"Good morning," he said finally, smiling suavely and stepping aside to let her in. The voice was just a little too smooth, as if he were reasserting his control over himself. "You're early—what happened to your little luncheon group?"

Jenny came inside, wondering, quite irrelevantly, why men were always so contemptuous of women enjoying each other's company, as if they should properly just fade out of existence when there wasn't a man around. She wished, just at that moment, that she could nourish a little resentment, but she couldn't—she seemed to be past having any right to pride.

She let him close the door behind her and stood in the center of the room, holding the strap of her purse with both hands. Erich came over and put his hands on her shoulders, but she twisted away. He didn't seem to care; it was just a gesture he had been expected to make. He smiled, apparently waiting for her to answer his question.

"I wasn't hungry."

The smile broadened into something very like a grin—he was flattered. He thought she was saying that she couldn't wait to be with him. And suddenly she discovered that she could resent him after all.

"I can't stay," she went on, staring down at her hands. "And I won't be coming back here." She looked up, because all at once her fear and shame had left her—it was only Erich she was talking to, and there was no way he could hurt her anymore. "I don't want to see you again."

The smile on his face became sympathetic, almost patronizing, and he seemed about to put his hands on her again. "Are you angry because I'm leaving?"

"No. It's better that way. Goodbye, Erich."

There, she had said it. What could he do, except perhaps tell someone that Jenny Springer had been his mistress? She would weather the gossip, if there was any, and then she would be free. And then she would do the right thing by Hal, whatever that might turn out to be.

That was what she was thinking as she crossed back to the door. And then she put her hand on the knob and opened the door, and there was Hal.

He was just standing there, in the carefully pressed olive green uniform he had put on that morning, his feet slightly apart and his hands down at his sides. She noticed that he had missed a little spot on the left side of his jaw when he had shaved that morning, and that the creases around his eyes seemed a trifle deeper. There was time to notice all of this because time itself seemed to have slowed to nothing, just like her heart. She wasn't sure that it hadn't stopped altogether. Perhaps it had. Perhaps in another instant she would simply fall down dead of surprise.

And then she noticed that in his right hand, which was hanging down limply at his side, just as if the nerves in his arm had been severed, he was holding his service automatic. That brought her back to life.

The pistol came up until it was aimed at a spot just a little under her breastbone.

"Get back in there," he growled, his eyes narrowing as his face grew rigid with suppressed rage. He took a step forward, as if he meant to prod her backward with the muzzle of his gun.

What did he want? What could he possibly be doing here?

She had forgotten all about Erich. When she glanced back over her shoulder to see what was making that peculiar wheezing sound, she was surprised to see him. He was standing behind her, bent like an old man, his breath coming in rapid, rasping gulps. His face looked as if it had been bleached white, and it was covered with sweat. In the course of a few seconds he seemed to have been transformed into a frightened, elderly wreck.

It was all just too silly. What was he so worried about?

With a clarity that surprised her, Jenny saw all at once that there was no longer anything she had to fear from anyone. Hal wasn't going to shoot her—he wasn't even going to shoot Erich. Hal couldn't kill anyone; he was just trying to work out some way to be a man still in his own eyes. Presently, when he had threatened and talked and satisfied himself that no one would think he was a coward—and he wasn't a coward, he was only hurt and humiliated—then he would put the gun down and they would all leave this place as if nothing had happened. And nothing would have happened.

And as for Erich—well, how could anyone be frightened of him?

"It isn't what it seems, Hal," she said, her voice perfectly smooth as she stood there, clutching her handbag. She tried very hard to keep from looking at the gun. "We'll go home now, and I'll explain."

"*You'll* explain! I like that."

The muscles in his face tensed into a cruel, painful grin. It was himself he was hurting—Jenny wanted to reach out and touch him on the arm, to give him some small sign of human sympathy, but of course it was too late for anything like that. So she remained where she was, being careful not to move or appear frightened or to seem to notice that her life was being threatened. The important thing was to keep from forcing Hal into anything he would regret later.

And then, as if surprised and annoyed at the intrusion, he seemed to notice Erich for the first time.

"Who's this guy?" he asked, pointing at him with the automatic—the thing might have been a pencil for all the harm he meant; he gave the impression he had forgotten he was holding it.

Erich looked at the pistol, and his eyebrows shot up. And then he actually smiled. He smiled and nodded, just as if they were being introduced at a dinner party.

"How are you?" he said. The man was an idiot.

Hal Springer and his wife exchanged a glance of mute incomprehension, and Jenny shrugged. They stood there like that for a moment, like the three points of a triangle—Jenny and Erich about nine feet apart, and Hal still just inside the threshold, the door still standing open behind him. No one, apparently, had thought to close it, so they were acting out their little drama in plain view of anyone who might walk past in the corridor.

It occurred to Jenny that perhaps she ought to say something, but she decided that, no, she wouldn't. It might be better this way—there were limits to how shrill things could become this way. They weren't quite alone. The open door was almost a sort of insurance.

And then, suddenly, they really weren't alone any longer. Behind Hal's back, as something no more distinct than a vague shape, there appeared a fourth someone. He simply stood there, peering into the room over her husband's shoulder, an observer, like the casual witness to an accident.

It was a man, that was all Jenny knew with any certainty in that fraction of a second. He wasn't a very distinct figure; he seemed to carry his own shadow with him. Just a tall, dark man, nothing more.

And then he looked into her face, seeming to recognize her, as if they had known each other always. His finger crossed the thin line of his mouth, demanding her silence.

And then Jenny's eyes began to round as she realized, through some process she didn't even begin to understand, that this was the furthest thing from a neutral spectator. This man was different, as different from Hal and Erich as if he had belonged to some other species. It didn't matter that Hal's back was turned; no gun in the world would have helped him, not against this man who appeared to think he could compel obedience with a gesture.

She tried to speak. She opened her mouth, but nothing seemed to come out. Like a mouse charmed by a snake, there was nothing she could do except to stare. To stare, and wonder that Hal didn't sense his own danger.

"Then you're the other man," Hal said, still pointing with his pistol at Erich. It was astonishing, but he just went right on —he was the jealous husband, even now. The whole world had changed in the last few seconds, and he didn't even know. "I hitched a ride into town and waited—I knew where they'd park. And then I just followed her. It was easy. And now you're the one I have to —"

He never finished. By then there was a hand around his neck, with the middle finger and thumb pressing against his larynx—he was being strangled, but with a curious delicacy.

In the instant when he realized what was happening to him, Hal made a muffled little noise and the pistol in his hand began to jerk from side to side as he seemed to be pulling the trigger. Astonishingly, there was no flash, no sharp smell of burning gunpowder, no bang. The pistol wouldn't fire; it merely twitched at the end of Hal's arm, as if it were frantic to get away.

Why didn't he try to break loose? The fingers at his throat seemed to hold him with no more force than a woman's caress, and yet Hal's eyes were wide with helpless fear. His mouth opened and closed and the hand with the gun slowly sank back down to his side.

And then he fell—his legs might have been kicked out from under him, it was so sudden.

It was all over, almost before you could have realized anything had happened. He was lying there on the floor, twitching. He trembled and jerked as if an electric current were passing through him. His face was buried in the carpet, and his gun was still clutched loosely in his lifeless hand. Jenny couldn't have said how she knew that he was dead, but somehow it was obvious. Hal had been killed, just as neatly and quickly as an apple is plucked from its stem. He was dead.

The man standing in the door frame took a step forward and pulled the door closed behind himself. He was tall, dark, and slender almost to the point of seeming sickly. He was also strikingly handsome, something Jenny noticed, even at such a moment, with a strange detachment. It all might have been happening behind a sheet of glass.

He was dressed in what looked like some sort of uniform; she was sure she had seen the uniform before, probably in the movies, but she couldn't have placed it any more exactly than that.

He reached over and picked up the pistol, which by then had slid out of Hal's grasp and was lying on the floor beside him. He held it up, the handle pinched between his first finger and thumb, and smiled. He looked as if he were about to apologize.

"As you see," he said, his eyes fixed on Jenny's face, "he had neglected to cock the hammer."

XXIV

The negotiations that followed were long and complex, one gathered, and conducted entirely in German.

The tall dark man who had killed Hal was a perfect gentleman. He took Jenny by the elbow and led her to a chair, where she sat and stared at her dead husband and wondered what was going on. From where he was lying on the floor, Hal stared back through eyes that were growing increasingly lusterless and accusing. A thin trickle of blood came from the corner of his mouth, but otherwise he gave no sign of the sudden violence of his death. He just stared at her.

"*Von Niehauser, wir können die Frau nicht erst töten und sie dann noch dazu hier lassen. Man kennt mich hier! Von Niehauser, die Polizei! Wie könnten wir hier entfliehen? Wie . . . ?*"

Erich was highly excited, gesturing wildly with his hands and sweating, while the other man sat quietly on the corner of the bed and listened. Once in a while he would nod, or speak a few words, or gaze at Jenny for a few seconds and smile his strange, apologetic smile. She gathered that his name was von Niehauser, but somehow it seemed unnatural to think of him as having a name at all. He hardly seemed human enough for that. He seemed to have forgotten that there was a corpse lying not a yard away from his left foot.

It was obvious that they were discussing what to do with her. Jenny didn't need to understand the words to know that. It was clear enough from the panicky look that came over Erich's face every time he forgot himself enough to glance in her direction. She had decided that they probably would kill her—it seemed the inevitable thing—but the thought left her curiously unmoved. After all, what difference could it make?

And, anyway, that would be up to von Niehauser, whom in her mind she thought of merely as "him," as if they were alone in the room. They might as well have been—Hal was dead, and Erich was nothing. And she was as good as dead, so that just left von Niehauser. Him.

She wished he would do something about Hal. It seemed so cruel to just leave him there like that. It seemed so unfair, so much the final indignity. She wished she had the courage to say something. . . .

As if he could read her mind, von Niehauser got up from the bed suddenly, stripped off the counterpane, and spread it out over the body on the floor. Then he sat down again and appeared to forget all about it.

Nothing made sense anymore. Hal was a lump under a bed quilt, and Erich had been reduced to little more than an incomprehensible stream of foreign words, and the final arbiter of her life and future, a man whom twenty minutes ago she hadn't known existed, was close enough that she could have reached out and touched him but hardly seemed conscious that she was there.

As she held herself perched on the edge of the chair, Jenny realized for the first time how limited had been her experience of the world. Tragedy was a word she had learned in a high school English class, and death was as unreal as the mystery of the Holy Trinity. Both her parents were still alive, had never known a sick day in their lives, and her older brother was a naval lieutenant stationed in London, where his job was to write speeches for an admiral to read to women's clubs. Perhaps that was what she had held so bitterly against Hal, that he had cheated her out of the knowledge of genuine fear.

God knows, nothing had prepared her for the man who sat on the corner of the bed she had shared with Erich Lautner, who hardly seemed to move as he listened politely to Erich's hysterical pleading, who answered in a soft, cultured voice, who killed as effortlessly as another man might have crumpled up a piece of newspaper. Who looked at her—when he did look at her—as if she were a child, or a part of the furniture, or invisible.

God knows, she was frightened enough now, but not of death. Hal was dead. Lots of people were dead, and they didn't seem to mind. But they hadn't ever seen this man von Niehauser. That the world should hold such terrors, that was what was frightening.

"All right, Lautner," he said finally, and, for the first time, in English. "Have it entirely your own way."

He rose to his feet, as graceful a process as you could imagine, and turned to Jenny and, this time, didn't smile.

"As you can imagine, madam, we have been discussing what should be done with you. Your friend Erich is quite emphatic that we take you with us, since to leave you here, either alive or dead, would, of course, instantly connect him with the death of your husband."

"Is this really necessary, von Niehauser?" Erich Lautner was leaning against the wall, with his elbow thrown over the top of the dresser. He seemed to be completely exhausted, and his eyes were red-rimmed and puffy as he watched the other man the way a dog might watch his master weighing a stick in his hand. But von Niehauser hardly seemed to hear.

"Yes, it is necessary," he said finally, but to Jenny rather than to Lautner. "We must all understand precisely where we are—a man has been killed. Murdered, if you will."

Jenny glanced down at the lump under the bedspread, and then quickly away. She didn't know where to look anymore. She would have liked to cover her eyes with her hands, but that seemed such a pointless thing to do. After all, everything would still be there again when she took them away.

"You're the devil," she murmured, hardly loud enough to be heard. "I think I must be going crazy."

"As to that, madam, I shouldn't like to offer an opinion, but I can assure you that my own association with the powers of darkness extends no further than the Security Service of the German SS."

And then he smiled once more, a weary, apologetic smile, and Jenny found she had to fight down a temptation to begin screaming.

"Erich, you see, is a spy," he went on, making a casual, contemptuous motion in the direction of the dresser. "He was recruited by Reinhard Heydrich in 1939 and ordered to defect to the West, and now I've been assigned to bring him home so he can tell our scientists all about that frightful weapon the Americans are building here in New Mexico. You see, we have hopes of building one ourselves—first. Or perhaps you didn't know what all those men are doing up there on the Los Alamos Mesa."

She shook her head. She did know, but that too was supposed to be a secret. She wanted to tell him that she didn't want to know, but she could tell from the expression on his face that this terrible man wasn't interested in what she wanted.

"It's a bomb. They plan to drop it from an airplane, and it will explode a hundred feet or so above the ground. A city the size of, say, Manhattan would be more or less completely destroyed, and our own estimates are that it would probably kill ninety percent of the population within a two-kilometer radius. Such a weapon would of course decide the war. I'm sure you can appreciate why we would prefer to gain possession of it ahead of the Americans."

"Why are you telling me this?"

"As I said, madam, because we must all understand where we are."

With what seemed like a single impulse, both of them looked at Erich Lautner, who straightened up suddenly, as if he had been caught in some shameful act. He took a handkerchief out of his pocket and wiped his face, glancing back and forth between von Niehauser and Jenny and then, finally, down at the body on the floor.

"You must see, madam, that for Herr Lautner and myself this is no insignificant business. He wishes me to keep you alive because he would prefer that when the police find your husband they should not immediately go looking for him. They will figure everything out eventually, of course, but by then the two of us will be far beyond their reach—you see, we plan to leave for Germany at once. He thinks your murder would be an embarrassment, and there is something to what he says. So, if you will allow it, we will take you with us. You do not strike me as an hysterical woman, so, if you refrain from forcing me to kill you, you might even survive to return to this charming place."

With the slow sweep of his arm, he seemed to take in more than just the room, or even just Santa Fe, New Mexico. The gesture implied the whole country, what she might consider home, life itself.

"But I want you to understand the full extent of your lover's guilt," he went on, quite as though Erich were in another room. "We met in my quarters last night, and he gave me a very considerable amount of information on the Los Alamos project, and after he left I made detailed notes. I carry them with me—here." The point of his middle finger rested on his left shirt pocket.

"If I am caught, this material will be found on my person and will be quite enough to make sure Herr Lautner is convicted and hanged for espionage, but I want you to know all this so that he won't have any notion that there is any course open to him but coming with me. If you die, you see, his involvement in both your and your husband's death will be plain enough. And if we let you go, I'm sure I can count on you to do the patriotic thing and go straight to the police. Either way, if by then the both of us aren't aboard a ship headed for Germany, he can bid farewell to his life. So you are useful to me, madam, as a guarantee that there will be no turning back."

The smile never left his face. He could speak of murder and spying and a bomb that could kill millions of innocent people, and still he could smile and call her "madam" and be as polite as the man who took your order at Macy's. Perhaps he was the one who was crazy. What kind of a person was it who could do such things, and think such things, and smile and not seem to care?

"I am a warrior, madam," he said, in the tone one might have used talking to a child. "And I am used to dealing with unpleasant choices."

"What should we do about him?"

"Do?" Von Niehauser cocked an eyebrow and let his gaze follow Erich Lautner's arm down to the lump of bedspread in the middle of the floor. "Oh, that. Why should we do anything about that?"

"Are you mad, von Niehauser? You forget, this is my room! It is registered in my name! How long do you imagine it would be before the police sent out an alarm and had me arrested?"

"Did you bring your car?"

"Yes, of course I brought my car. What has this to do with my car?"

The two men stared at each other for a moment, and then von Niehauser shrugged his shoulders and turned aside. "Very well, then. Put him in my room. Try not to cover yourself with blood."

Lautner didn't seem to know quite what to do. After hesitating for several seconds, he leaned over at the waist, and stumbled and nearly fell as he tried to pick up Hal's body. He was breathing hard. He stood there, crouched, a pleading look in his eyes. Finally von Niehauser knelt down and folded the bedspread around the corpse, so that everything was concealed. Then he picked up the bundle and set it lightly in Lautner's arms.

"Put him in the bathroom," he said. "Be sure to listen for the lock clicking shut behind you, and hang out the 'Do Not

Disturb' sign." He opened the door, made sure there was no one outside in the corridor, and stepped back to allow Lautner to pass.

"He's dead, Erich. He can't hurt you." As he spoke, there was a malicious narrowing of his eyes.

Thus, for a few moments, Jenny and von Niehauser were left alone together, at opposite ends of the narrow bedroom. Jenny remained in her chair, giving the impression she thought of herself as confined there for life.

"I have not been mistaken, I trust. He was your husband?" Von Niehauser made a slight movement toward the door with his left hand.

"Yes."

"I assumed as much. My apologies, madam."

Her head jerked up angrily and she searched his face for some indication that he was mocking her, but his expression was grave and composed.

"Thank you."

There was one of those awkward silences that happen to people when they have too much to say to each other. Even when she wasn't looking at him, Jenny could feel his eyes on her. They seemed to burn right through.

"What are you going to do with me?" She asked finally, when she thought she might not be able to stand it another second. "Are you going to kill me, or what?"

"I don't really know—either that, or let you go as soon as you can do us no more harm. I would prefer that, but it's for you to decide." He smiled. The smile was somehow reassuring, as doubtless it was intended to be.

"And all that about the bomb—was that true?"

"Yes."

Neither of them had moved when Lautner opened the door and stepped back inside the room.

"There's still some blood on the rug," he said, staring stupidly down at a dark reddish smear shaped like the footprint of some large reptile.

"Clean it up, idiot."

Lautner's car was parked on a side street, about half a block from the hotel. They didn't all go together; von Niehauser led Jenny back to his room, where the bathroom door was mercifully shut. He picked up a small suitcase and a long leather sleeve that pretty obviously held a rifle of some sort. Then he walked her down the corridor, and across the lobby, and outside onto the sidewalk. All the time he kept a painful but unobtrusive grip on her arm, just above the elbow.

"Don't try to run away," he said to her quietly. "Your husband's automatic is in my belt, and if you force me to I'll kill you before you've had a chance to run five yards."

It wasn't so much a threat as a simple statement of fact, delivered in a voice that compelled belief. Thus for Jenny there were no decisions—the hand around her arm was like iron; she couldn't have gotten free anyway. All she had to think about was how to keep from falling down.

"You drive."

He stood by the curb, still holding Jenny by the elbow, watching Lautner move around the front of the car to the driver's seat. Then he opened the front door on the passenger's side and helped Jenny inside. Then he got in the back.

"Nothing's changed," he said, leaning forward so that he was speaking almost directly into her ear. "If we stop at a crosswalk, and you open your door, you'll be dead before your foot hits the pavement."

The car lurched forward and then squealed to a stop as Lautner put on the brakes. He was gripping the steering wheel so tightly that his knuckles were white.

"Slowly, Erich, no one is after us. And when we are out of town, I want you to remember the wartime speed limits and not exceed forty miles per hour. We shouldn't like to be stopped by the police."

On the outskirts of Santa Fe there was a jewelry shop with a clock the size of a frying pan in the window. As they passed Jenny could see that it was only a little after eleven-thirty—she had thought somehow that hours must have passed, but they hadn't. Forty minutes ago she had been thinking about squaring things with her husband and preserving what they would have after Erich Lautner had left town. And now Erich was leaving, and her husband was dead behind a locked bathroom door, and she had been kidnapped by a German spy who seemed to have stolen the secret of how to blow up half the world—her half.

Maybe she really would go crazy.

She had never been anywhere south of Santa Fe, so she was surprised to see how flat the country was. From Los Alamos you had the impression that everything was mountains, as far as the eye could see, but Highway 25 was like an ironing board. Here and there in the distance a pile of loose boulders would thrust up two or three hundred feet through the sandy ground—there was no graduation; they were just suddenly there, as if someone had left them behind by accident—but the road simply skirted around them, almost ignoring their existence. You had the feeling that you could have taken the car out of gear and coasted all the way to Albuquerque.

There was only the desert. Sometimes a line of barbed wire would run parallel alongside for a mile or two, but there was no indication of why anyone would want to enclose such barren ground: no houses, no cattle, no trees, nothing. The cold had long since withered the grass, so there was only the infrequent patch of snow, usually no larger than a bedsheet, to break the yellows and pale reds of this landscape.

Truly God must have forsaken her here, she thought.

There was hardly another car on the road. It was the war, of course; people weren't supposed to travel long distances by car. Every ten or fifteen minutes something, usually a truck, would swoosh by in the opposite lane, but they never passed anyone going in their direction. In the long straight stretches you could look backward and forward and see yourself alone from one horizon to the other.

Even when they came into Albuquerque, it wasn't very different. In the city itself—she supposed you had to call Albuquerque a city—there was plenty of traffic, but they left that behind as soon as they got away from the cross streets.

And besides, what difference did it make? There wasn't a second when she couldn't sense von Niehauser's eyes on the back of her neck. The man had a way of making his silent presence felt, just as surely as if he kept a strand of wire around your neck and you could feel the tugging of his fingers.

And Erich—Erich, the accomplice, the German spy since before the beginning of the war—Erich was even more afraid than she was. The flesh under his jaw was puffy and sallow, and he was sweating and breathing through his mouth. His eyes kept flickering up to the rear-view mirror—not to check the road behind them, but because of the man sitting in the back seat. What frightened him most, capture or flight?

And all that about the bomb—was that true?

Yes.

It was with a certain bitterness that Jenny Springer remembered how she had looked down on her husband because he had not contrived to take a more direct role in the war. She had seen all that as brave men in uniforms who fought their hand-to-hand way up a silver beach in Italy, and here the biggest battle of all was being waged within a few hundred miles of her front door. And Hal had been the very first casualty, without ever even knowing it.

"Turn on the radio."

It was the first time anyone had spoken in over two hours. Erich's head jerked around to stare over his shoulder—perhaps he hadn't believed his ears. But it was Jenny whom von Niehauser had been addressing.

"Please, madam," he said, smiling sadly, the lines around his eyes so deep they reminded you of the cracks in a plaster wall. "It will be a long journey. Would you perhaps see if you could find a little music?"

She tried, and after a few seconds of fumbling she found a station out of Socorro that was playing a scratchy recording of Glenn Miller's "Tuxedo Junction." Von Niehauser didn't seem to object.

They listened to the strange, throaty sound of the orchestra, and Jenny remembered having read somewhere that Glenn Miller had joined up and was over in England, playing concerts for the troops. Everybody was doing his bit, it seemed—even Hal had done his bit—and here she was, too frightened even to open her mouth.

There was no one else. Von Niehauser was taking the secret of this grotesque weapon with him, over the border into Mexico, and there was no one else to stop him. No one else even suspected.

The music stopped after a few minutes, and an announcer read the weather. ". . . Patrol has issued a travelers' warning. Hazardous conditions will prevail over the southern part of the state. So this might be a good weekend to stay home and conserve gas, folks. Ha, ha, ha."

Suddenly, and for the first time, Jenny felt a glimmer of hope.

"I have to go to the bathroom," she said.

XXV

"Very well, madam." Behind her she could hear the crinkle of the map von Niehauser kept on the seat beside him. "Lautner, there is a place a few miles ahead, called Hot Springs. We will need to stop for gasoline at any rate."

So it was to be as easy as that.

They never did see Hot Springs. Only the sign, and a side road, and a Standard Oil station that looked like it would tumble down with a hard look—the pumps were the kind that worked by hand, and you measured the gas by watching the level drop through a glass container in the top.

"You will accompany madam to the toilet, and you will wait outside the door until she is finished," von Niehauser said in his quiet voice as the car slowed to a stop. Erich nodded stiffly. "And you will bring her back to the car. Remember what will happen to you if she gets loose, my friend."

"You folks want y'r oil checked?"

The attendant looked about seventy years old and at least three weeks from his last shave. Engine grease had worked its way into the cracks in his gaunt, weathered face, and his eyes were nothing more than pinpoints of smeary blue. He was wearing jeans and scuffed, stained boots and a heavy parka with a hood that made him look faintly like a Dominican friar. Jenny dreaded what the bathroom would be like.

"That won't be necessary," von Niehauser said, leaning forward until his head was nearly next to Lautner's. "If you could just fill the tank."

"Sure, pal." He glanced through the windshield and frowned when he saw Jenny sitting on the front seat. "Facilities'r in the back, if anybody's int'rested."

It was probably about a forty-foot walk from the car to the rear of the station, and there was a steady, biting wind from the south that made you pull your coat around your shoulders. There was only the wind and the high-pitched grind of their shoes on the sand, nothing else. Jenny kept her eyes on the ground in front of her and tried to forget that she was a prisoner under guard.

"Try not to be too long," Erich said. His collar was turned up and the cold had brought tears to his eyes—at least, one assumed it was the cold. He stood with his back to the wind.

The "facilities" were remarkably clean. The linoleum floor was worn with polishing, and the sink fairly gleamed. There was a little bar of soap, still in its paper wrapping, lying on a glass shelf under the mirror. Jenny picked it up, hesitated for an instant as she seemed to weigh it in her hand, and then peeled off half the paper.

MURDER. BLUE PONT., LIC. 254767—was that right? She hoped so. CALL POLICE.

She stood staring at the mirror. Was there anything else she should add? She had thought at first of writing "spies," but she was afraid they might think that was a practical joke. They might still think so.

God, she hoped that old coot would get the urge pretty quick.

She was almost ready to leave—in fact, she had her hand on the doorknob—when she remembered to go back and give the toilet a flush. She waited, her heart pounding, leaning with one hand against the wall. That was a close one.

She went back, picked up the soap again, and drew a line under the word MURDER. And that would have to do it—she couldn't see what else there was that she could possibly add. She had had her moment of liberty, and this was the best use of it she could manage.

As she turned the knob, as soon as she heard the latch click back open, she felt the door rush in on her. The edge caught her in the shoulder; it bounced off and slapped against the wall. And there was Erich, standing in the washroom doorway. He looked up at the message on the mirror, and he grinned.

"I knew you would try something," he said, stepping inside. He pushed the door closed behind him. "It is lucky for you, my dear, that von Niehauser doesn't know you as well as I do. He wouldn't understand this."

It was a tiny room, and Erich was pressing hard against her. She could feel the edge of the sink, sharp against her buttocks. Possibly that was all that kept her from falling down.

She couldn't stand to look him in the face, but there was hardly any choice. He kept his hand on her arm, kneading it with his fingers until the muscle ached. It was hard to breathe.

"What are you going to do?"

"Do? Why should I do anything?"

He was still grinning. She could see the yellowish stains on his teeth and smell his aftershave. She had to think. She . . .

"You are such a clever girl," he went on, reaching up to touch her face, catching her under the jaw when she resisted. "It might actually work, you know. And von Niehauser is mad—he's crazy. If he thinks I'm going back with him to that . . ."

And at last she understood. Good old Erich—he didn't have any causes in this world. She should have known.

"But there's a price, you know. You have to tell them that he forced me. You have to help me get the notes back. But you'll do that, won't you, Jenny? We both have our secrets to protect, don't we?"

He thought he had her now—you could tell by the triumph in his voice. You don't tell on me and I'll return the favor. God, what a fool, to think that any of that could mean anything now."

"Yes." She forced herself to smile. "When the police come . . ."

"You have to tell them . . ."

"Yes."

"He made me. I never . . ."

"Yes."

"He's crazy. He would have . . ."

"Yes."

And then he covered her mouth with his own, forcing his tongue between her teeth. And she let him. She would have let him do anything. Whatever it would have taken.

As they walked back to the car, with his arm through her own, they could see von Niehauser standing beside one of the gasoline pumps, talking to the attendant. They looked like conspirators.

"I was tellin' him," the attendant said, turning to Lautner as they approached. "Radio says there's a big storm comin' up from Mexico—be here by the mornin'. Hope you folks ain't got too far t' go."

His tiny blue eyes were worried—they were the only things left in his face that seemed to have any powers of expression at all.

"Twelve point five gallons. That'll be a buck twenty-nine—I don't set the prices."

Lautner counted out the money and the gasoline coupons, keeping his back to von Niehauser as he did it.

"You know, you really ought to do something about that washroom of yours," he murmured, like someone confiding a secret to a friend. "It's filthy in there—no place for a lady."

Perhaps the eyes weren't all that was left alive. It was his gas station, his pride. He looked like MacArthur contemplating the fall of Corregidor.

Somehow the stop for gas seemed to have worked a change in von Niehauser. He appeared more relaxed. Almost as soon as they were back on the highway, he pulled a paper bag out from between his feet and dropped it on the seat in front of him.

"The old man sold me some sandwiches," he announced. "And a few bottles of something called Squirt. It's nearly five—I thought you might be hungry."

"What is it?"

With his right hand, and keeping his eyes on the road ahead, Lautner opened the bag and felt around inside. He brought out a triangular package wrapped in heavy waxed paper. "Open it for me, Jenny."

It turned out to be tunafish. The odor flooded the car, making her feel slightly sick—she liked tunafish as a rule. It was strangely disgusting to watch Erich eat the thing as he drove.

"Have one, Jenny," he said. "It's good."

"No, thanks."

"How about you, von Niehauser?"

"Thank you, no. I seem to have lost the habit."

When he was finished, he asked for one of the bottles, which von Niehauser opened with the flat side of a folding knife he took from his pocket.

"This stuff is awful."

"Yes. Turn on your headlights, Erich. It's beginning to get dark." Their little party seemed to have fallen flat.

In the desert, the light lingers. At five o'clock the sky was merely a pale, luminous gray—true night was still almost an hour away.

But somehow the mere fact of the headlights seemed to make the air darken. It was only very gradually that you could see the faint, yellowish smear on the road ahead, but the sense of isolation was strong. You had the distinct impression that this arid, heartless landscape was collapsing in around you. The stillness was terrible.

"According to the map, we should be approaching the junction with state road 26. You will wish to turn to the right there."

Lautner nodded in the direction of the rear-view mirror, and his eyes flickered toward Jenny, who sat all the way across the seat from him, as if she couldn't get far enough away.

Where were the police? Hadn't that old fool gone into the washroom and seen the mirror? Had he imagined it was some kind of prank? What kind of idiot would think that? He had seen von Niehauser, hadn't he?

She had tried to keep some track of time since they had left the gas station, but it was difficult. She wasn't wearing a watch and, under the circumstances, she didn't think she could just trust to her impressions. There was only the car's odometer—Erich was driving a shade over forty miles per hour, and they had come about nineteen miles. That made it, what? Twenty-eight and a half minutes. A little less.

How would it work? If the State Police had a car out on the roads they would send that, but they had gas rationing too. Probably they had had to cut back on their patrols. They probably had an office in Hot Springs. Or they might send one out from Las Cruces—she had seen a road sign a few miles back, and Las Cruces was forty miles to the south. And now von Niehauser wanted to turn off onto a side road. If they came from Las Cruces, with the lead he had, they would probably miss him.

But if they came from Hot Springs—and if they believed her message—*they* wouldn't be held back by any speed limits. So they might catch him before the turnoff. Or they might have, if they had even sent a car. What were the chances of that now, after twenty-eight minutes? Not very good.

It was von Niehauser who saw them first.

"Didn't you notice anything, you fool?" he shouted. "Don't you use your mirrors? There's the junction—get onto the side road at least."

Jenny twisted around to have a look through the rear window—after such an outburst, would she dare not?—and she saw, very faintly, the glimmer of a headlight. It was a few seconds before she understood what could have alarmed von Niehauser so much, and then, gradually, she was able to make it out. Whoever was back there must be doing close to seventy miles an hour.

With a lurch that almost sent her sprawling into Erich's lap, the car made a sharp right turn onto state road 26. The sound of the tires was like a woman screaming—at that precise instant, just as they began to straighten out, she could hear the slow whine of a siren and she saw a red light flashing from the car behind them. It was the police all right, and they had figured out who they were supposed to be after. She felt like cheering.

"Slow down," von Niehauser barked. His face was set and expressionless, and he seemed coiled up inside like a snake. "We don't know what they want, and there's nothing to be gained by trying to outrun them. When we get a few hundred yards farther on, pull over. And try to remember that you are an innocent motorist—possibly they only want to issue us a speeding ticket."

He didn't believe that—you could read it in his eyes. The war is here, Jenny thought to herself. She was looking at a man getting ready to die.

Suddenly there was nothing left to cheer about.

It seemed to take forever. The car drifted to a slow stop—you could look out the window and count the tufts of dead grass as the engine growled and died away. Erich switched off the ignition and looked at her sideways, smiling faintly. He swallowed hard. He was sweating. But still, he smiled.

Von Niehauser, fortunately, didn't see. He was trained on the rear window like a cannon, as if he believed he could kill with just his eyes if he looked hard enough. You couldn't see anything except the back of his head, of course, but his very hair seemed to be on the alert.

It was then, watching him as he watched the car behind them, that Jenny began to grow genuinely afraid. Because the police didn't settle a thing, not just by being there. This one wasn't going to go along quietly.

"Do nothing. Merely wait." The voice seemed to be sounding from an immense distance. "Make them come to us."

The police car stopped about fifty feet back. The siren slid down about four octaves, growing steadily louder until it cut out at about a sixth below middle C. The red light kept on winking like a bad joke. There were two men inside. They were wearing the flat-brimmed hats that seemed to be standard with state troopers everywhere. They just waited. For what seemed like a long time, but probably wasn't more than five or six seconds, they simply sat in their car, as if they expected Erich to get out and come to them.

"Do nothing—merely wait." It was no longer clear that von Niehauser was speaking to anyone. He didn't look back. He didn't move. He hardly did more than whisper. "We are tourists, on our way to Deming where we expect to meet a friend."

Deming? Where in God's name was Deming?

And then the two highway patrolmen got out. The doors pushed open on both sides, and first one and then the other got out. They didn't hurry. One of them, the driver, was very fat.

Wilma Bragg had gotten stopped once when they were all on their way back to Los Alamos. It was about three months after Jenny arrived, when everything that happened still seemed unique and completely strange. Wilma hadn't given a signal, or something like that, and the troopers pulled her over. Only one of them had gotten out; the other one had stayed in the car. It had seemed the usual thing—why should it take two grown men just to issue a moving violation notice? But perhaps von Niehauser didn't know that.

Of course, it was impossible to misunderstand their intentions when, as they came around the front of their cruiser, they both drew their revolvers.

It was a bad moment in the car. Von Niehauser suddenly had Hal's service pistol in his hand—Jenny had had her eyes on him the whole time, and she didn't recall that he had moved; but there it was—and Erich was clutching the steering wheel with one hand and breathing in short, ragged gulps as he stared back over his shoulder at the two policemen. And Jenny was trying her best to remember what it was she had thought would happen when she scrawled that message on the washroom mirror. Not this. Certainly not this.

"We haven't got a chance," Erich said abruptly, his voice thick and gravelly, as if from years of disuse. "Did you hear me, von Niehauser? We'll get killed—you can see that."

Von Niehauser turned around, very slowly, and smiled. All the tension seemed to have gone out of him. He seemed at peace with himself. He seemed to welcome what was coming.

"At least there's no pretense here. And if we die, then we die."

Erich simply stared at him—struck dumb, it seemed, shocked into helpless silence by the staggering, inexplicable transparency of the thing. Von Niehauser wasn't going to surrender. As far as Erich Lautner was concerned, he might as well have been watching the man turn himself into a werewolf.

And then, quite suddenly, from one instant to the next, he screamed. It was a loud, high-pitched scream of more than animal terror; it seemed to make the stillness shatter like glass.

The sound was still trembling in the air when Erich's door popped open, something it seemed to do of its own accord. Erich just went with the door—all at once he was outside, crouched and running. He was holding his arms out at his sides, heading obliquely toward the policemen, and he was shouting something, but his voice was too shrill and cracked for anyone to make out what he was saying.

The events of the next few seconds seemed to stretch out over hours. Jenny was sitting on her knees on the front seat; she could watch it all happen so clearly, just as if time had been slowed down almost to nothing for her particular benefit. And there wasn't anything she could do.

It began when one of the policemen—the thin one, the one who hadn't been driving—raised his pistol and fired. Maybe he thought he saw something, or maybe he was just startled. Either way, no one was ever going to know. The bullet caught Erich square in the neck, and his shouting stopped, and he pitched over face first onto the road.

Jenny began to fill her lungs to shout something—there was just an instant when that still seemed to be possible—and then she stopped short. Something had changed. She couldn't define what it was, but something had happened, something that made her scream suddenly irrelevant. She could do anything she wanted and it wouldn't make any difference.

And then she understood. She was alone.

The back door was open, and von Niehauser was gone. He just wasn't there. She couldn't understand it. He was gone—he had left her there alone.

"God help us," she heard herself whispering.

She was perfectly aware that this was the moment to duck. What she should have done was to get her head down as quickly as possible, to hit the floor and stay there until it was all over, but she couldn't move. Nothing on earth could have induced her to move. She couldn't even turn her head away. All she could do was to witness in helpless fascination. Volition had nothing to do with it.

It was all over in an instant. There was a blur of sound that she dimly understood to be gunfire. The two policemen were firing wildly, not seeming to know which way to aim, and then the big one seemed to kick backward with his right leg, just as if it were being pulled from behind, and then his whole body began to twist wildly—he must already have been dead; he was being jerked around like a child's doll, and nothing alive could have moved like that. And he collapsed to the ground. He bounced—at least, it looked like he bounced—and then he was still.

What happened to the other one was less mysterious but, if that was possible, more terrible. He was standing by the side of the road; you could have thought he was at target practice. And then his arm fell down to his side, just as if it had grown tired, and he went on standing there as the bullets tore into his chest, making little black circles on the front of his light brown jacket. Once, twice—he didn't seem to notice them. And then once more. He finally looked down, as though to see what was happening, and then he collapsed forward, sinking onto his knees first. And then he went over on his face.

Neither of them moved. There was no sound.

She had no idea how long she sat there staring. Probably not very long, but it felt like half her life. And then, cautiously, afraid of what more there might be to see, she peeked out of the side window.

Von Niehauser was lying in the withered grass by the side of the road. And he wasn't moving either.

She began edging toward the open door on the other side, the one through which Erich had run to his death. It wasn't until she was outside, standing on the road, that she felt the sting from the wind; it carried a strange, acrid smell. She imagined for a moment it was the smell of blood, but she knew that was ridiculous.

There was a bullet hole in the rear window of the car—odd that she hadn't noticed that. Had they been shooting at her too? It seemed strangely unimportant now.

Erich was dead, there couldn't be any doubt about that. He was lying on his face, in a huge pool of blood that looked almost black. She turned him over and found that his eyes were still open. They wouldn't close all the way.

One of the policemen was still alive. The big one was lying on his side, and when she knelt down next to him his lips seemed to be trying to form some word. She waited there with him for the minute or so until he was gone too.

She sat down beside von Niehauser, if only because she was suddenly too tired to go any further. After a few moments she reached down to press her finger against the side of his neck—she had read somewhere that that was the best place to feel for a pulse. She didn't expect to find one.

And then, all at once, as if recoiling from her touch, he moved. She drew back her hand as though from something burning and watched as, slowly, and with obvious suffering, he rolled away from her and onto his side.

The pistol was still in his hand—and pointed directly at her head—and he was grinning, whether in pain or from some twisted feeling of triumph it was impossible to know.

"As you see, madam," he said, his voice nothing more than a tense gasp. "As you see, we are not quite finished yet."

XXVI

He was very bad. He had been shot twice; one bullet had shattered his left elbow and the other had taken him in the small ribs, just under his right lung. His arm was soaked in blood all the way down to his fingers. There was no way of knowing how it was inside his chest.

"But alive, madam. As you see, still alive."

It was painful just to watch him as he struggled to his feet—he must have been in agony. For a moment, as he stood braced against the side of the car, she thought he was weaving so badly that he might simply collapse. But he got hold of himself.

After a few minutes he seemed to forget all about his wounds. His eyes narrowed as he studied his surroundings, and finally, with a wave of his pistol, he ordered her to follow him as he began walking stiffly in the direction of the two dead policemen. He took the revolvers out of their hands and stripped the gunbelt from one of them—the thin one, who had died so hard. He reloaded one of the revolvers from the gunbelt and then threw the other one, along with Hal's automatic, into the field on the other side of the road.

"I was out of bullets—you should have killed me when you had the chance," he said, and then he glanced down again at the body at his feet and frowned. "We are only about a quarter of a mile from the main road. A parked police car might not attract any notice, but these corpses will. You will have to drag them out of sight, madam—I fear I have not the strength to do it myself."

He pointed to a ditch that ran along parallel to the road.

Jenny simply stared at him. It was the most appalling suggestion she had ever heard in her life.

But finally, when she saw that he meant it, that he was prepared to kill her if she did not do exactly as he said, she went over to one of the policemen and grabbed him by the coat sleeve. He wouldn't move.

"I have learned from experience that it is easier if you pick them up by the legs."

It was horrible. They left thick smears of blood behind them on the asphalt, their arms trailing limply along like pieces of heavy rope. Erich was the worst. The whole side of his face was caked with blood.

"It's over now, isn't it," she said, her breast heaving with more than merely fatigue as she rested against the police car, staring down at the three bodies that filled the ditch, head to foot, as if they were playing hide-and-seek. "You don't have the secret now. You don't have Erich anymore."

Von Niehauser merely smiled.

"I too am a scientist, madam. And before I came I knew which questions needed to be answered." He touched his breast pocket. "I have my notes and my memory—Herr Lautner and I had a long conversation the other evening. His presence in Berlin would have been a convenience, but it will not be vital. I think I know enough to help my people build their bomb."

So it had all been for nothing. They stood facing each other, perhaps no more than twenty feet apart, and Jenny found she had to blink hard to keep back her tears. Three people were dead, and nothing had changed. The war was still right here.

"And now, madam, the time has come when we must decide your own particular fate."

He stood there, in the center of the road, listing a little to one side, staying alive, it would seem, by sheer force of will. The man had two bullet holes in him, was probably bleeding internally, and he seemed to dismiss all that as if it hardly mattered.

"I ask myself what could have brought the police down on us," he went on, his face hardening. "I ask myself why Lautner bolted like that, what he expected from those two—I'm not such a fool as to imagine that he was all eagerness to help his country in its hour of peril. And then I remembered that gas station, where the two of you were alone."

"I left a message—Erich knew." What the hell. She squared her shoulders. She would at least show him he wasn't the only one who could fight back. He had obviously figured it out for himself anyway.

"Then you are a brave woman," he said. "Braver than most men, braver than Lautner. I don't blame you. I would have done the same thing in your place. Doubtless you could face death as fearlessly as most, but unfortunately this will not be your opportunity to prove it. Because, you see, I have need of you now. Get in the car."

She tried, except that, just at first, she couldn't seem to move. Was there such a thing as delayed fear? She had felt courageous enough when she was reasonably sure that von Niehauser planned to shoot her within the next fifteen or twenty seconds, but now, having been reprieved, she rediscovered her terror of him. She had the distinct impression that if she risked taking a step forward she would probably fall flat on her face.

Von Niehauser had a simple way out of the difficulty, however. He just cocked his pistol and aimed it at her head.

"I am not sure that my wounds will allow me to drive, madam. But if you decline to help me, I shall have no choice but to leave you here with a bullet through your face and manage on my own."

And that was how Jenny Springer found her legs. One foot at a time—right, left, right, left. It got easier as she went along. She was fresh out of heroism, she discovered; it was easier to stay alive.

"I haven't driven a car in two years," she said, settling in behind the wheel. She adjusted the front seat forward a few inches. The key, surprisingly, was still in the ignition.

"Then this will give you an opportunity to practice," von Niehauser answered dryly. He was on the seat beside her, and his pistol was pointed in the general direction of her heart.

"Shouldn't we do something about that?"

She glanced significantly at the bloodstains on the sleeve of his overcoat—the bullet had torn a huge ragged hole in the fabric, like a wound in its own right.

"I hardly think this is the place for that. I have a first-aid kit in my suitcase, and we only have another two hours or so to drive before we reach our destination—or, at least, a place where we can stop with relative safety. That will be soon enough."

It was the first time she had seen his face close up since they had stopped, and the skin around his eyes and nose was the color of buckskin. He was perspiring heavily. He looked withered. He looked like he was dying. Only two hours—two hours without painkillers, two hours in which to bleed away his life a little more.

Why should anything be that important to anybody?

She turned the key and listened as the engine coughed and came back to life. She would drive the car, because she hadn't any more excuses and, anyway, she was no match for this man.

They pulled away, leaving the main road and the dead behind them.

It was getting dark. They had long since left the paved roads and were bumping over a dirt track that was passable only because the ground had been frozen hard for weeks. Von Niehauser had tied his bad arm to his belt with a packing strap he had found in the trunk, but their lurching progress along this thread of a mountain road must have been almost unbearable for him.

The map was neatly folded on the back seat. He never looked at it—he seemed to have committed it to memory. The revolver rested in his lap, like a small animal that had gone to sleep.

The country had changed, almost as soon as they had left Highway 25. The land was rising again, becoming more broken and ragged as the mountains—abrupt and raw, with hard, sharp faces of broken stone—crowded closer and closer in on them. Except for the road itself, the last evidences of human presence had long since been left behind.

"The road will fork in a few miles. Stay to the left. I shouldn't think it will be much longer."

It was strange, considering that he had been shot to pieces and was probably half dead from loss of blood, but all along his attitude toward her had been conciliatory, even gentle. He talked to her as if she were a frightened child, and his voice seemed to reflect none of the terrible physical suffering that was etching itself so clearly into his face. The threats had never been repeated; the gun was always there but seemed to have been forgotten. It was almost as if he had decided they were allies, that he had made some decision to trust her. Or perhaps he was simply becoming accustomed to her, or the pain and the bleeding had taken their toll and he was beginning to get careless. At any rate, she had almost ceased to be afraid of him. And, if he wanted to trust her, that might be something that would come in handy later on.

He looked awful, worse and worse as the time passed. It seemed a labor for him even to close his eyes. But the mastery over himself never weakened—so maybe entertaining any hopes of catching him off guard were just so much wishful thinking.

At last, there it was, a NO TRESPASSING sign and a rutted trail that led away from the road to the crown of a hill, as barren a place as God ever made. There were no indications that anyone had been there in months.

The cabin, which they saw as soon as they had skirted around to the other side of the hill, was a tight little box made of rough boards. For some reason, the sight of it filled Jenny with a curious elation.

She nosed the car up to the side wall, which happened to be windowless, switched off the engine and the headlights, and waited.

"I am afraid I shall have to be so ungallant as to ask you to carry the bags inside," von Niehauser said quietly, sounding as if he had just awakened from a profound sleep. "You will find the front door unlocked."

She opened her door, stepped outside, and was surprised all over again at how cold it was—the wind at this altitude was much stronger and almost palpably laden with ice. The sky was black now, but there was a bright full moon that shone like a searchlight.

The cabin, as it faced south, seemed to be perched on the edge of a saucer. The land sank slowly for about a mile and then began to rise again until it ended abruptly in a chain of mountains that stretched in both directions for as far as you cared to look. In between, the ground was dotted with rocks, some of them the size of a refrigerator and some no bigger than a man's hand. One wondered what could have possessed anyone to build here.

She opened the trunk and got out the long leather rifle sleeve and a small leather suitcase held together with two beltlike straps. Erich's bag was there, a brown wooden thing with metal corners, covered with travel stickers; it gave her a strange feeling to see it, almost as if it had been his corpse tucked up there next to the spare tire, instead of just a battered box with a pair of canvas handles. She decided to leave it where it was. If von Niehauser wanted it, he could come and get it himself.

There was an old-fashioned iron stove standing in the precise center of the cabin floor, and an orange crate filled with kindling next to the door. Von Niehauser was already feeding a tiny flame when she came in. Within a few minutes you could feel the heat.

"And now, with your assistance, I can see to this," he said. He was sitting at the foot of one of the two twin beds that were jammed into that corner, at right angles from one another. He was untying his left arm from his belt, and when it dropped lifelessly to his side his head snapped away and a faint, whimpering groan came from between his clenched teeth. It was several seconds before he let his breath out.

And then, slowly, he began to undo the buttons first of his

overcoat, and then of the military tunic underneath, and finally of his shirt. He slipped his right hand inside and began feeling around, exploring the wound on that side, and then he moved his fingers to the back of his rib cage.

"Good—I can feel the bullet. It's resting directly under the skin, so there should be no difficulty in cutting it out."

His eyes rested on her for perhaps a quarter of a minute before it sank in that it was she whom he expected to do the cutting.

"Help me to take these things off."

He freed his right arm first, snaking it out through the three layers of sleeve and then picking up the revolver again, which he had kept beside him. Then he stood up, letting the weight of the overcoat pull everything else away until it was all hanging from his left shoulder like a bullfighter's cape. When he sat down again, she began working the left overcoat sleeve down his arm. She could tell from the way he was breathing that the process was a torment for him.

It wasn't until she had gotten it free, and saw the way the arm of his tunic was matted and stiff with blood that had dried to a blackish purple, that she understood what he must have been going through for the past couple of hours.

"We'll have to cut this away," she said, her voice shaking as she wiped her hands off on the front of her coat.

"I expect so. You'll find a pair of scissors in the first-aid kit in my bag."

The whole time, while she peeled away the pieces of cloth that had glued themselves to his flesh, while she cleaned out the wound, while she bandaged it and splinted his arm to a flat length of board that had apparently been used to hold the cabin window open on warm days, he never made a sound. It seemed to be a point of honor.

"And now the little detail of my back," he whispered, smiling his strange, apologetic smile as his face streamed with sweat. The ordeal had blanched his skin to a pale gray.

He pulled a small folding knife out of his trousers pocket. "The blade is too short to kill me with—unless one is much more skilled in these matters than I suspect you are, madam. I shouldn't advise you to try."

He pried it open with one hand and held it out to her.

He had been right about the bullet. It was a little lump halfway up his back, just a few inches from his spine. She braced herself, took half a breath, held it, and cut. The thing popped out into her hand, which was then very rapidly covered with blood.

When everything was over, and she had retreated to the end of the other bed and was struggling to get a hold on herself, he sat there, bracing his good arm against the other knee, looking tired but somehow oddly indifferent to what they had both been through.

"I should like to thank you, madam—it occurs to me that until this moment I have somehow neglected the courtesy of inquiring your name."

"Jenny," she answered, as if in her sleep. "Jenny Springer."

"Then thank you very much, Mrs. Springer. I am in your debt. And tomorrow my friends will come for me, and I will trouble you no longer."

He smiled, and closed his eyes, and allowed his head to sink down a little toward his naked breast, and for that instant he looked like one of those icons of death you saw all over Santa Fe, painted on the walls of the churches. Implacable death, who knows neither gratitude nor mercy. And then he opened his eyes and became human again.

The little door to the iron stove was standing open; otherwise they wouldn't have been able to see by that time. The two of them sat on opposite sides of the narrow triangle of reddish, wavering light.

"I wonder if there is anything to eat," he said suddenly. The remark was somehow as startling as if he had all at once declared the end of the world, and Jenny had to catch herself to keep from starting. "Perhaps we ought to have a look."

They didn't find any food, but they did find a gas lantern. They hung it from a hook in the center of the ceiling. Somehow, with the cabin flooded with light, the space within those four walls seemed to define them. She was merely she, freed for the moment from both past and future, and von Niehauser was merely a man who would not let his pain show. The events of the last several hours seemed to belong to other lives—all of that was far less real than the hissing of the gas lamp and the sound of the wind outside.

"I saw some painkillers in the first-aid kit," she said.

But he shook his head. His temples had grown hollow and there were black smears under his eyes, but still he shook his head.

"I've gone without them before. It's something I learned fighting in Russia—men don't die of pain; they die of other things. Besides, the pain will help to keep me awake. What would I need to do with you, Mrs. Springer, before I could allow myself the luxury of falling asleep?"

The silence that followed was almost a third presence in the tiny room. No, this wasn't just a man with a few holes in him, and the past was real.

"But there is no reason why you should not sleep." He made a small, diffident gesture toward the other bed. "And you needn't have any anxieties. I am not Erich Lautner, and even if I were . . . poor flesh has its limits."

For a moment she simply stared down at the floor, as if she hadn't heard, and then, for some reason, she glanced up at the gas lantern and had an idea.

"I think some of your sandwiches are still out in the car. If you're still hungry . . . I know I am."

"Then go and get them." His eyes narrowed and one corner of his mouth lengthened slightly, as if he could see through into her mind and was amused by what he read there. "I will retain the key, if you don't mind."

He held out his hand, and she hunted around in her coat pocket and surrendered the keychain.

"I wouldn't know where to run to anyway," she said. "I don't even know where this place is."

He smiled in a way that made it impossible to tell whether he believed her or not.

Outside, there was that damp smell in the air that she had learned, since coming to New Mexico, to associate with the approach of a winter storm. According to the radio weatherman, there was supposed to be a genuine killer coming up from the south—they had been headlining it for the past two days, and now it was possible to believe them.

And tomorrow my friends will come for me, and I will trouble you no longer.

They might, or they might not. If these mountains were under a couple of feet of snow they might not. They might think twice about picking up their German spy if the wind was forty miles an hour and they couldn't see to the end of their arm. They might not come then.

But von Niehauser had killed two policemen this afternoon, so maybe his friends weren't the only ones looking for him.

And they would need something to look for.

It was a slim chance. In twelve hours there might be nothing moving between Denver and Mexico City, but there were still those twelve hours. And she had to do something.

It was a simple enough matter—you didn't need the keys to turn on a car's headlights. There was a little switch to the left of the steering wheel. Parked on that side of the cabin, where there were no windows, the car was as invisible from inside as if it had been buried in a rockslide.

As she sat there on the front seat, she found herself prey to a conflict of emotions she wouldn't have been able to imagine even two hours ago. Part of it was fear, simple anxiety to survive —if von Niehauser found out, what wouldn't he do then? And he would find out. By tomorrow morning, in this cold, with the lights on, the car battery would be as dead as those two state troopers back there. As dead as . . .

So, if she threw that switch she was probably committing suicide. She wouldn't be crashing her plane into a fuel storage tank or pulling the pin on a hand grenade and holding it to her bosom—she had seen Lana Turner do that in a movie once; or maybe it had been Veronica Lake—but the effect would be much the same.

And then there was the sense of betrayal, as if, after all, it was a mean thing to do. Von Niehauser was . . .

I have my notes and my memory. . . . I think I know enough to help my people build their bomb.

She put her hand on the switch and twisted, hard. The lights came on with a click. She had gone halfway back to the cabin before she realized she had forgotten the bag of sandwiches.

"I see you've brought them," von Niehauser said, brightening visibly as she closed the door behind herself. He was just pulling on a clean shirt, gingerly nursing his splinted arm down through the sleeve. "How many are there left?"

After an instant of hesitation, as if she couldn't decide how he expected her to know, she opened the bag and looked inside.

"Three—and a bottle of Squirt."

"You might save me a swallow of that." He smiled. "I should hate to go to my grave without knowing what something with such a picturesque name tasted like."

She was astonished at her own hunger; she ate two of the sandwiches almost without stopping. Von Niehauser merely tasted the corner of one and then set it aside. Somehow it was impossible to think of him sitting down to a big meal.

Had he ever had a wife? Had he ever had anyone? Jenny found herself studying his face, wondering what recognizable human passions had ever crossed it. No, he wasn't Erich Lautner. He seemed to have refined out of his character everything that didn't relate to the business of being his country's agent: lust, mercy, fear, even cruelty. There seemed to be nothing left of the man except will, cunning, and a certain gentlemanly deference for people's feelings.

She was alive, she sensed, merely because she was useful to him—or, at least, not in the way. When the time came he would murder her easily enough, but without either pleasure or brutality. And he would probably apologize. It was like being with a civilized cobra.

"You are not, I think, from this part of the country?" He looked at her through lowered eyes and shrugged, as if to assure her that it was not his intention to pry. Having kidnapped her, one gathered, didn't qualify as an introduction.

"No. No—I'm from New Jersey. That's . . ."

"I know where it is. I traveled through it by train on my way here. But one can tell very little about a place from the window of a train."

He smiled as he said it. He didn't want to imply any criticism of her home state.

"I've enjoyed America. Aside from the police, everyone has been most cordial."

"Perhaps after the war . . ."

"There will be no 'after' to this war, madam." Von Niehauser seemed to draw himself in, like someone shrinking from contact with an unpleasant fact. "At least, not for such as myself. Perhaps here, it will be different."

He finished buttoning his shirt, a process that had been interrupted by the arrival of the sandwiches, and began tucking the ends into his trousers, which couldn't have been easy for a man with only one good arm. He didn't seem in a hurry to resume the subject.

"Why here?" she asked, not quite sure why she wanted to goad him on; it just seemed that they had been on the verge of something. . . . "Why should it be any different here?"

"Because all the battles have been far away. We in Europe —the French, the Russians, and now, it seems, finally, the Germans—we've been bleeding into the land where we were born. You Americans, you'll be able to forgive and forget; in five years the whole business will seem as vague as a dream. With us it's gone too far for that. The choices have become very simple—win or die."

"You sound like your Führer."

From the sudden flash of anger that appeared in his eyes as he looked at her, she was certain that he would retreat into silence. She felt a giddy twinge of fear as she recollected that, after all, this wasn't one of her husband's friends she was listening to, and they weren't sitting around over a couple of beers in the recreation hall at Los Alamos.

And then his expression changed. It was just something that happened around his eyes—the anger had been deflected from her, and had found some other object.

"Hitler is a flabby Austrian peasant who eats cream cakes with his secretaries and long ago stopped listening to anything but his instincts and his astrologers—people say he's mad, but I'm inclined to think that he's merely stupid."

His mouth tightened in a compressed little smile, as if it gave him some sort of relief to say such a thing, and then he shrugged his shoulders in a gesture of dismissal.

"Europe will be a dead world," he went on, almost to himself. "A dead world, no matter who wins. I grew up listening to my father telling stories of the last war, and this is nothing like that. This is a contest of dishonor."

She couldn't recall what had awakened her. Suddenly she was awake; that was all. She couldn't even remember having gone to sleep.

Von Niehauser had found a blanket that he could roll up and put behind his back, allowing him to rest in a chair. He was the first thing she saw. It was impossible to tell whether he was awake or not—his eyes were open, but he didn't appear to be seeing anything through them. For a moment she thought he might actually be dead.

No, he wasn't dead, but if he didn't get to a doctor pretty soon he might well be. He looked wasted and pale and painfully weak, as if he had run through his whole life in a single night. The bones in his face seemed almost to be sticking through the skin. He seemed to be breathing through a conscious effort, as if he had to remind himself to draw in the air.

As soon as she moved, his eyes came back to life. He smiled at her, but otherwise hardly moved at all.

"You're in a bad way," she said. "You need to see a doctor."

"I will live long enough." And then he smiled again.

She could hear something tapping against the cabin window, which faced south to the plain and the mountains beyond, and when she looked outside it was snowing.

She could see it spreading across the flat ground, swirling around the rocks and mixing with the parched, ocher-stained earth. Sometimes it would whip itself into dust devils of angry white that would travel for a hundred feet or so and then collapse. The sky beyond the mountains was black. In a few hours, no more, they would be in the middle of a howling storm.

It was hard, she thought to herself. It was hard. She stood there by the window, her arms folded across her breast, fighting down the temptation to weep.

The war was here.

XXVII

Romero hadn't been quite so confident that the risks involved in obliging Mr. Hoover would be as "insignificant" as Havens claimed. Agustin Gomá, as he was quick to point out, wasn't precisely one of the faceless masses.

"He will doubtless resent being detained, and he is a man who does not shrink from avenging smaller slights than that." The elegant crime czar with the broken hands stood in front of his living room window, looking down into the bottom of the gorge where the Rio Grande snaked its muddy way to the sea. "He is a man of political consequence, Mr. Havens. In my business it is not considered prudent to antagonize such men."

"Then you can kill him when we're finished. Believe me, no one will raise any objections to that."

Romero turned around from the window, frankly astonished. He was more than astonished, really—he was shocked.

"The *norteamericano* police seem to have changed the rules rather drastically from that to which we have all grown accustomed. Are you serious, Mr. Havens? Are you authorized to say such things?"

Havens grinned—he was acting, and he was scared to death; he was strictly on his own down here, but he had to make it sound like he had President Roosevelt's letter of authorization in his shirt pocket. So he nodded and grinned and bluffed it out.

"Señor Gomá is strictly expendable," he said, clasping his hands behind his back so that Romero wouldn't see them shaking.

"Señor Gomá is an agent of his country's enemies. No one will think to inquire into his death, and if anyone should we can blacken his name so completely that the Mexican government would probably feel obliged to give his murderer a pension. As perhaps I've suggested, we're playing for high stakes."

"So it would seem."

And so it was that George Havens, federal agent, found himself in the back seat of a '37 Ford, heading off into the desert with five of the toughest thugs he had ever seen in his life.

"When do you wish this thing accomplished?" Romero had asked, with the polite disinterest of a waiter inquiring if you were ready to order.

"Right now, yesterday—it's not something that can wait. Do you know where Gomá is to be found?"

"Yes—of course. When half a dozen of the local *banditi* suddenly come into possession of enough money to pay off their gambling debts and buy their girlfriends out of the bordellos, I make it my business to know the why of it."

He smiled—it was a tight, faintly condescending smile that said that the police were amateurs in such matters, that Mr. Hoover had done better than he knew to put his trust in the Razor of Juarez.

The men in the car seemed to have nothing to say, and no interest in their surroundings: they stared straight ahead, in perfect silence, during most of the drive. They were dressed in city clothes—woollen overcoats and neckties and felt hats—but something about them suggested that all that was merely a species of disguise. They were heading into the desert, into the wilderness where Pancho Villa had held off armies from both the north and the south, and one had the impression that these hard, wordless mercenaries were probably closer to that tradition of the mountain desperado than, appearances notwithstanding, to the poolhall tough in his candy-stripe silk shirt and his patent leather shoes.

Havens glanced at the speedometer—they were loafing along at a shade under forty miles an hour. Really, these people . . .

"Can't you step on it a little?" he snapped, leaning forward toward the driver. But the driver merely caught his eye in the rear-view mirror and smiled.

"No hurry, señor," he said pleasantly. "If they gone, they gone. But they no leave tonight."

With his right hand, he pointed across his body to the southern sky, where a peculiar greenish-black line ran along the horizon.

"Big storm coming. Tomorrow maybe. They wait for that to pass."

"Terrific."

They had been driving for well over an hour when Havens saw another car, pulled over to the side of the narrow dirt road and seemingly deserted. They drew up behind it and came to an abrupt stop; all four doors opened at once, and Havens found himself sucked outside by sheer momentum.

It was only when they were all standing around, and the driver had opened the trunk and was passing out shotguns, that the owner of the other car stepped out from behind a clump of yucca, still buttoning his fly with one hand while the other kept a casual hold on an antique Winchester 30-30. He nodded glumly, shook hands with the driver, who seemed to be in charge, and listened with evident skepticism to the murmured explanation that one gathered, from the number of times Havens felt the two men's eyes on him, was as much about the *yanqui* passenger as the upcoming job.

Finally the driver turned to Havens, attempting a rather unconvincing smile. "Zee hacienda is five, six miles more, señor. We take two cars."

"Have you got another shotgun?"

The driver's thin, ascetic face took on a worried expression. This, it would seem, wasn't covered in his orders.

"Señor, is no game," he said blandly, as if that were the last possible word on the subject.

Havens went over to the trunk, which was still open and

where there were in fact two shotguns, and picked up a Browning pump. He grabbed a handful of shells from an open box, fed one into the chamber and another three into the magazine, and clicked on the safety.

"Who said it was?"

The plan, so far as there was one, and so far as the driver had been able to render it into intelligible English, consisted of nothing more than driving right up to the house, bold as brass, hoping that not everyone would be concentrated inside and that, in the face of such suicidal audacity, Gomá and his troops wouldn't immediately assume they were under attack and would hold their fire until after they had lost whatever advantage was theirs by position. After all, even in Mexico you didn't kill people just for rolling up to your front door.

After that it was a simple pincer attack, one car covering the back while the other shot out the porch window. Guns booming, it was to be the storming of the Bastille.

There didn't seem to be any alternative, really. The house was in the middle of a huge stretch of flatland, with only the one approach road and no surrounding cover, so you could forget about the lightning commando raid from out of nowhere, but Havens still didn't like it. He didn't like the apparent indifference with which these soldiers of Romero's contemplated the very real risks of getting their heads shot off. People who were that cavalier about losing their lives didn't fill him with much confidence.

What was he doing, trusting the most important operation of the war—perhaps even the war itself—to a pack of reckless Mexican hooligans?

That wasn't quite fair. After all, all he had to do was give the word and probably every one of them would breathe a sigh of relief and head right back to Juarez. And if there was a better plan, he hadn't been able to think of it.

Truth to tell, it was principally Inspector Havens' conscience that was giving him trouble. He was beginning to realize—as an imaginative fact, which was the only way that mattered—just what it was he had bought with little brother Juan's neck. A great many men were probably going to be dead in another hour's time. What he had done was to order himself up a massacre.

"There she is, señor." The driver held a bony finger up to the windshield. A small, squarish speck was just visible on the edge of the horizon. "Keep the gun from sight."

The men on the back seat began rolling down their windows. There were no signs of anyone on the front porch.

It might work, Havens thought to himself, clutching the shotgun between his knees. It might really . . .

They were about half a mile away when the first of Gomá's forces stepped out through the front door and onto the veranda. He just stood there, his hands in the pockets of his heavy jacket, and then another man joined him. The second man raised an arm to shade his eyes—thank God, the sun was in their faces—he looked relaxed and unworried, and he didn't appear to be armed. Perhaps they were still only curious.

A quarter of a mile, and the front car, where Havens was sitting on the front seat, began to gather speed. They were close enough now that a man with a rifle might have had a chance of disabling them. The engine was roaring, and a huge cloud of dust was churning up behind them. The man in the door frame ducked back inside. Two hundred yards now, then a hundred, then fifty . . .

The driver swerved to the right with a great screeching of tires, and just in time. Havens heard the ping of a rifle bullet as it creased his door, but there was no time for anything as complicated as fear. They weren't twenty yards from the house now—as the side windows went flickering by, he could see people inside, like still photographs that succeeded each other so fast that they seemed to blur into one.

As they rounded the back, they saw a man burst out through the rear door. He was bent almost double and running, with a rifle cradled in his arms like a child. The car began skidding to a stop—the noise was sickening—and, as the man began to raise his rifle, Havens jerked the shotgun up from where it was resting against his leg, nearly throwing it through the window. Without thinking, without even aiming, he fired. The man stumbled and fell, almost under their wheels.

The car stopped, but the noise didn't. Like everyone else, Havens burst out and began running toward the house, exactly as if he expected the car to explode behind him. He had barely presence of mind enough to work the pump on his shotgun—the expended shell was a tiny red stain seen in the corner of his eye; for a moment he thought he might have been hit.

But it wouldn't have mattered. There was only him and the back door, nothing else. Him and the back door, about to collide.

And then there was someone else, and he did matter. He was just a shape in the doorway, but that was a gun in his hand. He raised it up—it seemed to take him forever—and then there was another sharp explosion, almost next to Havens' left ear it seemed, and the shape in the doorway fell over backward.

Havens made it through. He was in a little kitchen; that, and the relative darkness, registered on his brain, and then he stumbled on something and found himself lying across a body that seemed to have most of its head gone.

Outside, the sound of gunfire was almost deafening.

Where the hell *was* everybody, he thought. What was he doing here all by himself, with his nose stuck in the remains of somebody's windpipe? He kept waiting for someone to take a shot at him, to serve him in his turn, so he could lie there on the board floor with his brains scattered around like loose change.

And then he saw another door, and heard one of his men behind him, and got up and picked up the assault again.

"You okay, señor?"

Miraculously, it seemed, it was the driver, with his hand on Havens' arm.

"Yes—fine—terrific!" Havens heard himself shouting. And then a bullet fractured the thin wooden door in front of them, and he turned around and saw his companion with a surprised expression on his face and a hole in his cheekbone. Blood was leaking out through it, thick as oil.

Did I do that to him?

There was only time for the one fugitive thought. Still on his feet, the man was dying, right there in front of him. Havens found himself staring in appalled fascination.

He forced himself to look away. And then he charged the door in an unplanned, maniacal blending of fear and rage. It gave way in front of him as easily as if it had been made of paper.

Inside, in what was obviously the main room, he saw a man with a heavy, blockish face, wearing an overcoat, standing next to the fireplace, holding a pistol. Havens didn't have to ask who it was—he knew who it was. There was a tiny curl of yellow flame from the fireplace. Havens brought the shotgun to his shoulder and fired.

After that, the noise stopped. Outside, inside—everywhere. Havens ran for the fireplace, saw that it was a small packet of papers that was burning, pulled it out, threw it on the floor, and stamped out the flames under his boot heels.

Gomá was still alive. It was astonishing—his chest was torn open and looked like the waste barrel in a butcher's shop—but he was alive. Havens picked him up by what was left of his coat lapel and tried to shake him out of his trance.

"Where is he, señor? Where the fuck have you got von Niehauser?"

Gomá merely stared at him, with an expression of scandalized incomprehension.

And then he died. From one instant to the next, he just died.

Someone came through the front door. Havens had his shotgun raised, ready to blow him away, when he saw that it was one of his own. The two men exchanged an embarrassed grin—it was impossible to know why; Havens didn't feel the least little bit like laughing.

"Is it over?" he asked. Outside, as if in answer, he heard two blasts from a shotgun, prefaced by a short, high-pitched scream. The Mexican nodded impassively.

"Si, señor. Están muertos."

When he stepped out onto the porch, Havens saw three dead men stretched out in the dirt, one of them lying with his legs tucked up underneath him, as if he had been kneeling when he got it. One of the corpses Havens recognized as the man they had met along the road. The dust was spattered with blood. He decided it would probably be just as well if he didn't ask any questions about what had happened out here.

"Señor?"

The man was standing at the end of the porch, motioning Havens toward him with a flipperlike action of his left hand. He was wearing a dark blue overcoat and a gray felt hat, which went rather strangely with his heavy handle-bar mustache and his two-day-old beard. The clothes looked out of place here—not the man, just the clothes. You had the impression that any moment he would step sideways and out of them, just like out of those sets that photographers use at state fairs, where you stick your head through a hole and appear as a turn-of-the-century dandy balancing on a unicycle. Havens followed obediently along.

There was a barn about seventy yards behind the main house. It looked as though no one had painted it in years, and some of the boards used for siding hadn't been cut quite straight, so here and there weird slithering chinks appeared in the outer walls. Another man was standing in front of the door, with his shotgun slung across the crook of his arm, as if he had been posted guard.

It was dark inside. There were three or four horses in stalls right near the door; you couldn't see them properly, only the flicker of shadowy movement within the closed-up pens, but they were pacing back and forth and whinnying nervously—at intervals there would be a sharp rap of a hoof against the partition. Probably all the shooting had set them off.

Or maybe not. At the other wing of the barn, at the end of a rope that had been slung across the roofbeam, hung a strangely sinister mass that twisted slowly around from one side to the other like a set of wind chimes on a still day.

Havens took a step forward. As his eyes adjusted to the dim, filtered light, he saw that the mass was human, was a man tied and hanging by his leg—just the one; the other was splayed out at a grotesque angle. He could smell the blood long before he recognized Suñer.

They had beaten his head almost to pulp. They had made a game of it—the blood-smeared two-by-fours were lying in a little pile under the body. It could have been almost anybody. Havens wasn't sure, not really sure, until he read the label on the inside of the suitcoat—Adams & Co., New York—and noticed the polish on the fingernails of one hand.

"Cut him down." His voice wasn't much more than a hoarse croak. He turned on his heel and went back to the house.

"They are no especting us, no?" The man in the gray felt hat smiled at Havens, showing a row of fine white teeth as even as bathroom tiles. He held up a couple of fingers. "Only two kill. Five them, only two us."

Havens nodded, finding himself at a loss to do more. He had only fired a gun at another human being once before in his life, four months after he finished his training at Quantico, when a numbers runner in New York had panicked and tried to shoot his way out of a raid and Havens had hit the guy in the knee. He had even thought about quitting the Bureau over that one—everyone treated him like a hero, but he had felt like something very different—and now he had blown two men to pieces with a twelve-gauge shotgun. Probably for these guys it was like hunting jackrabbits.

He went back into the house and sat down next to where Gomá was lying on the floor, his eyes still wide open and the expression on his face registering a kind of surprised outrage.

"Is this what you thought you were getting into when you

went to war, pal?" Havens asked, leaning forward in his chair to study the dead man's alarmed countenance. "Me neither."

But he must have grown up some since the numbers runner in New York, because the major emotion that he experienced as he looked down at Gomá was a sullen, fretful resentment. The son of a bitch had forced him to shoot, and he had needed Gomá alive.

So what did he have? In a way it had been kind of a relief to find Suñer hanging out there in the barn—you come storming into a place and blow everybody away, it's nice to know they had it coming. And Suñer with his head beaten in validated everything that Suñer alive had had to say about Agustin Gomá. So at least it hadn't all been just smoke screen. At least they had come to the right place to get the right man.

And at the right time too. Havens had been more than a little afraid of finding the place deserted, but Gomá was still here. He hadn't yet crossed over into the United States and picked up von Niehauser, because if he had he wouldn't still have been lounging around with his bodyguards—he would have been halfway to the freighter or the submarine or the God only knew what else that was probably waiting around at that precise moment to take its cargo back to the Reich.

So everything was perfect—except that Gomá was too full of number-five birdshot to tell anybody anything.

And then Havens glanced down at the floor and saw what it was that Gomá had been trying to burn when he had run out of time. It was still folded, and the edges were pretty badly scorched, but it remained more or less intact.

It was a map.

XXVIII

It was one of those extremely detailed topographical maps, on a scale of about an inch to the mile. The upper half was burned so badly that it simply fell into tatters when Havens tried to unfold it. There really wasn't any way of seeing how the surviving fragments related to one another.

But the lower section was still in reasonably good shape. He spread it out on the floor and found Gomá's hacienda marked with a square of heavy pencil. There was another pencil stroke, stretching straight north until it began weaving its way through a line of mountains and then disappeared into the map's charred edge. Havens could look out the window and see the mountains; they weren't more than four or five miles away.

And beyond them, somewhere, von Niehauser was waiting.

"Could you take a car through there?"

He stood on the porch with the man in the gray felt hat, who seemed to be the only one of them who understood any English. The man shook his head apologetically.

"No, señor, *un caballo*—you need a horse."

He grinned, as if he thought the sound of the word was funny to beat hell.

"Can you and the others come with me?"

"No, señor." He shook his head again, but this time he was looking not at Havens but at the mountains behind him. "The border there. We stay here."

Havens was clutching the map in his hand. The trail that

Gomá had sketched out for himself was clear enough—all he had to do was look up to see the notch in the mountains through which he had planned to enter the United States. Everything was perfectly clear.

He took one of his Bureau business cards out of his wallet and scrawled a note on the back: "I'm following this trail. Start the search." Then he copied out the name and the address of the field supervisor in El Paso. Charlie Rice would have brains enough to know what to do.

He handed the card and the map to the bandit in the gray felt hat. "Can you take these to this man?" he asked, pointing to the name on the back of the card.

"*Si.* This I can do."

The Mexicans thought he was insane to go heading off into the mountains, with nothing under him except a horse. They pointed to the blackening line of the southern horizon and assured him he would be dead by the next afternoon if he allowed himself to get caught in the storm it prophesied. But in the end they saddled him up, gave him a carbine and hunted through the hacienda for a fleece-lined jacket and a pair of leather gloves. One of them even gave him his hat.

"You *loco*, señor," he said, holding his hand up above the horse's neck as he offered it to Havens. "But you fight good—*como un mexicano*, eh?"

Havens took the offered hand and shook it, strangely touched.

The mountains were colder than he had imagined. The wind came rushing down the steep rockfaces like water—it was easy to believe that a man could die up here.

By a quarter to six he had reached the summit of the long, snaking pass, where the trail was no wider than a footpath and sometimes seemed to disappear altogether in the rubble of countless rockslides. The light was beginning to fail, so he dismounted from his horse, a chestnut mare with a single white stocking, hardly larger than a pony but tough after the fashion of Mexican horses. They walked along in single file, as if they had been friends for a lifetime.

In the dim, reddish, sunset light, the mountains were the color of tobacco and as barren as the craters of the moon.

How far had he gone? Six or seven miles, no more. He was past the charred edge of Gomá's map, and all he could do now was to follow the contour of the land and keep his eyes open. Either he and von Niehauser would run into each other, more or less by accident, or they wouldn't. There was nothing either one of them could do about it now.

There was a hopelessness to it all. They had been dueling all this time over the secret of the most terrible weapon in the history of the human race, and it hardly seemed to matter very much. Havens had left eight dead men behind him at the hacienda, two of whom he had killed himself, and von Niehauser was at the end of his own long trail of corpses—what were they doing? What was it, except a contest to see who would have the honor of turning the world into a cinder?

You can develop a feeling about someone, even if you've never met him. Havens had only seen von Niehauser for a few seconds on a street corner once, had read the bare outline of his life in a military dossier, and had seen the remains of his victims, but he felt as if they were connected by some invisible thread of sympathy, like Siamese twins who had remained strangers. He didn't need a map—they had all those miles of mountains between them, but they couldn't have avoided each other if they had wanted to. That was what this whole sorry business was about, not bombs and the fate of Europe. What did all the dead they had left behind them care about any of that?

He looked back over his shoulder and saw that the sky was vastly darker behind him than in front. He could feel the wind right through his heavy coat, just as if he were standing there naked. The Mexicans had been right—there was a hell of a storm coming.

He wondered what it would be like to freeze to death in a place like this, to fall asleep huddled against the side of a cliff face and turn to stone. It was possible that no one would ever find him up here. He could vanish as completely as if he had never existed. And then the world would have to work out its own destiny, without the eager guiding hand of George Havens. Somehow the idea pleased him. To step down once and for all from being personally responsible for the salvation of the species—who the hell did they think they'd been kidding?

The horse nudged him on the back of the arm, as if to inquire what was slowing things up, and Havens turned around and ran a hand down the animal's nose, wondering what her name was or if people bothered with names for leathery old ranch ponies like this one. He hadn't been on a horse more than half a dozen times in his life, but this one hadn't taken advantage of the fact and for that he was obscurely grateful.

The darkness was almost total now. There was only the moonlight, and that could play funny tricks on you. He could hear the wind whining high up in the rocks; soon it would be impossible to go on and he would have to find somewhere to stop for the night. The Mexicans, who probably already thought of him as a dead man, had nevertheless packed up his horse with some food and a sleeping bag. They had told him he was crazy not to wait for the storm to pass, but if he lived it would probably be because of them. They were good men.

There was a twinkle of light ahead. It probably didn't mean a thing, but later he would get out his field glasses and have a look.

He would have bet anything that von Niehauser wouldn't be waiting for the storm to pass.

He looked down at his feet and was a little shocked to discover that he could no longer see them. He could walk right off the face of a cliff at this rate—it wasn't going to help the war effort any if he ended up a mangled corpse in some gully. He couldn't feel his feet either. It was time to knock off. There was a flashlight in the saddlebag—those guys had thought of everything—so he would poke around until he found someplace where at least he could get the horse out of the wind.

The sleeping bag was one of those quilted, feather-filled things that made you feel like a caterpillar larva. He didn't imagine he would get much sleep—you didn't sleep when you were lying on a sheet of rocks as sharp as ax heads—but once he had shivered himself warm he was comfortable enough. The only part of him that was exposed was his face. The horse was hobbled behind a pile of boulders that formed a sort of natural stable. He could hear her snorting every once in a while. They would last it out together until the morning, but after that everything was up for grabs.

If there was a big blow tomorrow, Charlie Rice would keep his troops at home. He hadn't been filled in on just how big the stakes were—Groves had forbidden that; the man had a perfect mania about security—and he wasn't going to risk anybody's neck just because Havens had assured him that finding this spy was "vital to the prosecution of the war." That was the phrase he had used: "vital to the prosecution of the war." Groves had seemed to think that would be enough.

So nobody from the El Paso office was going to take a chance on freezing to death. They would wait until the howling stopped, and then they would put the chains on the wheels of their jeeps, and maybe a couple of spotter planes in the air, and see what they could find. Havens couldn't really blame them.

The only problem was that von Niehauser didn't operate like a civil servant and wasn't likely to pay much attention to anybody's convenience, including his own. In a couple of days, when things had settled down, they could doubtless box him in quite nicely; but in the meantime a good lively storm might just give him his chance.

Charlie was an asshole. They were all assholes, the whole Bureau. They didn't have a clue about how to deal with a man like von Niehauser.

And he was an asshole himself. What was he doing, sitting

out here in a mummy bag, thinking that all by himself he had any chance of making the difference? He was just as potty as the rest of them.

The twinkle of light was still there. He had had his look and hadn't learned very much. In the dark there was no way of being sure, but whatever it was was probably a good three miles away.

It was an artificial light, and it was steady—that was all he could say for sure. He would look again in the morning.

With his back propped up against the smooth surface of the rockface, Havens watched the faraway glimmer and thought about how tired he was—this would be the second night in a row with little or no sleep—and wondered why he was so goddamned depressed. This was what he had wanted, to be in on the war. He wasn't shuffling papers anymore, or explaining to little old ladies in White Plains that the country hadn't been invaded, that the Brownies were merely having a weenie roast; he was in on the main action, just as surely as if he were actually on the bridge of that aircraft carrier in the Coral Sea. He was doing what he did best in the world, tracking down spies, and he had come to hate every minute of it.

Maybe von Niehauser really was different from all those gold stars on his Bureau efficiency reports, those poor clowns with whom he'd played cowboys and Indians before the war. Maybe now he was being reminded of his human limitations. Maybe that was what bothered him.

Or maybe, just maybe, he really didn't want to catch von Niehauser. You can come to identify too much with your quarry; that can happen too.

Or maybe he was just tired. God, the look in Gomá's eyes as the life leaked out of him! Was he likely to forget that any time between now and the day he died? He wondered if von Niehauser, who had killed at least four people that he knew about—and killed them standing close enough to know how they smelled—if he carried around any ghosts like that, or if he had gotten used to it. And what could his life be like if he had gotten used to it?

But Havens wasn't a hardened butcher of men—it was all new to him. At the time, at the moment when he had pulled the trigger, they had been nothing more than targets; it had been like shooting clay pipes at Coney Island, except that these clay pipes could shoot back. It wasn't until after, when he had had a chance to catch his breath and look around him, when he had been able to stop worrying about getting his head shot off in the next five seconds, that he had felt anything except a kind of crazy exhilaration—hell, he had enjoyed himself.

But it was a little different when you were looking down into a man's face and he seemed to be asking why you thought you had the right to do such things.

He sat listening, filled with a sudden uneasiness, but there was only the wind. It seemed to be high above him, as if it were skimming the mountain peaks—at least, that was how it sounded. In the darkness he couldn't see if the air was carrying any snow, and he was too sheltered to feel anything except the cold. Probably what he heard was the forerunner of tomorrow's storm.

He wondered if von Niehauser could hear it. He wondered if it scared von Niehauser, or if there was only the one chicken heart between them.

It was the blank spots in a man's biography that made the difference. Nobody—at least, nobody this side of the Atlantic—had any idea what von Niehauser had been doing with his life since the outbreak of the war, but those must have been the years that had turned him into whatever he was now. Probably, given his family background, he had been a soldier. Was that what war did to you?

Havens' eyes were beginning to sting, so he held them closed for a moment. It didn't make any difference; he couldn't see anything either way. He tried to remember what von Niehauser had looked like. He sat there with his eyes closed, trying to conjure up the image of a man he had seen for just a few seconds, over two weeks ago.

The Bureau had found a photograph—a snapshot taken at

an honors banquet in Berlin in 1936, the property of a German refugee who was presently working on cyclotrons in California. It showed a slim, rather naïve-looking young man in a dinner jacket, smoking a cigarette while he talked to his table partner. It wasn't the face of a murderer; it seemed to have only a remote connection with the face Havens had seen that afternoon in New York. The two might have been father and son.

Everybody changes in eight years, but not that much. The waitress in Maine wouldn't have been so bowled over by the von Niehauser of 1936—not that the younger version hadn't been handsome enough, but lacking the sexual fascination that comes only with a fall from grace. "Like ice," she had said. One of life's aristocrats.

The man Havens knew had been through the fire, all right. Nothing would ever surprise him again. For Joachim von Niehauser, life had lost its power to appall. He had already learned all the secrets about himself. That, apparently, was what the war had done for him.

And those were the years Havens had spent sitting behind a desk in Washington. You kept your innocence in Washington; there were no brushes with tragedy, and you could live there forever and stay just the same. Like a fly in amber.

No wonder von Niehauser had been able to walk around the whole FBI, just as if they hadn't been there.

Havens discovered that he had a headache. It wasn't a real deluxe number yet, but it was getting there. His eyes hurt. He focused on the tiny, distant fleck of light, faintly resentful that it should be there, that he should have anything to trouble him from horizon to horizon.

But it was going too. The darkness was winning out; you could watch the thing beginning to fade. For five minutes, Havens hardly blinked. And slowly, in stages that were so gradual that it was impossible really to notice them, that point of yellow light became fainter and fainter.

And then, abruptly, it was gone.

What the hell did that mean? Havens looked at his watch, which had one of those illuminated dials, and saw that it was after four-thirty in the morning. In another hour, it would be sunrise.

Who keeps a light on until four-thirty in the morning—and in a place like this? Possibly someone might live around here, but that didn't really go very far toward explaining the light; at four-thirty in the morning, most people were sound asleep. And that light hadn't been switched off—it had seemed to go out by itself.

Why does anybody leave a light to go out by itself? Clearly not for their own use, or they would get up and tend to it. Then for someone else.

Suddenly the obviousness of it struck him. He couldn't understand how he could have been so stupid as not to have seen it from the first. The proverbial light in the window—the thing was a signal.

And who up here would have a reason to be signaling anyone? Who else?

All at once Havens could feel his heart pounding and the sweat beginning to break out under his armpits. All at once he couldn't wait for the first gray traces of dawn, because he knew now that whatever it was he had come for was out there waiting for him.

XXIX

The wind and the sun rose together. The night just seemed to fade away, leaving the soft outlines of things in the white air. Little pieces of ice went stinging by him as Havens climbed out of his sleeping bag and crouched underneath the shelter of the rocks. It was so cold that he didn't like to take a deep breath.

He dug his field glasses out of the saddlebag and tried to find the source of the light he had seen last night, but it was useless. Things half a mile away were merely dim shapes, and in a few hours, probably, you wouldn't be able to see to the end of your arm. The storm was going to be everything the Mexicans had claimed for it. It would leave no room for anyone; the only thing left to do was try to get in out of it. So all Havens could hope for was that, wherever that light had been coming from, whether von Niehauser was there or not, it was someplace that had a door you could close.

He unhobbled the horse, slipped the bridle over her ears, and climbed on. He didn't try to direct her—he didn't have to. That animal wanted to get down from the mountain just as bad as he did.

After about half an hour they hit the flatlands again. The mountain just stopped; you could have traced its edge in the dirt. For a while they were a little shielded from the wind, but that didn't last.

The horse walked with her nose tucked down by her chest, and Havens turned up the collar of his sheepskin coat and buried his gloved hands in the pockets. Through eyes narrowed down to slits, he tried to home in on objects that lay straight ahead, guiding the horse with his knees if she started to wander. He didn't want to end up going round and round in huge circles out here, until he fell out of the saddle and froze to death. That sort of thing seemed perfectly possible.

But he tried not to think about that. He tried to think about von Niehauser, about how he would play it if by some miracle there really was a cabin or something up ahead, and if von Niehauser should be waiting inside. He supposed he should have something in mind.

Pleased to meet you, Herr Baron. And now, in the name of the people of the United States, I'd like to place you under arrest.

Maybe he would try that, as soon as he had thawed out enough to be able to make intelligible sounds again. But by then, of course, von Niehauser almost certainly would have killed him. Why the hell should he do anything else?

Havens tried to think of everything he had working for him, but it didn't amount to much. There was, of course, no particular reason for von Niehauser to imagine that he had been tracked as far as the New Mexico desert. And, of course, Havens had the advantage that von Niehauser had never seen him—not to remember, at least. It wasn't possible that he could remember him from New York, so when he stumbled through the door he could be anybody. He had taken the precaution of leaving his badge and identity card behind him in El Paso, so even if the Herr Baron decided to pat him down he wouldn't find anything except twenty dollars and a driver's license.

Of course, none of that might make any difference. Von Niehauser might be the type who was just inhospitable on principle. He might blow Havens away as nothing more than ordinary professional prudence.

Not that it would do him any good. And somehow Havens really couldn't see him stooping to that. Nothing he had ever found out about the man led him to imagine that von Niehauser was wanton in his homicides—the man killed to stay alive.

And the net was tight around him now. Gomá was dead, so his Mexican contact was canceled—there wasn't anywhere for him to run to anymore. And tomorrow, when the storm lifted, every inch of these mountains would be crawling with federal officers. Where was von Niehauser going to go?

It was with a tiny flash of surprise, like being startled by someone hiding behind a door, that Havens realized, and for the first time, what it was he was actually doing out here. He could have waited back at the hacienda—if von Niehauser tried to break out, where else would he come?—but what had driven him over the mountains and into this howling storm was the pressure of the manhunt he himself had set in motion.

Those guys from the El Paso office, with their jeeps and their high-powered rifles and their search planes, all they wanted was a body they could carry back in an ambulance, so the morgue photographs could be in the mail to Seat of Government and they could stop worrying about their performance reports for a while. They had their orders—nobody was prepared to take any chances on the subject breaking loose. All of them would shoot to kill, the first time. *I expect you'll run him to ground and that that'll be the end of it.* That was what General Groves had said.

Well to hell with Groves. Havens had made up his mind to try to take von Niehauser alive. And if von Niehauser didn't feel cooperative, that was going to be his tough luck.

But in the meantime, God it was cold! At least the wind was coming from behind him; otherwise he couldn't imagine how he would have been able to open his eyes, there was so much ice in the air. The horse didn't like it either—she kept making strange little snorting sounds, like a man blowing his nose into a handkerchief.

It was astonishing the way everything seemed to have been bleached out, like a photograph taken with the lens too wide open. It hadn't begun to snow yet, exactly. It was just so cold and the wind itself seemed to have frozen up into hard little crystals that stung like pieces of sand. Havens wished he had something to pull down over his ears. If von Niehauser killed him, he wasn't sure he would be able to tell the difference.

He forced himself to look around, to try to get some sense of how far he had come and where he was. According to his watch, it had been about twenty minutes since he had left the mountain; he looked back over his shoulder—it was just about impossible to keep from closing his eyes—and he could no longer see it behind him. The ground had seemed to be falling gradually, and then to have leveled off, and now it appeared to be rising ever so slightly. He didn't have any idea what that meant. He didn't know if these flatlands would just go on forever or what. He didn't have a clue about what was a thousand yards in front of him.

The hat that Romero's soldier had loaned him was a kind of Mexican version of the stetson, a little flatter in the brim and with the crown not creased quite so deeply, and he was wearing it jammed down as tight as it would go, so that the sweatband was almost covering his eyebrows. But there was no strap, nothing to keep it on except its own tenacity, and finally the wind was too much for it.

Havens moved—or thought perhaps that he had moved—and the thing went skimming off and was almost out of sight before his hand was halfway up to catch it. That was when the cold really began to get mean. Within only fifteen or twenty seconds it felt like somebody had grabbed hold of the back of his head with a pair of ice tongs. After a while, the pain was virtually the only thing he could think about.

And then, in an instant during which he was able to pry his eyes open to see where he was going, he saw the outline—really nothing more at first—of a small building.

How far away? A quarter of a mile? Less? There was a door and a single square window—as he got closer he could see the thin little cross of latticework that held in the four panes of glass. And there was a car parked by the side. It was something to head for. He didn't care if Jack the Ripper was hanging by his clawed feet from the rafters—all he wanted was to get under that roof and in out of the storm.

"Not far now, pal," he murmured, patting the horse on her neck—the poor brute was just plodding ahead with her nose down, exactly like a machine. "Maybe they've got a stable. And if they don't, you can come inside and drink tea with the gentry."

As he straightened up, he thought he heard something zing by his head. It sounded like an insect, but of course that was impossible. Probably it was just the wind, which by then was whining like a buzz saw. Probably his ears were beginning to play him tricks.

And then, the next instant, it was as if the whole world had suddenly turned a brilliant, electric white. There was nothing anymore, not another object in the universe. He was hardly there himself.

He wasn't sure he ever felt the impact. He thought, but it wasn't something about which he could be sure, he thought he could feel himself sinking; but that too had thinned out almost to nothing. It was like falling backward into a huge feather pillow that became a cloud, that became nothing, that dissolved you into nothing. And the question just had time to flicker across his brain, *Am I dying?*

And then the blinding white turned to red. And then to darkness. And then to nothing.

When he opened his eyes, the first thing he saw was von Niehauser. Havens was lying there—at first he didn't know any more than that, and then he heard the wind and felt the cold and knew he was still outside—and von Niehauser was looking down at him. He was wearing a heavy, double-breasted greatcoat and a British officer's cap, and he was kneeling. His right hand was clutching the barrel of a rifle, the butt resting against the ground so it supported him like a staff, and the reins of Havens' horse were twisted through the fingers of his gloved hand.

The horse was looking down at him too, her head just above

von Niehauser's shoulder. Von Niehauser, unlike the horse, was smiling.

"Good—you are alive then." It seemed to afford him some real measure of satisfaction, as if he had won a bet. "I had intended to kill you, of course, but I am not at all displeased with this outcome."

Havens tried to turn his head a few degrees, but the effort was so exquisitely painful that he felt as if his skull must certainly be lying around on the sand in big pieces.

When the sensation had passed off a little, he tried moving his fingers and was happy to discover that they still worked. And then his feet, first one and then the other.

That was when he noticed that his left hip seemed to be twisted out of its socket. Anyway, that was what it felt like. It hurt like a bugger, but it was a different pain from the pain in his head. It was an impersonal sort of pain, as if it really belonged to somebody else and was only out to him on loan. At any rate, he supposed he would find out all about it soon enough.

He wished von Niehauser would stop smiling at him.

Havens tried to say something, but his throat was like leather and the words just wouldn't come out. And then, without warning, he was racked by a great spasm of coughing that seemed to tear him apart inside and made his head feel as if it might burst. He turned over on his side, and a thick gob of blood and phlegm ran out of the corner of his mouth and onto the sand. After that he felt better.

"You shot me, you son of a bitch," he said finally, his voice a shaky whisper but at least audible.

Von Niehauser merely nodded. "Yes. I needed the horse. And, besides, I recognized you—you're the policeman from New York."

"Jesus."

"Don't sound so surprised, my friend. You should know that a hunted man can always tell when someone has recognized him."

"Jesus Christ."

For a long time neither of them moved. They seemed to be studying one another, as if each was satisfying an intense curiosity, as if each was confirming the accuracy of his conjectures. And then Havens swallowed, and tried to raise his head, and spoke again.

"Gomá is dead."

"Yes—I knew that the minute I saw you. Did you kill him?"

"Yes."

It was then that Havens noticed for the first time the way von Niehauser held his left arm stiff against his body, and how drawn his face seemed. He really was leaning against the barrel of his rifle, giving the impression that without it he might have had trouble keeping his balance. Everything about him suggested an almost overpowering weariness. Havens had almost made up his mind to ask what had happened, but then he remembered that this wasn't precisely a class reunion and thought better of it.

Instead, he brought a hand up to his head and started feeling tentatively around for damage. His right temple was badly swollen, and he could actually put a finger into the deep cut, like the lips of a repulsive, bloated mouth, that seemed to run the whole length of his skull. There wasn't very much blood; the cold seemed to have congealed it almost at once.

"I was aiming for your head," von Niehauser said matter-of-factly. "You see, I couldn't take the risk of hitting the horse. And in this wind . . ." He shrugged rather stiffly. He seemed to feel it was necessary to explain to Havens why he hadn't killed him outright.

"Don't think a thing of it." Havens smiled rather sourly. "What's the matter with my leg?"

"Oh—that. I think you must have torn something when you fell. Does it bother you terribly much?"

"I've felt better." Havens tried moving his foot again, and shooting pains ran straight up into his groin. "It doesn't seem to work."

It occurred to him that the conversation was beginning to sound ridiculous.

Because, after all, they were warriors separated by a deeper antagonism than possibly any two people on the planet. It had nothing to do with pride or personal hatred or the honor of their countries. They were struggling over the shape of history, and Havens kept hearing, over and over again, something that Groves had said. *If they can't have the world, they might be willing to watch it go up in flames.*

"You got what you came for, didn't you."

"Yes." Von Niehauser nodded, almost imperceptibly. There was nothing like triumph in his voice. "Yes, I got what I came for."

"And do you think now that you'll be able to build your goddamned bomb?"

"Yes."

Havens could feel a strange throbbing inside his chest. It was anger, he realized suddenly—and fear. It was von Niehauser, after all, who had the gun and the horse and the secret of fire. It seemed that the combined forces of American security, collectively and in the individual person of Special Agent George Havens, were a poor match for this solitary man with no resources beyond his own will and courage. The end didn't matter; on a purely personal level, von Niehauser had already won his victory.

But there was nothing of the victor to be seen now. The dignified, composed figure that knelt beside Havens in the howling wind seemed impervious to everything. If he felt his success, or the cold, he didn't show it. And whatever was wrong with him, whatever had etched into his face that look of resigned weariness, his suffering gave the impression of being more an attitude of mind than anything like the corruption of injury. Von Niehauser seemed immune from accident; he was merely tired of it all.

In one of those flashes of insight that sometimes come to people at the cutting edges of their experience, Havens realized that the man looking down at him through those dead eyes cared nothing about the war or the survival of the races of man or his own life. He was indifferent the way the dead are, and whatever drove him forward, whatever had brought him down into this pitiless cold and whatever would send him where he was going, it had nothing to do with fear or patriotism or the soldier's pride or the ambitions of common humanity. He was past that.

And then von Niehauser smiled again.

"I am sorry about taking your horse," he said, exactly as if he meant every word of it. "But the battery in my car is dead. I have no other way of getting out of here."

"Give it up."

Havens had managed to raise himself up to lean on one elbow—it seemed so undignified to talk about these things while you were flat on your back, and he saw clearly enough that, behind the faint playfulness, von Niehauser was very far from intending a joke.

"Give it up, Niehauser. Gomá is dead, so there's nobody to help you get away. If you try to cross into Mexico now, you'll never make it—you'll die out there; you can see what's coming just as well as I can."

"I have seen wind and snow before, my friend."

"Like this?"

"Yes, like this—and much worse."

"But you weren't alone then. And somebody hadn't shot you full of holes." He paused for a moment, and they both looked at the ragged tear in von Niehauser's coat, just to the right and a little under the first rank of buttons. There was no blood visible —it was a heavy fabric and doubtless all the spattering was on the inside—but neither was it possible to doubt how it had gotten there.

"So you have discovered my little secret," von Niehauser said finally. "Good for you."

Havens only shook his head.

"Don't try it. What chance have you got? Even if the storm somehow doesn't kill you, even if you got across to Mexico, the first break in the weather and this whole area will be crawling with federal agents who aren't going to pay any attention to borders anyway. You can't run that far."

But von Niehauser only smiled, the same smile that had never left his lips, as if he were being called upon to explain adult truths to a child.

"So you recommend that I stay, and die at the end of an American rope in two or three months' time? I'm sorry, but the possibility doesn't attract me. Besides, there is always the faint chance I might surprise us both."

He began to rise to his feet, leaning heavily on the rifle—he really was in a bad way. It seemed a miracle that he could even have walked the few hundred yards from his place of ambush.

But he made it into the saddle. The horse, which had grown restive as the storm rose with greater and greater intensity behind them, calmed under his hand.

"Goodbye," he shouted—it was now necessary to shout. The wind was like some cry of animal despair. "I know you cannot wish me luck, but I can thank you for remembering the truth. Goodbye."

"Niehauser! NieHAUSER!"

It was perfectly useless, of course. Even if he had heard—and in the midst of such a gale, where the snow whipped along the ground so fast that it was nothing except a blur, how could he have heard?—but even if he had he wouldn't have stopped. It wasn't very long before he disappeared completely, like a man who has stepped behind a curtain.

It was perhaps to his credit that Havens' thoughts at that moment were more about von Niehauser's survival than his own. When he tried getting to his feet, and discovered finally and forever that his left leg just wasn't going to take the weight, it was from some half-formed idea of going after the by-then hardly visible figure of his adversary. It wasn't until he collapsed back to the ground, and felt the wrenching pain that hardly left him able to breathe, that he began to get scared.

George, you could die out here too, he thought. He wondered if that was what von Niehauser had intended—if that could be why he wasn't dead already. After all, the man had given sufficient evidence to date that he was playing for keeps.

He twisted around and discovered that he could still just make out the peaked roof of the little cabin. If he could see it, maybe he could get to it. Maybe . . .

Not a chance. It was two hundred yards—at least. How could a man crawl that distance, even if his life depended on it?

Maybe he couldn't. But even if he couldn't, at least he could show von Niehauser that the Germans weren't the only ones prepared to die trying.

He had made perhaps seventy-five or eighty feet, and his hands, even inside his gloves, were torn and scraped, and his bad leg was pounding like an anvil, when he saw something moving ahead of him. He stopped for a moment—it wasn't a hard decision to make—and wiped the snow from his eyes and looked again.

*Some*thing had moved. But that really wasn't very surprising—every goddamned thing in the world seemed to be moving. The storm was playing tricks on him, that was all. Anyway, in this snow he was nearly blind.

And then, as he tried nerving himself up to see if he couldn't manage another three or four yards, he felt someone take hold of the shoulder of his coat. It was a strong tug—that was no trick.

"Try to get up," the voice said. It was shouting, and from only a few feet away, but it sounded as thin as a woman's. "Is your leg bad? Lean on me."

Jesus—it *was* a woman's voice. All of a sudden he found himself resting his arm across a pair of narrow shoulders in a tan coat that was almost white with snow. She wasn't very big, but the arm he felt around his waist seemed as though it intended to hold him up all by itself.

For the rest, he could wait. All he knew—all he cared about—was that all at once he had a chance to die old.

They didn't say anything more. They didn't have the breath to waste, and the wind and stinging ice didn't make them want to pause and get acquainted. Havens concentrated on keeping his feet under him.

He could see the cabin clearly now, and the car parked nose-in beside it. It gave him a reason to keep going.

Sixty yards. . . . One foot in front of the other, balancing to keep the strain off his leg. Fifty yards. . . .

He could count the boards in the front wall now. He could see the shape of the door handle. He could . . .

One step at a time. Twenty-five yards . . . twenty. . . . God, his leg hurt so bad he could hardly feel it at all.

Thirty feet . . . fifteen. . . .

He almost fell through the door—it wasn't even closed. He just collapsed onto the floor and crawled to the center of the room. There was a stove going. He could hear the hiss of the updraft. He couldn't feel the heat yet; he was still too cold to feel anything, but he didn't care. He didn't care about anything else in the world, except that he was inside. All he wanted to do was to remember how people breathed.

Finally, after he had heard the door slam shut behind him, after he could feel his hands again, when he could believe that it was finally finished with and he could stop worrying about his eyelashes freezing shut, he remembered.

He turned over onto his side—it wasn't easy, but nothing was easy—so he could see behind him, and she was still there, leaning against the door as if she thought the armies of the shady night were outside trying to get in, as if she thought there was nothing but her slender little body between the two of them and destruction. Three minutes ago, there hadn't been. It was an odd feeling to owe one's life to a pretty little woman with light brown hair and the eyes of a frightened child.

He cleared his throat, just to make sure that it still worked. It did—he could probably manage five or six words as well as the next man. And now he even had somebody to listen to them. So he might as well find out.

"Who the hell are you?"

XXX

It never stopped, all the rest of that day. The wind sent the snow snapping against the front of the cabin like gravel—it even got in under the door and went snaking across the floorboards until Havens stuffed the crack with old rags. You couldn't see out the window; it was frosted over, inside and out. Every once in a while a kind of shudder would pass through the whole structure, as if it too had reached the end of its strength and was about to collapse under the unwavering pressure of the storm. It was like being buried.

There was nothing to do except to keep the fire going. There was nothing to eat, but they were only hungry enough to be uncomfortable. There was nothing to distract Havens from the more-or-less continuous contemplation of his own physical and spiritual misery. He concentrated on his leg, which hurt like hell but from a purely functional point of view seemed to improve from the moment the fire started to thaw it out. It was only a bad sprain, apparently. Within two hours he could stand on it again, and by the middle of the afternoon he could get back and forth to stoke the stove if he used a broom handle for a crutch.

His head, though, was another matter. He hadn't realized that anything could hurt that much for that long. He could put his hand up next to his ear and feel his heart beating through the bruise. But he imagined he would live through that too.

And they were stuck. It would have been an act of madness

to have gone outside, and the car wasn't going to take them anywhere anyway.

"The batteries are really dead?"

"Yes."

"How come?"

"I left the headlights on."

It was said without any emotional coloring at all. She might have been telling him the price of the wallpaper. She just sat there, on the edge of one of the two beds that took up that part of the room, drained of every human feeling. Havens found himself staring at her, as if she were the eighth wonder of the world.

"On purpose?"

"Yes."

"And he didn't kill you?"

For a moment she didn't answer. She just turned her great blank eyes on him like a couple of searchlights. She seemed to think the question was stupid—if she thought anything about it at all.

"He didn't kill you either," she said finally. It would seem that was all the answer anybody should need.

And she was right. Von Niehauser hadn't killed him. He had gotten on his horse—and it was *his* horse, by right of conquest—and he had ridden off, knowing that there was someone to make sure that Havens found his way to safety. He had left one enemy to fend for another—it was all very tidy.

Or perhaps, by that time, he had given up on the notion of having enemies. Perhaps he had decided to renounce the luxury.

"Is there any chance of his getting away?" she asked, the way someone else might have asked, "Will it rain?"

"If it were anyone except von Niehauser, I'd have to say no chance at all. As it is, I don't know. I don't think so."

She might as well not have been listening. The man had murdered her husband, had kidnapped her, threatened her, led her into the worst kind of danger, and now, one gathered, how she might or might not feel about the fact that the odds were all in favor of his being as good as dead was going to have to remain her secret.

Because, of course, she had told him all about herself, the whole sordid story, almost the first moment they were alone together inside the cabin. It had come out in fits and starts, as if it were something she was pulling out of herself by force. It was a confession she was making. She was Hester Prynne on her own private scaffold.

"How bad is he hurt?" Havens asked, when the spectacle of all that self-contempt began to make him uneasy and he found it convenient to remember that he was an intelligence officer and von Niehauser was, in addition to everything else, an enemy agent.

"He's shot—here." She pointed to a spot about eight inches below her right breast. "And in the elbow. He's in a lot of pain, and I think he's probably bleeding inside. He was pretty weak this morning."

"But not weak enough to keep him from shooting me. And from coming down and catching my horse."

She looked at him as though he were reproaching her. "He didn't have to catch the horse. It just stood there waiting until he came and got it. And I couldn't have stopped him from shooting."

"I know that."

They didn't talk anymore after that.

The next morning, when he woke up and discovered that the wind had subsided, Havens pushed open the cabin door and found that everything was a glistening white, almost as far as he could see. The sun was out. Everything was over.

The snow was piled up in drifts in front of anything that had stood in its way, but otherwise it was only six or seven inches deep. They wouldn't have had any trouble getting around, except that there wasn't anywhere to go.

Mrs. Springer came out, and they stood together in front of

the cabin, looking south to the mountains. There was nothing alive out there, but they hadn't expected there would be. Havens wondered how many hours it would be before the search teams from El Paso found them.

"What'll you do after you get out of here?"

"After?" She stared at him as if the concept were strange to her, and then she shrugged her thin shoulders and took a ragged breath. It seemed to be the first time it had occurred to her that she had a future life to get through.

"I don't know," she said. "I guess I'll go home."

"Where's home?"

"New Jersey."

"I grew up in Brooklyn." He looked at her and smiled, wondering why he had said that.

"Yes?"

And she smiled too. She seemed almost human again, standing there in the snow with her hands pressed against the waistband of her coat. She would probably have some pretty bad times in front of her, but she would be all right.

"God, I wish we had something to eat. You sure there isn't anything in the car?" Without waiting for an answer, he went around to where it was parked and opened the door. There was nothing except a couple of bloodstains on the front seat. Havens turned away, wishing he had left well enough alone. He was beginning to feel cold, and his leg was bothering him again. He went back inside the cabin.

It was a few minutes after ten when he heard a loud buzzing sound and rushed outside again to see a search plane making its slow pass over the cabin. He waved his arms and shouted, perfectly aware that there was no way he could be heard; but the plane made a second pass and dipped its wing, so at least they knew he was there.

Half an hour later he could look down where the road would have been and see a jeep churning up the snow. It was wearing chains and wasn't doing more than fifteen miles an hour, and there were two men inside. Havens recognized the man in the passenger seat as Charlie Rice.

"What kept you?"

"Don't be a smart ass, Havens. Where's our spy?"

Havens raised his arm and pointed to the southern mountains. The expression on his face suggested a certain distaste.

"You mean he got away?"

"I mean that the last time I saw him he had a horse and was on his way to Mexico. That was yesterday morning."

"Yesterday MORNing?" Charlie's ponderous face seemed to broaden with anxiety. "Well then, he never made it. We've had guys waiting down there at that slaughterhouse of yours ever since last night, and he never turned up."

"He wouldn't go there—he knew that Gomá was dead."

"And how did he happen to know that?"

"I told him."

"You WHAT?"

"I told him." Havens made an impatient gesture that seemed to dismiss the subject. "Have the planes seen anything?"

"Not a thing. Who's the woman?"

She had been there beside him for perhaps half a minute and somehow he had never noticed her. In that instant, he discovered, he hated Charlie Rice like poison.

"This is Mrs. Springer," he answered, in his best official voice. "She and her husband ran afoul of our friend in Santa Fe, and Mr. Springer was killed. Von Niehauser took the lady hostage. She's the one who sabotaged his car." He stared at the car, as if he hated it too, as if its flat battery were some sort of visible wound that should have been obvious even to Charlie Rice. He knew that Jenny Springer was staring at him, and it made him feel uncomfortable.

"Have you got anything to eat?" he asked suddenly.

They didn't have much time. The search teams were converging around the cabin—two or three people would come up through the mountains from Mexico, retracing Havens' route—and in an hour or so someone would take Mrs. Springer into El Paso, where she would be questioned and examined by a doctor and would be able to make a start at putting her life back together. Havens insisted that he was going to stay with the search, arguing that he certainly would have known it by then if von Niehauser's bullet had done him any real harm. Since he was the officer in charge, no one was prepared to argue with him.

The best Charlie Rice could do in the way of food was a Thermos of hot coffee, and Havens and Mrs. Springer stood out in the sunshine and drank it while the others went inside to visit the stove. It was probably the last time they would be alone together.

"Stick as close as you can to the truth," Havens murmured, clasping the coffee cup between his hands and watching the cabin door suspiciously. "Just tell them that you and your husband went into the hotel together. You won't convince them, but that won't matter—they aren't really interested in anybody except von Niehauser and this guy Lautner. I'll see to it that your version gets written into the official record."

He handed the cup to Mrs. Springer, who seemed glad to have a reason for not looking him in the face.

"Thank you for lying for me." She paused and cleared her throat. Her voice was hardly more than a thick whisper. "You didn't have to. It isn't very important if they . . ."

"Maybe you don't think so now, but you will in a month or so. You don't owe it to anybody to appear on some police blotter as the scarlet woman; these things never come out very close to the truth anyway. And the Bureau can afford to cover for you—after all, you were the only one who managed to slow our friend down any. Also there's the small matter of my life."

She smiled, not very convincingly, and Havens thought perhaps he understood why von Niehauser hadn't killed her when he found out about the headlights. She was no coward, was this lady. And she wasn't going to lie to anybody about anything.

But that didn't matter either, because he was going to doctor the report under any circumstances.

Ten minutes later he climbed into the jeep, leaving a faceless young man from the El Paso office to take care of Mrs. Springer while he and Charlie Rice set off to look for von Niehauser.

He would have been in a mood for a little conversation, but Charlie turned out to be one of those people who couldn't drive and whistle "Dixie" without serious risk of a crack-up. Twice they almost got bogged down in snowdrifts before Havens decided that he had better shut up.

For a while he thought about how much his head hurt and whether he would be able to turn it into a couple of weeks' worth of disability leave after all this was over, but then he remembered his report and how many people would be waiting to read it and how the Army would probably want to spend the next several months turning over every rock in New Mexico because their precious security had been compromised, and he decided that by the time he was through with all that his head would probably be as good as new anyway.

And then he wondered what the Santa Fe police were making of Hal Springer's dead body right that moment, and what sort of a fellow he must have been that his wife had started ducking out on him like that. She didn't seem the type somehow, but then again maybe there wasn't a type. At least she wasn't making any excuses for herself.

The former Mrs. Havens' rebellions hadn't taken that particular turn—Karen had been more the pack-her-bag-and-back-to-mother type, but she had made plenty of excuses. If Karen had had to explain what she had been up to in that hotel room in Santa Fe, she would have lied her little head off. She wouldn't have been able to help herself.

But it seemed to Havens that just at present his life was filled with people who were perfectly ready to accept the consequences of their actions. Mrs. Springer for one—and then there was von Niehauser, who had wandered off into a snowstorm rather than accept a few more months of life at the cost of his peculiar Teutonic honor. Everybody, it seemed, was being very noble and at one with himself.

He wondered how at one with himself he would be when he had to explain to J. Edgar and Company just why he had warned von Niehauser that he could forget about a hero's welcome down in Mexico. From a strategic point of view it hadn't been the brightest action of his life, but somehow he had difficulty regretting it. Somehow it would have been appalling to let the man go off like that without his knowing the perfect emptiness of the gesture. Not that it seemed to have made any difference to him. And not that it would make any sense to Mr. Hoover.

It suddenly occurred to Havens that he had forgotten to ask Mrs. Springer just where home was in New Jersey. But the Bureau would keep tabs on her; she wouldn't be very hard to find. Doubtless he'd see her again, in one context or another.

When they reached the foot of the mountains, they had to get out and walk. There were patches of snow on the trail, but nothing bad—the wind had blown most of it down onto the flats. Charlie Rice, who probably hadn't been away from his desk in five years, set a slow pace, but Havens didn't complain. He could just manage with his leg, but only just.

They were about halfway to the summit when they met the team that had hiked over from the Mexican side. There were three of them, and they were just sitting around, lined up with their backs against a rock ledge like the three monkeys. They had been waiting there; that was obvious. One of them was smoking a cigarette. They weren't looking for anything anymore.

Five yards farther up the trail, and you could see the reason.

The body was lying face down, with its head turned to one side. The eyes were open, but enough snow had drifted around that you had to brush it away from the head to notice that fact. Von Niehauser looked as if he had died still trying to crawl forward on his hands and knees.

"What happened to the horse?"

Havens looked around at the three men, and finally one of them shook his head. They hadn't seen any horse. Maybe it had wandered off onto some other trail and died, or maybe it had somehow managed to find its way home. Horses were tougher than men, even this man.

The orders had been quite explicit. When von Niehauser was taken, there was to be no interrogation and, aside from a quick frisk for weapons, no search. They were to wait for Havens. Information about the precise nature of the operation was to remain as restricted as possible. That had been the way General Groves had wanted it.

"Why don't you guys go down to the jeep and fetch us up a body bag?"

Charlie Rice looked annoyed when he realized that he too was included in that suggestion. He stood up and dusted off his backside with the air of a man nursing a grievance. Havens waited until they were all well out of sight.

Von Niehauser had frozen to death. It wasn't much of a thrill pulling his pockets inside out. Havens turned him over, grabbing the khaki greatcoat by the right arm. It was like rolling a log.

He looked strangely alive, and his face registered nothing of the suffering Havens had seen there only a little over twenty-four hours ago. He looked as if everything he had gone through had left him merely amused and a little contemptuous. Havens tried to close the eyes, but they wouldn't close, and in an odd way he felt as if von Niehauser really had beaten him after all, as if the whole business had never been about bombs and secrets and the fates of nations, as if only now he was seeing that he had misunderstood everything from the beginning.

He found what he was supposed to be looking for in the inside coat pocket, five pages covered with a close, spidery hand. The rest was locked in von Niehauser's mind and would be safe enough there.

There was a tiny piece of black-and-white ribbon sticking out between the thumb and first finger of von Niehauser's gloved right hand, which was closed almost in a fist. With great difficulty, Havens managed to open the fingers and found a square, black-enameled medal in the shape of a cross. The four ends were wide and flat, and in the center was a small white swastika. It was only about two inches in width; von Niehauser had been holding it so tightly that its corners had cut into the leather of his palm.

Havens didn't know what it was, and he would never know what it had meant to von Niehauser, but he had an obscure feeling that this wasn't something that should go into a file envelope in the basement of Seat of Government, that it was nobody else's business. Probably this black cross was the last thing that von Niehauser had ever seen.

The wind was beginning to pick up again—perhaps today had only been a lull between storms. Havens put the medal in his trouser pocket and turned up the collar of his coat, waiting for the war to end.